The Art Collector's Daughter

Derville Murphy

POOLBEG

This book is a work of fiction. The names, characters, places, businesses, organisations and incidents portrayed in it are either the product of the author's imagination or are used fictitiously. Any resemblance to actual persons, living or dead, events or locales is entirely coincidental.

Published 2020
by Poolbeg Press Ltd.
123 Grange Hill, Baldoyle,
Dublin 13, Ireland
Email: poolbeg@poolbeg.com

A catalogue record for this book is available from the British Library.

ISBN 978178199-390-3

www.poolbeg.com

About the Author

Derville Murphy practised for many years as an architect before completing an MPhil in Irish Art History, TCD, and subsequently a PhD in Art and Architecture, UCD. In 2008 she founded art@work art consultancy. As an artist, she has exhibited widely, with solo exhibitions in 2005 and 2007 in the RIAI – her paintings are in several public art collections. As an academic, she has written articles in journals including the *Irish Art Review* and *Architecture Ireland,* and in 2016 she contributed to the RIA's edition of *Modern Ireland in 100 Artworks.* This is her debut novel.

Acknowledgements

Although I came to novel-writing late in life, it has always been my dream to enjoy a life of leisure, painting, and writing. Although the leisure bit has proved elusive, I have certainly enjoyed the latter.

As always, my husband Brendan has been my rock and encourages me in everything I do.

My daughters Amy and Niamh provided literary critiques, political correctness and social savy!

Deirdre Grant and Ger Canavan have provided constant encouragement, advice, and support for which I am incredibly grateful.

I owe a great debt to my book club pals Marguerite, Yvonne, and Mavis – and also to Helen and Ailbhe, who all gave me insightful feedback on my early drafts.

Thank you also to my friend, Ele von Monschaw, Paintings Conservator at the National Gallery, for her advice, and to Joan McManus for help with French translations.

The team at Poolbeg have been so good to work with. I would like to thank Paula Campbell, Publisher, for believing in me. And also, Gaye Shortland, Editor, who has been a pleasure to work with and whose expertise helped solve a particularly tricky plot hole.

I would like to give special thanks to Catherine Marshall, my mentor, whose encouragement changed my life and opened up new possibilities.

Finally, I would like to thank Patricia O'Reilly, author and Creative Writing teacher at UCD, for her inspiration, generosity, and support; and to the many friends and fellow writers that I met over the last few years in her class.

To Eithne and Matthew Furlong RIP

Prologue

He could feel the energy pulsating through his body. The brush was like an extension to his limb, a sentient instrument. It was her, she had broken the spell, cast out his demons, dispelled his recent stupor. They say some people have an aura about them. Although he didn't believe in superstitious bullshit, this child had something. Something his brush was defining but his mind had yet to understand.

He paused briefly and looked at the canvas as the image of her emerged, even at this early stage emanating a tragic, fragile beauty. She had been sitting patiently for him on the swing for about half an hour – longer than the usual floozies that he paid for the privilege. But now she was fidgeting.

"I'm tired, monsieur," she said to him.

"Mademoiselle, a few more minutes, please."

She moaned – she was tired. He didn't care. She would have to put up with it for a while longer. Something was happening for him. He spoke to distract her, his voice sounding surprisingly husky, as if someone else was speaking.

"Stippled sunlight through beech trees and the smell of roses wafting on a summer breeze. A young girl on a swing. The swing rising higher, and higher, and the child squealing in delight. Until one strong push and then, as if propelled, the child goes flying through the air, her white lace skirts trailing like the wings of a wounded dove before finally lying broken, shattered on the ground. A shimmering halo of red blood spreads around her fair hair ..."

"Is that a story?"

"No, child, I'm just musing," he said, not lifting his eyes from the canvas.

"I don't find that a bit amusing," she said petulantly. "I'm bored with sitting on this stupid swing. I'm going to find Papa."

Paul appeared shortly afterwards, his cigarette-holder dangling from the side of his mouth.

"Henrique, my friend, my daughter is not impressed. I'm afraid you are going to have to find older models."

Chapter 1

Paris
October 1939

The Café des Trois Théâtres near Pigalle in the 9th arrondissement was packed. Three men sat in a small alcove off the main dining area where the mahogany furniture, covered with burgundy velvet and gold tassels, created a Belle Époque meets Hollywood-glitz style glamour. Smells of garlic and eau de cologne wafted on the smoke-filled air. Sitting back in their chairs, legs crossed, two of the men wielded cigarettes in ornate holders. The companions were mellow – bellies full, they were savouring the moment.

"I wonder, my friends, will we be meeting here this time next year, drinking beer and eating Wiener Schnitzel? I do think you would look rather well in lederhosen," said Émile.

"It's nothing to laugh at," Daniel replied. "All our futures look perilous now Poland has fallen, and Britain and France have declared war on the Krauts."

"Even in neutral Éire?" Émile chided.

"Even in Ireland. Although we are small fish in a sea surrounded by sharks, there is no doubt we will suffer," said Daniel, his clipped manner of speaking at odds with his soft Irish accent. He was small and neatly formed with the clumsy tweed tailoring of an English country squire. "We rely heavily on imported grain and coal. Unless we get safe passage across the Irish Sea, many of our people will face starvation. But, Paul, you must be worried. You should have gone before now."

"*Mm*," replied Paul nonchalantly. Despite his studied elegance, a telltale tic flickered at the side of his mouth. He tapped his cigarette on the ashtray. "I must admit I have thought of nothing else. It seems to be a case of I'm damned if I do and damned if I don't. If I leave, they will confiscate my paintings – and if I stay, they will confiscate my paintings – and God knows what will become of my family."

"Picasso has already fled to Nice. He claims that he will sit out the war there and at least enjoy the sunshine. Can you not do the same?" enquired Émile, frustrated.

"I admire his optimism, but I don't see it quite playing out like that. Hitler won't rest until he has conquered the whole of Western Europe. I believe Rosenberg and his agents are working on an inventory already, identifying works in private art collections – Jewish art collections – that he will plunder for his crazy scheme. You know he intends to build the largest, most prestigious art museum in the world in Linz, where he attended grammar school."

"Yes, I heard that," said Émile, his expression grim. "Look, Paul, even I'm heading south. I have taken a lease on a villa in Antibes, Casa Fonteille. Odette and I will go there in the spring."

"And your auction house?"

"It will close for the foreseeable future. I will go underground, as they say in Hollywood."

4

"You really should leave, Paul," said Daniel. "Your paintings will be no use to you or your family if you are dead."

"*Mm*," said Paul, taking another slug of the brandy and leaning forward to put his arms on the table, carefully watching his two companions. "I think I have a plan. But I will need the co-operation and support of you both."

Émile coughed into his fist, his gold cufflinks sparkling in the candlelight. "Paul, this is not a time for heroics, or unnecessary risks. As a Jew –"

"For God's sake, Émile, you above all people know that I'm not a practising Jew."

"Unfortunately, that's not the way Hitler sees it – practising, or not, you are a Jew. Look, we will do whatever we can to help you, but within reason. I take it that this is connected in some way with your degenerate artists. Do you really believe that they are worth taking unnecessary risks for? In twenty years' time they will probably be forgotten like all the others."

"How can you say that? These artists have changed the art world as we know it," replied Paul passionately. "They will live on long after this war is over. They will never be forgotten!"

Émile sat back in his chair. "God loves a zealot," he said ironically. "Very well, my friend, tell us – what is your plan?"

Chapter 2

Compositionally, it was balanced. She had divided a slice of cheese, the plastic type, into three, draped each section over a fish finger and artfully arranged them on the plate with a mound of beans. As an image it could represent today's fast-food culture, maybe a suitable subject for Andy Warhol. But maybe not. He was more of a branded-products man: soup, Marilyn Monroe – objects of conspicuous consumption. Did Warhol ever eat fish fingers, she wondered? Claire ate them slowly, savouring each mouthful. He must have had plenty in his time, starving artist and all that.

It had been a disastrous day. It had been so hot in the dry cleaner's that when she first noticed the shirt and realised that she had, somehow, put it into the machine with a pair of red knickers, she had nearly passed out.

She looked down at her new navy canvas shoes – they were Jackson Pollocked, as her friend Henry would say. Literally, they were splashed all over with bleach.

She rubbed her aching arms. She had stirred that bloody shirt in three vats of bleach to get the colour out

6

of it, until eventually it was no longer pink. It ended up white – not sparkling white, more of a yellowy white.

The thought of his fury earlier made her stomach lurch. She put down her knife and fork and downed the last of the Valpolicella then added the empty plate to the pile of dirty dishes beside the sink. She moved to the sofa where she lay down, carelessly pushing the pile of magazines to the floor so that she could raise her feet on the small coffee table. But, as she closed her eyes, the memory refused to go away and returned to taunt her. The image of his face replayed like a silent movie. Mouth twisted in rage – he had looked at her like she was an imbecile. If he hadn't been so good-looking and treated her with such contempt, she would have seen the funny side of the situation. It had been funny – really. Later she would tell her sister Molly how he had been gobsmacked when he saw the shirt that she had spent nearly two hours trying to fix.

"What happened to my lovely pink shirt?" he'd said in his posh South Dublin accent.

"Oh, my God. I'm so sorry, I thought ..."

And then her boss Stefan, who had been aware of her frantic efforts all afternoon, heard the interaction, came over and made the situation even worse.

"Sir, so sorry. Will give you money for new shirt. How much cost, please? Very, very, sorry, sir!"

"*That's not the point!*" the young man had said, incensed. "I really liked the shirt. It was a Giorgio Armani. I need it tonight for a function." He glared at Stefan.

"Look, I have other shirts, dress shirts," said Stefan. "I give you money and lend you shirt."

"*I don't want somebody else's bloody shirt!*" he'd

shouted, so that a lady with a trout-mouth, standing politely behind him, turned and hurriedly left the shop.

He looked like he was about to punch Stefan.

"How much to go away, sir?"

"*What, me?*" the young man exclaimed furiously.

"No. Problem, sir."

"Oh, it cost twenty quid. But can't you see that really isn't the point?"

Eventually, he had left with a twenty-pound note. Stefan told her this would be deducted in instalments from her wages, together with the cost of a gift voucher for dry cleaning to be repaid by her working extra hours for nothing. As if the shirt-man would ever return! Through gritted teeth, she told Stefan what to do with his job, restrained only by the fact that, at some stage in the future, she might need a reference. But now she was skint, broke – down on her uppers. She would have to draw down some more of her savings to see her through the next few weeks until she could get another job. There wasn't even anything on the goggle-box to cheer her up.

As a distraction, she opened the post she had been avoiding for the past few days. They looked like bills, except for one letter she had not noticed before in a cream envelope. On the back was a forwarding address with the name Nicholas Courtney. She opened it.

Your name was given to me by Professor Dillon, she read ... *good student ... blah, blah ... would you be interested in recording the life and works of my late sister-in-law Sylvie Vasseur?*

Claire hadn't thought Professor Dillon even knew her name. Unfortunately, her academic career had been distinguished by mediocrity. Despite several valiant attempts to shine by choosing obscure subjects for essays, it had dimmed as the two-year programme progressed. So why had the batty professor recommended her? The only plausible explanation was that he must have mixed her up with the other Claire in the class. Although they were both blonde, unlike her the other Claire was clever and very attractive. He knew *her* alright. Still, she mustn't look a gift horse in the mouth.

She spent the next half an hour reading her Irish art history books, to find that Sylvie Vasseur, an artist, originally French, who lived and worked in Ireland, had died in 1965 aged 33, tragically, in a drowning accident.

And really that was how it all began.

Nicholas Courtney opened the rusty padlock to the wooden door with difficulty. "No one has been in here for years. It's been too painful for us. Too many memories."

Claire's eyes were drawn to the ceiling. The studio was in the style of an old-fashioned conservatory with part-height brick walls supporting a timber-framed, glazed structure above. Stained, yellowed butter paper, the type used in the past by draftsmen, was sellotaped to the glass overhead, although sections had fallen allowing dust-speckled shards of sunlight to permeate and dissect the space. But it was the overall unpleasant smell that assailed her senses. Rubbery plants, some dead, clung like prehistoric triffids, their fronds matted against the glass and emitting a rotting, vegetal odour.

Claire thought it was a generous space for an artist to work in as she tried to imagine what it had been like when Sylvie was alive. At the end of the room was a large wooden easel, positioned beside a raised platform, presumably used by models. Along one side ran a worktable. On it were rocks, fossils and skeletons of small, long-dead animals interspersed with palettes of dried and muddied oil colour. Tubes of paint were scattered everywhere, not neatly rolled up as Claire's were in order to use the last precious drop, but squeezed, twisted and hastily discarded. Books were piled on the floorboards – others were strewn open on the bench. She approached the worktop and carefully turned a page of an old *Encyclopaedia Britannica* with the heading **"Wooden Defences"**. There was a hole in the page where a diagram had been carelessly torn out.

Claire stepped back and surveyed the room, noting that the overall impression was one of total disorder – but despite this her eye was constantly drawn to arrays of objects forming intriguing displays. She remembered reading once that highly creative people are marked by a compulsive curiosity. A trait certainly embodied by this studio. It was like walking into a life-size version of a Victorian cabinet of curiosities.

"I hope you won't be put off by the state of the place, Miss Howard."

"Please call me Claire," she said with a smile. She looked for warmth in his eyes but could find none. The 'like-me' look that most people project on first introduction was absent.

"My sister-in-law was an odd combination of chaos and almost obsessive interest in detail. I often think it was this clash of opposing energies that fuelled her work." He took a packet of Gauloise cigarettes from

10

his pocket and lit one. Only after inhaling the resinous fumes deeply did he offer her the packet.

"No, thank you," she replied. "I'm trying to give them up. You said Brian Dillon gave you my name?"

"He suggested I contact you. You come highly recommended."

"Really," she said thoughtfully, before asking, "Nothing has been written about your sister-in-law before?"

"No, other than a few magazine articles at the time and an obituary by historian Dr John Fallon. You see, although a number of students have approached us over the years, we were not ready to face all of this."

"It must have been awful, such a tragedy. I can understand how it must have been difficult to come to terms with what happened."

"Well, now we need to. We want to sell the house. So, you see, we can't put it off any longer. We have to sort this out."

"What did you have in mind? Your letter mentioned that you wanted to record the contents of this studio, and her life and work generally."

"Well, yes, to start with. I suppose we were looking for advice on how best to go about it."

"Are there any other places that she worked apart from this studio? Did she have an office in the house?"

"She had another studio, much smaller, in a summer house in Wexford on the Hook Peninsula. I can arrange for you to visit. Well, what do you think? Will you take it on?"

"I'm certainly intrigued. I was always a great admirer of her work," Claire said artfully. "She was considered one of the most original Irish painters at that time – and of course her sudden death, so young, made her such a romantic figure. A cult figure almost. Maybe if I think about the best approach and try to put together a plan?"

"Sorry to be such a philistine – but cost? I'm afraid our resources are limited."

"It's hard to price work like this. It's probably better to agree a plan of activities and estimate the cost of each so that you can decide which you wish to do. I could get back to you within a week or so."

He nodded and, without smiling, held out his hand.

"Great," he said.

The following day, as she passed through the arch from College Green into Trinity College, sounds of traffic in Dublin's bustling city centre were left behind. She was transported back in time to another age – to the hallowed halls of academia. No matter how many times Claire entered the front square, flanked by red-brick Neo-classical architecture, each time she was impressed anew. Because, unlike other cities, such as Paris or Rome, Dublin had few grand public spaces, and this one, she thought, had the distinction that you came upon it quite by surprise, hidden within the heart of the city.

That day, the pebbled square was crowded with students, American tourists and guides with colourful umbrellas, like swarms of exotic butterflies. She had planned to ambush the professor before lectures and was rewarded with the sight of the familiar tall figure lumbering towards the Arts Block – his head down, avoiding eye contact with anyone.

She ran ahead of him and blocked his path, forcing him to look at her.

"Professor Dillon, a quick word if I may."

"Ah, yes, what can I do for you?"

"I don't know if you remember me. I'm Claire Howard, I was a post-graduate in the Master's programme last year."

"Oh yes, Claire. Yes, of course, I remember."

Although he remembered the name, she knew he didn't recognise her at all. Professor Dillon had soft pliant features, fulsome cheeks and a squarish face accentuated by rectangular, black-framed glasses. He appeared to be jovial and absent-minded, and he was most of the time, but his piercing grey eyes indicated a steely resolve that she had experienced occasionally in the past.

"I believe you recently recommended me to Sylvie Vasseur's family for a piece of research."

"Yes, I did. I hope that wasn't a presumption on my part?"

"No, not at all. I'm very grateful for the opportunity. But I was just wondering, Professor, if I could pick your brains a little bit?"

"Yes, of course."

He hesitated briefly, distracted, then from his voluminous academic gown he plucked out a red alarm clock with bells on top and examined it closely.

"I lost my gold watch recently," he said by way of explanation, "and I was hoping that my good wife might take the hint and buy me a new one for my birthday. It's a roundy one."

"Your birthday?"

"No, the watch."

"Oh, really." Stifling her laughter, Claire smiled sympathetically.

He referred anxiously once more to his timepiece.

"I have a lecture in ten minutes, but I'll meet you in the Buttery at half eleven and we can have a proper chat. Now I really must ..." and still clutching the alarm clock, he was gone.

In the hour to kill before meeting him, she visited the Berkeley Library to check up on newspaper accounts at the time of Sylvie Vasseur's death. Without too much trouble she found the feature by Dr John Fallon, the *Irish Times* obituary that she had already read and a few other newspaper accounts that covered similar detail. But the library card catalogue highlighted several articles in a Dutch art journal that she was unfamiliar with. By the time she had photocopied the articles, it was time to meet the Professor. She put them in her bag to read later.

"Yes, Sylvie Vasseur – odd situation there – thought you might be interested."

Professor Dillon had been waiting for her when she arrived. He had bought two mugs of tea. Hers was by that stage cold, but she thanked him anyway. The restaurant, with its low vaulted ceiling, had originally been a cellar. This morning it was thronged with long-haired students, uniformly dressed in shapeless woollen jumpers and denim jeans. They looked as if they had only recently crawled out of damp bedsits in Rathmines and Rathgar. Smells of stale beer and cigarettes hung on the air and were infused with the smell of the cheap cooking oil emanating from the kitchen's deep-fat fryers. The smells evoked memories for Claire of her own time spent there as a student. Was there also a slight whiff of weed, or was she imagining it?

The professor took up where he had left off earlier without any formality.

"To leave it so long to sort out her affairs seems strange. The Courtneys, her husband's family with whom she grew up, are keen art collectors. But apart from the grandfather who studied classics in Cambridge, none of them has an academic background – until recently, that is. Her son Sam left the world of commerce and is now a mature student, an undergrad in History of Art – 2nd year, I believe. Obviously, because of his mother, he's got an interest. But sorting out her estate and cataloguing her works requires a level of expertise that he does not presently have. For the family it was probably just too daunting an undertaking. It was her husband's brother, Nicholas Courtney, who contacted me looking for someone to catalogue the studio contents. He is a property developer and collects art. I met him years ago when he sponsored a Léger exhibition here at the college – and I have occasionally, over the years, advised him on his collection. And that really is as much as I can tell you. So, best of luck, Claire, keep in touch, and do let me know how you get on."

Just as she was thinking, but afraid to say, why me, why recommend me, he said, "Now I'm afraid I really must be going."

And with that he got up and left abruptly.

Chapter 3

Paris
7th July, 1940

Paul thought back to the night in the Café des Trois Théâtres the previous year when he had teased Émile about his flight to the South of France. He had not realised that the day would come when his friend's prescience would prove to be his own salvation. Putting his affairs in order had taken longer than expected. Jean-Claude, his assistant, had helped him – he couldn't trust anyone else.

Leaving the workshop, Paul walked into the spacious ground-floor gallery. He remembered his excitement all those years ago when as a young boy he had first seen and fallen in love with the building. Built originally for an antiques dealer who sold Persian carpets, his father had seen that its large windows made it a perfect space to display art.

Paul nervously lit a cigarette in his gold-and-amber holder and looked out across the desolate street. What a state of affairs Petain had set in train when he had signed the Armistice with Germany! He had succeeded in taking France out of the war. But at what price? The government had fled to Tours and then on to Bordeaux.

But it was hard to get a handle on what was really happening, the radio and single-sheet newspaper were filled with German propaganda. Paul took another comforting drag of his cigarette. He thought about how much had changed in the city in the three weeks since the Germans' arrival – before then, the Rue du Faubourg Saint-Honoré had been a bustling and fashionable thoroughfare. Today it had the air of abandonment of a mining town from the American Midwest. Anyone who could leave the city had already gone, millions had fled into the countryside. A curfew was in place from nine in the evening until five the following morning. During this time, the city was plunged into darkness. But even more disturbing was the eerie quietness of the place, the absence of the normal bustle of the city. The usual sounds of pedestrians were gone, no street hawkers, very little traffic, no construction sounds, just silence – a lacuna magnified by the occasional sound of low-flying aircraft overhead and armoured vehicles rolling around the city's cobbled streets. Paul shivered, it was as if the city was infected by a plague, and it was of a sort, a malaise of fear and desperation. Those remaining in the city were waiting, hoping for order to return.

Paul's stomach rumbled – he had left the small amount of bread they had for Hanna. Finding food was still most people's priority.

He watched in dismay as workmen hung a large swastika banner on the building opposite. Until recently an atelier for fashionable ladies' costumes, it had been requisitioned from his Jewish neighbour, Monsieur Mandel, by the Gestapo. The elegantly attired mannequins usually in the window had been replaced by a large

17

poster showing a grotesque representation of a Jew, his long taloned hands clutching the world. Underneath were written the infamous words from Edouard Drumont's despicable book, *La France Juive*: "*The Jews came poor to a rich country. They are now the only rich people in a poor country.*"

His father would not have believed it possible that this could happen to his beloved Paris. The old man had been a proud Frenchman, a patriot who had fought with distinction for his country in the Great War and had the medals to prove it. His Jewishness was a separate thing to him – it was his religion, his tradition, the way he chose to live his life. He would be horrified at these new extremes of blatant aggression towards his people. Although, Paul acknowledged sadly, it had always been there, in some form or another.

It was early yet. But he knew that the Einsatzstab Reichsleiter Rosenberg, the ERR, could descend on him at any time. A task force, as far as Paul was concerned, set up to loot the best of Western Europe's art and cultural objects.

He looked around the gallery at the exhibition and felt a cold sweat spread over his body.

The paintings on the walls were from his personal collection. Every one of them represented a different episode in his life. The more valuable works were in the smaller gallery upstairs.

All those years ago, when his father had established the business in the 1920s, the old man had built his reputation by collecting mid-19th century art. These *plein air* painters – predominantly French artists, led by Théodore Rousseau and Jean-François Millet, had turned their back on traditional, Italianate studio painting to paint nature directly in the outdoors. They had been based in the French village of Barbizon near the forests of Fontainebleau.

Paul's interest, however, was in the avant-garde and, after his father's death, he pursued this passion relentlessly, collecting artists such as Braque, Léger, Picasso and especially the Portuguese artist Mateus. Paul was not a dealer in the traditional sense, he was more of a patron. He believed in these artists and supported them by exhibiting their works, often paying over and above the painting's market value. He had been able to do this and still make a living by trading on his father's more marketable Barbizon collection. In this regard, the fact that there were two galleries was useful. If a buyer was not ready to embrace shocking modernist images, then Paul would quietly lead the prospective client upstairs and show him something more attuned to his taste.

Paul felt bile rise in his throat and the familiar tightening across his chest. He took a peppermint from his pocket and placed it on his tongue. He was exhausted with the strain of it all. Earlier that morning he had written to Émile. He could wait no longer. They would have to advance their plans. He would be joining him for an extended visit at the end of the week.

Paul walked across the gallery floor and stopped to gaze at his most precious painting. It was of a young girl sitting on a swing in a garden. The model was Sylvie, his daughter, and it was a gift from his friend, Henrique Mateus. Painted in bold outlines and flat plains of colour, the image was lively and yet, compositionally, perfectly balanced. He had managed to capture the child's indomitable spirit, her remarkable clear-blue eyes staring defiantly out at the viewer. The innocence of youth, Paul thought, trying to suppress the fear that constantly haunted him. It was eight weeks since he had left her at the Gard du Nord with hundreds of other Jewish children who were being evacuated to Britain, as fears escalated of the German troop's imminent arrival.

She had been so brave, the little one. But since then, he felt as if his heart had been wrenched out of his chest leaving a gaping hole there, one that daily he struggled to deal with. Hanna had not recovered either from the separation, even though the child had written to say that she had arrived safely in Ireland with Daniel and that his family were being kind her. Hopefully, she wouldn't have to remain there for too long.

He tried to put these thoughts out of his mind and pull himself together. He had business to attend to if he was to get his affairs in order by Friday.

Paul's thoughts were interrupted by the sound of the door opening as a Gestapo agent dressed in plain clothes entered the gallery and proceeded to look around at the exhibition. He stood, legs apart, at each of the works, examining each briefly, his hands behind his back, his expression supercilious. When he had finished his inspection – for that was what it was, thought Paul – he approached him.

"Monsieur Vasseur, it is hard to understand who would buy these kinds of paintings, particularly of such ugly women. No wonder Herr Hitler calls it *Entartete Kunst* – degenerate art." The German smiled, his expression sardonic.

Paul nodded, his head solicitously to one side. "Indeed, officer, it can be difficult for these artists to make a living alright. But I have a few more traditional pieces. Unfortunately, I have very few left at this stage. I've had something of a clearing-out over the past few years. What's left, I keep upstairs, for special customers, so to speak. Would you like to inspect those? And may I offer you a coffee, or something a little stronger?"

The agent's manner, ignoring Paul's offer, instantly became officious. "I presume you have heard of Hitler's recent order to put artworks belonging to Jews in safe keeping?"

"Yes, I have, but these works don't belong to me – they are owned by the artists themselves," he lied. "In any case, the exhibition is closed. I am in the process of taking down the works."

"Just as well, just as well. You cannot be upsetting your new neighbours." He nodded to Mandel's old premises across the street, then he clicked his heels and moved briskly towards the door.

When the German had left, Paul lit another cigarette and slowly circled the room, gazing at each painting, as if for the last time drinking in the images, absorbing their beauty. He paused once more at *Girl on a Swing* and carefully took it down from the wall. *My Russian friend has done well. Even Émile would be fooled. For a short while anyway.*

When he returned home that evening, he told Hanna that they would leave the next morning. They couldn't wait till Friday. Paul's sense of a lucky escape lent a new urgency to his actions. They were ready anyway – the furniture had already been put into storage, and they had sent their clothes ahead. They were travelling light. They would swing by the following morning and lock up the gallery.

Shortly after seven o'clock they passed through the city. Some of the shopkeepers were opening their wooden shutters, but it was still early for those left to go about their business. On the streets, a few stragglers, with bicycles and pushcarts laden down with bags, were bravely starting off on their journeys. But the Jews who could were long gone. Paul knew by delaying he had taken a terrible risk, but he had thought about every option, and this was the only way.

As they passed the courtyard in front of the Musée du Jeu de Paume they saw a column of black smoke but paid little heed. It was one of many bonfires all over Paris. However, when they saw soldiers heading towards the museum, trucks filled with paintings, he grabbed Hanna's hand which was shaking – his other hand, white-knuckled, held the wheel. Silently, the two of them prayed. After what seemed like an age, and several checkpoints later – where their false papers were examined and they were summarily waved through – they reached the Rue du Faubourg Saint-Honoré. His new neighbours had not yet opened. Many of the shops were closed, boarded up, and rubbish was spilling out of the bins onto the pavements as large brown rats ran across the cobbled street. A torso of one of Monsieur Mandel's mannequins lay smashed in the gutter. Paul slowed down the car as they passed Number 71 but did not stop. The wooden shutters were hanging off their brackets and the windows were shattered – the paintings were gone – the gallery was empty.

Paul looked at Hanna. "It will be alright, *bubala*. Now we can go."

The heat was intense and the air stifling as they left Paris from the Porte de Versailles heading south. At this stage, the sun was well risen in the clear blue sky. On the road the traffic was steady, with vehicles of all shapes and sizes shimmering in the heat. Cars, horses and carts, even a hearse, were stuffed to the gills with furniture and household possessions. Several cars had been covered with mattresses intended to absorb bullets. If it was chaotic now, Paul could only imagine what it must have been like in the days ahead of the German advance on Paris. He had read in the newspaper, following the Armistice, that the Germans intended to compartmentalise France into Northern territories under the Germans, and Southern territories to be controlled by the French. It was only a matter of time before it would be impossible to cross this demarcation line, even with their fake birth certificates and papers which had cost him a small fortune on the black market. On reflection, he felt their timing was perfect – they had left it long enough to deflect suspicion and buy them some time, but not too late for his plan to be effective.

Their sleek Citroën Avant had caused a few raised eyebrows. Although they were waved through the first checkpoint, Paul realised that staying in the car at night they were going to be sitting ducks, an easy target for looters and those desperate enough to do anything to survive. With a total breakdown of law and order, once off the German-controlled main routes, it was a case of every man and woman for themselves. Under the back seat of the car, their food was hidden carefully in a metal box. They had taken this precaution after seeing a dishevelled man, dressed in a suit and tie, swipe a chunk of bread from the hands of a pregnant woman just outside Paris. Shops and cafés were closed everywhere, and there were groups of people outside roadside cottages begging for water.

That first night, hidden amongst trees, he had taped black material to the windows of the car so that it felt like being trapped inside a tiny prison cell. Every sound outside was exaggerated, and despite being covered with thick, woollen blankets neither of them slept. At one stage he heard Hanna whimpering and he squeezed her arm, trying to console her.

"It will be alright, my darling, everything will be alright once we get to Antibes."

Despite his soothing words, he was worried. Hanna was not a fit woman by any means. Although still relatively young, she carried extra weight. She was too fond of sweet things, he thought fondly. The days ahead were going to be arduous. He knew they only had enough petrol to reach Bourges and, once they crossed the border, they would probably have to abandon the car and find another form of transport. There was no petrol to be had anywhere. That night, he mapped his route by torchlight, intending to travel on secondary roads where there was less chance of being stopped. At this stage, the Germans could not possibly have controls along the full length of the green line.

When they eventually reached Bourges, on the outskirts of the town they passed a soup kitchen and crowds of refugees were queueing with cups and pots to get sustenance for their starving families. As they approached the town's centre, they saw why – shops and cafés were boarded up everywhere. Undeterred, Paul carried out a quick reconnoitre on foot, taking Hanna with him, knocking on café and shop doors. But mostly their attempts were ignored. When people did open the door, usually the women, they were told there was no food available. At one café a blonde woman in a fur coat ahead of him, carrying a bedraggled poodle – both sweltering in the heat – was desperately offering exorbitant prices. She too received short shift from the woman of the house.

After an hour or so, Paul realised he was wasting his time and they walked back to the market square at Place des Maronniers where he haggled with a young man for two second-hand bicycles.

Afterwards, sitting with the bikes under the shade of a tree, they fell into conversation with a young woman and her daughter, who looked about the same age as Sylvie. Although, initially, Paul remained aloof, Hanna couldn't resist engaging them in conversation. The woman told them how they had been visiting her ailing mother in Paris when she heard the Germans were heading towards the city. But she could not bear to leave her to die alone. And now that the old woman had passed away, she was anxious to return home to her husband. When she heard they were both heading for Antibes, she told them that she was fortunate enough to be travelling by car, with a cousin of her husband's, a police inspector. She would arrive long before them. She didn't offer them a lift, and they didn't ask. But taking advantage of her apparent good nature Paul grasped the opportunity and hastily scribbled a postcard to Émile which she promised faithfully to deliver the next day.

The following morning, after a good night's sleep and a packet of sweet biscuits between them for breakfast, they abandoned the car in a copse of trees outside the town. Leaving Bourges with their newly acquired bicycles, they eventually crossed the green line, walking through fields south of the city, and then headed towards Vichy. They had been travelling for three days and that afternoon they allowed themselves the luxury of a bottle of fine Bordeaux that Paul had been saving for the occasion and a few extra hours' sleep.

Hanna was slow on the bicycle at first, and her navy woollen skirt chaffed her legs. Every two hours they had to stop for her to rest. During these breaks they ate the rest of their meagre food supplies, consisting of sausage and chocolate which they doled out in tiny rations. On the second day on the bikes, Hanna took Paul's spare trousers, cutting the seams at the side so they fitted around her tummy, using his belt to keep them in place and cutting off the legs, turning them into long shorts. She had never looked less attractive – or been more precious to him.

Each day they took a longer break at midday when the sun was at its strongest. But during these times of not moving, they could never fully relax. The Krauts were still seeking out pockets of resistance. Constant sounds of gunfire that sounded like cars backfiring could be heard in the distance. They clutched one another in terror as low-flying aeroplanes marked with swastikas, like monstrous raptors, flew overhead against the background of the azure blue sky.

At nightfall they slept in barns, sheds or, as a last resort, huddled together in ditches under a blanket. Hanna had always been afraid of the dark. To take her mind off things, Paul encouraged her to tell stories from her childhood, or the early days of their marriage when Sylvie was a little girl, stories that he had heard many times before. She repeated these incessantly. Eventually he couldn't bear to hear them again. But he didn't have the heart to stop her as they gave her such comfort.

One night they slept on a haystack and stared up in wonder at the stars. Sometimes they joined small groups of fellow travellers, but they found their fear and despair to be infectious so mostly they kept to themselves.

When they eventually reached Vichy, the administrative centre of Free France, Paul bought a horse and cart from a grain merchant for American dollars. It had almost cost enough to buy a small apartment in New York, he told Hanna. But it was such a luxury, and they begin to relax as they headed towards Lyon at a more leisurely rate and then south towards Provence.

Fort Carré, Antibes, 12th July

Émile's hands had been strapped together with a leather belt by the Gestapo agent who had dragged him here. His arms were suspended over his head and he was hanging from a butcher's hook in the concrete ceiling. He was in agony. He felt as though his bones were dislocated from their sockets and they could snap at any minute. His mouth was dry, and his lips cracked. He had soiled himself. The smell of his own filth made him retch. Although, at this stage, there was nothing but bile left in his stomach.

He had been in the cell in the old Fort Carré, a 16th-century star-shaped building on the outskirts of Antibes, for three days. Although it seemed like he had been there for longer. The Gendarmerie had knocked on the door of the villa at three o'clock on Sunday morning. Awoken by the banging and sounds of shouting, he and Odette had known that this could mean only one thing. Somehow, they had been found out. They had clung together in their bed, their arms wrapped tightly around one another, too terrified to move.

Below they had heard Sebastien, their Algerian servant, drawing the bolts and opening the heavy wooden door, followed by the sound of heavy footsteps on the stone stairs, and then the noise rising and heading towards their bedroom.

The men had kicked in the door, bursting the lock.

"*Where are they, the Jews?*" the lieutenant had shouted.

"I do not know what you are talking about, officer!" Émile had cried.

"We have been informed by your servant that you are expecting visitors. A Monsieur Vasseur and his wife who have travelled illegally here from Paris."

"Sebastien," whispered Émile, shocked.

They heard the door below open once more and someone running from the villa, then a single shot was fired, followed by a thud.

"It never ceases to amaze me how these African vermin would sell their souls to the devil," said the police officer.

Émile was so terrified that he thought he was going to vomit.

Antibes, 17th July

Ten days after they left Paris the Vasseurs arrived in Antibes, both brown from the sun. Paul looked emaciated, and Hanna, noticeably thinner, had shrunk comfortably into the shorts. Fair highlights from the scorching sun streaked her greasy, dark-brown hair. They were both sweaty and dirty and their shoes were white with dust.

Having sold the horse and cart at the market to a family fleeing to Britain via Bordeaux, they eventually reached the house that Émile and his family were sharing with its owner at four o'clock in the afternoon.

Casa Fonteille was set back from the road behind a high white wall and mature Cyprus trees. The wrought-iron gate in the arched opening was unlocked – once through Émile and Hanna were faced with an impressive Art Deco style villa, with steps leading up to the front door.

Paul rang the bell, as Hanna hastily tried to straighten her greasy hair with her hand.

But instead of his friend, he was greeted by a smiling Gestapo officer.

A cold chill ran over Paul's weary body as Hanna grasped him fiercely by the arm. He thought his legs would give way beneath him. Both were trembling – he knew neither he nor Hanna had the energy to run.

"Monsieur Vasseur, at last, we have been waiting for you."

Chapter 4

Knockaboy, New Ross, County Wexford
September 1940

It was the night-times she dreaded most. The room was smaller than her bedroom at home, yet somehow it felt emptier. Heavy curtains blocked out the moonlight except for a sliver at the top which shed a speckled wash of light across the ceiling. She pulled the blanket over her head creating her safe place, her private world, and switched on the little torch Peter had given her. So she didn't waste the precious battery, she only used it when she was really frightened, like tonight. Her night terrors had returned. Shapes moved amongst dappled light on the ceiling, headless bodies with outstretched arms – scary men coming to take her. Then the noises in her head started, engines revving, marching noises, getting louder, louder and closer. Memories of Maman as she said goodbye at Gard du Nord with tears running down her powdery cheeks, telling her how she must be brave, she was a big girl now, nearly eight. How she had crushed her with her bosomy hugs so that she could hardly breathe. Papa, struggling to put on a brave face, his eyes glistening. But she could see he was upset by the tell-tale twitch at the side of his mouth.

Then the nightmare of the endless train journey – *clickety-clack, clickety clack*. It seemed to say to her – *clickety clack, Sylvie Vasseur – you won't be coming back – clickety clack*.

Finally, she remembered the boat. And how she couldn't see over the rails. A kindly man had lifted her as they left port. But he put her down hastily when she started screaming as icy rain cut her face. Meanwhile, the coast of France had disappeared on the horizon without her even seeing it. But the rain, the driving rain, had followed her from Calais to Dover in England, then from Liverpool onward to Ireland – this country that smelled of cow dung and wet grass.

She pulled the blanket down, switching off the torch, and listened to the sounds of the sleeping house. It creaked, she thought, like an old man settling down in his bed. But tonight, she could hear the sirens in the distance, echoing across the estuary, even though Waterford was several miles away. She put her fingers in her ears, but she could still hear them, like those bad headaches she sometimes had that wouldn't go away. She knew Ireland was not in the war – *neutral*, Aunt Nora called it. But it hadn't stopped Hitler from bombing the Co-op in nearby Campile. She had asked her aunt if Hitler had followed her. Did he know where she lived? Aunt Nora had laughed at her and told her she was being foolish. But Sylvie thought that somehow he knew – and the recent bomb in Campile was meant for her. It was only a matter of time before he found her.

Peter's fair head appeared around the door.

"You OK, little one?"

"Yes," she said.

31

At least you are here, she thought, and she put her thumb in her mouth and once more tried to sleep.

It started after Mass on Sunday, a gnawing anxiety in the pit of her stomach in anticipation of school the following morning. A fear fuelled by thoughts of the black, crow-like master, MacErlaine. Although Maman had often spoken to her in English, it was difficult to understand all the words, and when the master spoke in Irish he might as well have been talking Russian. Perversely, he asked her to read, and when she did she could see laughter in the eyes of the other children. He didn't beat her though. The master knew what was good for him. Uncle Daniel had spoken to him the first time he had threatened it.

Nicholas, who was three years older than her, always left for school early, so he could meet up with his friends and smoke a cigarette they shared on the way. But Peter, who was only a year older, waited for her. Every morning, as they walked the two miles from Knockaboy, he helped her with her pronunciation by going through the words she had found difficult the previous day.

The road was long and twisty with low stone walls. Peter called them the "Hunger Walls". He told her they were built by men half-starved to death during the terrible famine a hundred years ago, when Bridget's granny had died leaving her mammy, only a baby, abandoned at the side of the road. Today, despite the war they had plenty to eat anyway, he told her.

The small flaxen-haired girl in her cotton dress and pinafore and the taller fair-haired boy, wearing a tattered woollen jacket and worn trousers, walked through fields of beet and golden barley, down to the hollow where the Catholic church nestled in the trees and then along the straight road, through the crossroads and into the village of Kilrothery. She looked forward to spending this precious time with him. Even though, on the way, the village boys called her names. Jew, Frog, and Kike were their favourites. She didn't really know why they did this – she was a Catholic now – but the calling of them was said with such menace that she was afraid – so afraid that she would start to tremble as soon as she saw them approaching in the distance at the other side of the crossroads. Then Peter would squeeze her hand and say, "It's alright, Sylvie. They're only names, they can't hurt you." But they did. And when she got to the small village school, the playground was the worst.

Of all the boys at Kilrothery National School, Christopher Mulligan was the scariest. Although he wasn't as tall or broad as some of the bigger boys, like Nicholas, he was strong and wiry and brown from being out all day in the fields. He was the son of a seasonal labourer. It was one consolation, Peter told her, that he would be gone by the spring when he left school to tramp the countryside with his father.

She remembered vividly how one morning he had pushed into her, knocking her, so that the satchel, containing the lemonade bottle filled with milk and the bread Bridget had given her for morning break, fell to the ground. Nicholas, at least six inches taller than Christopher, grabbed the youngster by the neck and pushed him till he fell backwards into the dirt while the other children stood back, gawping at the spectacle.

"Courtney, Mulligan – that's enough. Get in here this minute and let me give you a lick of the leather to douse your ardour!"

MacErlaine loomed menacingly over Mulligan, leather strap in hand, veins throbbing in his neck. He could hardly contain himself, then drawing on some inner reserve he turned abruptly.

Mulligan scrambled to his feet and, with Nicholas, followed the long, black back into the classroom.

"Roll up your sleeves and put out your hands," MacErlaine said while the other children silently took their seats.

Mulligan rolled up the sleeve of his boiled-wool jumper with difficulty, and Nicholas took off his jacket and rolled up the sleeve of his shirt. The master hit Nicholas first, ten lashes. Sylvie watched, tears running down her face as red welts appeared on his white hands. Then he dealt with Mulligan. It wouldn't hurt him as much, she thought, his hands were well hardened.

"Sit down now, both of ye, and I don't want to hear a word from ye all day. As for you, mademoiselle, it seems to me that wherever you are there is trouble. Go to Father Thomas and make your confession and tell him about your habit of inciting decent people."

Sylvie didn't know what inciting meant but she was sure it was a terrible sin.

She sat down beside Peter but the master roared, *"Sit up here at the front where I can keep an eye on you!"*

Nicholas and Peter looked at her sympathetically as she gathered her chalk and slate and moved to the front of the class, head bowed so no one would see her tears.

That morning MacErlaine told them how the Jews

hounded, and finally killed Our Lord Jesus Christ, like a common criminal. Sylvie kept her head lowered in shame. Uncle Daniel had told her on the day she arrived that she was *never*, *ever*, to mention the fact that she was Jewish. He said it was because of the terrible things that the Jews did to Our Lord, and that from now on she was a Catholic girl – a child of the Virgin Mary. He had arranged for her to be baptised by Father Thomas quietly one morning – with just himself and Nora there – when no one else was around. But they all seemed to know that she wasn't one of them.

Later she recited the Catechism with gusto so that they could all see that she was sorry for the sins of her people, and that she was going to try very hard to be a good Catholic in future.

When she asked Peter next morning what inciting meant, he avoided her pale-blue eyes.

"I think it just means you cause trouble for no reason." He let go of her hand and put his hands in his pocket, kicking a stone on the road. "It's probably because you're so pretty. At least that's what Nicholas says. Anyway, hurry up, or we will be late for school."

Knockaboy, 1950

That was when she came here first. How things had changed over the years. Christopher Mulligan for a start. She had met him in the village earlier that day. Aunt Nora had sent her in to fetch stamps from the post office and she bumped into him, literally. He was sorting the letters. He still wasn't as tall as her cousins, but he had an impish face that some of her friends found attractive. But not she – she wasn't the forgiving type – and, although she would be ashamed to admit it, she found him coarse and uncouth. She noted with satisfaction that his brown face turned red as he stuttered a greeting. Who had the problem with pronunciation now? She gave him a condescending smile and turned away.

He called after her. "Miss High and Mighty, you'll have to come down to earth too, you know, and sooner than you think!"

She looked at him quizzically.

"I hear your uncle's bank is in trouble. It's emerging with the Provincial."

"I think you mean *merging*, Christopher. It won't affect us at all, if you must know. Mustn't stop you from sorting those letters though. Cheerio!"

Christopher was the least of her concerns today – she was in a hurry to get back to Knockaboy. Nicholas was due home from Dublin, and she wanted to shorten the hem on her Sunday-best dress, try on the silk stockings Aunt Nora had given her for her birthday, and have the time to do up her hair.

Granville House in the townland of Knockaboy was a two-storey farmhouse, three miles from the village of Kilrothery and twelve miles from the town of New Ross. Set between rolling hills and the Irish Sea, it was typical of Irish farmhouses in Wexford. It had been gentrified over the last hundred years, "grown-up" as Aunt Nora would say. It had started off as a two-up, two-down labourer's cottage with a shed for the animals to the side. But, as times improved, the shed was converted, and the animals moved to an outhouse at the rear of the yard. Some years later, with the proceeds of a dowry, or a family inheritance, an extension was built by the next generation to even up the other side. So that now it was a four-up, four-down, slightly crookedy, ramshackle kind of a place. But, inside, Aunt Nora had decorated it like a palace. Peter told Sylvie that Nora's people were horse breeders from Kilkenny and were comparatively wealthy. When her parents died, she had inherited some of the furniture that had once graced their manor house near Graiguenemanagh which she had lovingly transposed to Knockaboy. Now it was a suitable house for an Agent of the New Ross & District Bank, she would say.

Aunt Nora had prepared a dinner in her eldest son's honour. It was to be a joint celebration as it was also Sylvie's eighteenth birthday. All week, with Bridget's expert help, her aunt had been baking Nicholas's favourite things. There was an apple cake, a Bakewell tart and a tea brack. The silver and brasses were polished and the Waterford glass in the dining room sparkled. The table had been set since ten o'clock that morning. Sounds of Nora singing Percy French's haunting melody, 'The Mountains of Mourne' came on a continuous loop from the kitchen. She sang it for happy, and sad, occasions, as the song seemed to suit any situation. During this maelstrom of industry, Uncle Daniel's study door was firmly closed as he attended to his business, or more often, Sylvie suspected, was indulging in an afternoon nap.

Upstairs in her room, Sylvie, sitting at the sewing table that Aunt Nora had bought her for her eighteenth birthday, was shortening the hem of her dress. It was kind of her aunt, she thought, but it would be far from sewing she would be doing in the future.

She thought with affection of how the Courtneys had taken her in and made her one of their own. They insisted that she called them Uncle and Aunt, and that she addressed the boys as cousins. As she sewed, she thought how Aunt Nora and Uncle Daniel were such a mismatched couple. It was only as she grew older that she came to understand this. Nora was stout, not as in the Guinness, which was also called stout, but in the physical sense – she was a heavy woman. She found this comforting as she reminded her of her own mother who likewise had a generous build. Her aunt's heart was also big and generous. The older woman permanently wore what she called a housecoat. It was like another dress really, in a faded flowery fabric and tied at the front with straps – and when someone important called to Knockaboy, like Father Thomas, the Collins, or the Eustaces who lived up the road, then she would whip off the smeared and grubby outer garment and underneath she would be neat as a new pin. She reminded Sylvie of the fat and brightly coloured Russian dolls that she had played with as a child.

On long winter evenings, Uncle Daniel, Aunt Nora and Mr and Mrs Eustace would play cards. The women would have a glass of sherry and whisper gossip about neighbours while the men drank whiskey and talked about important things, like sport and politics. People, their goings-on, and annoying idiosyncrasies, didn't seem to interest the men. After a few sherries Aunt Nora used to sink into the chintz-covered sofa and her chubby knees would start to spread until Uncle Daniel would say, "Nora, I can see your knickers," and she would pull down her skirt and laugh in a good-natured way at her sombre husband. But Uncle Daniel wasn't joking. Sylvie could see this and wondered why her aunt didn't. Uncle Daniel was a serious man, careful with his words which he dispensed in a clipped fashion that matched his neat moustache. And whereas she knew Nora, who was no relation, loved her – as much as she loved everyone really – she was never quite sure about Uncle Daniel.

It was implied to neighbours that he was a distant cousin of her father's. When she asked Uncle Daniel about this, he told her that her father and he had met at the Art Historical Society in Cambridge where they were both studying Classics – and, because they were distantly related, they had become friends. However, when Sylvie questioned him about the nature of their relationship, she felt the details he gave her were vague. He told her how her papa had subsequently studied Art in the Royal Academy in Antwerp and went on to become an art dealer in Paris. Whereas Uncle Daniel had joined the bank – but he also collected art, he said, for investment purposes – Sylvie was never entirely sure what that meant. Over the years the two men had kept in touch, particularly as art was a passion that they both shared. And when the war broke out, Papa had done the sensible thing and asked his old friend Daniel to take care of his only daughter until things calmed down in France.

In the beginning her parents wrote every week – she kept the letters under her bed in an orange-coloured Jacobs biscuit tin that Bridget had given her that first Christmas. But after a while the letters had stopped suddenly. Every day when Sylvie came home from school, she would run to Aunt Nora and ask if anything had come for her. Nora's eyes used to glisten as she said no, and she looked so sad. From then on, she noticed her aunt avoided talking to her about her parents. In desperation, she eventually plucked up the courage to ask Uncle Daniel about them. He said that they were both ill and had gone to a sanatorium in Switzerland, and that because of the war he had lost contact with them. He told her not to pester himself or her aunt – some things were better not spoken about.

When she was twelve, he had called her into his study and told her that her parents were probably dead, killed by Hitler. He told her to be a brave girl, that it was her cross to bear, and that God only gave burdens to those with broad shoulders who were able to carry them. He told her all of this while she sobbed, inconsolably, standing in front of him as he sat with studied emotional detachment at his desk. From then on, she used to cry herself to sleep in the realisation that she would never return to their home in Paris with the apple trees in the garden and the painted metal hen fixed to the coach-house door.

In those early years she used to play a game. She would imagine climbing up the three flights of stone stairs to their apartment in Rue de Sévigné. Walking through the front door, the first thing she would remember was the lingering smell of Papa's Gauloise cigarettes. In the hall she would see the watercolour painting of the village of Barbizon, near the Forest of Fontainebleau, where Papa told her the artists congregated to paint "*en plein air*" in the beautiful countryside. To the right of this, the grandmother clock stood, with its brassy chimes and comforting *tick-tock*, *tick-tock* sounds that marked the passing of their lives there. Then she would turn left into the parlour, where Maman kept her good china in a wooden-and-glass cabinet. And all over the walls were Papa's paintings. She remembered how her friends from school had laughed at them, said they could do better. But she had grown used to these childlike images and brash colours. Papa said it was "modern art". Her favourite was the painting of the woman in an exotically patterned dress with her cat, by Papa's friend, Henrique Mateus. He was old and wrinkled and he smelt of garlic and hair oil. He had painted her once, sitting on a swing when she was at a party in the house of Papa's friend, who she called Uncle Émile.

In her game she would then proceed into the dining room with its glass epergne in the middle of the elegant mahogany table that was surrounded by chairs covered in dark-red damask velvet. And finally, in her mind's eye, she looked through the door into the kitchen with its range where on cold winter mornings their maid Louise would make crêpes spread with apple purée and flavoured with cinnamon. Once she started it was as if a floodgate in her mind had opened and other memories would then flow through, such as the laughter of the servants in the communal basement and the smell of lavender, lemony soap and hot linen as the women did their laundry. Sometimes Louise let her turn the mangle to wring out the smalls. In the afternoons when Papa was at the gallery, Maman would take tea with Madame Dubois from the apartment on the first floor. She was a fine-boned, small woman who'd had polio as a child and walked with a limp. She was her mother's

41

closest friend. Sylvie often wondered what had happened to her. She too was Jewish. Her husband ran a bookshop near Place des Voges. She remembered how, if it was fine, the two women and her would eat ice cream and walk in the Tuileries gardens where they would sometimes meet Odette, Uncle Émile's wife with the sad brown eyes, and their young son Felix.

Eventually the memories faded and were replaced with new ones, Irish ones. Until it came to a stage that sometimes she struggled to recall her parent's likenesses at all. But then something – a smell, or a familiar face – would act as a trigger and the memories returned once more, as vivid and real as ever. Even now, ten years later, before going to sleep she would pray for her parents and vow that one day, when she was able to, she would return to France to find them.

But today Paris was far from her mind.

Peter popped his head around the door.

"I have a present for you. I wanted to give it to you before dinner."

"Come in, come in! What is it? Let me guess!" She grabbed the box which was carefully wrapped in red tissue and tied with a white ribbon. "Is it a book?"

"No."

She shook it and it rattled a little. "Hairbrush."

"No, but close. Why don't you open it?"

She tore the ribbon and the paper off the box and uncovered the shiny black metal case of a Cotman watercolour set and a small watercolour sketchbook.

"Peter! How did you know? This is exactly what I wanted. You are such a sweetheart!"

Peter looked slightly embarrassed as he kissed her

on the side of the cheek.

But as she turned their lips grazed. She jumped back in alarm.

"Oh, sorry, Peter! I didn't mean to!"

He pulled her to him and placed his hands around her face, kissing her full on the lips.

"Well, I did. And now that you're eighteen, I think we should do it more often."

She pulled back abruptly, leaving him standing with his hands in mid-air.

"No, Peter," she said, exasperated, "how could you even think I could feel like that about you? I think of you as a brother, no more."

Peter, crestfallen, turned away.

"Sylvie. I thought –"

"Well, you thought wrong, you eejit! Now come on, Nicholas will be here soon, let's not spoil my party."

When Sylvie met Nicholas in the hall as he arrived, she had felt a little shy at their physical contact as she welcomed him home with a sisterly hug. He had grown tall and broad in the three years he had been away at college and had acquired a new confidence. Looking down at her, his brown eyes laughing, he was obviously impressed by the changes he also saw in her.

"My little cousin, you have blossomed into quite a beauty. I bet all the clodhoppers around here are pestering the life out of you."

Sylvie smiled shyly as Peter, standing behind them, glared at his older brother.

Later that evening, when they had all finished the lavish dinner and Bridget was clearing away the plates,

Nicholas asked his father about the proposed merger with the Provincial.

But before Daniel had a chance to answer, Sylvie interjected. "Christopher Mulligan implied we will be down on our uppers."

"Loose talk doesn't help anyone, Sylvie," Uncle Daniel rebuked her. Then he continued in a more conciliatory tone. "There is no doubt that it will affect us though. Our stock has plummeted in value and our shareholders are getting nervous. I'm sorry to say that the last board of directors made some reckless investments in oil exploration which failed to materialise, in Russia of all places. The merger will help pull the bank through. But, although I own some property, the bulk of my personal savings were tied up in bank shares which are now worth a fraction of what they were. So from now on we will have to cut our cloth to suit our measure."

"How do you mean, Father?" said Peter.

"Well, cut back on expenses. Nicholas, I have made enquiries with a solicitor in New Ross who is willing to take you on. But, Peter, you might have to put off college for a year or two, until our affairs are in better shape and help me in the office. That would mean I could let Jim Kelly go."

Nicholas did not seem surprised, thought Sylvie, as if he had been forewarned.

However, Peter looked aghast at his father and the sudden annihilation of his expectations.

"But Jim has been with you for years," he said.

"Yes, but I simply can no longer afford to keep him."

"What about me?" said Sylvie, "I'd hoped to go to art college."

"Out of the question, my dear. The Metropolitan School of Art is a totally unsuitable place for a woman. I won't hear of it."

"But, Uncle, I have dreamt of being an artist since I was a child."

"Dreams, dear, dreams – very few of us have the luxury of living our dreams. Is that not so, Nicholas?"

Nicholas, who had been quiet during this exchange, answered, "Yes, Father. But hasn't Sylvie got her own money? I thought her father left –"

"*Enough*. Dinner is not the place to discuss the sordid subject of money, Nicholas. Now what culinary delight has Bridget created for pudding?"

The next evening Uncle Daniel had asked to speak to Sylvie after dinner in his study. She had been distracted and fearful of the prospect all day. She was afraid somehow Uncle Daniel had learnt of Peter's foolishness. What on earth was the silly boy thinking of? She had been annoyed about it all day. Peter was her rock, her best friend – she told him everything. Well, most things. She talked to him about her dreams of becoming an artist, and of one day returning to France to find out what had become of her parents.

It was six years since the war had ended. When she was younger her uncle had forbidden her to read the newspapers. But as she grew older, she would sneak into the Carnegie library in the village where she read everything that she could lay her hands on about what had happened. How the Allied forces had eventually liberated Paris from the Germans in August 1944. Although she had seen images in newspapers of women in Berlin with wheelbarrows clearing stone and rubble whilst all around them the buildings were in ruins, Paris appeared to have survived relatively unscathed. The city's boulevards, cafés and elegant shops were still for the most part intact. However, she knew from newspaper reports that her home was gone – it had been blitzed early on in the war. Where were all the people now who had lived there, she wondered. They couldn't all be dead. What had happened to Mr and Mrs Dubois? Although many had been killed in action in France and Belgium, or on the Russian Front, she was never entirely sure why her parents had disappeared. She knew that her parents were Jewish, although they didn't practise, unlike her grandfather. And she knew that Hitler had ordered the killing of Jews and she had heard the unbelievable stories about the gas chambers. However, she couldn't bring herself to accept that this was what had happened to her parents. Maybe Uncle Daniel's belief that they had died in a sanatorium was true. She remembered in one of their last letters that they were planning to stay with Uncle Émile for a while in the South of France. But she had no contact with him or his wife Odette since leaving France. When she finally got an opportunity to track them down, at least it would be a place to start.

Uncle Daniel's study was a sparse room. It had a window looking out to the garden but he, instead of enjoying the view and the opportunity it gave for quiet contemplation, had chosen instead to position his desk with his back to it. On one wall there was a bookcase of art books with glass doors that were locked and a large wooden filing cabinet where he kept his papers. Peter told her once that he had a safe behind the room's single artwork. For someone who liked art she always thought that his choice for this room was strange. It was an etching of a rather sad-looking rabbit.

When Sylvie entered the room, her uncle was sitting upright behind the desk and indicated that she should sit opposite him. He pressed the tips of his finely boned fingers together and looked at her from under thin well-groomed eyebrows.

"Well, Sylvie, you are eighteen years of age, a young woman. I thought it was time we discussed your future."

"Yes, Uncle, I have been thinking about this myself. I –"

He held up his hand to silence her.

"As you know, Sylvie, I am your legal guardian and, as your poor late father requested I brought you into my home and put a roof over your head, sparing no expense."

Sylvie bit her lip as he said this. She plucked up the courage to ask him the question that had been on her mind for some time.

"Did my parents leave me anything? I know their apartment was bombed during the war, but at dinner last night Nicholas seemed to suggest that they had left me some money. What about my mother's jewellery?"

"No money, nothing," he said firmly. "Their apartment was blitzed, as you say, and the gallery at Rue du Faubourg Saint-Honoré was leased over a period that has long since expired. Unfortunately, he spent a lot of money decorating it in lavish style. He even paid Mateus to design ceramic floor and wall tiles. At the time I warned him it was a waste of money, but your father had his own ideas. He thought with his heart not his head. Stocks and shares were sold before the war and turned into cash, American dollars, and gold. It was the only safe thing to do. He told me that he had bought jewellery and precious stones and had sewn these with any other items that your mother owned into her coat. I often wonder what became of the coat in their escape from Paris that summer – as I recall it was during a period of sweltering heat." Daniel's eyes glazed over briefly. "I digress, Sylvie. It was almost impossible to get money out of the country. One can only assume that all he owned was confiscated when he was arrested by the Gestapo. So, you see Sylvie, there is no money."

"What about all of Papa's paintings? I told you about the Mateus."

"Destroyed, my dear. I believe they were burnt shortly after the German occupation. 'Degenerate Art' is what the government called it. Hitler had no truck with modern art. He favoured sublime landscapes, art that was concerned with classical ideals of physical beauty – socialist or heroic realism they would call it today. So, my dear, like us all, unfortunately, you will have to earn a living – and that is what I wanted to talk to you about today."

In the last few years he had given her pocket money. Before she received it, she had to go to his study each Friday and account for how she had spent her previous week's money. She found the whole arrangement humiliating, telling him about underwear she might have purchased, or the cost of a new set of pencils. Last week she had to explain to him why she would want talcum powder to cover the smell of perspiration. Peter told her not to take it personally, that his father put him through the same ordeal. Peter said it was a form of control. She had looked forward to the day that she could escape this indignity and have money of her own. The news that her parents had left no inheritance did not come to her as a complete surprise. She didn't know where Nicholas had got the idea that she had money of her own. Over the years there had never been even a hint of this from her uncle and aunt. Although she was disappointed about the paintings, particularly the Mateus which she remembered vividly.

"I want to be an artist," she said boldly.

"Out of the question, my dear, as I think I told you last night." He leaned forward, elbows on his desk and his bony fingers touching. "I have thought about this carefully, and I think a commercial college might be the answer. I believe there is a suitable college in Dublin, run by the Dominican nuns in Eccles Street where they teach typewriting, shorthand and bookkeeping. The course is designed to groom young women for a job in the Civil Service, a professional's office or a bank. You can start at the end of the summer in September. I believe you can earn a decent living once you have completed the course and been awarded their certificate. Initially, however, I will continue to pay you a small allowance as your earnings will not meet your living costs. Miss Brennan, the postmistress in the village, has a sister in Dublin who has a boarding house near the college and has kindly promised to take you in."

"But, Uncle," tears welled up in Sylvie's eyes – she was not expecting this, to be summarily turfed out of her home, "I don't want to leave Knockaboy. You are my family – you are all I have."

"Well, as I said last night, Sylvie, things are about to change around here. There will be economies. Peter will have to work for me at the bank and, as I explained last night, I have arranged for Nicholas to be indentured to a solicitor in New Ross." He took his glasses off and laid them on the desk, sitting back in his chair. "Now I'm tired, Sylvie – that's enough for one evening."

"But, Uncle!" Tears were falling down her cheeks.

"No buts, Sylvie. I have made my decision. You are always welcome to visit but my obligations to your father have now been discharged."

Sylvie, her eyes blind with tears, made her way up the stairs to the privacy of her bedroom. She had expected an argument about art college which she hoped to win by pointing out that she could earn a living teaching. But, instead of discussing her education, her whole life had been turned upside down. She undressed hastily, fell on her bed, pulled the blankets over her head and sobbed into her pillow until, exhausted, she fell into a disjointed sleep.

She woke to hear a gentle knock on the door.

"Sylvie, it's Peter – may I come in?"

Wiping her eyes, she rose. Pulling her candlewick dressing gown around her, she opened the door and let him in.

"Jesus, Sylvie, Nicholas just told me! What a bastard! He talked to me too. At least you get to escape to Dublin. I will be stuck working at his bloody bank where I will rot away until I become old and miserable just like him."

"It's just – I hadn't thought about leaving. Not this way. To go to college, yes. But I always intended to come home to Aunt Nora, and to you and Nicholas, to what I thought was my home – till now. I will be so lonely in Dublin – I don't know anyone there."

Peter sat down on the bed beside her and put his arm around her shoulders.

"Look, Sylvie, it's been a shock. But he does seem to be in serious financial trouble. Mother says that we all must pull together as a family. He never was the most sympathetic, or tactful man, but it's just his way. Maybe commercial college won't be so bad. You will make friends, you always do. You are so pretty. And you might even make money. Maybe you could save and pay to go to Art College yourself. At least you will be away from him. You can visit at the weekends when you get lonely and, of course, I can visit you in Dublin."

Sylvie remained unconvinced.

"Nicholas is in with him now," said Peter. "They're roaring at each other – at least Nicholas is roaring. Although I can't make out what he is saying. Mother is wringing her hands in the kitchen, worrying what will become of us all. And Bridget is saying the Rosary. God, I hope we don't have to let Bridget go. God knows what mother would feed us."

Chapter 5

Antibes
17th July, 1940

Once inside Casa Fonteille the Gestapo officer led them up the white marble staircase and into the main reception room, where the owner Monsieur Gerard Cabbott and his wife Francine, who had sublet the house to Émile and Odette, were waiting for them. The Cabotts were seated on chairs whilst Émile and Odette stood behind a chaise longue. White, sheer curtains lifted with the breeze coming through the blue-louvred doors which opened onto the terrace and had views out over the Mediterranean. Although late in the evening, it was still warm. There was a smell of cinnamon in the air and, in the half-light, Paul glimpsed the tiny lights of fishing vessels that he imagined, with longing, were heading out across the sea towards the coast of Africa.

"Madame, monsieur, welcome!" the German officer said in a booming voice. "May I introduce myself to you – I am Major Heinrick Keppler and this is my comrade Lieutenant Foucault who is facilitating our investigation." He nodded perfunctorily at the French police officer and clicked together the heels of his black leather boots.

"Take a seat, you look tired after your journey."

Keppler was tall and broad-shouldered – and, although he was slightly balding, he had a youthful, bullish face with a short upper lip which gave his face a sneering expression.

"Although I appreciate the current difficulties travelling, you have taken your time. But don't worry, your friends here have been most hospitable."

Paul looked nervously at Émile, noting his pallor and the mauve-coloured shadows under his eyes – he did not look well. He could see the white knuckles on his friend's hand resting on the back of the chaise longue.

Paul helped Hanna sit down on a couch opposite them while the Gestapo officer stood near the door, addressing them all.

"Let us not waste any more time, my friends. We are here to discuss art. An enlightened subject, don't you agree, Monsieur Vasseur? I believe you have a taste for the avant-garde."

"Major Keppler," said Paul, with forced dignity, the sight of the Gestapo's officer's black uniform filling him with terror, "my wife and I have been travelling for over a week and we are both exhausted. Can we not postpone this ... meeting until tomorrow? At least let us freshen up and change into some clean clothes."

"No, unfortunately, that is not possible, monsieur. Herr Göring is not a patient man and he is anxious to hear about your private paintings. I have been telling my comrade, Lieutenant Foucault, how Herr Göring feels it is his personal responsibility to protect the patrimony of the French state from the reckless actions of those who wish to make personal gains in these unsettled times."

"Do you mean my father's paintings, the Barbizon works?"

"Yes, but also those of the degenerates – Picasso, Léger, Braque."

"The works of the modern artists you mention belong to the artists themselves. To my knowledge, they are still in my gallery in Paris. But the Barbizon paintings have already been sold, major. They were auctioned a few years ago."

"To foreign buyers, no doubt."

"I have no idea. Amongst auctioneers, client confidentiality is sacrosanct."

"Which auctioneer?"

The officer looked away from Paul, directly at Émile.

"Did you avail of the professional services of your friend here? Is that not what friends do?"

Émile stiffened and Odette clutched his arm.

"No, not in this instance. I knew I would get better prices abroad."

"So, where did you send them?"

"Several different houses, mainly in London and Geneva."

"And you can prove this, Monsieur?"

"Yes," said Paul, trying to avoid Émile's eyes.

"To export fine art without a license is illegal, monsieur, as you know."

"I have the licenses."

"These, unfortunately, are no longer relevant. Nevertheless, I would like to see them."

"As you can see," said Paul, holding out his hands, "we have travelled here with nothing but the clothes we stand in. My paperwork is all in Paris."

"Then you and I must return to Paris."

Odette looked to the ground.

"I will go with you," said Hanna, her voice barely a whisper.

"No, my darling, you must stay here with our friends." He looked at Émile who nodded.

"No, no, I insist, monsieur – she can come too." Keppler said this as if bestowing a great favour.

"You are Jewish, I believe, Monsieur Vasseur, although you could pass for French, even German, with your fair colouring. But not your wife, something about the eyes."

"We are not practising Jews, officer."

"Practising or not, once a Jew, always a Jew. It's in the blood, monsieur." He turned to Foucault. "Lieutenant, can I leave you to deal with these collaborators?" He waved a gloved hand at Émile, Odette and the Cabbotts.

"Of course, major," said the lieutenant nervously.

The Gestapo agent, his Luger drawn, with a nod of his head directed the Vasseurs towards the door.

As they left the room, Hanna looked back imploringly at Émile.

Chapter 6

It was all a bit odd. Claire thought to herself, although she couldn't quite put her finger on it. Since she had completed her Master's she had found it tough going. Jobs for art historians were rare and usually based on who you knew. The cream of the students was usually hired quickly after graduation as cheap labour to work on senior academicians' own projects, poring over archives and doing the donkey work. For most people it was a long and expensive apprenticeship. And here she was, with an interesting project that had dropped like manna from heaven. And what was even more satisfying, it involved working with real people, as in non-academics, which meant that she would probably be paid a reasonable fee for her troubles. Her sister would tell her she shouldn't overanalyse this situation – she should just accept it and get on with it.

She had read through the details of Sylvie Vasseur's death and was struck by the poignancy of it all – how the beautiful young artist was found drowned on a beach in Wexford. The coroner's verdict was that it had been a tragic accident. But one of the newspaper articles written at the time seemed to suggest that she may have killed herself.

Why would she want to do such a thing? Her life was by any standards successful. She had received critical acclaim within the Irish art world in a relatively short period, and her work was, at that stage, in several prestigious collections. In fact, the year she died one of her paintings had been bought by the Arts Council, a valuable imprimatur for any artist trying to establish their reputation. Also, she had been working towards an exhibition that autumn with the highly regarded Baggot Street Gallery. On a personal level, she seemed to have had a happy marriage, and a loving family who spoke movingly of her in the newspaper reports. "Loving mother, adored wife," that sort of thing. But then they usually said that, didn't they?

Claire tried to put thoughts of Sylvie's emotional state out of her mind, to concentrate on the task in hand – how she would go about this project. First, she'd do a tabletop research study, scope the artist's life and works from available sources, and then she would prepare a detailed inventory with photographs of the artworks and write a report compiling the two. It wouldn't be possible to examine the paintings without the initial research as you wouldn't know what you were looking for. This wasn't exactly as she had described the process to Nicholas, but in retrospect she felt that it was a logical way to go about it.

The following day in the bright and airy café of the National Library Claire sat in a seat by the window. She had arrived early and was sorting out her paperwork as she sipped black coffee when she saw Nicholas enter the room. She waved at him to catch his attention and he smiled at her in acknowledgement. He was still a good-looking man in his mid-fifties, his hair dark, although thinning. He looked like he exercised regularly. He was dressed carefully, smart casual they called it these days, but smart casual achieved by expensive brands rather than Claire's shabby chic which was as a result of economic necessity.

He walked briskly over and sat opposite her at the table, holding up his hand to call the waitress's attention.

"Hello, Claire, nice to see you again. I got your letter outlining your approach to this."

"I hope it was clear enough."

"Perfectly. Time though? How long do you think it will take?"

"I'm not sure – it depends on how organised your sister-in-law was in terms of records."

"I wouldn't hold out too much hope on that score. As you saw in the studio, she was all over the place, very disorganised." He paused. "I think it would be useful if my nephew Sam helps you do some of the physical sorting. He was a banker, following the family tradition. But two years ago, he left his well-paid job in the bank to go back to College and study History of Art in Trinity." Nicholas said this with a sardonic lift of his eyebrow. "He is also interested in contemporary art, and as you can imagine would be keen to learn about his mother's work. He was only fourteen when she died and was heartbroken at the time."

"Oh," said Claire uncertainly, deciding on the spur of the moment not to disclose her conversation with

Professor Dillon. "I prefer to work on my own really."

"Well, in this instance, possibly you could make an exception." He stared at her, – eyes unwavering. "Actually, it's a requirement, non-negotiable so to speak."

"Oh, OK. Right, well, I would need to meet him." She didn't want to lose this opportunity but was not really keen on babysitting someone she knew nothing about.

"Of course. Actually, I asked him to join us – see could you both get along. Oh, perfect timing – here he is."

Claire stared in horror as Pink-Shirt man ambled into the coffee shop and up to their table.

"Oh Christ, it's you! I don't believe it!" he exclaimed, equally aghast.

"You two already know one another?"

"Yes, unfortunately, we met last week, in my local dry cleaner's. Claire ruined my dress shirt."

Claire blushed profusely and shuffled uncomfortably in her chair.

But a broad smile spread across Sam's face. "I hope you're a better art-historian than you are a dry cleaner."

He put out his hand and she shook it weakly.

"Well, do you think you could work together?" Nicholas asked.

"Hopefully," said Claire nervously, at this stage all attempts at presenting herself as an aloof and confident professional evaporating. "Maybe we could go through the plan."

"Wonderful! Coffee, Sam?" Nicholas asked as the waitress approached their table.

Sam was already there by the time she arrived. He was sitting on a chair reading the newspaper with two disposable cups on the workbench beside him.

"Ah, Claire, I got you a coffee, not sure whether you took it black, so I got milk separately."

"Oh, that's really kind of you."

"No problem. Listen, I realise I have been foisted on you. But she was my mother – it's my legacy if you like."

"I can understand that. Well, for today, let's just try and tidy things up and see where everything is."

"OK."

"Right, if you could stack the canvases there. Will I show you how best to handle them?"

"Please."

"Well, put these on first." She gave him a pair of cotton gloves. "Hold the canvases by the sides and stack them stretcher to stretcher. I'll start systematically working along the bench, sorting objects from rubbish. Then we can tackle the drawers."

They worked silently at first, Claire occasionally glancing at Sam to see if he was doing the stacking properly.

Then she asked him, "Were you aware of your mother's work growing up?"

"Well, I remember doing my homework here in the studio as she painted when I was about six or seven. She sometimes got me to draw things like shells and bits of twigs. I used to love collecting skeletons as a child, ghoulish really. She encouraged me to draw them. In the summer we used to spend a lot of time at Nicholas's bungalow on the Hook Peninsula. Peter used to come down at weekends."

"Peter was your dad?"

"Well ... No, actually, he was my stepdad."

"Really?"

"Yes. It's a long story, and one I'd rather not talk about if you don't mind."

"Sorry, I didn't mean to pry," said Claire, intrigued, and reluctantly changed the subject.

"How's the studying going?"

"Not too bad. I have to complete a 2,000-word essay on Celtic decoration by the end of June, but I've the bones of it sorted at this stage."

"If you need any help – to read over and edit – feel free to ask."

"Would you have time?"

"Between archiving and dry cleaning, you mean?" She smiled. "Actually, I gave up the dry-cleaning job. I handed in my notice. So, I do have some spare time."

"Oh, I hope that wasn't on my account," he said earnestly.

"No, don't worry. I couldn't stand the heat. And you know what they say."

He laughed and Sylvie was struck by the fact that this extremely attractive man was also rather shy.

"Thanks for the offer. I'll bear it in mind."

By five o'clock it had become overcast and the light levels in the studio were poor.

"Look, why don't we call it a day?" said Claire.

By the end of the first week they had made good progress. The worktop was now visible, and Sam had brought in a steel shelving unit to stack the archival cardboard cartons. The canvases were sorted down one end of the studio and the papers were loosely arranged in cardboard boxes waiting to be sorted in more detail.

"How are you at photography?" Claire enquired.

"Not bad," he said, smiling.

"Well, for this exercise, you just need to photograph each piece and attach it to an individual form outlining the artwork's details. We will use these to put together a catalogue of the work. Later we can get the paintings photographed professionally. While you do that, I'll sort out the paperwork."

"Let me carry those boxes for you – they're heavy."

"Thanks," she said. "I'm not as fit as I should be."

"You look in pretty good shape to me," he said, blushing.

Once more she was taken aback. She had assumed, with his good looks, he would be more self-assured.

"I've really enjoyed this last week, working with you," he said shyly. "I've learnt a lot. More than in all those hours of lectures anyway. How about a drink later?"

She had insisted on going home to the flat and changing. Lying in the bath – the shower was banjaxed again – she agonised about what to wear. She hadn't expected him to ask her out. Most of her wardrobe her sister described as arty-farty. At this late stage, she didn't have time to borrow something suitable from Molly. In the end, she chose a short black denim skirt with leather boots, a lacy shirt, and a half-decent long woollen coat her mother had bought her the previous Christmas.

"You look great," he said when they met later that evening outside Toner's bar in Baggot Street.

So did he, she thought, but said, fingering her woollen coat, "Oh, this old thing, I got it from Oxfam."

"Really?" he said, recoiling almost imperceptibly at the thought.

He showed her into the snug and ordered drinks.

"So what made you give up your job in the bank and study art history?"

"Have you got all night?" he said sheepishly.

"Well, I have another date lined up at ten, but he's quite unreliable, probably be arse-holed by then."

Sam looked alarmed.

"Joking."

They spent a pleasant evening together, her reminiscing about her time in Trinity, sharing stories about Professor Dillon. She told him the one about his alarm clock.

"He was a friend of my grandfather's, you know," he said. "He used to advise him about art. The Prof studied at the Cortauld – his family are connected to the Pinkertons – the famous auctioneering house."

"I thought that Daniel Courtney was a banker."

"*Mm*, yes, he was, quite a wealthy one by all accounts. But he had an interest in art – always up at the Dublin auctions, buying and selling. In a modest way, of course. Sometimes he even advised bank customers what to buy as investments. But he got into financial difficulties during the early 60s. Well, as you know, Ireland was only emerging then from the financial desert of De Valera's era. But through dealing in stocks and shares privately, he turned his finances around. Nicholas was involved in a lot of his business dealings, him being a solicitor."

"And Peter?"

"No. Grandfather never really forgave him for marrying my mother. You know she was taken in as an evacuee by my grandfather during the Second World War when the Germans occupied Paris. He felt that they had both let him down. And, in fairness, at the time, people were genuinely quite shocked – the fact that they grew up together as brother and sister. I seem to remember being told that they couldn't get married in a church, had to go over to England, to a registry office. Then, after my mother's death, Grandfather left Peter in limbo, financially I mean. Peter was such a lovely gentle man. He was broken-hearted. Took to the drink really. He died a few years later – cancer got him in the end. But I think it was largely caused by the trauma of her death."

"That's so sad, Sam." She put her hand on his arm, squeezing it slightly.

"Enough of my tales of woe. How about you?"

"Well, you know a lot about me already. I'm an under-employed art historian who sometimes works part-time as a dry cleaner."

He smiled. "Family?"

"Boring, in comparison. My father is a civil servant, my mum plays serious golf – badly. I have one sister Molly who works at the make-up counter in Arnotts and deplores my lack of style, and I live in a damp, dreary bedsit in Rathmines. See, really boring."

He smiled at her and took a sip of his drink.

"Look, Claire, Nicholas invited me to an art auction in the tennis club next week. Would you come with me? It would make it bearable if you could. I hate those things. It's just Nicholas has been helping me out with fees while I'm in college and I feel I should support him."

"Yes, that would be lovely. Would I have to dress up?"

"They are fairly formal things, I'm afraid – so, yes, you would have to wear something a bit more ..."

"Grown-up."

"Yes," he said – and he laughed, once he saw she was not offended.

The auction was on at the Fitzwilliam Lawn Tennis Club, a fundraising event. Sam had picked her up outside her flat in a taxi – he had insisted. Looking in the mirror before leaving, she was glad of this luxury because she felt overdressed to be swanning around Rathmines at night. The dress she was wearing had been borrowed from her sister. Turquoise-coloured, it accentuated her blue eyes. It was fitted and comfortably cut to flatter her curves. A suitable outfit, one that had been selected after hours of consultation with Molly. It wasn't too dressy, but it was formal enough. Enough of a concession for her to make to this type of ostentatious pomp which she normally hated.

"You look beautiful, Claire," Sam told her when she got into the taxi.

And although she felt he was just being polite, she luxuriated in feeling unusually glamorous.

"So, what's this 'do' going to be like?" she asked.

"It's one of those events centred on an auction where businessmen bid for artworks for extraordinarily large sums of money that only goes to prove how little they know about art," Sam said genially.

"I must tell you – I don't really approve," she replied. "Artists are generally giving their works for free. Even though most of them are living on less than the minimum wage and can ill afford the gesture." She had just started reading Thorstein Veblen's theories of conspicuous consumption. "In fact, the organisers should just give the money directly to the homeless people and avoid the necessity of an ostentatious charade."

"You are probably right. But maybe don't share those thoughts with Nicholas – not tonight anyway." He grinned.

"Is Nicholas married? Will his wife be there?"

"Good Lord, no, she won't. He and his wife Evelyn are separated. Have been for years. She got wise to his philandering very early on in their marriage. They have a daughter, Sarah. She must be in college at this stage. Nicholas only sees her occasionally. He never seemed too interested. The wife, or ex-wife, lives in Chicago in the lap of luxury. Plays golf, does a lot of charity work. She's a nice lady. Too nice for him."

"Does he have a partner now?"

"No, no one special. He changes women with the seasons, as soon as he gets bored with them."

"Really," said Claire, her mouth thin and disapproving.

By the time they arrived, the function room was crowded, and Sam hastily showed Claire to her seat.

Nicholas rose to greet them, raising his eyebrows when he saw Claire.

"Claire, what a surprise. You two are obviously getting along well, despite your initial reservations."

Claire, momentarily taken aback by the snide comment, rallied. "Oh, an art historian's caution, one I overcame very quickly once we got to know one another better."

A glamorous woman, blonde with bouffant hair and a pink jewel-encrusted cocktail dress, also rose to her feet, smiling encouragingly.

"Hello, Claire, my name is Valerie, how lovely to meet you. You can sit beside me and tell me what to bid for – I believe you are an expert."

"Oh, I wouldn't say that."

They all took their seats.

The host for the evening, a well-known auctioneer and notable impresario, called for people's attention. In strident tones worthy of the Abbey Theatre he stressed the charitable nature of the function to raise funds for the homeless and, with a great deal of humour and bonhomie, bidding proceeded at a brisk rate. But it occurred to Claire that some of the men who were bidding would pass a homeless man on the street without making eye contact.

"Not bidding, Nicholas?" Sam asked.

"Well, as it happens, I have my eye on something. You'll see later."

Lot Number 34 was a series of coloured pencil drawings by Mary Swanzy. Nicholas, bidding against one other rather dispassionate punter, got them for a song.

Finally, it was over.

Claire was relieved as Valerie had kept asking her in loud whispers, "What do you think that's worth?"

Eventually, Claire had asked obtusely, "To the artist?"

"No, no, how much money is it worth?

"Well," Claire had replied, "go by your instinct. The only thing that really matters is that it's for a good cause."

Valerie had stopped asking after that.

Flush with his successful purchase, Nicholas was trying to push his way through the crowd to get drinks.

"Hey, John!" he called to a friend at the bar. "You're wanted urgently at home!"

Alarmed, John, red-faced and balding, turned and headed frantically towards the public payphone in the hall. As he left his spot at the bar, Nicholas sidled into the space he had just left.

Sam, watching, threw his eyes up to heaven.

"That's so mean!" Claire exclaimed, but regretted saying it immediately.

"Yeah, he's like that – he thinks it's funny," said Sam with resignation.

"Nicholas is used to getting what he wants," Valerie added archly.

Despite disliking his brashness, Claire had to admit that Nicholas was an entertaining host, regaling them with amusing tales. Even though they were usually told at someone else's expense, Claire could not help laughing. He was generous too. Several times, he had dismissed her offer to buy a round of drinks. He had paid for everything which made them both feel obliged to stay with the couple and engage in small talk after the buffet finished.

A couple of hours later, Sam walked Claire home. It was a beautiful evening, still warm as they ambled up the tree-lined Appian way, through Ranelagh towards Rathmines village. They arrived there just as the pubs were discharging boisterous punters, swollen with drink, onto the empty Victorian street.

When they reached the front door to her flat, Sam briefly clasped her arms.

"I really enjoyed this evening Claire. I hope we can do it again. But, sure, I'll see you tomorrow anyway at the studio."

Then before she had time to ask him up to the flat which she had spent three hours tidying, he was gone. She was disappointed. She had thought he fancied her. But maybe he was just being nice – getting to know her. Hard to read these privileged types, she thought to herself. There was no doubt that these 'West Brits' were an entirely different breed.

Chapter 7

Dublin
18th January, 1951

The red light flickered under the Sacred Heart statue as the clock on the wall struck three. Only one hour to go. Miss Russell was talking, but Sylvie wasn't listening. Instead, she was thinking desperately about her situation. She would have to knuckle down if she was ever to escape from Eccles Street. Achieving a certificate was a prerequisite of Uncle Daniel continuing to pay her miserly allowance, which she needed now more than ever.

Sylvie was struggling to concentrate as the teacher droned on. Miss Russell – who had a strong Newry accent – was a spinster. She had crimped iron-grey hair and glasses shaped like birds' wings which sat at the end of her nose. Sylvie watched her nostrils flare as she talked, frequently puckering her lips so that she looked permanently surprised. Today she was wearing her habitual uniform, a neat twin set and pearls. Her skirt, woollen, was neatly pressed and her shoes had sensible low heels. She never wore make-up.

"Miss Vasseur, do sit up straight. Slouching is bad for the digestion and looks slovenly. No self-respecting secretary sits like she is suffering from severe abdominal cramps."

"Yes, Miss Russell. Sorry, Miss Russell."

"Now, girls, I want you to type the text on the board in front of you. I'm going to count to ten – then you can start – and when you are finished make a note of your time and put up your hand."

Sylvie, staring at the board to the flurry of sounds of typewriter keys echoing around the room, went through the exercise on autopilot. But as the *clickety-clicks* diminished until she could only hear her own keys, she realised that she was the last to finish. She looked in dismay at the clock: two minutes. It was worse than last week's result.

At the table at the front of the room Miss Russell stood to receive the pages of typing.

She looked at her witheringly. "Miss Vasseur, are you aware that your performance is supposed to be getting better, not deteriorating? If things have not improved significantly by the end of the month, I'm going to have to ask the principal to contact your father and let the poor man know he is wasting his hard-earned money."

"He's dead, Miss Russell," Sylvie said acerbically.

"Oh, I'm so sorry," she said as though Sylvie had told her she lost a favourite umbrella. "In the war?"

"Yes."

"I see. Well, Miss Vasseur, all the more reason to concentrate on gaining respectable employment. I don't know what has happened to you. You started off here well enough. I thought you were going to achieve a modicum of success. But, in the last month or so, you seem to have lost even the small amount of commitment you originally had." She paused and asked in a lowered voice. "Do you have any problems, dear?"

"Problems?"

"Yes, family problems, or young men, that sort of thing. I have noticed your mind wandering lately. I hope your head is not full of Hollywood nonsense. You know, true love and all of that foolishness." Without pausing for Sylvie to answer, she continued, "A young woman needs to be able to support herself these days, unless she is fortunate enough to secure a husband. Despite what these 'filums' say. Love is all very well, but it doesn't pay the bills. Now go along, dear, and do try to present a more *business-like* appearance."

She looked Sylvie up and down.

The cheek of her! Sylvie thought that she was looking rather stylish. The dress she was wearing had come in a parcel that Niamh O'Reilly's unmarried Aunt Kathleen had sent over from America to Knockaboy. She worked as an elevator operator in Macy's Department Store in New York and had first dibs at the sales. Niamh had given the covetable item to Sylvie as it was several sizes too small for her. Most of the American hand-me-downs were awful with brash colours and man-made fabrics that looked strange in Dublin. In Ireland, colours tended to be muted to suit the rain and drizzle, and most people's clothes were worn and shabby as a result of constant washing. But she thought this dress was rather nice. It had a chocolate-brown bodice with small gold buttons and a mottled brown-and-black full skirt. She knew she was a bit overdressed for Eccles Street, but she was meeting Nicholas later. And although her heart was racing at the prospect, she was also dreading it.

The two brothers had called on her within weeks of her

moving to Dublin and continued to do so. For them Sylvie was an excuse to escape from the tedium of Knockaboy where, like most other parts of rural Ireland, daily life was orchestrated in its minutest detail under the watchful eyes of the Catholic Church. The highlight of the week's social calendar was usually the gathering after Sunday Mass in the village church – or bumping into girls at the picture palace on a Saturday afternoon in New Ross. Even there, the Church exercised iron control. The sexes were segregated for the matinee performance by orders of the Monseigneur, a man so principled that *Gone with the Wind* was banned for fear of encouraging lax morality amongst the young people of the parish.

But there was another reason the brothers came to see her. They took every opportunity to escape from the unfolding drama of Uncle Daniel's worsening money troubles. She was aware that he had sold a farm he owned in Tully Cross to pay his debtors. And to make it worse, he didn't seem to get on with the new management in the upper echelons of the Provincial Bank. They had made him report to an agent in New Ross, a man who, by all accounts, was even more grumpy than Uncle Daniel. All in all, since she had left, according to the brothers, the atmosphere in Knockaboy was grim.

Nicholas got up to town the most frequently, using visits to the law library to study as an excuse. Peter less so – usually only when Uncle Daniel was going to some Saturday morning art auction on the Dublin Quays. On those occasions, Peter would make an excuse to stay over to visit a school friend who was working in the city.

The brothers stayed at a young men's Catholic

hostel in Abbey Street which was only a stone's throw from Sylvie's boarding house in South Frederick Street.

That first night, Sylvie had met them together. Initially, she felt ill at ease with Nicholas, and was not quite sure why. He was looking at her in that leery way again. When he touched her, she could feel an energy between them, and she thought he lingered a little too long when he kissed her in greeting. To overcome her confusion, she directed most of her attention to Peter. But this only served to amuse Nicholas, and she suspected he knew how much he unsettled her.

Nicholas had taken them both to Sheries diner on Abbey Street for tea. And then afterwards, daringly, he had suggested a drink in the lounge of the Abbey Mooney public house up the road. There the three of them spent a companionable evening, catching up on the comings and goings of Knockaboy. Sylvie and Peter listened enthralled as Nicholas, charming and witty, entertained them with impressions of people. Father MacErlaine was a favourite. The old priest had recently decreed that couples at the afternoon tea dances organised by the parish had to "stay apart and leave room for the Holy Ghost. No hands are to meet bare flesh," Nicholas mimicked in a broad Wexford accent. He regaled them with tales of his mother's batty behaviour, and his father's detachment. Sylvie reciprocated by telling them stories about Eccles Street. After a glass of Babycham she relaxed, and her earlier awkwardness with Nicholas melted away. She told them how the course included a class on grooming where she had been taught how to arrange a man's tie, and to serve tea, and how a lady never attended to her appearance in public. But at the same time, she told them how the girls were advised to be assertive in interviews. And she described how the principal, Sister Concepta, sent girls home if they were not respectably dressed. Make-up was forbidden – it was considered common – and the elderly nun would put her virgin-white hankie against a suspect cheek to check that there wasn't a trace of powder on it. But it was her advice to the young women to always carry a newspaper that drew the most hilarity from the brothers. If you were forced through circumstance to sit on a young man's knee, which you should avoid at all costs, the nun advised them that you could at least protect yourself by putting a newspaper between you. They had laughed at this, especially when Sylvie told them about Noreen, from a sheltered background, who had asked would this stop her from becoming pregnant.

The next time, when Nicholas came up on his own, they followed the same routine. But, as he walked her home along O'Connell Street – him wearing a fedora and his long American-style raincoat over a smart grey suit – he took her arm and leaned in so close that she was afraid he could feel the hammering of her heart. A longing for him that recurred when she thought about him, as she did frequently, during the following days.

"Who was that handsome young man we saw you with?" the other girls teased. "He has a roguish look about him," they said knowingly, and Sylvie thought they were right, he did.

The first time he kissed her she felt like she had died and gone to heaven. They went to see a re-run of

Casablanca. She was Ingrid Bergman and he was Humphrey Bogart. She was in love. He treated her like she was a princess, his manners courteous and considerate. Sitting in the pictures, she realised why the priests were so set against it. Trapped in the darkened space, and feeling his warm flesh pressing into hers, her mind was filled with sinful thoughts and all of her senses were pulsating. She was staring ahead and willing him to take her hand as she watched the couple on the screen kissing passionately. Then as if, intuitively, he felt her desire, his hand had travelled tentatively across her shoulders, creating a trace like an electric current with his fingers, until reaching the nape of her neck he stroked the soft skin just below her ear. And as the screen goddess had said, "I love you – I will always love you," he turned, and his lips found hers and he kissed her hungrily. He had pushed his tongue into her mouth and, although she fought the urge to gag at this unexpected intrusion, her senses had exploded as his other hand stroked the flesh between her thighs through the material of her thin cotton skirt. From then on resistance had been futile. They met regularly that winter, at the pictures, in St Stephen's Green. As well as continuing their passionate groping, they fell into an easy and companionable relationship. On dark street corners, and in the back rows of theatres and cinemas he explored the delights of her body through layers of wool and silk. They laughed at jokes together, and shared memories of growing up in Knockaboy. He goaded her about Peter's obvious devotion but conceded that Peter was nicer than him. She admitted that he was. She refused to betray Peter by joining in with this banter.

One Sunday in the middle of December he took her to

Wicklow in his father's car which he had borrowed while his parents had gone to England to visit Nora's sister who lived there. And despite the cold, in the cramped back of Uncle Daniel's Wolsey, surrounded by the sublime landscape of the Glen of the Downs, they had made love.

Ten days later when she returned home for Christmas Uncle Daniel announced that he had arranged a new job for Nicholas with better prospects working for a solicitor he did business with in Cork. Nicholas told her he would not be travelling to Dublin for a while.

After a fortnight or so, missing him so much that she felt a pain weighing down on her chest, she visited Knockaboy at the weekend hoping to see him. But he wasn't there. She spent the weekend in her room, or going on long solitary walks along country lanes, despite Niamh O'Reilly's persistent attempts to lure her to the dance hall in New Ross.

"Haven't seen young Nicholas Courtney lately," Miss Brennan, her landlady, said knowingly when she returned to Dublin. "Although, I heard from my sister in Kilrothery that he's seeing one of Darcy's daughters – you know, the doctor in New Ross – well, she's living now in Cork. She's the flighty, dark-haired one, very attractive. Imelda. I believe she works in the bank. He was always a cute wan, that Nicholas. The apple didn't fall far from the tree."

"What do you mean?" Sylvie stuttered, stunned.

"Well, his father didn't marry for love, they say. Maybe I shouldn't have said that, you being related to them."

Nicholas was late. Normally they met in Sheries diner and he walked her to Mooney's pub, but his note said that he was under time pressure and he had suggested that they meet in the pub. The lounge was busy, and she felt uncomfortable as three young men sitting close by were obviously eyeing her up. To make things worse, opposite her on the banquette seat, a woman with permed, mauve hair sitting with her baldy husband, glared at her disapprovingly with a look that would curdle milk. She pulled up the neck of her blouse, sorry that she had left the top button open.

When Nicholas eventually arrived, twenty minutes late, she was agitated, conscious of the damp patches that had spread noticeably under the sleeves of her blouse. She had almost finished her Babycham.

"Sylvie, so sorry I'm late. The Cork train was delayed, cows on the tracks at Middleton. Again!"

"Oh, that's too bad. I was just about to leave – those men have been ogling me."

"Ogling, bedad. Well, why wouldn't they? Aren't you looking as beautiful as ever?"

His flattery drew a weak smile from her in response. He was here, she thought, beginning to relax. She looked at him shyly.

"How was Cork? How's the job?"

"Grand. The boss is a bit of a stickler, but the work is interesting enough, wills and property transfers mainly."

"And have you made any friends there – you must be lonely in the evenings." She turned slightly to look at him directly.

"Oh, there are a few chaps from Trinity there," he said, not making eye contact. "I meet up with them for a drink after work sometimes – if I'm not too tired. Unfortunately, I still have to study, you know."

"I believe one of the Darcy girls is working in the Bank of Ireland on the South Mall."

"Yes, yes, she is."

Fishing a silver cigarette case from his pocket, he chose one and slowly lit it, and then inhaled deeply.

"In fact," he said after what seemed like an age, "I bumped into her a few times when I was out with the lads."

"Oh. And? Is she well?"

"Very well. In fact, I quite like her."

"You – quite like her?"

"Yes, I do, actually. I don't know if the gossips have already been at work, but I wanted to talk to you about things. About us. Look, Sylvie, our friendship – I think we should take a break from seeing each other quite so often, at least for a while."

"Friendship, is that what you call it?" she said angrily.

The young men who were ogling her earlier were now staring at them both with rapt interest.

"Sylvie, calm down."

"Don't you dare tell me to calm down, Nicholas. *You bastard!* How could you?" Tears started to stream down her face.

"Jesus, Sylvie. You're making a show of yourself. Let's get out of here."

He stubbed out his cigarette, pulled her up by the arm, roughly, grabbed her coat and headed for the door.

Outside on Abbey Street, passers-by on their way home from work stared at the distraught young woman.

He manoeuvred her against the wall, his body covering hers.

"Look at me, Sylvie, and do try to stop crying."

Sylvie refused to look him in the eye. He took her

chin and forced her to look at him.

"Sylvie, we should not have done what we did. It was wrong, we were wrong. You are like a sister to me."

"Funny way to treat your sister."

"You know what I mean. It's just, you're so attractive, and because I know you so well … I mean, I let my feelings get the better of me in the Glen of the Downs. It shouldn't have happened. I'm really sorry, Sylvie."

"Are you telling me that these past few months have meant nothing to you?"

"No, we had fun. I thought that was what you wanted too."

"How could you think that of me, Nicholas? Don't you know I really like you – God knows why. I have for a long time. In fact, in fact … I think I love you, Nicholas," she pleaded. "I wouldn't have done that with you otherwise."

He let her go abruptly, pushing her away. He took his cigarette case from his pocket and lit up, the act terminating their intimacy.

"Oh, you may think that now, but you will meet someone else one day, and then you will realise what real feelings for someone actually are."

"I suppose you feel that way about Imelda Darcy?"

"Don't be ridiculous, Sylvie. Look, she's not that important. What's important to me is that I'm honest with you. I'm sorry if you misunderstood my intentions, but you know a relationship between us is just not possible. It would only be a matter of time before Father found out and then there would be hell to pay."

"When he hears first, I know he will hit the roof. But can we not talk him around, change his mind?

You know, if we told him we were going to get married."

"*Whoa there!* Marriage, who mentioned marriage! Jesus, Sylvie. There is absolutely no way on earth that Father would agree to it! He would be absolutely furious! I know we're not really cousins. Daniel only told people that to explain why he took you in. But even though we are not related, we have grown up together. It wouldn't look good. People would be shocked. Anyway, my father has other plans for me. Look, Sylvie, I'm really sorry – it's just I don't think of you in that way."

"How do you think of me then? Like one of those women who walk at night along the Grand Canal – a floozie, a loose woman?"

"Stop it – you're being emotional."

"I *am* bloody emotional. I'm pregnant, Nicholas."

He looked at her, horrified. "You can't be! I thought we were careful."

"Not careful enough."

"Oh God! Christ!"

He stood back, inhaled deeply on the end of his cigarette then threw the butt on the ground, grinding it with his foot.

"How late are you?"

"About three weeks, I think."

"Jesus. You will have to get rid of it."

"Get rid of it. No. Absolutely not."

"Look, Sylvie, I have some savings I can give you. You can go over to London and stay there. There's a hostel in Paddington that takes in girls like you who are in trouble."

"You seem to be very knowledgeable about this, Nicholas."

"A friend of mine found himself in the same position."

"*It's not you who's in the bloody position!*" Sylvie sobbed.

"Jesus, Sylvie, please stop crying." He took out a hankie and gave it to her.

She blew her nose noisily.

"Look, let me take you home. I'll think about what's best to do and I'll meet you tomorrow. Bewley's on Grafton Street after work, say half five, upstairs where it's quieter."

After a restless night reviewing her options, the next day she took his money. She even asked for more, which he sent the following week by postal order. She couldn't believe she had been so gullible, so stupid and weak. She still had feelings for him but now she also hated him. She knew his treatment of her defied every moral principle of their shared upbringing. What would her poor dead parents think of their only daughter, who was little more than a whore? She was not sure she would be able to look a priest, or Aunt Nora, in the eye ever again. As for Uncle Daniel, she shivered in anticipation of his contempt.

Nicholas had given her the address in Paddington. By the time they parted in Bewley's she had come to a resolution of sorts. She really had no other choice. She would finish her certificate in mid-May and by that time she would be six months pregnant. She would take the mailboat to London and work for as long as she could, and then see could she find a convent that would take her until after she had the baby. That was as far ahead as she could think about for now.

Her room was smaller than at the last boarding house. She had known that it would only be a matter of time before Miss Brennan noticed and told Uncle Daniel of her circumstances. She had given her notice and left at the end of the month, saying an opportunity had come up to live in a lodging house with reduced board – in return babysitting for the landlady in the evening. A tale intended to allay the Wexford woman's suspicion. In truth, she had moved to a flat in Amiens Street near Connolly Station. She continued to ring Aunt Nora once a week and had given her the new address.

Not surprisingly, she hadn't heard from Nicholas. But several times she had to fob off Peter's attempts to meet up. At first, she gave the move as an excuse, declining his offers of help – and then she told him she was busy studying for her exams. Until now she had also managed to hide her condition in Eccles Street – even though she had seen Miss Russell staring quizzically at her attire. The spinster must have wondered at Sylvie's sudden fondness for shapeless blouses and oversized woollen cardigans. The other girls didn't seem to notice her clothes, but they had told her to slow down, take it easy, that she looked pale – dawny, as Aunt Nora would say. Their smart comments indicated that they thought she was out gallivanting with her handsome young man till all hours. If only they knew, she thought bitterly.

The sickness was the worst, but as the doctor predicted it had eased over the last few weeks. She lay in her narrow bed and cradled her growing stomach. She knew that despite the neatness of her bump, she was four months pregnant, and she would be unable to hide her pregnancy for much longer. A loud knock on the door interrupted her thoughts.

"Miss Vasseur, a telephone call – a Mr Courtney for you."

Sylvie pulled the knitted woollen blanket down from over her head and rose slowly from the bed.

"I'll be down in just a minute, Mrs Cody." Heart thumping, she grabbed her flannelette dressing gown and pulled it around her swollen belly.

Cautiously opening the door, she realised too late that the older woman, her head in curlers wrapped in a scarf, was still outside, waiting for her. She followed as Sylvie carefully went down the three flights of stairs to the hall. In her haste, Sylvie had forgotten to put on her slippers and the lino was cold on her feet. When she reached the hall, the older woman reluctantly went into the kitchen and closed the door behind her. Only then did Sylvie lift the receiver.

"Hello?" she said tentatively.

Her heart sank at the response.

"Sylvie, it's Peter. I've been really worried about you. I haven't heard from you in ages. I'm up in Dublin. I thought we could meet in Sheries and catch up on all the news."

"Oh Peter, it's so lovely to hear from you." Tears welled in her eyes at the sound of his kind, cheerful voice. "It's just I can't meet you this evening, I have the most awful –" she tried to think of something that would last the duration of his weekend, "dose … a stomach bug."

"Oh, that's too bad. You poor thing. But I don't mind, I never catch anything. Mother says I have an iron constitution."

"Well, it's just ... I can't keep anything down, I have to be near a bathroom."

"Look, Sylvie, I'll be over in half an hour. We can stay in your room and have a chat."

"Well, actually, Peter, I'm not allowed male visitors in the boarding house. Mrs Cody is terribly strict." Sylvie glanced at the closed door in the full knowledge that her landlady was probably listening at the other side.

"Well, I'll just have to wrap you up warm and take you out so. I'll bring a brown paper bag for you to honk into."

"Don't be ridiculous. Look," she said, trying to be stern, "I just don't feel up to seeing anyone. Sorry, Peter, goodbye." And she put down the phone.

Mrs Cody, coincidently thought Sylvie, opened the kitchen door and came out just as she finished.

"Family?" she asked.

"Yes."

"Don't they know?"

Sylvie shook her head. She had never actually told the landlady she was pregnant. She didn't have to. Her trips to the bathroom every morning, to empty the basin she puked in, had given her away. After one such episode the older woman had thrown her eyes up to heaven, blessed herself, and had muttered, "Another poor lamb to the slaughter." It occurred to Sylvie that there had never been sight or sound of a Mr Cody. But a few days after this interchange, Mrs Cody had made a point of telling Sylvie that her boarding house was for single working women only. It was not suitable for children. "No room for prams, don't you know," she had said. Despite this warning, she had been kind to her and subsequently brought her home-made scones and biscuits left over from her bridge parties. Sylvie got the impression she had seen it all before, many times, over the years.

"Look, Mrs Cody, if you don't mind, I'm tired. I think I'll go back to my room and get some rest."

It was ten o'clock on Saturday morning. There was no point now in going back to bed. She straightened her sheets, pulling up the blankets and woollen cover. Then she washed herself in the handbasin in her room and dressed in a serviceable blue dress and cardigan. She put a shilling in the meter, indulging in the luxury of having the gas heater on for half an hour or so, just to take the chill off the room.

As she finished her boiled egg, which she made on the single gas ring, she heard a knock on the door.

"It's only me, Sylvie!"

It was Peter.

She opened the door.

"Peter, you shouldn't have come, I told you I was sick."

"Well, I've come to mind you. But I must say, you don't look too sick to me. A little pale maybe. How about a hug for your poor old cousin?"

Feeling his arms wrapped around her, inhaling his familiar smell of Imperial Leather soap and hair oil, tears started to run down her cheeks.

"Peter, I'm so glad to see you. I have missed you so much."

"Sylvie, there, there! You poor thing," he said, stroking

her back. "Have you been terribly homesick? Well, don't worry. I'm here now, and I will make everything better. Don't I always? Come here to me, you eejit." And he took her face between his hands and gave her a gentle kiss on the mouth.

But she froze, her pale-blue eyes staring wildly into his.

"Sylvie, what is it? Are you sick? Tell me. Has something happened?"

"Peter, you are going to despise me," she said, turning away from him.

He grabbed her by the shoulder and turned her around.

"I would never despise you, Sylvie. Nothing you could ever do would make me despise you."

She broke away from him again. "I'm pregnant, Peter!"

He looked stunned, then crushed.

"Oh, no! My God, Sylvie." His hand covered his mouth.

"Peter, please ..."

"The father?"

"He's gone, a pilot in the RAF, in Dublin on leave."

"Does he know?"

"Doesn't want to know, more like," she said bitterly.

"God, the bastard!" He paced the small room. "Look, I can borrow money from Nicholas, and we can arrange for a convent somewhere down the country where you can have the baby."

"No, Peter, no! Please don't tell Nicholas! No one in the family must know. Uncle Daniel would disown me. Aunt Nora and Bridget, everyone in Knockaboy, would feel nothing but contempt for me. I couldn't bear it."

"Oh, they would understand, eventually," he said somewhat unconvincingly. "How about going to the priest, here in Dublin?"

"Don't be ridiculous, Peter, you know what they do. They would just incarcerate me in one of those bloody laundries which, from what I hear, are just another form of prison. No, I have thought about it carefully. To be honest, I have thought about nothing else. I'm going to London. I have saved some money over the last couple of months. And I'll get a job, hopefully someone will feel sorry for me, and then book myself into a convent for the birth. Then I'll think about adoption."

"Adoption, Sylvie? Could you? Could you put your baby up for adoption?"

"Look, Peter, don't you think I haven't agonised about this – me of all people, losing my parents as I did? There is just no other way."

"Well, there is actually. You could get married."

"To whom, Peter?" she said with exasperation. "It's not as if there's a long line of eligible men queuing up to marry me."

"To me, of course."

"Oh, don't be ridiculous."

"I have never been more serious in my life. I have always loved you, Sylvie, ever since you were a small girl and held my hand on the way to school. I hadn't dared hope you would be interested in me. Not since you brushed me off the last time. You are so beautiful, you know, my gorgeous girl!"

With that he embraced her, kissing her passionately on the lips.

She pushed him away.

"Peter, I'm truly touched by your kindness," she said, tears falling down her cheeks. "And as I have already told you, I do love you, but like a brother. I cannot think of you in any other way."

"Look, Sylvie, for me initially that is enough, but maybe in time your feelings will change. And, right now, you are alone with a baby on the way. If I'm willing to take a chance, you should be too. If not for your own sake, at least for the child's."

Sylvie fleetingly considered his proposition but then said firmly, "No, out of the question."

But in her mind the seed of the idea had been sown. It was a way out of this nightmare. She knew what happened to single women who had babies and went to London – they rarely came back – they spent a lifetime in exile. She knew about life over there too, she had seen it all in the movies: God Save the Queen, back-to-back housing, and of course all that fog. She had images of herself working in a typing pool, eventually marrying a man who drank beer and played darts in the local pub and living in a two-up two-down in Clapham. No, that wasn't for her. Maybe marrying Peter could work. Peter was a good man, a kind man. Nicholas would be furious of course, but he would just have to come to terms with it. Serve him right! Peter would make a loving husband. But what about the sex, she thought desperately. She could probably avoid it initially, at least until well after the baby was born. There was no doubt it would be awkward at first, but maybe this is how marriage was supposed to be, based on friendship and mutual convenience. Maybe, as Peter suggested, love and passion would develop in time.

Miss Russell was right, she thought bitterly, romance certainly does not pay the bills.

Wearily she turned to Peter.

"Look, I'll think about it, but now I'm really tired. Can we meet tomorrow?"

She spent another restless night, waking up several times, sweating profusely, her sheets knotted and twisted. Images haunted her of being in a laundry, turning a gigantic mangle and standing in a pool of blood with Uncle Daniel leering at her. This was followed by a scene where she walked, naked, into the church in Kilrothery and Father MacErlaine shouted from the pulpit, "*Get out of God's house, you dirty Jezebel!*" And as she walked back down the aisle, the people from the village spat at her. Amongst the crowd was Nicholas, his sneering face spitting along with all the rest.

The following day when she met Peter, she had made up her mind. She would accept his offer. Shyly she told him, and he lunged across the table in Bewley's knocking over the cakestand of iced fancies to kiss her once again.

"Sylvie you have made me the happiest man alive. You will never, ever regret this."

Sitting in his father's study, waiting for him to return from New Ross, Peter wiped the beads of perspiration from his forehead with his handkerchief. He had been practising what to say on the drive down to Knockaboy. He was not looking forward to the meeting.

"Ah Peter, what a pleasant surprise. How are you? I

wasn't expecting you home till Tuesday. How was Dublin?"

Peter rose to greet his father.

As he entered his study Daniel grasped Peter by the upper arms, his usual form of demonstrating affection with his sons. He then sat down at the other side of the desk, carefully arranging his jacket so that it didn't crease.

"Your mother said you wanted to speak to me – in private. So, what is so important that it couldn't wait until after dinner?"

"I have some news, Father."

"Oh," said Daniel, leaning forward slightly. "What kind of news?"

"Good news, I hope." He paused. "I'm getting married," he said sheepishly.

"Married? This is rather sudden. I didn't even know that you were walking out. Catholic, I hope?"

"Yes, she is a Catholic."

"Well, come on, son, spit it out. Who is the lucky woman?" his father asked apprehensively.

Peter inhaled deeply and sat upright in the chair.

"Sylvie, Father, it's Sylvie."

"*Sylvie!* Peter, you cannot be serious!"

"Yes, Father. We have spent a lot of time together while I was up in Dublin over the past few months, and we fell in love, and well ... now we plan to marry."

Daniel's face was puce, his expression thunderous. He jumped up from the desk and towered over his son.

"*Impossible, Peter! You cannot marry Sylvie!*"

"Why not, Father?" Peter replied, gaining strength in defiance.

"Because, because ... she is your sister."

"Not technically – not legally."

"In God's eyes, and in everyone else's for that matter. You have lived under the same roof since you were children, for heaven's sake!"

"But she's not a blood relation."

"*I will not have it! Do you hear me! I won't have it!*" Daniel thumped the desk with his fist, the impact causing his silver pen in its ornate holder to vibrate.

Peter was shocked by his father's response. "I'm sorry you're so upset, Father, but the thing is I'm legally an adult, and I'm free to marry whomsoever I choose. With, or without your consent, I intend to marry Sylvie."

Daniel drew back and sat down once more. He pulled at his moustache anxiously.

"You are making a big mistake, Peter."

"Why, Father? You love Sylvie – at least I always thought that you did."

"Sylvie is a flibbertigibbet, always has been. She hasn't an ounce of sense, that girl, full of notions. I can see now that she has seduced you with her brazen ways. Make-up, lipstick, flaunting herself at decent people. I told your mother – she'll come to no good, that girl."

"Father, stop this! I won't hear you talk about the woman I love like that."

"Love – love, what has love got to do with anything? Love is for idiots. Life is like any other business venture – if you have any sense you invest for the long haul."

"She's pregnant, Father," said Peter.

"Jesus Christ, Peter! I don't believe it – a son of mine. You idiot!"

He put his hands over his eyes, his shoulders trembling. He said nothing for a moment, trying to collect his thoughts, then he lifted his head and looked directly at Peter.

"Look, Peter. You don't have to marry her. There are other ways to deal with girls who get themselves in trouble."

"Father, I cannot believe you would talk about Sylvie as if she were some tart that I picked up on the quays in New Ross."

"Peter, you are young. This would be a terrible mistake – for you, for this family. Sylvie has a flawed pedigree."

"I don't understand what you mean?"

Daniel ignored his question.

"Look, I will give you a thousand pounds if you don't marry her. Go to England, to London, get a job there for a while. Do what young men do. Why tie yourself down while you have your whole life ahead of you? You will soon get over whatever infatuation you have. Peter, if you marry Sylvie, mark my words, you will bring disgrace down on this family. Peter, you *cannot* marry her."

Peter was furious at this stage. "I intend to marry Sylvie with, or without, your blessing, Father."

"Well, if that is the case then get out of my house and don't come back." His father's eyes locked on his. "I hope you don't live to regret this day."

Daniel rose and went to stand looking out the window towards the trees at the back of the house, indicating that their meeting was over.

Chapter 8

Sandymount Strand, Dublin
May 1953

Sylvie pulled the collar of her jacket up around her neck. It was a warm day, still early in the summer, but the sea breeze made it feel cooler than it was. Sitting on a bench near the Martello Tower café, she watched the child playing at her feet. Nearby, two small children were running around as their mothers, sitting on the grass, chatted amiably together. She had caught the toddlers' ball and asked their names and told them Sam's. Although they were a few months older, she had hoped he would engage with them, but he continued to ignore them. Beyond the children, Sylvie noticed absentmindedly how the concrete swimming baths seemed to float incongruously like a meringue in the middle of the shallow bay – while, at its edge, a lone male figure paused before diving into the hidden man-made depths, as if he was diving into the centre of the earth. The water must be freezing, she thought. And, despite the fact it was still only May, in the shimmering distance she saw three intrepid bathers seeking deeper water, wading out towards the horizon.

The Englishwoman wasn't there today. Maybe she

had come earlier. Sylvie was disappointed that she had missed her. She had met her on an afternoon like this a few months earlier when they had ended up sitting on the same bench. She had a dog, a small white terrier called Chipper. Sylvie had tried to engage Sam with the dog, and they had started chatting. They covered the "Do you know so and so?" stuff very quickly – and then the older woman talked to Sylvie about art, and life, but mostly art. Her relentless cheer had drawn Sylvie to her, and the fact that she told her stories about living in Paris as a student during the war. Stories that stirred memories and gave solace to Sylvie. She grew to look forward to meeting her. It was also something to tell Peter in the hour or so before going to bed in the evenings when they managed to spend time together. Because lately she felt she had very little to talk about. She felt like she was slowly dissolving, that her spirit was withering away. She had no friends in Dublin. Niamh O'Reilly had gone to London to work, and she had not seen or heard from her for ages. She hadn't had the time for making new friends over the last couple of years and, if she were honest, she hadn't had the inclination. She was bored by the company of the other young mothers who, most afternoons, sat in the leafy shade of the horse-chestnut trees in Sandymount Green – they seemed to talk endlessly about tantrums and toilet-training. At this stage she knew that, for her, minding Sam simply wasn't enough. There was also the fact that sometimes, when she looked at him, she was reminded of Nicholas, and the hurt and anger would well up inside her once more. She had to tell herself that he was only a child, he could not be held responsible for his father's actions. She wondered, and not for the first time, whether this was normal, or if there was something wrong with her. Hopefully these feelings would fade in time. It was some consolation that he looked more like Peter – at least *he* would never guess.

At about half past two, Sylvie's heart lifted, as, in the distance, she saw the stocky woman ambling along the coastal path towards the tower. She was carrying her easel, with a leather satchel hung military-style across her chest.

Sylvie thought Jennifer Ambrose was probably in her sixties – she could be younger – and she looked as if she had known a hard life. Her face was lined and dominated by dark brown, slightly bulging almond-shaped eyes, and a full mouth outlined permanently with red lipstick. She looked exotic. She always wore a black beret – not rakishly perched on the side of her head like the models in the *Vogue* magazines that Sophie read on her occasional visits to the hairdresser's – but pulled down tight over her ears so that her died curly blonde hair fanned out from underneath it. She had a bohemian style about her. The well-cut Mackintosh she wore was spattered with paint and around her neck she wore a batik scarf in bright purples and pinks.

"Afternoon my, love," she said in her cockney accent as she approached the bench. "You've kept my spot. What would I do without you?"

"Nice to see you, Mrs Ambrose."

"Jenny, my love, I keep telling you, everyone calls me Jenny, except my Maxwell who calls me Jennifer when he's in a piss with me."

She started to undo the easel, laying the box flat on

the ground then pulling out the legs and adjusting them till they looked like an upended stick insect, before flicking the whole lot over and positioning it on the grass behind the bench. "*Voila!*" she said as she pulled out the upper arm and the easel was assembled.

Out of her satchel she took a small canvas and beside Sylvie, on the bench, she placed a jar of white spirits and some linseed oil together with a wooden palette, some rags and a flask of tea.

"Been here long?" she asked.

"No, only thirty minutes or so. I was afraid I'd missed you."

"Maxwell delayed me. We were talking about our autumn show, what we needed to get done. Lord, there is such a lot of organising, I don't know why we pay the gallery a commission at all as we seem to have to do all the work ourselves."

"Can I help?"

"That's very kind, my dear, but you have enough on your plate."

"Well, that's just it, I don't I'm afraid. Peter works all day at the insurance company, then he works in Foley's bar in Ringsend at night. I'm on my own in our one-room flat with Sam most of the day and, adorable as he is, I do miss adult conversation. Look," she continued hesitantly, "I've been thinking about this. Last week you told me anyone can learn to paint once they understand colour theory. Could I be your guinea pig, could you teach me? I told you I wanted to go to art college. With the little one, that's unlikely to happen now. But, maybe, if I helped you with all the boring administration for your exhibition, you could teach me to paint?"

"Well, my love, that's an interesting offer. Most interesting." For once Jennifer was lost for words. "I'd have to think about it, but no doubt it 'ud be a challenge. I'd have to talk to my beloved. Look, leave it with me and I'll get back to you."

She looked out to the horizon.

"Shimmering sands and slippery seas, bee-eutiful!" she exclaimed.

Sam had toddled up to her and was generously offering her the carcass of a dead bird he had found.

"What do you make of that, my love?" she said.

Then, ignoring him, and seemingly oblivious to everything, including Sylvie, the older woman started to mix her paints.

Maxwell, rather rudely, Sylvie thought, did not open the door fully but turned around and bellowed up the stairs.

"Jenny! Jenny! Some woman is at the door looking for you! Says her name's Sylvie!"

Sylvie heard footsteps coming down lino-covered stairs before the door was flung open and Jenny, resplendent in a black-velvet, jewelled turban and a long denim apron, beckoned her in.

"Oh, don't mind him, dear, he's anti-social. Do come in. Maxwell, you know who she is. We talked about this yesterday."

Sylvie tentatively entered the hall. The Ambroses lived in a Victorian red-bricked, terraced house in Gilford Road just off the seafront. The hall was dark, but light was pouring in through a window at the far end of the tiled passageway.

"Come in, lovey, you've managed to lose Sam, I see."

Although Jenny made the right noises at Sam, Sylvie sensed that she struggled to be convincingly maternal, and she suspected that Jenny didn't really like children.

"Yes. Peter's Aunt Elsie who lives in Bath Avenue offered to mind him for the afternoon."

"Wonderful! We shall have you all to ourselves so. Come into the sitting room."

She entered a bright room, with French windows looking out onto a lush flower-filled garden and the side of a Victorian-style glass conservatory.

"That's my studio. I'll show you shortly, my love. But now, how about a nice cup of coffee?"

Maxwell, who was hovering at the door, was of medium height – a good-looking man with a full head of white hair and dark straight brows over confident brown eyes. He was tanned and fit-looking for his age. However, he appeared discommoded by Sylvie's visit. At Jenny's suggestion, he disappeared into the kitchen, returning a few minutes later with a French cafetière and some iced buns.

"Oh, real coffee, what a treat!" Sylvie said enthusiastically. She was used to the cheaper, instant variety with its bitter taste of chicory.

After pouring the coffee, he sat down in a chair across from Sylvie, and he remained silent as Jenny rabbited on for a while about the exhibition. He nodded every now and then but did not take his eyes off Sylvie's face for a second. She started to feel uncomfortable.

He finally interrupted Jenny's flow.

"Sorry, Jenny, sorry, it's just you didn't tell me ..."

"Tell you what, you old goat?"

"That she was so beautiful." He paused, then asked tentatively, leaning forward with clasped hands held nervously, "Do you think, Sylvie, that you could model for me?"

Sylvie said with a broad smile, "Of course, no problem, as long as I can keep my clothes on."

"Oh," he said, disappointed.

"Of course, dear. Don't mind him. It's whatever makes you feel comfortable." Jenny beamed at Sylvie. "Well, my dear, Maxwell and I have discussed a plan for your art education." And she tapped the notebook on her lap with the palm of her hand with determination.

From then on Sylvie fell into a routine. She would take Sam up to the house every morning. First, she would have coffee with Jenny – Max was a late riser – and while Sam played in a playpen which Jenny had bought in a second-hand furniture shop, they would agree what needed to be done that day. When Max eventually rose and had breakfast, he would drive into town and collect any artists' supplies they needed, bring any finished canvases to the framers in Baggot Street and collect the ones already framed. And, while Sam had his morning nap, Sylvie would compile the list of exhibition invitees, look up their addresses from the telephone directory, direct the printing of the invitations and type up the envelopes.

Sylvie had never thought of herself as organised, quite the opposite in fact – her own paperwork was in a mess. But she knew that she could be organised when she chose to be. And she needed to be, as she soon realised that Jenny was incapable of sorting anything.

Systematically, Sylvie got through all the jobs that Jenny had been procrastinating about for so long. She typed up the artist's statement penned by Max (although this was rewritten and retyped many times), contacted Penelope in the gallery to agree details for the reception, and ordered the wine, cheese and crackers. After a few days, Sylvie encouraged Maxwell to put a shelf over the writing desk in the studio and keep an address book and files with administration details there, so that the whole operation would be easier to undertake the next time.

In the afternoons the couple's cleaner, Rose, would come in and take Sam in his pushchair down to Sandymount village and mind him for the rest of the day. Sylvie would then put on an apron that she kept in Jenny's for the purpose, and embark on her art education, mainly under Max's watchful eye. Some days Jenny would be the model for Sylvie to practise life drawing.

As a teacher, Max was patient and generous, never giving her instructions directly. Instead, he might suggest to Sylvie that she change a line here, or there. But mostly he taught her how to really look at things, and to think carefully about what she saw.

"Look at the way that the sun bathes Jenny's skin and gives it a peachy glow," he would say, "and where its absence casts a mauve shadow in the skin's folds." He showed her how capturing the effects of light could energise a drawn object and bring it to life – how there were no hard lines defining things and how the very edges of things were blurred. He talked about colour theory: contrasting colours, how certain colours lent others more vibrancy, and how others made those beside them recede – how different combinations created different dynamic effects and communicated different energies.

At coffee break, and over lunch, they would discuss artists and art movements. Max told her how he had taught in an art college in Manchester for many years, and how he had met Jenny there before a family inheritance meant they could both retire early and move back to his home in Dublin. He talked about the Barbizon School, the Impressionists, Post Impressionists and the various modern art movements of the 19th and 20th centuries.

On Friday afternoons Jenny would make herself scarce, taking Sam down to the beach. Then Sylvie would pose for Max, not naked, but eventually she was comfortable enough with the older man to agree to be partially draped. But she never told Peter about this aspect of her education. And during those long hours standing still, Sylvie would tell Max her story. She told him about her father's gallery. Max was so impressed when she said, "Braque was a friend of Papa's" and "Picasso used to come around often to our apartment in the Rue de Sévigné for dinner". But when she had told him that she had been painted as a child by Mateus, he was enchanted, and they talked about it for days afterwards.

Max asked, "Do you know what happened to the painting?"

"No, I've no idea – my uncle thinks it was destroyed by the Gestapo during the early days of the occupation. The German soldiers made a bonfire. Another, 'Bonfire of the Vanities', Uncle called it, where they burnt a lot of looted art."

Max had told her that Hitler, unlike his treatment of artists of whom he did not approve in Germany, had become a little more tolerant of certain artists in Paris, such as Mateus and Picasso, allowing them to continue to paint and exhibit as the war progressed.

Over the course of the last six months, Sylvie realised that she had grown to depend on the older couple. At the weekends she would miss them, their jokey banter with each other and their engaging conversation. They were always asking, "What do you think about this?" or "What would you do if?" Peter, in contrast, was only interested in listening to sports on the radio, or relaying family gossip from Knockaboy. Sylvie began to find him tedious, boring even. She had started to read the newspaper every day which she had never done previously. Initially this was to find out about art exhibitions and society gossip, but the Ambroses stretched the limits of her interests. They discussed books, theatre, even politics. She joined Pembroke library and, in the evenings, when Sam slept, she read literary novels that the couple recommended: Marcel Proust, Jean-Paul Sartre, Albert Camus, and books about art – so many books about art. She had started painting in oils, semi-abstracted landscapes and figurative work, impressions of Sandymount Strand, of Sam, of the yellow jug on the windowsill in Jenny's kitchen, anything that caught her fancy. Sylvie had never felt so alive. She was brimming with pent-up energy. However, this newfound joie de vivre quickly dissipated when she returned home in the evenings.

The first-floor flat on Serpentine Avenue was small

and cramped with lingering smells of the previous night's dinner. Because there was no storage, most of their clothes and meagre possessions were kept in paper carrier bags and canvas holdalls, making the room look permanently unkempt. Summertime was the worst as it was hot and stuffy – the single sliding-sash window was hard to open. But now, as the weather was getting colder, the gas-heater caused the windowpanes to mist up and swirls of black condensation mould to form on the walls. Trying to wash it off only made it look worse. It was no place for adults to live, Sylvie often thought, let alone a child. Sparsely furnished, it contained a kitchen sink and a single cupboard unit on which sat a two-ring gas-hob with two shelves overhead. Adjacent to this was a red Formica-topped table that folded in two, like a card table, and two steel tubular chairs. A sofa, covered in rough, knobbly, brown wool defined the middle of the room – opposite, on a sideboard, was the wireless. And close to the sofa, with just enough room to climb in, was their double bed, a steel-framed affair with springs that stuck into their private places and screeched on impact like a dying cat. And at the end of the bed, in unfortunate proximity, was Sam's cot. She had insisted on this ploy in the hope of diluting Peter's ardour. But as a result, Sylvie often woke up in fright in the middle of the night to see the toddler's blue eyes staring mournfully at her from between the bars.

When she eventually got Sam settled in his cot for the evening, Sylvie usually collapsed on the couch and attempted to listen to music on the wireless. However, the noise of passing trains meant that reading was usually a better option. So that by the time Peter returned home from his evening shift in Foley's, she was usually asleep, or at least pretended to be. And although he persisted in his attempts at lovemaking, he met with her constant excuses. She told him she was too tired – and he, also exhausted and afraid of waking the child, accepted her rejection without demur and promptly fell asleep.

By the time the Ambroses' art exhibition came around in October, Max had suggested she submit two of her own works, which she did – and to her surprise she sold them. Although she didn't make much profit after she had given the gallery their cut, it was enough to invest in a few decent-sized canvases and her own set of oil paints. Up until then, her materials had been provided by Max and Jenny.

The exhibition opening had been exhilarating. Sylvie had talked to so many interesting people, many of whom, to her surprise, also seemed to be interested in her. Max and Jenny, both members of the Royal Hibernian Academy, appeared to know everyone. The whole night, one or the other of them would pull her by the sleeve and say, "You must meet so and so". Or, they would introduce her to someone with a flourish, "This is Sylvie – she was painted by Mateus as a young girl". By the end of the evening, she was tipsy with the wine and heady with all the attention.

When she eventually returned to the tiny apartment, Peter looked hot and bothered. He had taken the evening off from work to mind Sam who had a temperature, and he had paced the floor with the bawling child for most of the evening.

"Ah, Sylvie, you decided to come home."

"Oh Peter, I'm so sorry – it's just that it was the most wonderful evening."

"Great, so now you can mind Sam."

"Why don't I make you a cup of tea, or maybe we could have a glass of wine and I'll tell you about the exhibition."

"Not now, Sylvie. I'd say that you have probably had enough to drink for one evening."

"Why are you so bloody bad-tempered?"

"I'm tired, Sylvie, exhausted if you must know. Like you claim to be, most of the time."

"God, you are so boring! Sometimes, I don't know why I ever married you."

She regretted saying it immediately.

"I'm so sorry, Peter! I didn't mean ..."

But the damage was done. With a face like thunder, he opened the newspaper and retreated behind it, maintaining a stoic silence for the rest of the evening.

By the time she got into bed, his back was facing her. Although she knew he was still awake, he didn't say goodnight or "I love you" as he had every night since they got married.

The following morning when Sam's cries woke her up, she felt a cold space in the bed beside her – he had already left to go to work.

That afternoon she came home from Max and Jenny's early to make him a special dinner, a beef stew that she knew he really liked. She had even splashed out and bought an apple cake in the grocer's shop in the village. But when he eventually arrived after his night shift, an hour later than usual, she could smell the whiskey on his breath as soon as he walked in the door. He told her he wasn't hungry and went straight to bed.

Sheries was busy on Saturday morning with early morning shoppers. It had been raining and a cloying smell of damp clothes and fried food filled the air. In the rush earlier to dress Sam and make his breakfast, Peter had forgotten his umbrella and he was wet and irritable. Sylvie always insisted on sleeping in on Saturdays. A time that, in the early days of their relationship, used to be for them, a time when they would be together, wrapped in each other's arms, he licking the sleep from her eyes and cupping the soft cheeks of her buttocks in his hands, pulling her swelling belly gently into him. But that was then, he thought sadly, things were different now. Earlier, he had left the child dressed and fed, trying to snuggle in beside her, as she – ignoring him, forearm shielding her eyes – tried to prolong her nocturnal release.

Even coming to Sheries this morning had been a mistake, as it too reminded him of happier times and how things had changed. Nicholas, who was always in a rush, had suggested it, as he could get there easily from the Four Courts Law Library.

When his brother eventually arrived, fifteen minutes late, and they inspected the menu, Nicholas insisted on a full Irish, a luxury Peter couldn't really afford. Although he soon regretted admitting that.

"It's only a bloody fry-up, Peter," Nicholas had said as he protested. "It's hardly going to break the Bank."

"Sorry to be such a misery guts – things are difficult with money at the moment. It's hard to make ends meet. We are trying to save the deposit to buy a house. The flat is so claustrophobic with Sam getting bigger."

"Have you considered Sylvie getting some part-time work. She kept up the French, didn't she? Remember she was friendly with the French teacher in the convent in New Ross who used to give her newspapers and books to read. And now, with her typing, I would have thought she should have no difficulty getting a job."

"Yes, you would think so, but it's not that straightforward. Although Sam is that bit older and we could leave him with Aunt Elsie who would be glad of the few bob, Sylvie won't hear of looking for work. She has become obsessed with bloody art. She can think of, or talk about, nothing else. That old bat, Jenny, the artist she met – I was telling you about her the last time – she has a lot to answer for. She's filled her head with a load of bloody nonsense. About how she should pursue her own dreams, instead of mine, and develop her latent talent. Jesus, Nicholas, I'm too bloody tired these days to dream – all I want to do is get a good night's uninterrupted sleep."

Nicholas, ignoring his gripes, asked, "And is she any good?"

"Are any of them any good these days?" Peter replied. "In the past you could appreciate a charming landscape, or the face of a pretty woman. These days it's all just abstract images in colours that are occasionally pleasant, but mainly downright dull. Sylvie often asks me if I can see what her painting represents, and I usually disappoint her by saying no, I can't. Then she thinks I'm being deliberately obtuse and flounces off like a spoiled child."

"It's an acquired taste, I believe," said Nicholas

knowingly. "I wonder, could she make a living from it?"

"Well, she exhibited with the Ambroses this year at their autumn show and she did actually sell a few works, but if you did a cost analysis on the materials versus labour, then no, it's not a profitable pursuit. She's happier – I suppose. But there's a distance growing between us, and this art thing is only making it wider."

"Well, Sylvie always was contrary." Nicholas paused, elbows on the table, his fingertips touching, and adopted an earnest expression. "How is the bedroom side of things?"

"Fine, that's not the problem," Peter said curtly.

Nicholas seemed to consider this, smoothing the trouser leg of his expensive slacks.

"Well, if painting pictures and discussing art is making her happy, that can only be a good thing. Why not try and meet her halfway, become more involved in her world?"

"Maybe," Peter said doubtfully. "It's hard to listen to all of that crap. Listening to Father for all those years was hard enough. But yes, I suppose I might try that."

"You look pretty worn out, old chap. Surely with what you make in the insurance company you could give up the evening work in the pub."

"Not altogether, I'm afraid. Insurance clerks are not in the same financial league as solicitors. We still have a way to go before we have the deposit. But yes, I probably could cut back on the hours – possibly not do the weekends anymore."

"And how's Sam doing?"

"Great – he's adorable, big for his age compared to

the other kids we meet in Sandymount Green, and he's such a strong little fellow," Peter said proudly. "Although, to be honest, sometimes I feel he's a bit neglected, always stuck in a playpen or belted into his pushchair while Sylvie farts around painting."

Nicholas raised one eyebrow. "I think you could do with a break, brother. Maybe the two of you should go down to Knockaboy for the weekend, try and mend some fences there."

"No thanks!" Peter exclaimed. "I'm not that desperate. The way Father talked to me when I told him we planned to marry! I still haven't forgiven him. Don't think I ever will. And then there's the further insult that neither of them came to the wedding. I know it was only in a registry office – and in London, but he hops over there often enough for business when it suits him. Imagine offering me a thousand pounds not to marry her – an incentive, he called it. And mentioning her flawed pedigree, if you don't mind. But when I tried to draw him out, ask him what he meant, he clammed up. I thought that he and Sylvie's father were best pals. It seems that there was more to their relationship that meets the eye."

"Well, I suppose that Father exaggerated the relationship between them to legitimise Sylvie's status as an evacuee," said Nicholas thoughtfully.

The waitress arrived at the table and cleared their plates.

Peter took a cigarette case from his pocket and offered one to his brother.

They lit up and inhaled slowly.

"It's amazing really, that Father never really talks about Sylvie's parents," Nicholas continued. "I mean, it was such a big thing for them to take in a child, and a Jewish child at that."

"I must get the ould fellah drunk one evening and cross-examine him."

"Good luck with that!" said Peter with a laugh.

Chapter 9

Dublin
June 1957

He had seen her earlier through the large plate-glass window in the Baggot Street art gallery. Peter had told him she was working there for a few days looking after Jenny and Max's latest exhibition while Penelope, the owner, was away at a London art fair. That day, Nicholas had business to attend to in Haddington Road, regarding a new office block he was developing in Ballsbridge. The meeting was a contentious one with the design team arguing about fees and it had lasted for over an hour. After it finished, or at least when he'd decided it was time to end it, on a whim he'd gone for a drink in Toners pub.

Nicholas was sitting in the snug so that he had an uninterrupted view of the gallery on the other side of the street. Lately, he had been thinking about her constantly. The novelty of sex with most of the women he had dated wore off quickly once he had overcome their natural Catholic reluctance. But even after six years he still remembered Sylvie. Still fired up from the meeting, he felt himself becoming aroused in anticipation of seeing her.

He checked his watch – it was half past five. As he had hoped, she came out of the door and started to pull down the shutter over the window to close for the evening. Nicholas downed the rest of his whiskey and hastily left the pub. As he navigated the traffic to cross Baggot Street, he kept her in his line of vision. Her hair was longer than he remembered and tied up in a ponytail at the back of her head with a black-velvet ribbon. She was wearing a sleeveless dress, fitted, with a billowing skirt in some pale floaty fabric which showed off her long brown legs. He was pleased to see that her body had not been affected by motherhood. Although, he thought, her breasts looked fuller. She was still lithe and sexy.

"Sylvie, what a surprise! Fancy meeting you here!"

"Nicholas!" she said, startled.

He hunkered down to help her, savouring the sight of her exposed thighs when the wind caught the thin fabric of her skirt as she crouched down and grappled with the padlock on the shutter.

"Leave me alone, I don't need your help," she said, pulling down her skirt. "I don't want to talk to you."

"That's not a very friendly way to greet your favourite brother-in-law, Sylvie."

"Tough, that's the way I feel."

"Look, we are going to have to meet up at some stage when Peter eventually makes it up with the folks. So, can we at least be polite to one another?"

"If I must, I will. But right now, I don't have to. So go to hell!"

She was standing now and about to go back through the gallery door.

113

"Look, Sylvie," he grabbed her arm, "can we talk? We need to talk. Sam –"

She froze. "No, Nicholas, we do not. Sam is nothing to you. Do you hear me? *Nothing*."

"Sylvie, he's my son."

Her face suffused with rage, she spoke through gritted teeth, "Sam is Peter's son. If it had been left up to you, he would have been flushed down someone's toilet!"

"Oh, for God's sake, Sylvie, there's no need to be so melodramatic. That was shock, it was my first reaction. I would have come around to it after a while. At least I supported you financially, to do what you thought best."

"Supported me? Paid me off more like. It seems it's a default position with your family."

"Look, Sylvie," he said ignoring the jibe, "can we at least be civil?"

"No."

And she shut the door in his face.

Sylvie rang Peter and asked him to come home early. She knew she had to try if this was to work, and she wanted it to work. Peter was a good man, a kind man, and a wonderful father to Sam. She remembered how they had made love for the first time. Peter could not contain his excitement, his pent-up desire – thankfully, it was all over quickly. But for her it was a traumatic experience. She had felt defiled. To her, he was her brother. But once she overcame her humiliation, because that was what she felt, the rare times they did make love she was comforted by their intimacy. She tried not to think too much about it, or to compare their coupling to the passionate lovemaking she had experienced with Nicholas.

114

That morning Max had been coughing and spluttering with a cold, and he had called off the life-drawing session planned for that afternoon. Sam, as usual, had gone to Aunt Elsie's after he finished school in Sandymount. Sylvie had called in to her and asked her to keep him till eight o'clock.

It was Friday evening, the start of the weekend. For once Sylvie had time to clean up and to cook bacon and cabbage, one of Peter's favourites. Although normally she couldn't bear the smell of it in the flat, tonight she had made an exception. She had even bought a bottle of Liebfraumilch, a rare treat for them these days.

When dinner was finished and the kitchen cleaned up, they walked up to Bath Avenue to collect Sam, chatting companionably about the day's events.

"I bumped into Nicholas today on Grafton Street," Peter told her. "He has finally been hooked."

"Really, who? Anyone I know?"

"I doubt it – he moves in more exalted circles than us. She's the daughter of a beef-baron, I believe. Lots of dosh."

"What about Imelda Darcy?"

"Oh, he spoiled his bib there. She caught him kissing her sister, I believe. Anyway, she's old news, there have been several others since."

"Jesus, Peter, he's unbelievable, your brother."

"Yes, he is," he said admiringly. "I don't know how he gets away with it."

"He obviously *doesn't*," Sylvie retorted.

"Well, darling," rather obviously changing the subject, "I was thinking, tomorrow why don't we take Sam to the Municipal Gallery? I believe there's an exhibition there of Post-Impressionists, including your friend Mateus. I suppose we need to start our son's cultural education. You can give me a few lessons too while you are at it."

"Oh, Peter! Yes, Jenny and Max were talking about it. Yes, that would be lovely."

"Good, and maybe, if it's alright with you, we could also meet up with Nicholas and his new woman. When I met him, he suggested we make a foursome and go for a jar. I mentioned it to Aunt Elsie, and she offered to babysit."

She opened her mouth to protest but said nothing.

Later, when they eventually settled the child for the night, Peter pulled her to him and she responded, tentatively at first, and then enthusiastically. They made love soundlessly, all the time aware that Sam, like a time-bomb in the room, could wake at any minute. Afterwards, they lay in bed sharing a cigarette and savouring the moment.

Maybe things will be OK, Sylvie thought. But then she remembered the unsettling incident with Nicholas the previous week. And now she faced the indignity of having to meet him and his new girlfriend – poor cow, whoever she was – and play happy families with Peter. She tried to get these unnerving thoughts out of her head.

"Sam's father, Sylvie?"

"Oh no, Peter! We just had such a lovely time! Don't let's spoil everything."

"It's just, I know you didn't get to know his father well, but I would like to think he was like me, from a similar background. You know, none of my friends have any idea that Sam's not mine. I mean look at him, he's the spit of me. Even Nicholas hasn't got a clue."

The child, with his fair curly hair was sleeping, his thumb firmly in his mouth.

"Peter, promise me," she pleaded, "promise you won't discuss Sam's father with Nicholas, *ever. Promise me.*"

"Don't worry, darling, my conversations with my brother are fairly superficial."

Sylvie felt self-conscious in her shabby dress and cardigan amongst the wealthier patrons of the Shelbourne Hotel's Horseshoe Bar. To make matters worse she noticed Peter's shirt collar was frayed.

"Hello, you two." Nicholas arrived flushed from the cold outside, looking as nonchalant as ever, his coat draped over one arm and on the other a glamorous companion. She was wearing a fox-fur collar over a fine wool, fitted dress with velvet-covered buttons. Although she was attractive, she was not as good-looking as Sylvie had anticipated. She had short dark curly hair and a warm, soft round face, with smiling eyes, anxious to please. Sylvie didn't know whether or not this was going to make the evening more bearable. She suspected she would have found it easier to dislike her.

"Sylvie, Peter, let me introduce Evelyn Jackson."

"Lovely to meet you both." The woman put out her gloved hand to shake Sylvie's, then Peter's.

"Can I get you a drink, darling?" Nicholas asked.

"Sherry, please," she replied.

"Same for you, Sylvie?"

"Yes," she said curtly.

Peter glanced nervously at his wife as Nicholas left. Then he turned to Evelyn. "Nicholas has told us all

117

about you," he said warmly. "How lovely to finally meet you. Do you know, it has been a double blessing, because we also get to socialise with my brother? He's normally so busy. At work, I mean."

"Well, it's so nice to meet you too, and I'm pleased to be of service," Evelyn, smiling, replied.

Nicholas returned from the bar, armed with their drinks, and sat down beside Evelyn.

"We have some news for you," he said coyly. "Darling, do you want to do the honours?"

Evelyn beamed. "We just got engaged, this very afternoon!" She tore off a long black glove to reveal a ring with a sizable diamond solitaire.

"What a wonderful surprise – about time you settled down, big brother," said Peter, obviously delighted.

"Who said anything about settling down!" said Nicholas. "Only joking, darling."

Sylvie felt her stomach heave.

Somehow, she got through the evening.

But from then on, at Nicholas's instigation, and Peter's obvious pleasure, the two couples fell into a habit of meeting once a month. Initially, Sylvie tried to make excuses. But Peter asked her, for his sake, to make the effort with his brother, particularly as they were ostracised from the rest of his family. To keep him happy, she reluctantly agreed, and she tried to put what had happened between Nicholas and herself behind her. However, it simply was not possible. She hated these evenings and she usually managed to curtail them to an hour or two. But despite herself, Sylvie got to like Evelyn, who, she discovered, worked in a PR company. But although Evelyn enjoyed her successful career, all she really wanted was to marry Nicholas, and have a family. She couldn't wait to have children. In fact, Sylvie found her mildly obsessed with the subject – encouraging Sylvie to talk about Sam – what he was like at various stages of babyhood. Occasionally, Sylvie tried to change the subject and talk about current affairs, or society gossip. She even attempted to talk to her about her painting. But she recognised, as Evelyn's eyes glazed over, that Evelyn was not really interested. As soon as it was polite to do so, Sylvie would make her excuses that they had to relieve the babysitter. Usually, it was when Peter reached the stage when he had become unbearable – when he started disclosing confidential information about customers of the insurance company that he knew Nicholas would find interesting – or badmouthing his colleagues.

On these evenings, Peter drank too much, trying to impress his older, more successful, brother while Nicholas stayed relatively sober. Sober enough for him to catch Sylvie's eye occasionally. His knowing looks unsettled her, and when they returned to their one-room flat she would make excuses when Peter, fumbling and worse for wear, attempted to initiate lovemaking.

Chapter 10

Dublin
September 1959

Penelope had been impressed with Sylvie's organisational skills for Max and Jenny's exhibitions over the last few years, and especially during the time she filled in for her when she was in London. So, when her assistant Janet left to get married, she offered her part-time work in the gallery for three afternoons a week. It made such a difference to Sylvie. As well as being paid for those three days, she would wash her hair, dress up smartly and escape from the confines of her narrow world. By that stage, with Max and Jenny's help, she had also built up a level of skill in her painting. But that was creating another problem. Sylvie's canvases were stacked around the tiny one-roomed flat. She was afraid to hang things on the wall in case the landlord made them redecorate when they eventually left.

One evening Peter in exasperation asked, "Why don't you have your own exhibition and get rid of some of the bloody things? Get some money back from your expensive hobby."

Jenny and Max had encouraged her to show her work to a wider audience. So, when she eventually plucked up the courage to show Penelope the series of oil paintings she had completed of Sandymount Strand, she was delighted with her reaction. Penelope was impressed, thought she had real talent and offered her a slot in January. This was usually not a great time to sell paintings as the office workers who were their regular customers were paying off overdrafts after the excesses of Christmas. But, still, Sylvie was delighted to be given the opportunity and threw herself into a frenzy of painting.

When she told Evelyn about the exhibition the next time the couples met at the Shelbourne Hotel, Nicholas's fiancée was delighted for her. It was also a relief for Sylvie to have something other than Evelyn and Nicholas's forthcoming wedding to talk about. Nicholas had managed to string the engagement out for so long at this stage that Sylvie didn't know why Evelyn put up with him. She suspected that she had finally given him some sort of ultimatum. The wedding breakfast was to take place in the Gresham Hotel and Evelyn had planned the event, and everyone's role in it, in meticulous detail. However, Sylvie was pleasantly surprised to find that her prospective sister-in-law threw herself just as enthusiastically into planning her exhibition, promising to round up all her friends to visit the opening and, hopefully, to buy artworks.

During the following weeks Evelyn used her PR expertise to advise Sylvie as to which papers and magazines she should send notices to. She also offered to see if a contact she had with the *Evening Herald* could persuade their art correspondent to attend.

Around that time, Nicholas made a suggestion to Sylvie and Peter.

"Look, you two, Evelyn and I are getting married next June, and all her family will be there, and I want my family to be there too. So, it's time that you patched things up with Mother and Father. How old is Sam now – eight? It's been too long already. Let's see if I can use the wedding as leverage with Father."

"If Uncle Daniel only wants to make things up just for appearances' sake then he can go to hell," Sylvie said in a low controlled voice.

"Sylvie, Sylvie," said Nicholas wearily, "he's an old man, set in his ways. Cut him some slack. I know he regrets the harsh words that were spoken, and Mother misses you both terribly. She also would love to be a part of Sam's life. So how about inviting them both to Sylvie's opening night? It would be a start. Come on, little brother, you're bigger than all of this."

Peter looked uncertainly at Sylvie whose expression was grim.

"Well, darling," he said tentatively, "maybe it's time we sorted things out?"

January 1960

The gallery on Baggot Street was a converted shop and modest in size. Only two dealers in Dublin catered for modern art, and both dealt in the main with established names like Jack B Yeats and Louis le Brocquy. Very few Irish people liked, or even understood, modern art. Sylvie thought that the gallery must be an expensive pastime for Penelope, funded, no doubt, by her father who she had heard owned a stud farm in Kildare. And, with his connections, it was not surprising that the room was heaving with Dublin's well-to-do professionals whose offices were in the fine Georgian houses on nearby Merrion and Fitzwilliam squares. There were also quite a few West Brits, Ireland's landed gentry whose way of life and cultural values were still firmly aligned with those of their forefathers across the water.

Earlier Sylvie had examined her paintings, and although she was sick with nerves at the prospect of the evening ahead, she felt enormous pride in what she had achieved. Framed and hung on white walls, her colourful paintings presented surprisingly well. Penelope kept saying, "These are simply luscious, darling". It was a particularly good way of describing them. Sylvie had painted Sandymount Strand at the same time every evening for over a year. Most of these were only sketches, but she had worked up twenty or so into finished artworks, each in heavy impasto showing the effects of changing light, the season and different weather conditions. It made a powerful display. Already there were several red dots beneath works bought by well-known collectors who Penelope had allowed in for a private preview before the show officially opened.

Amongst the eclectic gathering, Sylvie thought that Uncle Daniel and Aunt Nora looked decidedly uncomfortable. Nora's coat was tight around her chest and the buttons gaped. Her hat, the type that needed a pin to keep it in place, was perched on top of her round head like a pillbox, with a scrap of black net hanging down in front. One of Mrs Coleman's creations, Sylvie thought. It looked hastily made. Mrs Coleman worked in the undertaker's and made hats for special occasions as a side-line.

"How lovely to see you, dear. I've missed you."

Aunt Nora's eyes filled with tears as she encircled Sylvie with a big bosomy hug.

Sylvie instantly forgave her. Not that she had said anything in the first place, but her acquiescence in Daniel's intransigent position had infuriated Sylvie.

Meanwhile, during this emotional display, her uncle stood fidgeting with his gloves.

Peter came over to take Nora to say hello to a relative from Kilkenny and, as they moved away, Daniel, his face grim, put out his hand.

After a moment's hesitation Sylvie's hand met his.

"It's good to see you, Sylvie, and in better circumstances than the last time. Congratulations on the work. You were always good at art in school, if I remember, and you seem to have flourished. But then, I shouldn't be surprised, it's obviously in the blood."

"Did Papa paint much?" she could not resist asking.

"Yes, watercolours, usually sketches when he travelled. He always carried a sketchpad with him."

"I do remember him sketching when we were on holidays in Antibes – I must have been five or six. He used to sit on the sea wall outside the town and paint the view towards the castle."

"Really, how interesting. I believe you are friendly with the Ambroses and that it was they who taught you to paint. I know his work, he's extremely talented, and a good sort of chap."

"Yes, he is, they have both been very kind to me."

Daniel coughed awkwardly. "Look, I'm sorry, Sylvie. It was all a bit of a shock. You were both so young. And it didn't seem right. In retrospect, I overreacted. I met Peter earlier today, I'm sure he told you. I realise that things have been difficult for you both financially. To make things up, as a peace offering of sorts, I have given him money for the two of you towards buying a house. It's a start anyway. I know you still have a way to go before you have enough for a deposit. Your aunt misses you both terribly, and Sam too of course. But there may be other children. In which case we –"

But before he could finish, a tall young man with horn-rimmed spectacles and a mustard corduroy jacket several sizes too big for him bounded over to them.

"Mr Courtney, good to see you. I didn't expect to see anyone I knew here."

Reluctantly, Sylvie thought, Uncle Daniel introduced her.

"Sylvie, I would like to introduce Dr Brian Dillon to you. He's just finished his PhD in the History of Art in Oxford. He has given me advice in the past regarding artworks I was selling for a client."

"A Léger, if I remember rightly."

"A Léger ..." said Sylvie. "That name rings a bell."

"Yes, a very famous artist. He –"

"And how is the research going, Brian?" Daniel interrupted. "You were looking at German Degenerate Art if I remember rightly."

"Stalled, Mr Courtney, pressure of work, too much on my plate at the moment." The professor looked at Daniel, then back at Sylvie as if about to say something. But then he seemed to think better of it and started to move away. "Anyway, must go, got a train to catch to Cork, I'm lecturing in the Crawford tomorrow."

The young man disappeared out through the glass door into the black night.

"Nervous sort of chap," said Daniel.

Sylvie turned to her uncle. "Léger – Uncle Daniel, I didn't realise that you dealt with such famous artists. I thought they were mainly Irish, you know, Sadler, Edwin Hayes, that sort of thing. I never knew that you were involved in international art of such high calibre."

"I try not to talk about it too much. Loose talk and all that. And, of course, the work belongs to bank clients to whom I owe confidentiality. Years ago, your father used to advise me. Now I'm stuck with that young fellow. A bit odd, like most academics, but he knows his stuff."

"Miss Vasseur, could I ask you a few questions, please?"

Evelyn's contact from the *Evening Herald* had arrived.

It had been a busy day at the gallery and Sylvie was looking forward to getting home for the evening. She had sold quite a few paintings on the opening night. Since then sales had been sluggish. But today a hotel owner from Galway had bought six paintings which he insisted on taking back with him on the evening train. She had to take the paintings he had bought down, wrap them, and rehang new works to fill the empty spaces. She was tired and elated by it all. It had been a hectic couple of weeks. She only had until Friday when she would have to take them all down. But it was a good start, better than she had expected. Penelope had been so pleased she had covered her costs and made a reasonable profit that she had promised Sylvie another slot in the exhibition programme later in the year.

Sylvie looked out apprehensively at the heavy tea-time traffic on Baggot Street. It was raining, and she would get soaked walking home. She had forgotten her umbrella in the rush to get Sam ready for school that morning.

"Sylvie, I was afraid you would be closed."

"Nicholas, what a surprise," she said coolly as he strode into the gallery, closing his umbrella.

"I was hoping you could help me out," he said. "It's Evelyn's birthday tomorrow and I thought that one of your paintings would make a good present."

"Oh, well, I suppose that would be nice," she said ungraciously.

She rose from her desk where she had been completing the paperwork for the afternoon sales and stood beside her paintings.

"These are a new series I've done, I just put them up today. They are inspired by Howth Harbour – abstracts, of course – trying to capture the effect of the low sun and the reflection of boats' masts in the water."

"Yes, I can see, how interesting. Evelyn's living room is a beige colour, and the carpet has a pink-and-beige floral pattern. Which one do you think would go with it?"

"I thought you were a collector?" she said frostily. "That's not the way to choose art. You should know that. You should choose something that you like, that you respond to. Didn't your father teach you anything?"

"I think you will find that my father is equally pragmatic in these matters. My purchases tend to be based on investment potential. Of course, I like the Impressionists, and even Picasso and Mondrian at a stretch, but I find that in a lot of the modern stuff the imagery is unsatisfactory, neither a recognisable subject, nor a pattern. I find it less appealing. But

Evelyn really likes this sort of thing." He waved his hand around the walls. "I must admit that we were both impressed with your work at the opening. So, I thought it would make a nice surprise for her birthday. And that maybe you'd give me a generous discount, seeing as I'm family?"

He gave a wry smile and Sylvie looked at him sardonically.

"Of course."

He finally chose a lovely night scene, with the distinctive shape of Ireland's Eye in the background. The painting had strong ultramarine and cerulean-blue tones applied with Sylvie's signature impasto finish.

"Now we must seal the deal."

"What do you mean?" she said curtly.

"How about a sherry in the Shelbourne? You are closing, aren't you? When I was talking to Peter earlier, he told me that he was in the Limerick branch today and won't be back this evening. He also said you were a bit down in the dumps because Jenny and Maxwell were going to France for the summer and planned to rent their house – and that you will lose your studio while they are away. But I think I have a solution to your dilemma."

"Well, that's very kind of you, I'm sure. But to go for a drink is out of the question. I have to collect Sam from Aunt Elsie's."

"I took the liberty of phoning Elsie, and asking her to keep Sam for a few hours, that I needed to talk to you about family business."

"You had no right to do that, Nicholas. *How dare you!*"

"Sylvie, calm down."

"Don't you *dare* tell me to calm down."

He grabbed her wrists. "Sylvie. You are overreacting. Look, I want to talk to you. We should talk. I can't bear this atmosphere between us. Things are not going to change and we both need to move on. And, as it happens, I do have a suggestion for you about your studio."

The Shelbourne bar was quiet, the Tuesday evening crowd comprised mainly afternoon shoppers from nearby Grafton Street, ladies laden down with bags from Brown Thomas who were just having a quick tipple before heading home to the suburbs.

Sylvie sipped her sherry apprehensively.

"Before we talk about your ideas for the studio," she said, "I want to get things straight about Sam. He is nothing to do with you. As far as Peter is concerned, his father was an RAF pilot, a one-night stand. He is Sam's father now. I have never asked you for a penny towards his upkeep. And, if you must know, I cannot bear our frequent social outings pretending nothing happened between us." Her hand was shaking and her lip had started to tremble.

"For Christ's sake, relax, Sylvie," said Nicholas, looking around nervously. "Look, I deeply regret what happened, and it was unfortunate that you ended up marrying my brother. I'm not sure you really thought that one through."

Sylvie, furious, got up to leave, but he pulled her back down with a jolt.

"Steady, tiger! Be sensible, things have moved on, I'm about to be married, settle down. I just want to get on with my life. Funnily enough, I'm rather fond of that younger brother of mine. Can we not just be a little nicer to one another?" He paused and she glared at him. "Look, I have given up any right to play a part in Sam's life other than as an adoring uncle. I give you my word that I will not say, or do, anything to change that situation."

"And not in the future?"

"Not now, not ever. It would just cause too many problems within our family. Don't you see? For me, I mean."

Sylvie looked at him with contempt.

"Happy now?"

She nodded curtly.

"Now the studio. I have a bungalow on the Hook Peninsula – I just bought it. It's about a mile outside Slade village. It was designed and built by an architect as a holiday home. But he ran into financial difficulties. So I got it for a song. It's basic but comfortable and is done up rather nicely. Slade is so picturesque, as you know, with the harbour and the Norman castle. Remember when we went there as kids? It's an artist's paradise, I would imagine. I was wondering if you would like to use it as a studio this summer."

"What about you and Evelyn, don't you want to use it?"

"Unfortunately not. I jumped the gun a little there. Evelyn isn't so keen, finds it too desolate. She'd rather go to Kilkenny where there's more happening. I bought it really because it's near Knockaboy. So, if you want to use it, consider it yours for the summer."

"Well, that sounds interesting," she said reluctantly. "But I couldn't leave Peter for that length of time." Not at the rate he'd been drinking lately, she thought to herself.

"Well, he could come down at the weekends, maybe arrange his business so that he's in that neck of the woods on a Friday. Take a long weekend. You could make it work."

"That is very tempting. I must admit that I will be lost without the studio. Let me think about it – and talk to Peter of course."

"OK, no pressure. How about one for the road. To happier times ahead."

"OK, fine," she acquiesced.

On leaving through the hotel's revolving door the cold night air hit her, and she felt a little lightheaded.

Nicholas, leaning close to her, stroked her cheek. "I really enjoyed our chat. Almost like old times."

He bent to kiss her on the mouth. Too late she tried to turn her face away.

"I still have feelings for you, you know, little sister."

He turned, still smiling, and walked down the street, leaving Sylvie with her heart racing, furious and aroused.

When she got back to the apartment, Peter was there waiting for her.

"Where the hell have you been? And where is Sam?"

"Peter, you're here! Sam is in Elsie's. I met Nicholas for a drink. He told me he was talking to you earlier, and that you were staying the night in Limerick on business."

"What? I don't know where he got that from. I told him I was doing work in Limerick – he must have misunderstood. You know I would have rung you and told you, if that was the case."

"Sorry, Peter, sorry. It's just Nicholas bought Evelyn one of my paintings for her birthday – the one based on Ireland's Eye. He asked me to go for a drink and it seemed churlish to say no in the circumstances."

"Well, you could have bloody rung me and let me know."

"But I thought –"

"Oh, forget it. Anyway, I'm starving. I'll go and collect Sam, and you can start the tea."

Later that night, he spooned into her arched back, his hands on her breasts, feeling her nipples through her cotton nightdress, and bit her earlobe gently.

"I'm too tired tonight, Peter." She moved slightly, brushing him off.

"You're always too bloody tired."

She could smell the whiskey on his breath.

"Did Nicholas mention he has bought a bungalow near Slade," he asked.

"Yes."

"And that he could give it to you for the summer, so you could paint?"

"Yes."

"Well, did you accept his offer?"

"No, I said I'd talk to you first," she said warily.

"Well, maybe it's a good idea. To spend some time together, on our own, away from all of this."

Sam, in his trestle bed, started coughing.

"See what I mean," Peter said. "He's been irritable all day according to Elsie – she thinks he's starting another bloody cold. The sooner we buy our own bloody house the better." He paused. "Sylvie, can I ask you something."

"What?"

"Do you love me?"

"Oh no, Peter, not that conversation. Not now."

"Sylvie, I know you're tired. But sometimes when you look at me, I feel that I mean nothing to you. I only feel we really connect when we make love and then, even then, sometimes I wonder."

"Peter," she rolled over and put her arm around him, "we've had a tough time with Sam living in this flat, with you working day and night. But things are getting better for us. We seem to have turned a corner with the money your parents have given us towards buying a house, and I have my art now which is going well – I'm starting to sell. Things will get better."

"But do you love me?"

"Yes, Peter. I do love you. Just stop asking me all the time. Look, let's go and stay in Nicholas's bungalow for a week or two, maybe over Easter, if it's free, and see how it works out. Now, I really am exhausted. I've had a long day." She kissed him on the mouth and once more turned her back.

Chapter 11

Near Slade, Wexford
April 1962

When Nicholas had told her his bungalow was remote, he wasn't joking. Outside, she couldn't even see the lights of the O'Reillys' cottage, the nearest neighbours. But she thought she could hear their dog barking in the distance. She pulled the thick woollen curtains across the window, noticing how the large pane of glass quivered as the wind howled outside. Then she sat down once more on the couch in front of the fire and picked up her book. Unable to concentrate, she put it down again. The weather had turned, as if in sympathy with recent events. It had been unseasonably cold for April, and today was the third day of continuous rain, where low, dark-grey clouds pressed down upon the landscape. She remembered how she had laughed last week, in balmy temperatures, when Mikey Mac the fisherman had warned her that storms were on the way. She threw another sod of turf onto the fire. There was no point staying here now. It was raining heavily, and the wind was now roaring around the bungalow – great gusts of it. At one stage she felt the roof was going to come off as the North Westerly blew across the narrow land mass. It seemed to be picking up moisture-laden air from the sea and lashing it down on the land in bucketfuls. For the last few days there were no signs of local life.

When they had ventured out earlier, Sylvie and Sam had not met a soul, no one to press the flesh of her hand and say, "I'm sorry for your troubles".

Penelope had called her from the gallery last Friday morning to tell her the terrible news. The Ambroses had both died in a car crash whilst on holiday touring Savoy in a mountainous part of France, a collision on a bad bend on a windy mountain road. The other driver had been drinking. After receiving the news, Sylvie had been overcome with a grief that had robbed her of all her energy. A grief made tangible by the inclement weather. Peter had come down for the weekend when he had heard the news but had left on Sunday evening to return to work in Dublin.

Leaning back on the couch and closing her eyes, Sylvie thought back fondly over the last nine years, and how the Ambroses had become more like her uncle and aunt than Daniel and Nora had ever been. They had introduced her to their world, and through art had given her life meaning and direction, whereas before she felt she had none. Now she was an established name in the Dublin art scene in her own right – and this summer she had two works accepted for the Irish Exhibition of Living Art – a group of independent-minded artists who sought to challenge the autonomy of the Royal Hibernian Academy.

But what occupied her mind, and contributed to her current restlessness, was the news she had heard only yesterday from their solicitor. He had travelled down from Dublin to Slade to meet her and explain the extraordinary final act of kindness the couple had bestowed upon her. Unbeknown to her, they had made her their sole legal heir. Although the inheritance came with certain responsibilities – she was required to create an inventory of their work – Sylvie was under no illusions that this would be a straightforward or easy task. It entailed sorting out Max and Jenny's stuff: years of accumulated drawings, paintings and paperwork. But the legacy meant, effectively, that she was now the owner of their beautiful house in Gilford Road in Sandymount with its magnificent studio. Since Daniel had given them the money, they had been saving every penny, and now two years later they had just started to look for a small, terraced, two-up two-down property in Ringsend. Instead she could move into the home of her dreams, and live a different, more privileged life than the mean existence they had enjoyed up until now. For once she was independent – she needed no one, and it was this aspect of her situation that now occupied her mind. She was thinking about returning to Dublin the following day.

On the easel at the other end of the room was a large painting, an abstract inspired by the Hook Lighthouse and the sea. She was pleased with it.

Apart from the last few days, overall it had proved to be a productive couple of weeks. Sam had enjoyed it too. She had noticed earlier that his hair was bleached from the sun and his normally pale cheeks had developed a ruddy glow. She had invited a school friend of his over to the bungalow. The boy was staying in a caravan in nearby Fethard-on-Sea, and, conveniently, his parents had reciprocated and taken Sam to the beach most days, giving Sylvie the opportunity to work.

At the other end of the bungalow, he was fast asleep. His friend had gone home the previous day and he had spent a solitary morning in his room, making a Lego fort, and arranging his collection of fossils and skeletons. It was time to leave anyway, school started back on Monday after the Easter break. He had already started nagging her about seeing Peter. Sam was so close to him and in many ways he was very like him. He certainly looked like him. But in other ways, he showed traits that worryingly reminded her of Nicholas. His temper, for example, which would erupt volcanically every now and then. Despite this, for an eleven-year-old he was remarkably innocent. Although his obsession with dead animals was unusual to say the least. When she had raised her concerns with Peter, he had dismissed them and told her how he had collected dead spiders when he was a boy and had been very proud of his collection. She still worried, and in the evenings she encouraged Sam to try and draw the tiny skeletons with her and she would make up stories about them, turn them into characters that she hoped he could identify with. But he invariably ignored these attempts, told her they were childish. She supposed they were. It was hard to accept that he had grown up so quickly. She remembered back to when he was younger, how she had struggled – trying not to associate him with Nicholas. Time had helped in this regard, and Sam, when he chose to be, could be such a charming boy.

That afternoon, fed up with the morning's incarceration

in the bungalow, she finally cajoled Sam, after the usual tantrums, into braving the elements. Kitted out in Mackintoshes, Wellington boots and plastic hats, they had spent the day at Carnaevon wandering in the rain along the sodden beach, eventually discovering a horde of treasure: shells and bones, and the skull of a cow that had fallen off the cliffs on a night such as this. After all that, he was exhausted and had gone to bed early. When she'd put her head around his door half an hour ago, she found him fast asleep.

A knock on the door startled her. She wasn't expecting visitors. Cautiously she went and stood at the front door.

"Who is it?"

"It's me, Nicholas, let me in. I'm getting bloody soaked out here."

She undid the chain and opened the deadlock, her pulse racing.

"Nicholas, my God, you're drenched. Why are you here? Is anything wrong?"

"That's a fine welcome. Let me take my coat off and dry myself off. Any chance of a drink around here?"

Proprietorially, he threw his soaking raincoat and hat on the chair in the hall and marched into the living room to rub his hands over the fire.

"Well, why are you here?" she said coldly.

She had met him several times with Peter since their encounter over a year previously when he had kissed her outside the Shelbourne Hotel. These were strained and awkward occasions for her, but they did not seem to faze him one jot. Fuelled by Nicholas's constant repeating to Peter on their boy's nights out that Sylvie did not seem to like him that much, Peter had pleaded with her not to be so cold with him. Nicholas's knowing, hurt smiles when he met Sylvie only served to infuriate her more. However, she continued to use the bungalow on the Hook – both she and Peter loved the area and it was handy to visit Knockaboy. But this was the first time she had met Nicholas alone since that night, and she was still furious with him.

"Oh, I had business in New Ross, and I didn't feel like driving back to Dublin on such a filthy night. So, I thought you might be kind enough to give a bed to a traveller in distress. It *is* my house after all."

"Out of the question, please leave!"

"Sylvie, be reasonable, it's bucketing down out there, and half of the roads are flooded." He rubbed the back of his head with one hand and gave her his most charming smile.

"Look if you don't leave, I will."

"What, wake up poor Sam and drag him out in this storm? I didn't think you were such a cruel mother."

Sylvie was close to tears. "Very well, have a drink, then go to bed. You can sleep in my bed – I'll sleep on the couch."

"What kind of a man do you think I am? I'll sleep on the couch."

She walked over to the bookshelf in the alcove and, taking down the bottle of whiskey, poured him a glass with a shaking hand.

"Have one yourself, why don't you?"

"I don't drink whiskey."

"A small glass won't hurt."

Still trembling, she poured herself a finger.

"I heard your good news. What amazing luck – who would have known the two old codgers were worth that much. I suppose you'll leave Peter now. You don't really need him anymore, do you?"

"The two old codgers were my dearest friends and Peter is my husband and, believe it or not, I love him," she said, shaking with rage.

"*Mm*, really? Still having a bit of trouble in the bedroom department, I believe."

"*How dare you!*" She raised her wrist to throw the glass at him, but he caught it. But not before the glass fell and hit the floor with a thud, then rolled away on the carpet.

"I want you, Sylvie. I've always wanted you, and I think you want me too."

She struggled to get away from him, but he was too strong. He kissed her passionately, and she felt herself responding, and as he pulled her back onto the couch with one hand beneath her skirt rubbing the throbbing, soft skin between her legs, she stopped fighting.

Chapter 12

Dublin
April 1965

She lifted the brochure for holidays in France from her desk in Max's study, her study – she had to constantly correct herself. She had picked the brochure up that afternoon in the travel agent's. She would go home. But was Paris still home? If she were honest, memories of the city were at best hazy, informed by news footage on television and photographs in magazines. No, she never felt at home – wherever she was, she felt like a foreigner, not quite the same as everyone else. Art had helped – artists tended to celebrate difference – they didn't fear it like most people. The flights were so expensive, she thought. To hell with it, she could afford it. Now that things had settled down, this summer she could finally fulfil her dream and go back to Paris, take Sam, show him where their apartment had been and visit her father's gallery. She hadn't mentioned this to Peter yet. She didn't see him as part of her plan. Time enough to fight that battle. They had only just started speaking again after weeks of his sulking when she told him she'd bought Rose Cottage, her new rural retreat. Not that she didn't love Gilford Road, because she did.

But Wexford was special. She sat back in her chair. Yes, she thought to herself, Wexford felt like home. Not Knockaboy so much, although she had some happy memories growing up there with Aunt Nora and the boys, but the countryside around it.

She picked up, then signed a cheque for the builder who had carried out the alterations to the cottage. She put the cheque in an envelope to post on Monday. After she had inspected the work he had done at the weekend.

When Nicholas told her he was selling the bungalow to fund some new project he was working on, she was surprised at how disappointed she was that they could no longer go there – but she could hardly complain. She thought back to summer Sundays as a child when, after Mass, they would all pile into Uncle Daniel's black Austin, Aunt Nora in the front and the boys and her in the back, and they would drive down to the Hook Lighthouse. While Uncle Daniel and Aunt Nora read the newspapers and smoked Woodbines in the car, she and the boys would be let out to run across the fissured, limestone outcrop that formed the headland below the lighthouse and jutted out into the wild Irish Sea. It was a confluence of currents, Uncle Daniel told them, the coming together of the three sisters – the Suir, the Nore and the Barrow – three rivers that poured into Waterford harbour and joined forces to flow together out into the ocean. The wildness of the waters echoed in the currents in the air above, and people standing on the rocks had been known to be blown out to sea by the sheer force of the wind. And sometimes, in the winter, when the wind blew across the tops of the waves, inward over the land, a coffee-coloured froth would fill the road like a wayward cloud had fallen to earth. She remembered the pleasure they had as children kicking the knee-high foam and licking its salty residue as it smeared their faces and soaked through their woollen gloves so that they couldn't feel their fingers as their hands became bone cold.

Even thinking about the place lifted her mood, its austerity bewitched her, the way the land, sea and sky could coalesce into one another. Then, at other times, they would separate into individual elements, with a thousand variations of a scene – like an old-fashioned kaleidoscope. Aunt Nora used to say that each evening there was a different sunset, like no other that went before it.

Her eyes glanced over a silver-framed photograph Peter had given her last year for Christmas, that she felt obliged to display. It was of Nicholas, Peter and herself as children on the beach in Duncannon. They all wore shorts and hand-me-down Fair Isle jumpers. Their hair was chopped short, and unevenly, in one of Aunt Nora's legendary bowl haircuts, and there were buckets and spades at their feet. Each of the boys had a hand on her shoulder, Peter's blonde head taller than her, and Nicholas's dark one taller again. Her head was tilted slightly towards her older cousin. Her expression was unsmiling, Peter's innocent and Nicholas's mischievous. She pressed the tips of her fingers onto closed eyelids to block out the image. But it was still there in her mind.

She hadn't intended to have an affair with Nicholas, but she simply found it too hard to resist. After that first night – 'the night of the storm', she thought with grim humour, and it was, in a physical and metaphorical sense – it had been too risky to use his bungalow. So they met, usually, at some seedy inner-city hotel. Afterwards, she felt defiled, dirty, and she soaked for hours in the bath attempting to wash away her shame. But she never fully succeeded. She hated herself for deceiving Evelyn, who for all her business acumen was emotionally naive and chose to believe whatever excuses Nicholas gave for his frequent absences. Sylvie was not foolish enough to believe she was the only one. But then, she thought, Evelyn had got what she wanted – she had willingly given up her glamorous job to marry Nicholas and spend her time at home in the suburbs with their small daughter. Maybe, Sylvie tried to persuade herself, this was part of their bargain. But her main concern was that she was finding it increasingly difficult to continue to pretend to Peter that there was nothing wrong in their relationship. Some days, she thought she should never have married him. But it wasn't that simple, there was Sam to consider. He was so attached to his dad and Peter idolised him. She thought getting the house in Sandymount would have solved all her problems, their problems. And in some ways the last few years had been such an exciting time. The memory was still palpable of walking through the front door of the house in Gilford Road for the first time, knowing it was hers. It was one of the happiest moments of her life, knowing she would not have to worry about money ever again.

It had taken months to clear the house of Jenny and Max's stuff. Who knew one woman could own so many scarves and folderols, as Aunt Nora used to call them? Sylvie had filled countless bags of clothes and shoes to give to the travellers who called regularly to the house. Jenny and Max's paintings and sketchbooks were another matter. She had given the sketchbooks and the better paintings to the Hugh Lane Gallery. She kept a few of the more colourful abstracts by Jenny and used them to decorate the house. But the nudes were another matter. Really, there were only so many nudes anyone could hang on their walls, and Max had been partial to nudes. In the end she offered these to friends of the couple who were delighted to have them as mementos. She had also spent months creating an inventory: a list of each artwork, where they were, exhibition catalogues, newspaper reviews and correspondence. She had a production line going burning wastepaper in the brazier in the back garden. But now that was finished, the house was finally hers. Although, she felt guilty – it was almost as if she had purged the couple from their home. The house had been painted and decorated to suit her taste, and compared to theirs it felt minimalist, but still cosy. At the end of a day's painting in her new studio, she enjoyed nothing better than sitting down in the living room in front of a coal fire, sipping a glass of Riesling and enjoying the comfort of her new surroundings. But, despite her good fortune, guilt about her infidelity cast a significant cloud on her horizon. Most of the time she felt weighed down by sadness. She didn't love Peter and she didn't love Nicholas either. For her, the sex and the adrenaline rush with Nicholas were an escape from the despair of her loveless marriage. In contrast, she knew that for Nicholas it was about the chase, taking what he couldn't have – shouldn't have. Nicholas was one of those men who lived constantly on the edge and was willing to risk everything for the thrill of it all. She would have to tell Peter the truth, even if it meant her world would come crashing down. He didn't deserve it. But she couldn't live like this anymore.

Later that morning, Sylvie was in her studio trying to tidy up before starting on a new painting. Then she remembered she wanted to hang her father's etching of the rabbit on the back wall – the one that had hung for years in Knockaboy in Daniel's study. Aunt Nora had arrived with it in a taxi, unexpectedly, the previous day. Her aunt had got a lift from Wexford to Dublin with her neighbour who had a doctor's appointment in Merrion Square. Still saddened by Daniel's sudden death earlier in the year, the older woman seemed anxious and distracted. Her hair, limp, needed a perm.

"This has been on my mind for some time, Sylvie. It's the etching that belonged to your father. I remember Daniel telling me Paul wanted you to have it when you were twenty-one. Well, we weren't in contact at the time if you remember …" her cheeks flushed with embarrassment, "but, even so, Daniel should have given it to you sooner. God knows I nagged him about it often enough. I knew that you would like to have it." Opening her handbag, she took out an envelope and handed it to Sylvie. "I also found this amongst his papers. It was sent from Paris shortly after you arrived. There's a postcard in it for you, saying that he has sent the etching. I suppose he had second thoughts and put the postcard in the envelope to be discreet – those were dangerous times."

Sylvie was almost overcome by emotion but, quelling both her anguish and her anger, she laid the precious gifts aside and tried to soothe her aunt who was visibly upset.

After, when her aunt had left, Sylvie opened the envelope with its Paris postmark and French stamp, wondering why her uncle had opened a letter addressed to her and why he had never given it to her.

On the front of the postcard was an Art Nouveau stylised image of lilies. On the back it was dated July 7th, 1940.

On it her father had written in French:

Dear Sylvie,

I have sent Daniel an etching of a rabbit, to remind you of a similar painting, 'Flora', that you were so excited about in my gallery, the day that you helped me when Maman was sick. I have asked Daniel to give it to you, if we are not there, to remind you of happier times and how much we both loved you.

Love, Papa

Sylvie instantly recalled the day he was talking about. She remembered it vividly, as if it were only yesterday. She was about seven years old. Maman had the flu and had been in bed for a week. It was a Saturday, there was no school and she was to spend the day with Papa. It was winter, and even though there was a stove in the gallery it was so cold she had to wear her coat and fingerless gloves.

A very old, elegantly dressed lady had come in with a pastel drawing of a beautiful young girl. It was set in a burgundy oval mount. On the back was written

'Flora' by Philippe Bastin. The woman told them that it was of her as a young girl. She wanted it reframed. After she had left, Papa, removing the metal tacks, had opened the back of the frame. He had let her lift out the backing board and, to their amazement, taped to the inside was a letter. Papa read it out to her – he probably shouldn't have – but they had both been so excited. It was a secret letter, a love letter from the artist to Flora. The letter explained how he had been commissioned to draw the girl, a daughter of a wealthy Parisien banker. However, as he drew her, he had fallen hopelessly in love with her. He was enchanted by her beauty and beguiled by her soft and gentle nature. But he could not declare his love – she could never be his – she was betrothed to another, the son of a business associate of her father's. He hoped he was wrong, but he sensed she was unhappy and that this was not what she wanted. He knew that the frame of the drawing was of poor quality, and he hoped that one day she would need to replace it. Then she would find the letter and know that, unworthy as he was, he had truly loved her.

Sylvie remembered that when the old woman returned to the gallery, Papa had given her the letter. She read it carefully, and as she did so her crinkled, blue eyes had filled with tears which spilled down over her powdery cheeks. She did not remark on what had occurred. She simply paid Papa and left the shop, and he had never met her again. But for weeks afterwards, Papa, Mama and herself had talked about the incident, trying to fill in the blanks of the couples' extraordinary story.

Now, Sylvie sighed at the memory. Perplexed, she looked once more at the rather sad etching of the rabbit lying on her layout table. This etching and the drawing of the young girl from all those years ago had absolutely nothing in common. Whatever had her father meant? Unless …

Just as a crazy thought occurred to her, Nicholas walked in.

"Oh, does the rabbit have a new home?" he asked, looking at the etching.

"Yes, your mother brought it here yesterday."

"Why?"

"Because it belonged to my papa, and it seems he wanted me to have it when I was twenty-one." Sylvie tried to quell her rising excitement. She had no intention of sharing her wild speculation with Nicholas. "I don't know why Uncle Daniel could not have told me that before now."

"Is it worth anything?"

"No, it's only a print," she managed to say calmly, "but you know I have nothing else belonging to my father. No photographs, books, anything like that to remember him by,"

"It must be the same for a lot of Jewish families. They must have lost everything during Hitler's reign of terror."

"I suppose." She tilted her head to one side, looking back at the print, "It's such a sad little rabbit."

"Oh, there's no need for you to feel sad now – I am here."

He put his arm around her shoulder, pulled her to him and gave her a long lingering kiss.

When she eventually opened her eyes, to her horror she saw Peter looking into the conservatory from the living-room window. Time seemed to be suspended as she felt his silent primeval scream of betrayal cut through her. Then seconds later, he was there in front of them, eyes wild with anger, his mouth twisted into a grotesque sneer.

At first, in her fright, Sylvie didn't hear what he said. But then the words *"whore ... bitch"* registered through her confusion. *"I took you in when no one else would, you and your bastard son!"*

"Look, Peter, let's be grown up about this." Nicholas put his hand on Peter's shoulder to calm him down.

Peter, incensed, punched him forcefully on the chin, knocking him down against a large glazed china urn containing a rubber plant which crashed against the wall. Blood trickled from the side of Nicholas's cheek as he lay dazed on the ground, and the sound of Sylvie's piercing scream reverberated in the still air of the glass-walled chamber.

Peter sat down on the chair, head in hands, and sobbed uncontrollably.

"How could you – and with my brother, Sylvie? How could you?"

Eventually his tears stopped and he got up, wiping his swollen eyes and nose on his jacket sleeve. He left wordlessly, not looking at either of them. Nicholas stood up, dabbing his bloodied cheek with his handkerchief.

"Please, Nicholas, just go after him and make sure he's all right," Sylvie pleaded, and he hurried out.

Although still shaking from the incident, she felt strangely at peace. Finally, she had got what she deserved. Now she would just have to deal with the situation.

Her thoughts returned at once to the idea that had come to her about the etching – what if it contained a letter, just like the drawing of Flora all of those years ago?

Though she knew Nicholas might return quickly, she couldn't restrain herself another moment. She turned the print upside down on her layout table and, using a scalpel, cut the tape fixing the backing board to the frame. Lifting the board out, she exposed the back of the print.

There, underneath, taped to the board, were several pages of handwriting on faded blue paper, the type of paper used for airmail. With trembling hands, she cut the tape and removed the pages.

It was a letter written in French and addressed to her.

Hastily reassembling the print, she set it aside face-up so Nicholas would not notice. She would deal with it later.

Then she began to read her father's words from all of those years ago.

Paris, July 1940

Dearest Sylvie,
If you receive this letter, then things have not gone as I planned. I am now sitting in my gallery on the Rue du Faubourg Saint-Honoré. The German army has occupied Paris and it is no longer safe for your mother and me to remain here. I have only a matter of hours before I must

leave the city. When you are reading this, please God, you will be safely in Ireland where my dear friend Daniel has promised to look after you as if you were one of his own. But should we not be in a position to take you home in the future, through no fault of our own, you also need to know that Maman and I have left a significant legacy for you of Grandpapa's Barbizon paintings by Théodore Rousseau, Paul Huet, Constant Troyon, Jean-François Millet, and Charles-François Daubigny. But also, the more important legacy, I believe, is the collection of twelve paintings by the modern artists from my gallery. Many of these you will have seen. Amongst them are 3 Picassos, 2 Braques, 3 Légers, and of course the painting most dear to me, the one of you painted by Mateus. An accomplished copyist I know, a Russian artist who normally paints religious icons, made copies of all the paintings, sure as I was that these works were known about and already on some Gestapo list of acquisitions. I hung these fine copies in my gallery. The originals I removed from their frames with the help of my assistant Jean-Claude. The Barbizon works have been sent for safe keeping to Émile Bonnard in the South of France. He will take care of them for you until you come of age. The modern paintings we reframed and hid behind cheap William Turner prints of a view of Venice. These will be shipped to Ireland this evening to be kept in trust for you until you are twenty-one. Should anything happen to Daniel, as a precaution I have left this letter under this rabbit etching. I will also send a postcard to you, reminding you of the incident with the old lady and the hidden message. I can only hope it will inspire you to investigate the artwork and find this letter. I have advised Daniel that the etching is worthless and that I wish you to have it for sentimental reasons only.

I have so much I want to say to you, my dearest child, and so little time to say it. May God be with you, Sylvie. I pray that you will live a long and healthy life and sometimes hopefully you will remember your dear parents who both loved you more than you could ever know. Be safe, my dear, be strong, and try to be good.

Your loving Papa

Sylvie sat down on the floor and sobbed, racked with a grief pent up over the years, one that she had never had a chance to fully express. Consumed with loneliness and despair, she thought about what had become of her, how disappointed her parents would be. She knew she had not been strong, she had not been good, far from it. But as the sobs eventually subsided, she began to realise with alarm, which swiftly turned into anger, that she had also been robbed of her birthright.

Nicholas returned, flushed, ten minutes later. He had followed Peter who was heading towards Sandymount village, but Peter had jumped on a bus and Nicholas had been forced to give up and return to Gilford Road.

"He'll cool down eventually. Don't worry, Sylvie, we

can sort this out. We might have to stop seeing one another for a while, but in time ..."

He put out his hand to stroke her cheek, but she pushed it away.

"No – no, Nicholas, that's it. It's over between us. I want you to leave. Now."

"But, Sylvie!"

"*Now, Nicholas!*"

He shrugged and left.

Sylvie set about hanging the etching, dark thoughts agitating her mind. Uncle Daniel had told her categorically that her parents had left her nothing. So, what did this mean? What had her uncle done with the paintings?

Suddenly, she was very tired, completely physically and emotionally drained. But she knew it was important that she stayed focused and considered what had just happened very carefully.

She thought longingly of escaping to Wexford. She would take Sam there tomorrow. She imagined Peter would return home at some stage tonight, no doubt the worse for wear with drink. She needed to get away, let him calm down and give him a chance to accept that their relationship had been a sham and was now over.

She also needed to decide what she should do about what she had just learnt in her father's letter.

Chapter 13

Paris
February 1982

Leo Bonnard was trying to get some paperwork done in the small room at the back of the drawing office where he kept an electric typewriter, together with the personnel and office-management files. It was a place to go to when he simply wanted some peace and quiet, away from the constant inane nattering of his staff. But today the sound of workmen drilling was making it hard for him to concentrate even in this sanctuary. Finally, the drilling stopped. He sat back in his chair and closed his eyes, savouring the silence. The workmen were converting the small gallery upstairs into an apartment – a pressing economic necessity – the rent would help pay some of his outstanding bills. It made sense. The space, used for client presentations, had been a luxury that he could no longer afford. Since the slump in the retail fit-out market, business had been slow for some time. He'd already let three staff go. It had been an agonising decision. In the end he had decided to keep his glamorous receptionist – to lose her would betray his difficulties to the world. Instead, he reluctantly let go one senior architect who had been with him since he had opened three years before and one draughtsman – he simply did not have enough work for them – and his secretary Lydia. Her leaving had been a mixed blessing. On the one hand he found her constant chatter draining. But, on the other hand, he missed her typing skills. Now, as a result of her departure, the young architects were dealing with their own letters. Not without a fair degree of grumbling, it had to be said. Stephanie, twenty-four, claimed she hadn't studied architecture for five years to end up typing and refused outright to do it. She handwrote and faxed everything. Bruno, who was more amenable, adequately managed typing with two fingers.

"Monsieur Bonnard, excuse me." A shaved head and a tattooed arm appeared around the door. "There's something upstairs that I think you should see."

"Look," said Albert, pointing to the edge of the stairwell opening. It was decorated in colourful ceramic tiles with a leaf motif, blue on a yellow background, that his grandfather Émile had told him were designed by Henrique Mateus – the Portuguese artist that the gallery's original owner had represented in Paris before the war. He had asked the builders to remove these carefully and set them aside for reuse.

"You see here, these tiles are actually a front piece for a concealed box slotted in between the timber floor joists, and there's something in it."

Albert, using a flat steel knife, opened the box carefully, to reveal a dusty, black leather-bound book inside.

"Do you want to do the honours, monsieur?"

Leo carefully took it out, blowing away the black

dust – coaldust, he thought, from when the first-floor gallery was an apartment and heated with open fires.

"This is incredible," he said, lifting the cover carefully.

It appeared to be a journal, dated the 14th January 1940 on the first page and inscribed in a careful script with the name *Paul Vasseur*.

"He is a relative of yours, monsieur?"

"No, not a relative – he was my grandfather's friend. They had been at university together, in Cambridge. He owned this gallery originally. How extraordinary! This is dated a few months before the Germans occupied Paris. Thank you, Albert, this will be so much more interesting to read than paying electricity bills. Maybe leave this section of the work for the time being until I have a chance to examine this further."

Back in his office, Leo put on a clean pair of the thin cotton gloves he normally wore to clean his drawing pens and with a cloth carefully wiped the dusty cover. As he opened the journal and more dust particles filled the air, he sneezed.

Then with fascination he read Paul Vasseur's account of the months leading up to the Nazi occupation of Paris. He described how over a period of three months he had planned an exhibition of his own private art collection at the gallery. The format of the journal was mainly an elaborate to-do list: reframe this work by... varnish that one by ... touch up gallery after previous exhibition. He described the works as "old" and "new". The old, Leo gathered from the names of the artists listed, were Barbizon painters, mainly landscapes by Théodore Rousseau, Jean-François

Millet and Charles-Francois Daubigny. The new paintings were by modern artists: Picasso, Léger, Braque and Mateus. Unfortunately, however, the journal ended abruptly on the 3rd April 1940.

At the back of the journal there was an inventory of sorts which listed the artworks. For each painting there was a black-and-white photograph, an invoice relating to where it was bought, and information to do with the work's provenance. Leo was no art expert, but he knew these artists' work – they were household names for God's sake. The Barbizon paintings were of various rural scenes set in the region around the forest of Fontainebleau. He particularly liked the Millet of cornfields against a cloudless sky. You could sense, by the curve in their backs, the exhaustion of the gleaners, as they stooped to pick up the stray stalks of wheat. He turned the pages to the modern paintings. One was of a young girl on a swing. It was instantly recognisable as a Mateus, the Portuguese artist. A pretty painting, not his cup of tea, but he knew it must be worth a fortune. No, he preferred the Picasso, a nude, probably from his blue period. He could identify with the abstract imagery of the reclining figure. It was strong and voluptuous – he could imagine it hanging in one of his modernist interiors.

Leo sat back in his chair and thought about his grand-père, a cold and somewhat formal man. He vaguely remembered, when he was studying the history of art, Grand-père telling him about his friend Paul Vasseur's valuable art collection. But Leo had no idea that it was of this calibre. These artists were worthy of inclusion in any national museum of art. He recalled how Grand-père had told him Paul sent his daughter to live in Ireland during the war. Sylvie, he seemed to remember she was called. But Grand-père had never kept in touch with her. Strange that, thought Leo. He supposed, like many from that generation, he hated looking back to the past, filled as it was with unbearable memories. He certainly never talked about those years. Sadly, his grandfather had died when Leo was only fifteen. Leo remembered several times trying to talk about the German occupation to the old man, but somehow he always managed to change the subject.

Leo wondered what had happened to the paintings. In all probability, they were confiscated by the Nazis – he had heard stories over the years of the difficulties faced by Jewish survivors trying to reclaim looted art. Leo also considered the various other scenarios that could have occurred. Paul might have got the paintings out of the country and sold them before the Germans arrived. That was possible. Or even more intriguing, their whereabouts might still be unknown, and knowledge of them lost in the confusion of that time. But, if he had managed to get them out of the country, or to a place of safety, then surely Grand-père would have told him? And surely Paul's daughter Sylvie must know? Maybe she sold them off one by one. Yes, that was more likely. Anyway, whatever happened to them, one thing he was sure of – Sylvie would want this precious item belonging to her father.

Leo closed the journal, releasing another waft of black dust, smoothed the leather cover then placed it carefully on the bookshelf unit to the side of his desk. He should try to contact her – she was probably still alive. He reckoned she would now be in her 50s. Unfortunately, his father Felix couldn't help him track her down – he had died three years ago. He smiled when he thought of his father. Although the kindest and most loving of men, he had shown little interest in the extended family. However, if there had been the remotest possibility of the paintings surviving, or indeed any news of the Vasseurs, then Grand-père would have discussed this with Odette. A visit to his grandmother was long overdue. He would drive down this weekend and visit her in the nursing home near St Paul de Vence.

Odette had made an effort with her appearance for her grandson's visit, with red lipstick applied to her thin lips and hair newly permed into a metallic-grey helmet. She was wearing a dress of pale grey with beads on the bodice and a matching coat that made her look like she was on her way to a wedding. She stood out from the other occupants of the dayroom, a motley cardigan-ed crew whose loose clothing was chosen for comfort rather than style.

At eighty-two, his grandmother was crippled with arthritis, but neither her mind nor her spirit were in any way diminished.

"Leo, my handsome boy. I thought I was seeing things, and that it was your father walking through the door."

"Good to see you, Grand-mère. You're getting younger-looking every time I see you."

"If that is the case then maybe you will take me out of this godforsaken place."

"Grand-mère, you know that's not possible. How

160

would I ever get a wife with an old crone like you living with me? Seriously, you know I can't look after you properly. You need nursing care and the nuns here wait on you hand and foot. And if they don't, please tell me and I'll stop paying their exorbitant fees."

The old woman nodded grudgingly. He had told her the only reason the Catholic convent home had taken an atheist like her was because he had designed the place for a reduced fee.

"*Humph*," she replied, looking around at the other residents in the room to see if they had heard what had been said, unable to conceal her pride in her grandson. "So, what was it that you wanted to ask me so urgently that you drove halfway across France to see me?"

"Well, Grand-mère, it's the strangest thing. I was doing renovations in the gallery, taking out the old staircase that links the two spaces, and the builders found a hidden box between the floor joists. In it was an old journal written by Grand-père's friend Paul Vasseur. It was dated 1940 in the months leading up to the occupation of Paris and it has lain in that secret place ever since."

"My god, and what was in it?" she said, startled.

"Well, that's the extraordinary thing. Remember Grand-père telling us that Paul had two collections? One was of landscape paintings belonging to his father – he called these the Barbizon paintings – and the other was of modern paintings by Picasso, Braque, Léger and Mateus. Well, in the journal Paul explains how he was planning an exhibition of both collections. I was wondering what happened to the paintings – they would be worth a fortune today. I seem to remember

Grand-père telling me Paul Vasseur sent his daughter as an evacuee to Ireland? Maybe he sent the paintings with her, or maybe they are still squirreled away in some store, untouched for all these years. Anyway, I thought that I should try and contact her and send her the journal."

Odette closed her eyes briefly and winced as if remembering with difficulty.

"Courtney was the name of the family. Sylvie was only eight. She was the Vasseur's only child and very pretty – they spoiled her dreadfully. According to your father, she was a wilful little thing. I believe the artist, Mateus, painted her on a swing. He was very friendly with Paul before the war. As you know, Paul represented him in Paris." The old woman's eyes glazed over and seemed to focus on some indiscriminate point in the distance. "We had rented a villa in Antibes that spring, intending to stay there until things settled down in the city. But in May, Paul and Hanna wrote and asked to join us. Of course, we said yes." Her mouth puckered disapprovingly. "Paul sent their belongings, furniture and clothes, ahead – whatever they could really. So that when they finally fled Paris, they only had the clothes they stood up in. And then, as you know, they were arrested by the Gestapo as soon as they reached the villa. It turned out that an Algerian servant of ours was a spy for the French police, and he tipped them off that they were coming. Then a soldier was stationed in the house for a week at least before they eventually turned up half dead from exhaustion. They had a harrowing journey from Paris, I believe, by bicycle mostly. Poor Hanna was not strong. They were arrested and detained at a holding centre in Dancy outside of Paris, and then transported to Auschwitz where they were sent to the ..." Tears ran down her cheeks and she tried to stifle a sob.

Leo patted her veined and bony hand. She wiped her tears with a lace-edged handkerchief and paused for a while, looking out the window into the distance, her mind transfixed in another time and place.

"I remember your grand-père's despair in 1945 when it was finally confirmed that they were gone," she said eventually. "He blamed himself, you know. God knows why. There was nothing he could have done. We survived, thank God. Although survived doesn't really describe the way our generation lived in the world. We were all irrevocably damaged, one way or another. Your generation doesn't really understand. It was only after the war that the enormity of it all sank in. On one level we couldn't believe what had happened, and on another we felt somehow complicit. We were all scarred by looking into the face of evil."

She paused again, rubbing her eyes delicately with big-knuckled fingers.

"Paul could pass as French, German even – he was fair with blue eyes – Hanna could not – she was undeniably Jewish-looking with dark-brown eyes and olive skin. A very striking woman."

"And the child, Sylvie?"

"Well as you know, your grand-père died in 1973. But after the war I felt guilty about the poor child. Her parents Paul and Hanna were both only children – they had no family so she was effectively an orphan. For Paul and Hanna's sake, I thought we should contact her. But Émile used to say to me that his own family in France were enough trouble without going looking for more. But I remember some years ago, in the mid-1960s, that she died tragically. It was in all the papers at the time, at least the British ones. Your father used to get those to read the financial news. We all followed the reports with great interest because her death had occurred in mysterious circumstances. She had become an artist – well, it was in the blood, wasn't it?"

"Did Grand-père or Papa go to the funeral?"

"No, they didn't. They weren't interested. Although, funnily enough she had written to Émile shortly before she died. I never read the letter, but I remember him telling me that it was something about her father's art collection alright, but he thought she was barking up the wrong tree. I clearly remember him telling me that they had been destroyed in the early days of the occupation. They looted the galleries owned by the Jews first, including Paul's. They took landscapes, classical subjects that Hitler favoured but not modern art – 'degenerate art' as Hitler called it. Those simply did not survive in those early days. Later, they realised that even 'degenerate art' had a sale value. So many precious family heirlooms were stolen by the Nazis. Not just paintings – jewellery, china, antique furniture." The old woman twisted the loose gold band of the solitaire diamond ring on her bony finger. "But his Barbizon collection, as he called it, was destroyed in transit to his store in an air raid in Lyon."

"And none of them ever came up on the market after the war?"

"No, as I said, your grand-père said they were

destroyed. Maybe Paul told him. I can't remember how he knew." She shrugged her shoulders dramatically. "It was not unusual. Although some of the art the Germans looted was repatriated after the war, a good deal of it was never found. Destroyed or hidden away in bank vaults – I should think."

"Is there any chance that Sylvie's letter might be still in Grand-père's papers?"

"Yes, possibly. If it's there, it should be in a file marked *Family Correspondence* in the box-room of our apartment. But Leo, Sylvie is dead. Keep the journal as a memento – it's no use to anyone else."

"Did she marry, have any children?"

"No, not that I know of."

"Ah, pity. All the same, I'll ring Nathalie and go over and check out the letter."

"*Mm*, do that – your sister will be pleased to see you. Now, Leo, down to business – wife business. So why has a handsome, charming man like you not got a girl at your age?"

As soon as he opened the door of his family's second-floor Haussmannian apartment on the Boulevard Barbes, the cloying perfumed smell transported him back in time. As a child, he used to think it was an old person's smell. Years later he realised that it was the sweet smell of his mother's mimosa on the balcony that his sister now tended so lovingly.

Nathalie was late. He sat down on one of the tan leather Barcelona chairs and surveyed the apartment, admiring his own work. He had renovated their old family home for her a few years ago. It was now a pared-down minimalist version of the Belle Époque style that he remembered as a boy. Then it had been full of gilt antique furniture, mirrors and lustrous fabrics. It was never a homely place. He opened the casement window, stepped out on the balcony and surveyed the street below, hoping to have sight of his sister. Even the street where he had once played had changed. Then, it had seemed quieter, more sedate. Now the street was a hive of activity, day and night, infused with the colour and swagger of new cosmopolitan neighbours and sounds of African street hawkers selling their wares. His mother would have said it had gone down in tone. Instead, he thought, it had come alive.

He returned to the drawing room and sat flicking through one of the fashion magazines on the coffee table until he heard a key turning in the lock. He rose from the chair as Nathalie entered the apartment.

"Leo – good to see you, little brother," she said, although he towered above her. "Grand-mère told me all about it. She was on the phone to me as soon as you had left the convent. How exciting – did you bring the journal with you?" She was laden down with shopping, as usual.

Leo kissed his elfin-like sister on both cheeks and, taking her bags from her, took them into the kitchen. She sat down in the chair he had vacated.

"God, these chairs are so uncomfortable," she said. "They kill my back."

"Nathalie, you above all people should know that you have to suffer for style!" he called from the other room.

"Anyway, forget about furniture – show me the journal!"

Leo returned to the living room, took the journal out of his leather briefcase and, moving the magazines, placed it down on the glass table in front of her.

She opened it carefully and began to read the first page which described the gallery on Rue du Faubourg Saint-Honoré and the art collection.

"I'm going to get it transcribed and I'll give you a copy," said Leo. "While you look at this, I want to look in Grand-père's old filing cabinets in the box-room. Grand-mère remembers a letter coming from Sylvie Vasseur during the 1960s."

In the small room off the hall, which was used as a store, he opened the first of three filing cabinets. In it were ledgers from his grandfather's auction house. But at the back of the second cabinet were two manila folders with tabs marked *Family Correspondence*.

He took out the two files. In them was an assortment of letters and invoices dating back to before the war and a single postcard from Bourges dated June 1940 from Paul Vasseur. Leo was intrigued. Grand-père was not a sentimental man.

Dear Émile, it read, *On our way, all according to plan. Tired but determined, both well. Yours, Paul.*

Paul must have written this during his escape from Paris with Hanna. The postcard was worn and dirty at the edges. Then he noticed there was no stamp. Who must he have bribed to deliver it? A shiver went down his spine. He could hardly imagine what it must have been like for that generation. How must it have felt, to have heard German tanks rolling around the streets of Paris? He thought of Paul and his wife, and what had become of them. It didn't bear thinking about. If they had known what horrors lay ahead.

A thin blue air-mail envelope, addressed to his grandfather Émile caught his attention. The return address was 24, Gilford Road, Sandymount, Dublin 4, Éire. It was written in English.

28th April 1965

Dear Monsieur Bonnard,
I am not sure if you are aware of my existence. My maiden name was Sylvie Vasseur. I believe that you and my father, Paul Vasseur, were once close friends. My father was an art collector. He had a gallery on the Rue du Faubourg Saint-Honoré. From research I have carried out here in Dublin, I believe he was successful in his day, and represented many famous artists.
I was evacuated to Dublin from Paris as a child before the war and lost contact with my parents shortly after the Armistice and did not hear from them ever again. Many years later I learnt they had both died at Auschwitz.
The reason I'm writing to you is to ask for your help to understand what became of my father's art collection. I recently came across a letter from him, describing how he sent a number of paintings to Ireland at the time I travelled here. The paintings were by Picasso, Léger, Braque and Mateus. Any help you can give me in shedding light on their whereabouts would be much appreciated.

Yours sincerely,
Sylvie Courtney, née Vasseur

Leo folded the letter carefully, put it back and then took out a newspaper cutting. It was in English, from *The Times* newspaper dated, June 6th, 1965. As he read it, he realised that Sylvie had died a couple of months or so after writing the letter.

The cutting read:

The body of Sylvie Courtney (known as Sylvie Vasseur) was found yesterday washed up a County Wexford beach, in Southern Ireland. Miss Vasseur, a well-known artist from Dublin, who had a summer house on the scenic Hook Peninsula, went missing a fortnight ago in mysterious circumstances. A boat believed to have been used by Miss Vasseur was found washed ashore at the time on Bannow Bay where it had drifted following storm-force conditions on the Irish Sea. The body was found by an elderly couple out walking their dog on a secluded part of Carnaevon strand across the bay from Bannow.

A second cutting two months later said:

The inquest on the death of artist Sylvie Vasseur, held in the courthouse in New Ross, County Wexford, was inconclusive. Although the deceased had suffered head injuries, the coroner said that these were consistent with a fall from a boat. She was known to swim regularly in the evenings, and the autopsy established that alcohol had been consumed by the deceased. Death by misadventure was the finding. The deceased woman's husband, Peter Courtney, and brother-in-law, Dublin property developer and solicitor, Nicholas Courtney, were in attendance.

So she had married a Courtney, thought Leo, how intriguing. Possibly one of Daniel's sons. He should really try and contact him and send him the journal. But how sad for her to die like this, particularly as her parents had gone to such extremes when she was a child to protect her. He would take the files back to his apartment and go through them more carefully.

Chapter 14

Dublin
July 1982

Claire looked around, surveying the studio. They had made great progress over the previous three weeks. The canvasses had been neatly sorted and photographed by Sam. Flat cardboard archival boxes containing individual drawings had been stacked on the steel shelves, and sketchbooks had been carefully wrapped in black tissue paper then boxed. Larger cartons under the workbench contained artists' materials and maquettes. And at the door rubbish sacks were arranged in an ordered pile. Sam had spent two days pulling down the yellowed butter paper and scraping off the ancient triffids stuck to the glass roof, so that now the space was light and airy. The downside to this was that by mid-afternoon it was like a hothouse. The decaying smell had also disappeared, replaced with the scent of lavender that Claire had picked from the overgrown garden and placed in jam jars around the studio.

Claire felt a great sense of achievement even though she was tired – it had been a slow and tedious operation. Now she felt that she had a real understanding of Sylvie Vasseur's work, what she strove to achieve as an artist.

She had concluded that Sylvie was primarily interested in colour and light. Her landscapes were misty and ethereal. They had a lyrical quality about them that reminded Claire of a contemporary of Sylvie's, the painter Patrick Collins. But her palette was warmer than his. Like another obvious influence, Camille Souter, she was not afraid of colour. But unlike Souter's objects and images of the everyday, Sylvie was more interested in the feelings these places evoked.

Despite this understanding of her work, a sense of Sylvie as a woman continued to elude Claire. There were photographs of her everywhere, always alone. She wondered if Sam was hurt by the absence of pictures of him as a child. Was she a narcissist, Claire wondered? There was something about her that she could not make sense of – something that she could not quite put her finger on. As Claire looked at the photographs she had found, laid out on the bench, she thought that there was no hint of her being coy for the camera or wanting to please. On the contrary, she looked like she loved the lens, a woman confident in her own beauty – her gaze defiant. She had slightly hooded eyes and in the black-and-white photographs it was hard to tell whether they were blue or brown. Her features had the refined elegance typical of middle-European Jews Claire had seen in photographs of families before the war. But what made her look even more exotic was her fair hair – she wore it long and loose, or twisted in a careless knot at the top of her head. Her choice of clothing did not shed any clues either – for the most part they were asexual white shirts and baggy linen trousers. There was no doubt, though, that Sylvie was a beautiful creature, tall and long-limbed, a striking woman.

As Claire had been sorting out the studio, she had been somewhat surprised to find that there were no personal letters. The paperwork they had collected, mostly invoices for materials and gallery correspondence, had filled two cardboard boxes so far. Would Sylvie have kept personal stuff somewhere else, in a study maybe? Or had they been removed immediately after her death by the gardaí as potential evidence?

"Hi, I made you coffee." Sam appeared from the house, carrying two steaming mugs.

"Great, thank you, just what I need to clear my head. I know I asked you before, but it is rather surprising that there was no correspondence or letters found after your mother died.

"Well, I could double-check with Daniel."

Claire paused. Nicholas had been explicit at the start. Her job was to catalogue and record only. Any private papers were to be handed over to him immediately. He had even gone so far as to draw up a contract for her, emphasising this point. At the time, she had found this amusing and had told Sam about the condition.

"Nicholas is a solicitor," he had said. "They just love complicating things. He's probably afraid that you will find love letters, or something that might embarrass the family."

"Oh, did she have a lover?" Claire had asked tentatively.

"Yes – I thought you would have figured that out by now."

"Who?"

But Sam had just shrugged his shoulders and turned away.

She wondered about that now and was about to press him further when he changed the subject.

"Now what would you like me to do today, madam?" he asked. He sipped his coffee and looked around approvingly at the progress they had made.

"Oh, sort out the materials so we can donate the reusable stuff to some artists I know." She paused, gathering her thoughts. "Did Peter ever talk to you about her?"

"Not a lot," he said, putting down the coffee and looking at the photographs laid out on the bench. "He told me she was a restless spirit, and that art gave her purpose. He felt she never really got over the loss of her parents, that there was a sadness about her and a recklessness, almost as though nothing really mattered to her." His arms straight and back bowed, he leaned over the bench. "He was in awe of her, I think. He adored her, but he got upset talking about her so I never really liked to press him too much. He promised one day that we would go to France, see where she was born and grew up as a child. But we never did. He was a bit of a dreamer. And then there was the drink."

"How about Nicholas?"

"No, not really. I do remember one time after she died him looking at a photograph of her, and saying to Peter, 'MacErlaine was right, she incited decent people'. I thought it was an extremely odd thing to say."

"And who was MacErlaine?"

"I didn't ask."

Claire was distracted and at this stage wasn't really

listening to him. In the foliage of an overgrown spider plant, she caught a glimpse of a folder that had fallen down the back of the workbench, so that it was concealed from view. On impulse, she decided to say nothing to Sam.

That evening back in her apartment, Claire poured herself a large glass of wine and sat down with the cardboard folder at the kitchen table. Using a feathery paintbrush, she brushed away dusty cobwebs, dried leaves and loose black pin mould. Inside the folder the documents were bundled together in no particular order, some on flimsy copy paper, and others on writing paper with crinkled edges and Basildon Bond watermarks. She organised them according to date, noting that some of the handwriting was going to be a challenge, and that some of the typed documents had faded.

The first document was a letter in English from a Monsieur Émile Bonnard on cream embossed paper with the address 71, Rue du Faubourg Saint-Honoré, Paris, dated 18th May 1965 and written in black ink in a florid script.

Dear Madame Courtney,

Thank you for your letter. It was a great comfort to my wife Odette and me to learn that you are still alive and well and living in Ireland. Over the years I have often thought of trying to contact you, so it was to my shame, and my great delight, to hear from you. What a pleasant shock it must have been to find your father's letter. What a wonderful memento! If it was not too much trouble, I would so much appreciate it if you could send me a copy of the letter's contents. I would love to show it to my grandson Leo who has a great interest in our family history.

As you probably already know, your father and I were at Cambridge together where we studied Classics. We met at the Art History Society and, both being French, we became great friends. We also met Daniel Courtney there, and we three kept in touch when we left college. We would meet every year at the same restaurant in Paris, the Café des Trois Théâtres in Pigalle and have dinner together. After Cambridge, your father and I went on to become business associates. I was an auctioneer in Fine Art and antiques, and he was a dealer, so we had a lot in common.

In 1939 and being aware of the German's treatment of Jews in their own country, Paul knew that the day would come when he would have to leave Paris. His intention was to travel to New York and set up a gallery there. To fund his new life, he planned to sell his Barbizon collection and that I would auction them. Amongst these were works by Theodore Rousseau, Jean-François Millet and Charles-Francois Daubigny. These were his most valuable paintings which he kept in the upper gallery in Rue de Faubourg St Honoré. Over that year he had organised high quality copies to be made of these paintings. The originals were kept in a store outside Paris. The idea was to buy him time while he organised his affairs.

Once the copies were made, he sent the originals to me in the South of France for safe keeping ahead of the German advance on Paris. But, unfortunately, the train they were being transported in was blown up by the Luftwaffe in an air raid on Lyon. So that I never received them. Paul was devastated when he eventually heard of this on his arrival in Antibes.

The modern paintings that you enquired about, in comparison to the Barbizon paintings, were not so valuable at that time. But they meant more to him than merely works of art. He had supported these artists throughout their careers and encouraged them, lent them money when they were down on their luck, and paid their medical bills when they were sick. He could not bear to part with these paintings. It is my understanding that these and the Barbizon copies were confiscated by the Gestapo in the early days of the German occupation of Paris when they pillaged the Jewish-owned galleries. That is before Hitler's team the Einsatzstab Reichsleiter Rosenberg (ERR) organised a team of specialists to systematically rob all private and public collections alike. In all likelihood, Paul's modern paintings were burnt during those first few weeks in the Jeu de Paume in what some people subsequently called another, 'Bonfire of the Vanities'. I certainly never saw any of these paintings again.

You asked about the Mateus in particular, Girl

on a Swing, one of the artist's finest works. I remember the day it was painted, in my garden at a party to celebrate my wife's birthday. He started painting you but after some time you became tired and bored and refused to stay. You told Mateus so in no uncertain terms. I do hope you have lost none of that spirit.

Regarding his other assets, when he left Paris Paul had planned to take a considerable amount of cash and gold, and to sew precious jewels into their clothes. His 'running-away money' he had called it. By that stage, it was almost impossible to take money out of the country. I presume this was all stolen subsequently from him by the Germans when they arrested him in Antibes. After the war, I took on the lease of your father's gallery. It was a fine building in a good location. Paul had commissioned Mateus to design the interiors. He had chosen the colour schemes, and designed glass panels in the windows in yellow-and-blue stained glass with a leaf motif – and borders of matching ceramic tiles throughout. I knew at that stage Paul was never coming back, and the gallery was in a good location. It seemed like the right thing to do. I know he would have liked to think of me being there.

Although I have enjoyed writing this letter, despite the painful memories it evokes, I must finish now. My eyes are getting tired. Should you ever find yourself in Paris, dear Sylvie, my wife Odette and I would be delighted to meet you.

Yours sincerely,
Émile Bonnard

Claire put the letter to one side and flicked through the next few documents. Sylvie had also written to the Neue Pinakothek, a Munich art gallery, asking for information about the whereabouts of the Mateus. A polite reply from the curator informed her that, although they had heard of the work, they had no record of it since it was shown in an exhibition in Galleries Vasseur, in April 1940 in Paris.

Letters sent to Christie's in London, and the Louvre in Paris received similar replies.

Returning to the file, Claire opened a manila envelope. On the outside was written in Sylvie's handwriting, *Papa's Letter.*

The letter from Paul to Sylvie explained how Paul had made copies of the twelve modern paintings by Picasso, Braque, Léger and Mateus, hidden the originals in framed Turner prints of Venice and shipped them to Ireland to his friend Daniel Courtney.

Claire, stunned, put down the letter as its implications began to dawn on her. If Paul had made copies of the modern paintings as well as the Barbizon works, and these had been sent to Daniel ahead of the German occupation, and only the copies had been burnt by the Gestapo in the fire at the Jeu de Paume, as Émile's letter had suggested, what had happened to the originals? From Émile's letter it appeared that Sylvie had not told him that her father had also made copies of the modern paintings. Was it some sort of test?

Of course, it was possible that they did not arrive,

that the modern paintings were discovered, as Émile suggested, before they even left France. She felt this was unlikely as the works were sent ahead of the German advance. However, the ship delivering them could have been bombed in transit across the Irish Sea by the Luftwaffe or by a German submarine. She would have to brush up on her history to understand the course of the German invasion.

But, more to the point, the fact that Daniel had received the etching of the rabbit seemed to suggest that he had also received the others. Sylvie also must have come to this conclusion.

Claire poured herself another glass of wine and put her feet up on the table. Was Nicholas aware of this letter, she wondered? She thought briefly about telling him, then dismissed the idea. She neither liked nor trusted the man. And what about Sam? She did like him, was attracted to him if she was honest. But there was a reserve about him, and she still did not fully understand the dynamics of his relationship with his uncle. Sam might very well insist she should tell Nicholas. She knew she should, that it was the right thing to do – it was none of her business really. But then she thought about Sylvie. She had begun to really empathise and relate to her. She had such a difficult life, to have lost both her parents so young and been sent to a foreign country to live amongst strangers. And if Uncle Daniel was anything like Nicholas, and from what she had heard so far she had no reason to doubt this, then she must have had a loveless childhood. Her marriage to Peter, from what she had managed to glean from Sam, had not been that successful either. No, thought Claire, Sylvie Vasseur had not been blessed with a happy life.

Claire shivered, the hairs on her body standing up. She felt in some strange way the presence of Sylvie's spirit. *Please don't give up on me just yet*, she seemed to say. She would think about it and read the rest of the file tomorrow evening – then decide what to do.

The next morning when she arrived at the studio she felt the onset of panic in the pit of her stomach. Nicholas was already there. Walking through the garden, she could see him bent over the work bench. Her work bag was heavy with the weight of Sylvie's folder. She remembered Sam had told her he was going to be late as he had an early lecture in Trinity.

"Claire, good morning." Nicholas raised his head and smiled, but the smile did not reach his eyes. "I see you have made significant progress since the last time I was here. At least you have got rid of the dead animals. The place is beginning to look quite organised."

"Good morning, Mr Courtney," she said. "How was your holiday in France? Sam told me you were hill walking." She put her bag down on the bench and took off her jacket. At ten o'clock it was already warm in the studio. She felt his eyes scan over her body then, disinterested, look away.

"Call me Nicholas. Yes, I was in Carcassonne, the medieval walled city, stunning scenery, a fascinating part of the country. Anyway, interesting though it was, I didn't come here to talk about my holiday. How's the work going?"

"It's a slow process, I'm afraid, but Sam is a great

help – meticulous and organised. Just what a good art historian needs to be," she said, trying to sound professional but friendly.

"*Mm*," he acknowledged. "And what have you discovered amongst the morass?"

"Oh, we found several folios of beautiful watercolour studies, mostly seascapes of Sandymount Strand. They look like they were early works, painted during the time Sylvie worked with the Ambroses. They would make an interesting exhibition. There are twenty-four completed, some haven't been exhibited before. There are also about thirty or so unfinished canvases of various subjects."

"Do the unfinished canvases have a value?"

"Yes, they have academic value. But it wouldn't be advisable to sell them. For some reason or another, she wasn't happy with them and didn't think they were of a good enough standard to represent her oeuvre."

"Couldn't we just pay someone to finish them off, and then flog them?"

She looked at him in alarm.

"Relax, Claire, I'm joking. I'm not such a philistine as you think."

Nicholas took a box of cigarettes from his pocket and lit up, using an old-fashioned Zippo lighter. The action was studied and he reminded her of a preening cat. He had aged well, Claire thought. He had a debonair look about him and dressed in well-cut stylish clothes. This morning, he was wearing a linen jacket, and light-coloured slacks. He usually wore a tie but today his white shirt was open – intentionally, she suspected, to show off his newly acquired tan.

"Find anything else? Diaries, notebooks, that sort of thing?"

"Yes, lots of notebooks. Some poems actually, rather good – would you like to read some?"

"No, not really."

Claire caught her breath – she could feel her colour rising. His confidence was intimidating.

"No," he said, "I was more interested in memoirs, things that related to her personal life. I know she had started to contact her French relatives – she was very keen to find out about her father, what happened to him during the war. He was a well-known art dealer in Paris, had a gallery on Rue du Faubourg Saint-Honoré."

Claire, steeling herself, looked him in the eye. "No, I haven't found anything like that, but we haven't really got to sorting through her papers yet. There are about five or six cartons of them – Sam and I were going to start today. It's taken us all this time really to categorise and catalogue the works of art."

"Well, if you do come across any family letters let me know. Remember our agreement. Professor Dillon assured me I can rely on your professional integrity."

"I wouldn't listen to that old codger, Nicholas," said Sam, entering briefcase in hand. His tone was brittle, tense.

"Sam, good to see you are earning your fee in this project and keeping regular hours."

"Early lecture, your friend Professor Dillon as it happened. Interesting, he was talking about 'Degenerate Art'."

"Interesting subject, you must tell me all about it.

There was an exhibition a few years ago in Dublin of Oskar Kokoschka's work in Leo Smith's gallery, an artist who was a great influence on Yeats. Although I believe they never met. I bought a watercolour by him a few years ago at an Adam's auction and sold it on for a tidy profit in London. Anyway, back to business. I was just talking to Claire – you are starting to sort out your mother's papers today, I believe." Nicholas put his cigarette out carefully.

He even moved like a panther, thought Claire, slowly and deliberately, his body taut with pent-up energy.

"I wonder would you find that too upsetting, Sam? Maybe I could help Claire today. I'm not too busy, a client cancelled at the last minute. You could take the day off and catch up on your studying." He said it as if it were an instruction not a request.

Claire looked at Sam in alarm.

"No, absolutely not," said Sam, standing up straight.

Claire realised that Sam was taller than his uncle. Their eyes locked. Claire was not quite sure what was happening and why. It was certainly a battle of wills. Up until now she hadn't thought that the laid-back Sam had it in him to stand up to his uncle.

Nicholas looked quizzically at Sam and reluctantly seemed to acquiesce – the moment was over.

"Very well, but we need to get this finished as soon as possible. I'm not made of money, you know. Hard though it may be for you to believe." Having directed this at Sam, he left.

"What was that all about?" Claire asked when Nicholas had gone.

Sam shrugged. "Just his usual bully-boy tactics."

They spent the day going through the box-files of correspondence. They had already sorted these into categories: relating to exhibitions, correspondence with academics and institutions, the Arts Council, invoices and loan forms, and miscellaneous personal papers.

Claire took the exhibition correspondence and Sam took the personal papers.

Very quickly, Claire became absorbed in the task in hand, making notes of the various dates and locations where Sylvie showed her works.

Until she became aware that Sam was sitting with his head bent over and his shoulders shaking.

"You OK, Sam?" she asked gently.

As he raised his head she could see tears in his eyes.

"Oh Sam, Nicholas was right – this must be very difficult for you."

Embarrassed, he cleared his throat and sat up straight. "You know, she had such a hard life. I wish she had lived and I could have made things up to her. It just struck me suddenly that she had no soulmate – no one loved her. She was desired all right, but no one really loved her."

"What about Peter – he loved her."

"Yes, I suppose he did, but he resented her as well, and the fact was he knew she didn't really love him."

"Who did she love?"

"Me – I think. Although she was not an affectionate person, I always felt that she loved me. I think she had been traumatised by the loss of her parents, and to have grown up an outsider in our family must not have been easy. Not to mention the fact that she was a foreigner. They say damaged people have different boundaries – they lose the fear of social censure that keeps most of us in check."

"What do you mean?"

"Well, she didn't seem to care what anyone thought of her – she had an affair with Nicholas, and there may have been others."

"*Nicholas!*" Claire was shocked. That was so distasteful.

"I thought you would have figured that out. He seemed to have some hold over her, I could never figure out what. I was hoping to learn something from her papers, but so far there's nothing of any importance – a few letters from Knockaboy from Aunt Nora, and her friend Niamh when she was working in London."

"Sam," Claire said nervously, "there is another file. I found it lodged between the workbench and a dead spider plant yesterday. It had fallen off and was concealed there where the foliage was fuller. I took it home last night to clean – it was covered in mildew."

"Why didn't you tell me about this sooner?" He sounded extremely annoyed.

"Sorry, Sam, I was going to tell you. I haven't had a chance to read it all through." She lifted the file from her bag and placed it on the work bench. "Some of the faxes and typewritten documents have faded a little but the letters seem intact. They seem to relate to France, attempts she made to track down her family. And there are some interesting letters relating to your grandfather's art collection."

"Letters? Why didn't you mention this to Nicholas?" He suddenly grabbed her by the wrists and glared at her, his eyes alight with anger.

"You're hurting me, Sam!" she said, alarmed at how quickly his temper had escalated.

He let her go abruptly but continued to stare belligerently.

"I know. I should have," she said, rubbing her wrists, "but I wanted to tell you first ... I was curious. Over the last few weeks I've really begun to understand her – admire her. And I thought, because of the legal agreement Nicholas made me sign, that he would confiscate them. Then I would never find out what really happened to her – to the paintings."

Sam's anger melted away, and he put his hand gently on her arm.

"Sorry for losing my temper, Claire. But I'm not Nicholas. I know how much you have invested in this whole project. I would never shut you out. And, to be honest, I can't do this without you." He smiled sadly, looking disappointedly at her. "So, no more keeping things from me."

Thrown by his loss of composure, she moved away from him, breaking their physical contact. "Sorry, Sam."

"It's OK, Claire," he said kindly. "Look, let's go through this file together and see if we are any the wiser."

Sam was so excited about Paul's letter to Sylvie and Émile's letter to her all those years later that he insisted they sojourn to Sandymount House, a pub in the village, for a drink to mull it all over. The Victorian pub was quiet – it was a Tuesday evening – and they settled companionably into a snug divided by carved mahogany and stained-glass screens from the bar. Their earlier altercation was forgotten.

"If the paintings were sent to Daniel," said Claire, "then he must have kept them somewhere. In Knockaboy?"

"No, I don't think so," said Sam. "After my mother died, my father was consumed with despair and drank heavily so Nicholas parked me in Knockaboy for the rest of that summer with my grandmother. I spent a lot of time on my own. So I know the house well, and I can't think of anywhere that my grandfather could hide them without my father or me knowing about them. The attic is a possibility, I suppose. Daniel always kept it locked. My father was up there once or twice with him, but he told me it was just full of my grandmother's old rubbish. She was a bit of a hoarder, you know. Daniel also had a safe in his office, but that is only suitable for documents, and not large enough for twelve oil paintings, even if they were small. Possibly he could have put them in his bank's vault."

"Was Daniel still alive in April 1965 when Sylvie found her father's letter?"

"No, he died earlier that year, in January."

"But surely there would have been some record of them in his papers when he died?" Claire paused. "Who was the executor for your grandfather's will?"

"Nicholas." Sam frowned.

"Has he ever mentioned the existence of any paintings?"

"No, never."

"Should you ask him?"

"Possibly, but currently what do we know? That the paintings existed, that Paul sent them to Ireland. But what if the rabbit etching was sent separately, or later, and the others never arrived? Maybe they were discovered in transit, and what Émile suggested is what happened – they were either burned by the Gestapo or they confiscated them. Or maybe they arrived. If that was the case, what happened to them? In fact, if they did arrive and Nicholas was aware of their existence, it's unlikely that he would tell me now after hiding the fact for all these years."

"But they are rightfully yours and presumably they are worth a small fortune. People have been killed for less. Oh –" She broke off, suddenly thinking of Sylvie. "Oh, Sam, I didn't mean to infer that your mother was –"

"Murdered? Well, you wouldn't be the first to suggest that. The circumstances surrounding her death were unusual to say the least."

"Maybe we're getting a bit melodramatic here," said Claire. "Let's get back to the paintings. We also only know the artists' names, not the titles of the works, so it's not possible to trace anything. But there must have been a catalogue of the paintings from your grandfather's final exhibition. That might be a place to start."

"Yes, it would be something. We need to do some more homework before confronting Nicholas. Where would you find gallery listings from the 1940's?"

"Not sure," said Claire, "but I have a friend, Alice, who works in the Berkley Library in Trinity, and I'm sure she could point me in the right direction. I could go there first thing in the morning and see you in the studio tomorrow after lunch."

At this stage they had both finished their drinks so they rose to go.

"I'll walk you home," said Sam. "It's a lovely evening and I need to burn off this pent-up energy."

189

When they eventually reached her flat in Rathmines, after a leisurely stroll through Herbert Park, he kissed her on the cheek, and she felt her pulse race in response.

"You know, we make quite a team," he teased.

A young woman passed by, long-legged in a short skirt, blonde with big hair. She smiled provocatively at Sam who smiled in response.

Claire thought sadly that the young woman obviously didn't see herself and Sam as a potential couple. Claire felt small, plump and dowdy.

"Goodnight, Sam. See you tomorrow."

She turned her back to him abruptly and unlocked the door.

Claire was in high spirits when she arrived at the studio the following afternoon, the previous evening's disappointment forgotten.

"Sam, my friend Alice gave me the name of a French art-historian – a guy called Jacques Corentin she met at a conference – and I rang him. Fortunately, his English was better than my French. It seems that after the war about 60,000 works of art that had been looted, or sold under constraint, were brought back to France. Some easily identifiable pieces were returned to their rightful owners. But many of the artworks had no known history. These are on exhibition, or in storage in several French Museums, such as the Louvre, Musée D'Orsay and Centre Georges Pompidou. Unfortunately for us, there is no official register of these works. Although many Jewish bodies are suggesting that the Government should publish one."

"Does that mean we have to contact each museum?"

"Pretty much."

"That's quite a task," said Sam, "but doable, I suppose. But first we need to know what we're looking for, which means checking the Vasseur catalogues. Did he suggest where to find these?"

"Yes, he said they have a collection of gallery catalogues at the Bibliothèque Nationale in Paris. Also, I got him to check the Paris telephone directories and there is an architect, Leo Bonnard, based in Rue de Faubourg Saint-Honoré, your grandfather's old gallery. Which means, I guess, that we have to go to Paris!"

"Really," he said, not responding with the enthusiasm she had anticipated.

"Oh, maybe it doesn't suit you?" Claire tried not to sound disappointed.

"No, not at all, it's just that I have an essay for college, but I suppose I can work on that anywhere. And there is also the cost. We can't very well ask Nicholas."

"Well, I have some money set aside that my grandmother left me. I can lend you some – enough to cover the expenses – and you can give me the money back at some stage."

"Well, I'm not sure," he said reluctantly.

"Oh, for God's sake, Sam! Let's just do it! It will be a bit of *craic*, even if we find nothing useful," she said excitedly, high on the prospect of it all.

He looked at her pensively. "OK, let's do it."

"You'd better tell Nicholas that you're going to France on a college trip to the Louvre, and we're suspending operations for a week."

"Sounds like a plan."

* * *

Searsons was busy. Nicholas had clicked his fingers several times at the lounge boy who was studiously ignoring him.

"I'll get it," said Sam with resignation.

He approached the bar where he waited patiently for several minutes before he was served. When he returned to his seat with a Jameson's whiskey for Nicholas and a pint of Harp lager for himself, Nicholas's face was thunderous.

"A toe up the hole is what that half-wit needs. I must have a word with the manager before I leave. This place has gone downhill since they built all of those office blocks on Baggot Street."

"They're just busy tonight."

Nicholas took a gulp of the whiskey. "How are things going with the dumpling?"

"I wish you wouldn't call her that."

"Next thing you'll be telling me you've grown quite fond of her."

"I have actually," Sam said truculently.

"Well, don't complicate things, will you? Find your sexual gratification elsewhere. We have enough on our plate as it is. Time is running out – we need to catalogue your mother's works so we can sell the house, you can pay me back all the money you owe me, and I can pay off some of my bills."

Sam put his hands over his head.

"Come on, Sam, don't start moping again. What's done is done. What do they say? Build a bridge and get over it."

Chapter 15

They had got cheap tickets from USIT, the student travel agency. When the chartered plane rolled into sight across the hardstanding at Dublin airport, it was pink. Inside, the seats were covered in a purple-and-pink check fabric and were squashed together, so that Sam was sitting with his knees almost touching his chest. Claire felt sick and the lurid colour scheme did not help. She hated flying. And when the plane eventually took off, the plastic interior panels started to rattle, and she thought she would pass out with fright. She clutched Sam's arm, at the same time apologising profusely, while he tried to distract her by pointing out the old airport building, now model-sized far below.

"It's considered to be one of the best examples of pre-war, International-style Architecture, you know."

"Really," said Claire, not even looking out the window.

Once airborne, although she had technically given up smoking several weeks before, she lit up a cigarette and inhaled deeply, intermittently sipping the wine that Sam had ordered for her from the drinks trolley. Eventually she calmed down.

An hour or so later, the plane descended through a blanket of cloud as the late-afternoon sun illuminated the silvery vein of the River Seine as it meandered around Ile de la Cité.

"Look, there's Notre Dame," said Sam.

She peered across him out of the window, as she tried to make out the cathedral below.

"I've never been to Paris," she told him, her gaze returning once more, nervously, to the rattling internal panels.

"An art historian who has never been to Paris. We will have to make sure that this experience is a memorable one so."

As they headed north-east of the city towards Le Bourget Airport, Claire's fear was temporarily forgotten – her hopes soared.

That evening they ate in Chartier's restaurant, a Parisian institution. Lights sparkled on wineglasses and gilt-framed mirrors, and the sound of laughter reverberated throughout the high-ceilinged dining room. Claire could almost taste the smell of garlic. She was mesmerised with the scale and bustle of the place, with people seated closely together on tables arranged in a continuous trestle. She thought how this would never work in Dublin, as it was quite likely that you would end up sitting beside someone you knew. However, proximity didn't seem to bother the French. The couple next to them seemed to be having a row, talking and gesticulating with animation. But Claire observed, surreptitiously, that they were also touching each other intimately, and she decided that their exchange was more of a passionate negotiation than a disagreement.

She watched, fascinated, as the waiters scribbled down the orders directly onto paper tablecloths and then, after each set of guests departed, they pulled them off in one deft swoop, like flamboyant magicians.

"Stop staring, Claire. Or at least close your mouth," Sam teased. "What will you have to eat?"

"Not snails anyway."

"No? They're rather good here."

He studied the menu carefully. "I'll try the steak tartare, I think. I only ever eat it in Paris."

"Maybe I will have that too."

"You do know it's raw meat?"

"Oh God no, that's so disgusting! I'll have fish."

When the waiter came, Sam ordered in reasonably fluent French. Claire valiantly attempted to do the same but with less success.

"Your French is excellent," she said afterwards. "Did you ever come here with your mother?"

"No, but I have visited several times in recent years. She was planning to take me the summer she died. We never got to go in the end. When I was small, she often spoke to me in French. I think, for her, it kept those memories of her life in France alive. In school, I always worked hard at it, just to please her."

The wine arrived and they sipped as they chatted about how they would spend the next two days to most effect. The architect, Leo Bonnard, on the Rue du Faubourg Saint-Honoré was first on the list. They reckoned that he must be some relation to Émile, possibly his grandson, or a great-nephew. They planned to call in the next day to arrange to meet him and see if he could shed any light on what had happened to the paintings. They would also need to apply for a temporary reader's ticket at the Bibliothèque Nationale to look for the exhibition catalogue.

After they had drunk a second glass of wine and were both relaxed, Claire broached a subject which continued to fascinate her.

"You obviously have a difficult relationship with Nicholas – so why he is supporting you?"

Sam straightened up in his chair and fidgeted with his knife, pushing the remnants of the mushroom starter around his plate.

"Guilt, I suppose, after my mother died, and then my father."

"Why should he feel guilty?"

"I think he loved them both, in his own way. My father was a troubled soul. You know, I remember him bullying my mother one minute, then being painfully nice to her the next. Looking back, it was as if he was terrified that she would leave him. He was weak really. Although, I think she made him so. If she had really loved him, made him feel more secure in her affection for him, it might have been a different story."

"How can we ever really understand our parents' relationships, or even know them as people?" Claire mused. "We are programmed to idolise them when we are young and then, when we are teenagers, detest them when biology requires us to become emotionally detached. I suppose most people eventually reach an equilibrium and accept that their parents are flawed human beings who are just trying to do the best they can.

But I'm sure there are others who are so damaged by their experience that they never even try to understand them – they only resent their parents' failures."

"I suppose you're right," replied Sam somewhat morosely. "Do you blame your parents?"

"No – I used to blame them for all my flaws: my untidiness, my childbearing hips, my constant anxiety, but not anymore," Claire said trying to lighten the tone. But then she couldn't resist asking, "How did it affect you, losing your mother so young?"

"I don't really like talking about it, Claire – it doesn't serve any purpose."

"I'm sorry. I'm making you uncomfortable."

He looked at his fellow diners on either side. When he saw they were engrossed in their own conversations, he reluctantly continued.

"I always felt that, although she loved me, I wasn't enough for her. Then when I lost her I lost hope. I could never make it up to her, make her happy."

"Oh Sam, what a sad little boy you must have been."

"Yes, I probably was, but as I said that was all a long time ago."

"Is there anyone special now in your life?" Claire asked, casually.

"No, but I'd like there to be." He smiled at her. "This conversation has become far too heavy, Claire."

"Sorry, I don't mean it to be – it's just I would really like to understand her." She paused, then asked, "What happened after your father died?"

"Jesus, Claire, you're like a dog with a bone!" He sounded exasperated. "He struggled, drank too much. Our electricity and telephone were always being cut off.

And I had to leave Blackrock College about a year later when I was fifteen because he couldn't afford to pay the fees."

"I thought your mother was left money by the Ambroses?"

"She was, but because of his drinking he lost his job in the insurance company. After that he seemed to go through her money very quickly. He was also one of the bookies' best customers."

"And Nicholas, did he not help?"

"Would not, could not, a mixture of both. He felt that no matter how many times he paid off my father's debts, he would continue drinking and be back for more money. When my father died, I was only sixteen, still had my Leaving Certificate to do, and Nicholas packed me off to boarding school in Galway. Nicholas led a rather peripatetic lifestyle then, you see – still does, skiing in Italy in winter, summer in the South of France. And then there were always women, and a spotty, grunting teenager in tow would have cramped his style."

"I can't imagine you being either spotty or grunting," she said kindly.

"I'll show you photographs to prove it. When I left school, he got me a job in the bank, and I stayed in lodgings."

"How did Nicholas make his money – he is obviously very wealthy."

"Law, initially. He has a successful legal practice, and then he got into buying and selling property. He's rather good at it, by all accounts."

"Mademoiselle, your cod, and steak tartare for you,

monsieur." The waiter had arrived, his arm stacked with plates.

"No more questions, Claire – let me eat in peace."

After a leisurely breakfast at the hotel, and avoiding the rush-hour traffic, Claire and Sam arrived mid-morning at Rue du Faubourg Saint-Honoré. It was a narrow street where carefully groomed Frenchwomen ambled past shop windows filled with expensive couture arranged in extravagant displays.

"Odd place for an architect's office, I would have thought, amongst all of these dresses and handbags," said Claire.

"Or enlightened," said Sam. "They say Frenchwomen wear the trousers."

"Not many trousers on show here. In fact, I feel rather shabby – their clothes seem to be so co-ordinated, and they all have perfect hair and make-up – it must take them hours to get ready."

"They are rather stylish," said Sam unhelpfully, casting a dubious sideways glance at Claire's long tiered gypsy-style skirt.

Number 71 was set between a shop selling leather goods, and a well-known Italian high-end chain store. The word "*Architectes*" was etched on the opaque glass and repeated continuously in a single line along the base of the window.

"Could make more of a presence – rather understated, I would have thought, amongst all of this glitz," Claire commented.

"A minimalist, no doubt."

Sam opened the glass door and let Claire through into

a well-lit reception area. The walls were painted white and in the centre of the space was a reception desk in black limestone with stainless-steel trims. To one side, Barcelona chairs surrounded a glass table that Claire recognised was designed by Paola Buffa, a highly regarded Italian architect and designer, and in the other corner a small round Eileen Grey table was artfully positioned beside an Eames chair. Leo Bonnard was a serious modernist, thought Claire.

The sleek receptionist, tall and dark-haired, was dressed in a white shirt and well-cut black flared trousers. The overall impression was that she too had been carefully chosen to conform with the ethos of the interior design.

"*Bonjour, Mademoiselle et Monsieur. Puis-je vous aider?*"

"*Mademoiselle, je parle seulement un peu le français. Parlez vous anglais?*" Claire asked.

"But of course. How can I help you?"

"My name is Claire Howard, and this is Sam Courtney. We wish to see Monsieur Bonnard."

"You have an appointment."

"No, but I'm an old friend of his," added Sam.

"Oh, he is with someone now, but I will see if he can meet with you later."

She lifted the phone and spoke in rapid French, presumably to Leo. Then she turned to them and said, "He would like very much to meet you. He suggested that you wait for him in a coffee shop at the end of the street, Le Petit Boulanger. He will join you there in twenty minutes. Tell the patron that you are his guests and he will look after you."

Claire and Sam sat outside. For them it was a novelty,

as even in the height of summer outdoor eating was not a feature of the streets of Dublin. They ordered Madeleines and two café au lait. As they were being served, a young man arrived at their table. He was mid-height, dark-haired, with clear grey eyes and dressed in black jeans, a white T-shirt, and a black leather jacket. A confident man, smiling and outwardly charming, but Claire's initial impression was also of an inner steely reserve.

"Mademoiselle, and Monsieur Courtney, I'm Leo Bonnard." He shook hands firmly with Claire, and then with Sam, before sitting down.

"I'm so pleased to meet you. You have no idea how much," Leo said sincerely to Sam.

"You have heard of me?" Sam was taken aback.

"I'm sorry to say that until today I was unaware of your existence. I knew of your late mother, and recently learned that she was married to a Peter Courtney – one of Daniel's sons?"

"Yes, Peter was my father," said Sam. "Unfortunately, he died not long after my mother."

"So sorry to hear – they must have been difficult times."

"It was a long time ago," said Sam.

"And, of course, both of your grandfathers, Daniel Courtney and Paul Vasseur, were very close friends of my own grandfather, Émile Bonnard. They were together at Cambridge before the war and they met every year afterwards for dinner, in the café near Pigalle called Café des Trois Théâtres."

"Yes, my grandfather, Daniel, told me."

Leo took a packet of Gitanes from his inside pocket and offered one to Sam and Claire who both declined.

"What brings you to Paris, my friends?"

Sam looked nervously at Claire.

"My mother, actually," he said.

"We're researching Sam's mother," said Claire. "Sylvie Vasseur was quite a successful artist in Ireland when she died in the 1980s."

"Ah yes, rather tragically, I believe. I'm so sorry."

"Thank you," said Sam.

"I've been commissioned by Sam and his family to catalogue her works," Claire explained, "and it seemed like the right thing to do, to see could we find out more about her father's activities as an art collector before the war. Particularly his involvement with Mateus, Picasso and Braque."

"Yes, of course. But this is, in fact, a most extraordinary coincidence." Leo suddenly became quite animated. "You see, a few months ago I found a journal written by Paul Vasseur when I was refurbishing my studios."

"Oh, that's amazing," Claire said, wide-eyed.

"Yes, incredible. It was in a box hidden behind some tiles – we found it by chance. It described how he was planning an exhibition of his valuable art collection – two collections really, one of modern art and the other Barbizon landscapes. As you could imagine, I was really excited by the possibilities that this presented. However, my grandmother told me that the Barbizon paintings were destroyed in transit in an air-raid on Lyons. And that the modern collection had been requisitioned and destroyed by the Nazis. If I had known then of your existence," he nodded at Sam, "I would have sent you the journal."

Sam acknowledged this with a nod.

Claire then told Leo of their own discoveries of Sylvie's letters and of Émile's responses. When Leo heard about how Paul's letter was found and the existence of the copies, he was clearly intrigued.

Sam listened thin-lipped as Claire told Leo everything.

"So, Sam and I thought that we should try and find out what we can about Paul's last exhibition. It would help in a biographical essay that Sam hopes to write about Sylvie's life. The journal would also be a wonderful addition to Sam's mother's archive. But there is, of course, a remote chance that a few of the paintings might have survived the Gestapo's hands and may still be in existence today. So, we were planning to see if the Bibliothèque Nationale has a Vasseur's catalogue from the period so that at least we can identify the names of the paintings."

"This is all fascinating, my friends," said Leo, looking anxiously at his watch. "I would really like to discuss this further with you. But, unfortunately, I have an appointment in a few minutes, to open tenders for a factory I'm working on outside Paris. Could we meet later, for dinner maybe? Then I can show you the journal. Also, I would like to suggest something to you. A proposal that has just occurred to me that might be of help."

Claire readily agreed.

After he left, Sam called for the bill, then turned to Claire.

"For Christ's sake, Claire, we have only just met the man and you are confiding my family's business to him."

"Sam, he's the grandson of your grandfather's oldest

friend. He seems like a really nice guy. And to be honest we could do with some help."

Despite Claire's attempts to cajole him, Sam sulked for the next hour or so – then, as they wandered through the Tuileries gardens enjoying the late afternoon sunshine, his anger gradually evaporated.

Leo had booked a table for three at the Café des Trois Théâtres for eight o'clock – "to continue the family tradition," he told them playfully.

"Do you know, my friends – the interiors have not changed much since our grandfathers met here before the war. The patron once told me that although he decorated every few years, to keep the place looking fresh, the pre-war interiors are almost intact. I often come here – it reminds me of Grand-père. They have an excellent wine list, and it's usually not too busy if you come after the shows have started."

When their food arrived, they chatted about the delights of Parisian eateries. Leo recommended several restaurants in the vicinity that they might try. After the main course the waiter brought a cheese board, and Leo and Sam ordered port. Sam seemed unusually tense during the meal, so much so that Claire had to make an extra effort to make up for his churlishness. She had also drunk more than enough wine and was feeling a little lightheaded. She passed on the port, or another liqueur, and opted for an espresso, in the hope that this might sober her up before they settled down to business.

Then Leo cleared a space and laid the journal on the table. "So, here it is, your grandfather's journal, a lot cleaner than when I first found it. I had it cleaned professionally by an archivist friend of mine. It has a list of the paintings from both collections with images and details of their provenance. Assuming that the Barbizon paintings were destroyed as my grandfather described, this is the section that you are interested in – the modern collection." He opened the journal carefully.

Sam moved his chair so that he had a better view and they spent several minutes looking through the file.

Leo watched in amusement at the expressions of awe on Claire's face.

"Oh my God, an actual Picasso, I don't believe it!" She held up an image of a reclining nude.

"His blue period, I think," said Leo.

"And this Braque, from when he was involved with the Fauves – I have never even seen it before." She looked up. "This collection is, would have been, hugely significant." She returned to look at the images, but almost immediately her eyes widened once more in wonder.

"Sam, this must be your mother as a child – it's the Mateus!" She eagerly passed the file to Sam.

Sam looked at the painting of a young girl on a swing, painted in Mateus's unmistakable style of flat planes. Even though it was in black-and-white you could see his use of contrasting colours, energised by vibrant decorative detail. The girl's eyes looked directly at the viewer, her expression assured and challenging.

"That's my mother alright," said Sam.

Claire noticed that he seemed to be in a trance. She touched him gently on the arm.

"So now we know the names of the paintings, it should be possible to establish if they were destroyed, or not," she said.

"Unfortunately, it's not so easy," said Leo. "I'm sure you have heard of the Monuments Men. They were a group of experts set up by the Allied forces to protect art works and antiquities during the allied advancement. After the war, the Monuments Men collected all the art looted by the Nazis and attempted to return the individual pieces to their rightful owners. Fortunately, the Germans were assiduous record-keepers and kept detailed lists of the works they looted. So it was possible to repatriate some of the works where the owners were generally known. But for others, it was extremely difficult. The original owners needed to have documentation to prove their claim. As you could imagine, paperwork was the least of their concerns when they were arrested, or when they fled ahead of the Nazi advancement – many others, as you know, died in concentration camps. The heirs of these people often found it difficult to make a case. So, a significant number of artworks found in France ended up in French museums, and to this date they are unclaimed. Works found by the Allies in France, suspected to be looted, are part of the Musées Nationaux Récupération (MNR) programme. As part of the peace negotiations each country was given ownership of Nazi assets found in their jurisdiction, and each had its own solution to the problem. The difficulty in tracking individual works of art is that the paintings could have been destroyed, or auctioned abroad, or sold privately. To further complicate things, several senior Nazis also collected artworks for their own private collections. Goring was the best known of these. His collection was vast. In fact, at the end of the war he tried to use it as a bargaining tool with the allies. The Allies found two trains filled with valuable paintings and antiques in a tunnel in Berchtesgaden, a town in the Bavarian Alps. Unfortunately, it had been looted by the locals and quite a few of the works have never been accounted for. This is only one example, there are many others, where people came by works of art somewhat questionably which are, probably, stored in attics all around Europe. Now those people are ashamed they have them and are afraid of the consequences of coming forward to the authorities. But, at the same time, they don't want to give them up if they think they are valuable."

"We realised it wasn't going to be easy," said Claire. "I did some research before we came here. But Paris seemed to be the most likely place to start our search. We had hoped to find Vasseur's final exhibition catalogue to identify the names. Although, thanks to you, we have these now, it would still be good to have one. We should also check the various museums for the individual paintings."

"Yes, that is probably the first step. How is your French?"

"Good enough to order in a restaurant, but not good enough to write an essay," said Sam.

"Well, why don't I write a standard letter of enquiry for you and get a list of all of the museums from the yellow pages?"

"Maybe we should contact the auction houses, in case the works were sold in France?" said Claire.

"*Mm*, I think you might have to go to the Bibliothèque Nationale for those. You might get the original exhibition catalogue there as well. Historically, for auctions, there were usually notices of important artworks sales in the newspapers, and the highlights of the prices they received. And the auction houses would have produced catalogues, or at least leaflets, of the works to be sold. I know my grandfather kept some. I'm not sure how many. But they won't tell you who bought them. Client confidentiality in the art world is sacrosanct."

"Is there no record of who bought them?" Sam asked.

"Not that I'm aware, but that is something that you could check in the library," replied Leo.

"If there was, it might let us know whether they were still in existence. My goodness, imagine, if even one of them survived!" Claire said in excitement.

"You would be a rich man, my friend," said Leo, turning to Sam.

"I'll drink to that," said Sam, lifting his glass,

"I hope you are on good commission, Claire?" Leo said, one black eyebrow raised.

"I think I'm going to have to negotiate one."

"Let me do that for you, Claire, it would be my pleasure." He smiled at her, then at Sam.

But Sam was not amused.

Claire flushed and looked away, but not before she noticed the frisson between them.

"We should really be getting back to our hotel," Sam said stiffly, "it's getting late."

"Oh, I wouldn't like to keep you out past your bedtime. Let me call you a taxi."

"That's kind of you but I think we will walk," said Sam.

"Well, if Claire is not too tired?"

"I'm fine, thank you, Leo – a walk is just what I need."

"Let me walk part of the way with you."

"Oh, there is no need, we know the way," said Sam.

"Of course, but it's such a beautiful evening and we still have things to discuss."

"Fine," said Sam curtly.

"*L'addition, s'il vous plait*," Leo said to the waiter.

Outside, it was still warm, and they walked past Opéra, back towards the small hotel where they were staying on the Rue Gaillon.

"Look, Sam," said Leo, "I'm fascinated with all of this. I have been thinking. Maybe I can help. I have a young architectural student working with me and, apart from the factory, we are not that busy right now. I'm waiting for a client to approve design proposals for a new office fit-out. So how about I send her to the library every morning to look up old newspapers and auction notices, to see if we can come up with anything? She could also look for the original exhibition catalogue. Meanwhile, I will look through my grandfather's files. What do you say?"

"That is very generous of you," said Claire.

"Not at all, I'm fascinated by the story. I also feel, because of our family's relationship, that I am also invested in it." Noting Sam's alarm, he added, "Not financially, of course."

"It will be like looking for a needle in a haystack, you know," said Claire.

"I know. But nothing ventured, nothing gained, as they say."

They had reached the junction of the Rue Saint-Augustin.

"I will leave you here, my friends," Leo said and kissed Claire on both cheeks. "It has been a pleasure to meet such a beautiful and charming woman. And, Sam, I feel you are like a long-lost cousin. You know, I'm so pleased to have the opportunity to be involved in your adventure." He kissed him also on both cheeks. "Enjoy the rest of the evening, my friend."

"Goodnight, we will be in touch," Sam replied frostily.

They walked on in silence, each mulling over the day's events.

As they reached the hotel entrance Sam turned to Claire. "Would you care for a nightcap?"

"Oh, why not? When in Paris."

They settled down in chairs near the window and ordered two glasses of Chablis from the wiry waiter with bushy black eyebrows.

Claire was feeling more than a little tipsy at this stage.

"Leo is charming, don't you think?"

"I suppose, in that over-the-top way that Frenchmen have."

"I think they call it being in touch with your feminine side," said Claire playfully.

"Really. Seemed like a bit of a poof to me."

"I'd say he's anything but, Sam."

Sam leaned over and kissed Claire briefly on the lips. "I've been wanting to do that for ages."

"I thought you didn't fancy me at all." She threw her arms around him and they kissed passionately.

"*Ahem!*" The waiter looked down at them, his eyes twinkling. "Your drinks, monsieur, mademoiselle."

"Excuse us," said Sam.

"Don't worry, monsieur – this is Paris after all."

After they had finished their wine, Sam paid the waiter.

Then he got up and reached his hand out to Claire. "Bed, mademoiselle?"

"Oh my God, a romantic Irishman – you'll be buying me flowers next."

The next morning, as the other guests huddled together in the adjacent dining room, despite the chill breeze they had breakfast on the terrace restaurant of the hotel. The waiter who had served them drinks the previous evening was wearing a long crisp white apron. He removed the wax-covered Drambuie bottle that had served as a candleholder the night before and laid down a clean red-and-white checked tablecloth, returning minutes later with bowls of milky hot coffee and croissants fresh from the oven.

"I really enjoyed last night, Claire."

"Yes, me too."

He smiled at her nervously. "I hope it was not just a once-off."

"Hopefully not." She smiled back at him, surprised at his lack of confidence. She found it touching that he seemed so anxious to please, this extraordinarily handsome man who seemed to have no idea how attractive he was.

"OK," she said enthusiastically, "what is our plan for today?"

Entering the reading room at the Bibliothèque Nationale, Claire was filled with awe. Suffused with light and colour, thin, cast-iron columns supported, frond-like, domed cupolas with glazed circular windows at their centre. Colourful wall panels decorated with images of sky and foliage reinforced the impression of being in a tropical greenhouse full of books. The desks were arranged in rows, each with its own reading lamp with a green glass shade.

"It was designed by Henri Labrouste," she told Sam. "It's one of the finest examples of –"

"*Silence, si vous plait*," a passing librarian carrying several heavy tomes admonished Claire.

Claire bit her lip. "OK," she whispered, "let's concentrate on auction catalogues first. We can ask about exhibition catalogues later."

At the main desk, in response to Sam's queries, they were advised that as well as copies of all national newspapers before, during and after the war, the library also held microfilm images of sales catalogues from the various Paris auction houses. The librarian helpfully explained in English that these were not a complete repository, as some auctioneers kept better records than others, and that some chose not to share these records. Some included handwritten annotations that might include the name of the seller or buyer, and how much the work sold for. These catalogues could come from the auctioneer, or a collector who had attended the sale. This meant that for some auctions there were several different copies of the same catalogue, each providing different information.

"And how do we get access to the microfilms?"

"They are on cassettes. You have to fill out the forms and order each one of them, monsieur."

"Can we do that today, madame?"

"But, monsieur, there are at least one hundred and fifty cassettes of the information you require during this period. Also, it takes a day to get the cassettes from the stacks where they are held remotely."

"I see," said Sam, crestfallen. "We will have to come up with some alternative arrangement – we are returning to Ireland tomorrow."

"Looks like we'll have to take Leo up on his offer," said Claire.

"Unfortunately."

"Why do you say that?"

"I was hoping not to have him too involved."

"Why ever not?"

"It might be awkward to explain the situation with Nicholas. He might try and contact him directly."

"Well, Nicholas will have to find out eventually, Sam. Maybe we should bite the bullet and tell him now about Leo's list."

"I'd rather not just yet, Claire. If you don't mind."

"Well, it's up to you. But I don't fancy being exposed to Nicholas's wrath when he finds out."

"Don't worry, d –" Sam stopped himself.

"What were you going to call me? Was it the name of some ex-girlfriend?" she teased.

"No, Claire, sorry, slip of the tongue," he said absentmindedly as he paused to collect his thoughts. "I think it's time we checked out the Wexford studio, don't you? We'll be waiting a few weeks at least, by the sound of it, for Leo's assistant to go through all of those files, and for him to come back to us, so it would probably be a good use of our time."

Chapter 16

Sam sat in front of Professor Dillon's desk as he studied the paper. His cramped office in the Arts block looked out over the trees and railings facing Nassau Street. A Victorian carved bookcase filled with books arranged higgledy-piggledy looked out of place in the modern office building. Files were strewn everywhere, and a plate with a half-eaten dried-out sandwich was perched on top of a pile of essays.

"Interesting points about speed, and the age of travel and how this influenced Turner's use of colour and impressionistic style. A well-structured argument, but your grammar is appalling, Courtney. Didn't they teach you anything in school? The standard of English grammar in undergraduates' written work never ceases to amaze me."

Sam's heart sank as he saw that his paper was covered with the professor's trademark red-ink corrections. He looked under the table, noticing that Dillon was wearing a pair of unmatched socks, one red and one navy blue. He smiled to himself, thinking about how he would tell Claire later.

"It's nothing to smile about, Courtney, it's simply not acceptable. You will need to improve significantly if you are to pass your exams this year and proceed to third year. Your uncle will be so disappointed. I met him last week in my club." The professor paused, a puzzled expression on his face. "He had an alarming woman with him – she had a helmet of blonde hair, looked almost structural. Anyway, he was asking how you were getting on. He was telling me about your college study trip to Paris." He took his glasses off and looked sternly at Sam.

"Oh, really," said Sam, disconcerted.

"Yes, really. This college trip must have been a very exclusive affair, as I'm not presently aware of any organised college tour to that particular city."

"Well, professor, I twisted the truth slightly. I wanted to take some time out, go to the Louvre. I didn't want my uncle to think I was slacking."

"Ah!" He leaned back in his chair. "Paris is quite a romantic city. I remember spending an agreeable time there when I was younger, with my better half. You know, she's an entomologist, studies spiders. It was very enjoyable, but challenging, as I remember. I was looking up at the architecture, and she was constantly looking down on the ground. We met somewhere at eye-level when it was dark and called a truce." His eyes glazed over, consumed with pleasant memories.

Sam tried not to laugh. "I did have an agreeable companion as it happens."

"*Mm*, very well, Courtney. I know life isn't lived in a library. Although, unfortunately for me, most of mine is. But I need to see better results from you, otherwise we will be having this same conversation this time next year. Oh, by the way, how is Miss Howard getting on with cataloguing your mother's works? Your uncle told me you were helping her."

"Yes, it's going well, slow though, as you could imagine."

"So, I gather. Your uncle is anxious that she finishes up soon. I know his funds for the research are limited. Have you been to the studio in Wexford yet?"

"No, we plan to go there next week."

"I'll be interested to hear how you get on. I think her most interesting work was created there, in the series on the famine cottages. *The Hunger Walls,* I think she called it."

"Yes, I remember. I remember her talking to me about it as a child."

Chapter 17

Sylvie
May 1965

Peter was still staying at a friend's flat in Rathgar. Following his stormy departure, he had reappeared in Gilford Road a few days after Sylvie had returned from Wexford. She knew he would. Like a whipped puppy, he begged her to take him back. She told him it was too soon. They had met afterwards a few times and talked. He had promised to change, promised the sun, moon and stars: he would spend more time with her, be more affectionate, talk more to her. All the things about him that she found suffocating. But in her heart, she knew she couldn't do it anymore. She could no longer live the meagre life they had together – joyless – measured out in meaningless daily rituals. Nor could she endure Peter's constant imagined slights, and her own gnawing grudges against him – all of which conspired to wear her down. But neither could she continue her relationship with Nicholas, her stolen pleasure, exquisite and torturous at the same time. There was also Sam to consider. Peter, to his credit, adored the boy, and Sam seemed equally attached to Peter. She often suspected that, if it came to it, the teenager would rather be with Peter than with her. He had sulked for days when Peter had left. Once they returned from their rather dreary break in Wexford, she had been afraid that he would insist on going to stay with him. Until she explained to him that this was only a temporary arrangement.

A few weeks later she had been forced to phone Peter as final demands for unpaid bills were building up on the dresser in the hall. They had a joint account, and she noticed he was drawing from it more than he was putting in with his monthly salary. When she eventually steeled herself to call him, he claimed that he had incurred extra expenses moving into the flat and committed to paying her back. But he never did. She didn't care about the money, not really, and started paying the bills herself. Despite the hassle of having to look after the day-to-day stuff that Peter had always managed, she felt a huge relief in regaining her freedom. Even if it was only temporary. However, she felt sorry for Peter. She knew he missed Sam dreadfully – he phoned him most days. The teenager was also constantly asking her when his father would be coming home.

As her life began to return to some kind of order, thoughts about her father's letter and the implications of what she had learnt preyed on her mind. She had written to his friend Émile, who had responded saying he was sure that the paintings had been destroyed by the Nazis. But what if he was wrong? Because if the print that hid the letter was sent with the paintings and Uncle Daniel had the print then it was reasonable to assume that the paintings had also arrived in Ireland. If Daniel was aware of the paintings, maybe someone else in his circle also knew of them. Someone who had a deeper knowledge of the art world than Daniel's collection of coffee-table art books would imply. But who? Then she remembered the academic he was acquainted with whom she had met at her first exhibition opening.

Pamela was effusive as usual when Sylvie called into the gallery in Baggot Street the next day. She was wearing green-and-mauve silk flowing trousers and matching green-plastic disk earrings. She could almost have been an exhibit herself amongst the display of kinetic art that was currently on show. An elderly gentleman examining one of the works for sale was looking extremely puzzled. He glanced over enquiringly at Pamela, trying to catch her attention. But she studiously ignored him.

"He's only a tyre-kicker," she said, smiling.

Sylvie proceeded to tell her about the new cottage, and how she was going to spend the next few months there with Sam as soon as he finished school.

"It's called Rose Cottage. It's on the Hook Head near Churchtown, in Wexford. It's quite remote – it will be wonderful to get away from it all."

Pamela smiled woodenly. Sylvie suspected it was her idea of hell.

"Well, I suppose, at least you'll get lots of work done."

"Hopefully. I have an idea about a study of famine cottages."

"Oh, how interesting," enthused Pamela. "I'll be dying to see the results."

Sylvie was amused at the irony of the response. "I wanted to ask you something. Do you remember at my first exhibition, a few years ago, there was a professor from Trinity College who was a friend of my Uncle Daniel's? Brian something or other?"

"Oh yes, Professor Brian Dillon. Nice guy, bit of a bore though, doesn't half drone on. He's an expert on mid-twentieth-century French Art."

"Do you have a contact number for him?"

"Yes, of course, he's on our mailing list. I'll get it for you."

"Thanks, Pamela. I just wanted to pick his brains about something."

They had arranged to meet in Bewley's Café, the Victorian tea rooms, a Dublin institution – his choice. She had suggested several dates to fit in with his diary before they had finally agreed. She got the definite impression Professor Dillon was trying to avoid meeting her.

When she arrived at the appointed time, she asked the waitress if she could sit beside the large Harry Clarke stained-glass window – and, as she sipped her coffee, she admired the elfin beauty of the figures and how the coloured glass cast a diffuse amber glow in the crowded room. It was one of her favourite places, and always reminded her of student days and long wet afternoons spent drinking coffee and sorting out the problems of the world. Today the café was bustling with lunchtime shoppers, surrounded by bags at their feet from the nearby department stores, Brown Thomas and Switzers.

Through the crowd, Sylvie recognised the professor's ambling figure as he navigated his way between the dark-brown bentwood chairs and tightly packed tables.

She waved at him to catch his attention. He was wearing an oversized, mustard-coloured tweed jacket, green corduroy trousers, a checked-orange flannel shirt and a brown knitted tie. The colour of his jacket jarred with the tones of his shirt.

He sat down beside her, clicked his fingers at the waitress in an abstracted way that Sylvie found offensive, and ordered coffee.

"Sylvie, it's pleasure to meet you again. I was sorry to hear that your uncle passed away – he was still a relatively young man."

"Yes, a heart attack. It was quite sudden. In fact, so much so that he didn't really have time to put his affairs in order."

As the waitress, in her black dress, white apron and starched cap, returned with the coffee and a tiered, china plate of iced fancies, Sylvie watched the professor, and even though his eyes did not meet hers, Sylvie felt that she had his full attention.

"Oh, really?" he said when the waitress had gone.

"Yes – in fact, that was what I wanted to talk to you about – to see if you could help me. I seem to remember when we met the last time at my exhibition, a few years ago, he mentioned that you advised him on the sale of an artwork – a Léger if I remember rightly."

"Really?" he said, adopting a puzzled expression.

"Can you remember anything about it?"

"Vaguely." He lifted his china cup jerkily to sip his coffee but in doing so his sleeve brushed against a small glass vase of primroses, knocking it over, spilling water over the plate of iced cakes and the white linen tablecloth. "Oh, I'm so sorry, so clumsy of me!"

He pulled a large blue handkerchief out of his pocket and was attempting to mop up the mess when the waitress returned. She took control of the situation, removing the cups and saucers to a nearby vacant table and re-laying their table briskly.

During this time, the professor sat back in his chair, anxiously rubbing the loose flesh under his chin.

"To get back to the Léger," said Sylvie.

"Yes, yes. I recall now, he came to me with a Léger, it was a nice painting. He was looking for advice on how to sell it."

"And did he?"

"I'm afraid I have no idea."

"Do you remember the title?"

"No, sorry, the name escapes me."

"Any idea where it came from?"

"He told me it belonged to one of his bank's clients."

"The client's name?"

"Sorry," he said, mouth pursed, eyebrows raised.

"And where did you advise him to sell it?"

"Oh Christie's, or possibly Sotheby's. There is always a market for a good Léger. He's one of my favourite artists, you know."

"Surprising then, that you cannot remember the title," she said, smiling.

"Not really. I often look at paintings for people, give them advice. I've looked at hundreds of them over the years. I simply cannot recall all of them. Look, I'm terribly sorry, but I'm afraid I will have to scoot. I have a faculty meeting in ten minutes." He wiped his mouth with his napkin then started to rise from the table, stopping abruptly then sitting down again. "May I ask, why are you asking all of these questions? Have you found records of a Léger in your uncle's estate?"

"Yes, I have found records – but not in my uncle's estate, my father's."

"But your father died many years ago. I understood there were no papers."

"You have heard of my father?"

"Well, yes," he said, clearing his throat. "Dublin is a small place, everyone knows everything about everyone else. I had heard stories, of course, about your father, the art collector, whose paintings were burnt by the Nazis. Indeed, your uncle, or cousin Nicholas may have told me. Now, I really must go, Miss Vasseur."

"I'll pay the bill!" said Sylvie, calling after him as he turned and left. He had obviously no intention of doing so.

He turned back. "Thank you so much. Cheerio."

As he left Sylvie picked up a pink iced fancy and nibbled it slowly.

Her next call was Knockaboy to see Aunt Nora. She left Dublin early the next day and drove down without stopping in the battered, powder-blue Hillman Minx she had inherited from the Ambroses. The exhilaration of driving at speed with the windows open, the wind blowing her hair and the sun on her face, made her feel young again. The heavy weight that had been dragging her down for the last few years was starting to lift, and things were improving. Thoughts of a new life, and the freedom to do as she pleased were intoxicating. Buying the cottage seemed such an extravagance. But, she rationalised, she could always sell it if things didn't work out. After all, she also had the house in Sandymount which she could let at a push and maybe just keep the studio. Although Peter had been livid when he found out, he had to accept it was her money. Initially, he had advised caution and offered to invest the money for her in stocks and shares. To hell with that, she had thought to herself at the time, why not enjoy the money while she could? It was also at the back of her mind that the more of her money that was tied up, the less inclined Peter would be to ask to "borrow" money which he had been doing frequently of late. Before he had moved out, she had found slips from the bookies in his trouser pockets when she was doing the washing and suspected that he was becoming a frequent customer. Another man would have insisted that the Ambroses' inheritance be lodged into a joint account. But, to his credit, he knew how much the independence it represented meant to her. And then possibly he acknowledged, to himself anyway, his own weakness with money.

Things were now, certainly, much better financially. She had a good income from her art – enough to live on anyway. It would be so pleasant to spend another summer in Wexford with Sam. The time spent there in Nicholas's bungalow during their affair had reminded her how much she loved the area. It would also give her time to consider her next steps.

Shortly after finding her father's letter, she had written to his friend Émile, with whom, she had been told as a child, he had spent his last days in the South of France. She was still waiting for his response. The thought of one, or possibly more, of her father's paintings surviving was tantalising.

She had considered telling Peter and Nicholas about her discovery. But had decided against it for the moment. If the paintings had been sent to Ireland, then it was possible that Uncle Daniel could have been complicit, in some way, in their disappearance. Would Peter have been aware of their existence and not tell her? She found this hard to believe. He was a lot of things, but he was not deceitful. Nicholas, however, was another kettle of fish. And, as his father's solicitor, he must have known of any dealings he would have had in valuable artworks.

In Knockaboy, Aunt Nora was delighted to see her, and brought her into the large kitchen at the back of the house. Sylvie shivered as she passed the picture of the Sacred Heart in its heavy gilt frame. Although images of Christ's exposed, throbbing heart were to be found in nearly every Irish Catholic home, Sylvie had always found this image disturbing. As a child she had avoided looking at it. But, to her aunt, it was the family talisman and she operated her domestic domain under its benevolent eye, constantly referring to its auspicious powers.

Sylvie noticed her aunt had lost a lot of weight since Uncle Daniel's sudden death. She had taken off her housecoat in Sylvie's honour and her shapeless cotton dress was now several sizes too big for her. She also seemed a little more distracted than usual. She had made fresh scones for her visit, misshapen, unappetising lumps that were still warm from the range. She ushered Sylvie to sit down at the large kitchen table which was covered by a well-worn, flowery, plastic tablecloth. Sylvie savoured the comfort of the familiar surroundings. She knew, without looking, that a cigarette burn was hidden on the cloth under the butter dish. Beside the butter was the Waterford glass dish of homemade strawberry jam with a christening spoon – given to Peter by a long-dead aunt – sitting neatly on the side. As Sylvie sat down, her aunt turned down the volume on the radio as the theme tune for the popular soap drama *The Kennedys of Castleross* blared from the radio on the dresser.

"Well, Sylvie, it's well you're looking, being an artist seems to suit you. And how is Sam? You haven't brought him down to see me for ages. I suppose another grandchild for me would be out of the question?"

"Absolutely. Sam is now fourteen, a truculent teenager. I can just about cope with looking after him. Anyway, I told you before, I'm not the maternal type."

"Don't worry, dear, you will warm to your own, everyone does."

"Auntie," Sylvie changed the well-worn subject, "I came here especially because I wanted to ask you about my father."

"Oh dear, that poor man. It always upsets me to think about your parents. They were terrible, terrible times."

"Yes, I know." Sylvie put her hand over the older woman's as tears spilled out of her eyes. "It's about my father's art. You know he had a wonderful collection of art."

"Yes, I remember Daniel telling me. It was destroyed by those awful Nazis." She took a large man's hanky out of her pocket, wiped her eyes and blew her nose.

"Do you remember, Auntie, in 1950, the year things started to go wrong for Uncle Daniel – the bank merging, the dreadful new boss, and his losing a lot of money on stocks and shares?"

"Yes, the year you left – it was such a difficult time for us all. Remember, poor Peter couldn't go to college. I always regretted the fact that he missed out on the opportunity for a proper education."

"Yes, and I wanted to go to Art College," Sylvie reminded her gently.

"Did you, dear? I had forgotten that. We even had to sell Daniel's car and let Bridget go."

"But you seemed to recover, financially I mean, a few years later."

"Yes, it was in 1952 – Daniel made some shrewd investments, in oil, I think, and suddenly we were in funds again. He even bought me a fox-fur collar. So unlike him, he was always careful with money. I was so proud of it – I wore it every Sunday at Mass. It was the envy of Mrs Cusack, I can tell you. Although, with her double chin she wouldn't have been able to carry it off."

"I met a Professor Dillon yesterday," Sylvie said, trying to keep her aunt focused. "He used to give advice to Uncle Daniel about selling art."

"That's right, dear, your uncle sold art for some of the bank's customers. Your uncle was always interested in art, but at that time he started buying books about the subject. I think he saw it as a way of earning extra income. He used to bore the pants off the Cusacks talking about it. Yes, he became quite the expert, always going up to follow the auctions in Dublin. He bought the lovely picture of the daisies for me there in that auction house on the Quays." She looked up at the painting on the wall. "It's my most prized possession. It reminds me of him, you know, that and the fox fur. Mrs Cusack has always admired that painting."

Sylvie glanced at the painting of the daisies. It was an accomplished but unremarkable watercolour by an artist from Wicklow, mounted in a slender silver frame.

"Could I look at Uncle's books?" she asked. "I wasn't interested in them when I was younger, but obviously I am now."

"Yes, of course, my dear."

Her aunt fetched the key for the glass-fronted cabinet where Daniel had kept his art books. It was always kept locked. They both went into the study.

"He was so organised, not a bit like me," said her aunt, looking around the spartan room.

Arranged neatly in the bookcase were books on Twentieth Century French art: The Fauves, Cubism and Expressionism.

Sylvie took out a book showing the work of Mateus and flicked through its colourful pages, and then another about Léger.

"Could I borrow these two, Auntie?"

"No problem, dear. You can keep them. Nicholas is the only one who has ever bothered with them. But I'm sure he wouldn't object to you having a couple as mementos of him. He tried to be good to you, you know. To do the right thing. He found it hard to show his feelings – he just wasn't a very affectionate man."

"I know, Auntie," said Sylvie, closing the book and giving the older woman a big hug. "At least you made up for it."

Over the long drive home Sylvie thought about what to do next. As she mulled things over, she thought about the Courtney's change of fortune in 1952, the year after

228

Sam was born. Daniel had changed his car and bought a silver-grey Jaguar – and Aunt Nora and Uncle Daniel had spent their summer holidays in the Great Southern Hotel in Killarney, for a whole week. She remembered being surprised at the time as Daniel had always dismissed talk of holidays when they were children. He would say, "Are we not within a ten-minute drive of at least ten of the best beaches that Ireland has to offer? Why would I want to waste money going anywhere else?" She also remembered that Nicholas had started driving a flashy red Austin sports car with leather seats and a soft top – and started entertaining expensive women in the dining room of the Hotel Metropole in O'Connell Street. What if they had sold some of her father's paintings to fund this new-found lavish lifestyle?

When she arrived home in Sandymount later that evening, as she put the key in the hall door her phone rang. It was Nicholas.

After the usual pleasantries, he said casually, "I believe you met Professor Dillon. I bumped into him yesterday evening at my club. You were asking him questions about a Léger belonging to your father?"

Sylvie's heart leapt. She was on to something.

"Yes, I thought it was about time I tried to find out about my family. It's a subject that has haunted me for years. Uncle Daniel always discouraged me from talking about them. So, I have written to my father's friend, Émile Bonnard. I would like to meet him, to talk about my parents. In fact, I was thinking of going to France."

"How interesting, Sylvie. Paris in the summer, sounds most romantic. There is an intimate little hotel that I know, just opposite Île de la Cité. I'll take you there, if you like. I could be useful in more ways than one," he said provocatively.

"No, Nicholas. I told you already, and I meant it. It's over between us. *Kaput*. I need to sort out my relationship with Peter. Things are still fraught between us."

"How is he?"

"You care?"

"Of course I care, he is my brother."

Sylvie ignored him. "Look, this thing with my parents is something I want to do on my own."

"Mother mentioned you had taken some of the art books from Knockaboy."

"Reading up on the art my father was interested in."

"Very well, but I could save you a lot of time. I'm a bit of an expert myself, as you know."

"Thank you for your offer, but time is not an issue. I'm enjoying the process of finding out."

"Very well. Look, Sylvie, I'm also fascinated by all of this. I suppose it's part of my family history too. And I still care about you, Sylvie. So, keep me in the loop. Please."

"Yes, if you like, I will. Now I must go. I'm tired. Goodbye, Nicholas." She replaced the receiver on the phone and smiled to herself.

After unpacking the car, she sat down with a glass of wine and a hastily made cheese sandwich. Sam was staying over with school friends for a few days. She decided that if she was to succeed at all in this investigation, she needed a crash course in the history of art of the period. She would start with Daniel's books and go into the National Library in Kildare Street the next day and see what she could find out there.

* * *

After filling out forms and being supplied with a reader's ticket, Sylvie climbed the curved stone stairway to the first floor of the library. In the light-filled, Victorian reading room with its glazed dome, ancient-looking reference books lined the walls and the central area was filled with wooden desks. A pleasant smell pervaded, a cocktail of ancient dust and beeswax.

Sylvie approached the counter and spoke to a long-haired, pasty-faced librarian and told him what she was looking for. A few minutes later, the young man returned from the back-office storage area with a general history of art of the period and several magazines.

"I often find that it's easier to read magazine articles," he said. "They are written in more straightforward language and usually distil the information to include only what is essential in order to understand the subject."

"That's very kind of you. May I borrow these?"

"No, I'm sorry. This is a reference library only, but you can stay here all day if you like and read them."

She lasted three hours, reading the magazines first as the librarian had suggested. But by lunchtime she had read only five of the pile of about twenty magazines. She had not eaten breakfast and was afraid her stomach would start to rumble. Needing sustenance, she headed out of the library onto Kildare Street. Pleased to stretch her legs and inhale the fresh air, she walked up towards St Stephen's Green and the Country Shop which served good-quality coffee, wholesome soup and brown bread. The café also displayed Irish

crafts and featured artists' work. It was a place that she usually bumped into someone she knew. Today was no exception. She was only in the door when she heard familiar raucous laughter, the sort that caused everyone within a fifty-foot radius to giggle uncontrollably in response.

It was Deirdre Mathews. An artist with whom she had shared a twin room a few years previously in Kilkenny, where they were both showing work at an art exhibition.

Sylvie waved at her friend but sat at a table at the other side of the room. She was not in the mood to make small talk to the group Deirdre was with. But, undeterred, her friend crossed the crowded cafe and sat down at the table beside her.

"Haven't seen you for ages, Sylvie. I heard you had decamped to Wexford."

"Yes, I was there for most of last summer and really loved it. It's an inspirational place to work – no distractions."

"And how is Peter?"

"Oh so-so. To be honest, we are going through a rocky patch."

"I'm sorry to hear that – I hope things work out for you both."

Sylvie smiled in response but wasn't ready to acknowledge to the world the fact that she was considering leaving her husband.

"So, what are you working on, still immersed in landscape?"

"Actually, I'm working on a new series of paintings based on famine cottages."

"How fascinating – interesting subject matter."

"*Mm*, it is. When you consider that Lillian Davidson's painting of a starving family burying their child was painted in the 1940s. Our generation seems to have turned their back on the subject. But I also have another interest right now. I'm looking at Degenerate Art."

"How do you mean – pornography?"

"No." Sylvie laughed. "Artists of the 1940s whose work Hitler considered unacceptable: Picasso, Léger, Mateus."

"Oh, artists your father collected."

"Yes."

"I suppose you've talked to that professor in Trinity, Brian Dillon. He is an expert on that period. I seemed to remember reading an article a few years ago that he wrote in the *Irish Art Journal* – it was about the French art scene after the war. Though, I must tell you, Sylvie, that fellah is as odd as two left feet. They used to call him 'Tit-face' when I was a student."

Deirdre started laughing hysterically, instantly setting Sylvie off in response. She could see that the nickname suited the professor perfectly with his soft, fulsome cheeks. But as she was laughing, she made a mental note to check whether the *Irish Art* magazine article was amongst those the librarian had set aside for her.

When she returned to the library, she found the issue Deirdre had referred to near the bottom of the pile. She glanced at the text briefly, but what immediately caught her attention was a photograph that accompanied the piece – it was black-and-white and taken in the professor's study. Not his room in Trinity, thought Sylvie, it must be his study at home. He was sitting at a desk surrounded by books, smiling with that lopsided grin of his. Trying, but failing miserably, to look debonair. But behind him was a painting. Only a small part of it was captured in the image but Sylvie gasped with the shocked realisation that she had seen this painting before – it was her father's. One that she clearly remembered as a child – it had hung in the hallway of their apartment on Rue de Sévigné. It was one of the paintings her young friends had laughed at, saying they could paint so much better.

Back home in Gilford Road, she finished clearing up the dishes after dinner. In the living room, Sam was spread out on the couch. His long legs were hanging over the armrest. He was watching television while his goofy friend, Georgie, was lying on the floor reading a magazine about dinosaurs. Sylvie sighed to herself – the two teenagers seemed to take up so much space. But at least he now had friends. He had always been such a solitary child, didn't seem to need anyone else, except her that is. She found this aspect of motherhood frustrating. The Victorians had the right idea – leave them to the staff to bring them back washed, dressed and ready to go to bed. Although, she smiled to herself, he was a bit big for that. She noticed that Georgie was wearing jeans and a sweatshirt, while Sam was still wearing his school uniform even though she had asked him to change out of it several times already. He's going to need more new trousers soon, she thought, exasperated. He had gone from being one of the shorter boys in his class in Blackrock College to being one of the tallest in a period of eighteen months. All told, it had been an expensive year – the fees for the place were high enough – but she hadn't counted on the costs of constantly replacing uniforms. Still, his growth spurt had given him confidence and earned respect from his peers. She often wondered what it was about him when he was younger that he didn't make friends easily with other boys. Was it his serious nature? Or was it that he was such a good-looking boy, angelic almost, with his blonde hair and blue eyes? Street angel – house devil, Aunt Nora used to say. One time he had come home from school in a temper and had confided in her that the other boys teased him and call him Jane. But not anymore – because, despite being a mediocre student, he excelled in sports – and with his broad shoulders and strong legs he was particularly good at rugby. This prowess made him a hero amongst the other boys. But also, and it had to be said, it gave him an attitude that made her long for the gentle child he used to be. Although there had always been that temper.

"Sam, have you done your homework? It's time for Georgie to go home." She had decided to strike while the iron was hot.

"We were let off ecker today, Mum. One of the old priests died and we have to pray for his soul."

"Waste of time asking you to do that. But you could use the time to revise for your history test."

"Mum! That's not fair. I'm in the middle of something!" he replied truculently.

She could see by the glint in his eyes that he was starting to get annoyed. Wanting to avoid the possibility of his anger escalating, and a row developing, she said in a cajoling voice, "Upstairs, now, Sam – please. Home,

Georgie!"

She watched Sam lumbering upstairs, ducking his head at the landing bulkhead, and Georgie leave, banging the front door. Then she lifted the phone and rang the number.

"Dillon residence," a voice answered.

"Professor Dillon please."

"Who's calling?"

"Sylvie Vasseur."

"Are you a student?" the voice said petulantly.

"No."

"Is this personal?"

"No, it's business."

"Very well."

A silence ensued. She could hear urgent whispering in the background until eventually the professor lifted the phone.

"Sylvie, I didn't expect to hear from you again quite so soon."

"Nor did I. It's about the Léger."

"What Léger?"

"The one in your study. My father's Léger."

"I'm afraid I don't understand what you mean."

"Oh, I think you do."

"I don't know what you are insinuating, Miss Vasseur, but I don't like your tone."

"May I come around?"

"Absolutely not."

"Can we meet to talk?"

"If you must, but my schedule is quite full for the next few days. I cannot meet you until Monday week at the earliest."

"That's fine. In Trinity?"

"No, same place as before. Bewley's at ten o'clock. We can talk then, and you can explain to me what this is all about."

"See you then, professor," said Sylvie, hanging up.

She wanted to talk to him face to face. She wanted to see his reactions. She wanted to tease out from him how it came about that he had the painting. He was unlikely to tell her the truth without some encouragement – whether that was pretending she knew more than she did, or her threatening him, she wasn't exactly sure. She would have preferred to meet him at his office. A public location gave him the opportunity to end the discussion whenever he saw fit. But it was the best she could achieve at the moment. It also gave her time to prepare. She returned to the living room and considered her options as she picked up the teenagers' discarded magazines. After a few minutes she returned to the hall and bellowed up the stairs.

"*Sam, pack your bag! Let's take advantage of the dead priest and take a week in Wexford! I'll say you were sick.*"

We can both study for our history tests, she thought to herself.

Chapter 18

Paris
21st May, 1965

The Café des Trois Théâtres was buzzing. It was opening night at the opera of the *Tales of Hoffmann*, and the room was full of smartly dressed men and women in evening dress.

Nicholas was tired. He and the professor had arrived in Le Bourget airport on the four o'clock flight. The strain of their forced conversation had left him with a splitting headache.

"Good evening, Monsieur Bonnard," said a distinguished gentleman who paused as he passed their table, the medals on his chest glistening.

"Good evening, Minister – enjoy Hoffman, one of my favourites."

As soon as the older man was out of earshot Nicholas turned to Émile. "It would have made more sense, Émile, if you had come to Dublin," he said testily.

"As I recall, I did not precipitate this problem, my friend."

Nicholas did not respond – his expression was grim.

Émile then addressed the professor. "I find it hard to believe that an intelligent man like you would have allowed the painting to be photographed and published in an art journal. What on earth were you thinking?"

The professor's jowled face was glistening with sweat and his breathing was laboured. He was wearing a leather tie that looked inappropriate with his check button-down shirt. He tried to ease the collar which appeared to be too tight.

"Look, as I have already explained to Nicholas, they took several photographs. I specifically asked for the ones they took of me in my drawing room to be used when I realised the problem – but you must admit only his daughter could have recognised the painting from what was visible. I think my wife, without my knowledge, subsequently agreed to the photographs of my study."

"That was most unfortunate, careless even," said Émile. "Because now, after all of these years, we have a serious problem."

"Look, I have been thinking about this very carefully. I think we should tell Sylvie the truth," said the professor, wringing his large, soft, square hands.

"The truth," said Nicholas sneering. "You idiot! The truth will ruin us all."

"It's just that, as I was the one who authenticated Daniel's ownership of the paintings, I can simply say that since he died new information came to light and that I was mistaken."

"If you believe that will solve our problems then you are even more stupid than I gave you credit for," said Nicholas.

"How dare you speak to me like that!" the professor said, sitting up straight in the chair and clenching his fists, his lower lip trembling.

"Let us think this through," said Émile calmly. "We are all complicit in this, and there are consequences. But first, where is the Mateus?"

"It's safe in Knockaboy – it has never moved from there," said Nicholas.

"That's good. I would suggest, Professor, that you claim your Léger was given to you in lieu of fees for services rendered by Daniel. You might get away with it. But the others – the Picasso, other Légers and Mateus – Sylvie would, in time, be able to track down through the auction-house catalogues of the various sales. She could seek their return through the courts as stolen art. The links between myself and Paul are well known – eventually I would be implicated, and my reputation and my business would be ruined. There are also the Barbizon paintings to consider – technically they could be classified as Nazi-looted art."

"They had nothing to do with me, that was before my time," the professor interjected.

Émile looked at Nicholas then back at the professor.

"No, that is true, and I was the one involved in their sale – but, remember, once the story is out you will be considered guilty by association. Endorsing Daniel's ownership of the modern paintings will be enough to discredit you."

The professor put his hands over his head. "I will lose my tenure – I will never get another academic post."

"Daniel, at least, is dead, disclosure will hurt him the least," said Émile, smoothing his moustache and taking a sip of his brandy. "Can we use that fact? Could he be the fall-guy, as the Americans say? Maybe for some financial incentive for the family?"

"No, absolutely not," said Nicholas. "I would still have to deal with Sylvie, and she will sue me for everything I have. You have no idea what a tigress she is – she will not take this lying down." He smiled bitterly.

"I only have a week before I have to meet her again," said the professor, loosening his tie.

"Can we pay her off?" Émile asked.

"No, that won't work either. Unfortunately, she's not motivated purely by money."

"We will have to make sure that she does not talk by other means so," said Émile calmly.

"Look, I don't like the way this conversation has turned," said the professor, starting to rise from his chair.

"Sit down, you idiot," said Nicholas, restraining him with an iron grip.

"Gentlemen, please." Émile took a cigarette from the box on the table, lit it and took a long drag. Then he turned to Nicholas. "We don't have much time. I have already responded to her letter to me and tried to put her off. But with this new information she will be back in touch, no doubt. I presume I can rely on you, my friend, to make her see sense."

"Yes, I think so," said Nicholas.

"Very well, I will be in touch. Meanwhile, professor, for all our sakes, but particularly for yours, please try to hold your nerve."

The following morning Nicholas called into Bonnard's auction house on the Rue du Faubourg Saint-Honoré. He found Émile in the downstairs gallery sorting through paintings for a forthcoming auction. Émile turned to the two men wearing brown overalls and white cotton gloves who were assisting him.

"I have some business to attend to. I will be back in an hour or so – carry on without me."

He took Nicholas to the café at the end of the road.

After they had placed their order with the waiter for coffee, he turned to Nicholas.

"I was so sorry to hear of your father's death last year. Unfortunately, I was unable to go to the funeral. My own health is not that good these days. But I was a good friend to him, you know. All those years ago when your father was in financial trouble, I helped him out. I hope that you will remember this if the shit hits the fan."

Nicholas leant his head to the side and smoothed his straw-coloured linen trousers.

"Of course, Émile, you were good to my father. But not out of the kindness of your heart. A few years ago, my father told me that it was for a price – if you can call it that. It was for his silence on another matter that you were anxious to erase from history."

Émile's face suddenly turned red, contorted with rage, and he banged his fist on the table, not noticing the alarmed look of a fellow customer. "Your father blackmailed me, Nicholas, he was a ruthless man. You don't understand, they were desperate times, we did what we had to do to survive!" He lowered his head as if suddenly defeated. "It was all very well for you Irish with your neutrality," he looked up, sneering, "sitting on the fence and letting the rest of Europe fight your battles."

"Your insults are wasted, Émile. Irish politics are of no interest to me. However, my money and my family's reputation are. Look, Émile, the fact is we both have a considerable amount to lose, more than that idiot Dillon realises."

"Very well, Nicholas, deal with it. But be under no misapprehension – if you don't, I will, and my methods may not be quite so acceptable."

Chapter 19

Rose Cottage, Wexford
25th May, 1965

As she tidied away her paints, Sylvie thought about the disturbing phone call she had received from Evelyn the previous evening. She hadn't pulled any punches, called her cold and heartless and told Sylvie in no uncertain terms how she felt that she had betrayed their friendship. Sylvie felt sick. She could still feel that hollow feeling in her stomach when she recalled the vitriol the betrayed woman had unleashed. She wiped the table with a cloth soaked in white spirits, slowly, soothingly, watching the spilt paint meld into swirls of grainy colour. She had never intended to hurt Evelyn who had only shown her kindness. But maybe she should have watched her husband more carefully. Only a fool would have expected Nicholas to be faithful. Evelyn had told her she was moving to America. Lucky her, thought Sylvie, to be able to walk away so easily. At least she had her own money. Hope she takes it with her. It would serve Nicholas right. But she was sorry to lose Evelyn as a friend, she had been amusing. And she had to admit that with her connections she had been useful, promoting her work on more than one occasion.

But she shouldn't dwell on these negative thoughts, what was done was done. By the time she had finished the washing-up she had put Evelyn and Nicholas out of her mind, replacing those depressing thoughts with the altogether more enjoyable prospect of spending time painting here in the summer. It had been so pleasant this last week while she waited for the professor to grace her with his presence.

The cottage was on the road down to Hook Head Lighthouse – one of the oldest lighthouses in the world, according to Mikey Mac. She had met the old man while out walking and had assumed his name was short for McCarthy, or McConville, but was amused to hear that it was short for Mackerel. He was a fisherman – the nickname distinguished him from farmer Mikey, who lived outside Slade village, not far from the bungalow Nicholas had sold. Mikey Mac was also the local, self-appointed weatherman. He made it his business to listen to the morning shipping forecasts, and to relay the outlook for the next few days to everyone he met. When Sylvie could not sleep in the middle of the night, she often saw the stooped figure ambling along on the road. She thought of him as a friendly hobbit and felt comforted when she saw him on these nocturnal prowls.

The stone cottage was small, an open-plan living and dining room at the front, and a tiny kitchen at the back. Upstairs were two bedrooms and a bathroom. The larger room was hers and the smaller room was Sam's. This studio, in the back garden, had been a dark shed that the previous owner used as a workshop. Before moving in, the local builder had fitted a large roof light in the corrugated steel roof, a new shower in the bathroom, and a range in the kitchen.

Here, in her studio, she felt she could shut out the feelings of guilt she carried constantly with her. Because despite everything, she knew Peter was a good man, that he loved her, and had been there for her when she needed help and had no one. She had betrayed him by marrying him in the first place.

The current work was good, she knew it. She always knew. She used to think of it as the painting singing to her, but she didn't associate this feeling with the sounds of music, it was an emotional thing. It was when the sense of visual fulfilment was pure. It did not jar. No one part of it was deficient, or crude, it emanated a harmony that pleased her eye, and its message hit the purest notes within her soul.

Sam was camping overnight on the Great Saltee Island with friends, whose father had a boat. Sylvie was looking forward to a peaceful evening on her own. She could hear the farmer's tractor cutting grass to make silage in the field between the cottage and the cliffs. A few drops of rain trickled down the window and she noticed the gnarled whitethorn tree in the garden starting to sway. The weather had been fair during the day, but the forecast predicted storm-force winds later. She reached over the sink in her studio to close the window, savouring the sweet smell of cut grass. These physical sensations stimulated her. Before, her painting had been consumed with the sea, how it segued and contrasted with the sky as the seasons changed. But the inspiration for the latest paintings was embedded in the land. She had completed the series of studies of the peninsula's famine cottages, small, crumbling stone hovels where Irish peasants had eked out a meagre existence from the barren ground. They had been abandoned during the famine in the 1840s when a blight hit the potato, the country's staple crop. Two and a half million people were forced to emigrate, and one million people starved to death. Peter's talk of the Hunger Walls when she was a child had made a deep impression on her, and nowhere did she feel closer to those abandoned souls than on the Hook Peninsula. The work was also a move for her towards the figurative, as the shapes of cottages and their ghostly occupants were clearly discernible. She looked around the walls, there were twelve canvases in all. The gallery in Baggot Street were excited about them. Pamela had already been down to see the work in progress. Sylvie would need to take them to Dublin to get them framed in time for the exhibition in December. But that was months away, it was now only May. Sam would be on his holidays soon. At least this year he had school friends who lived in the area to entertain him.

The last week had given her time to think. If the professor had her father's painting, then from whom did he obtain it? Did he buy it, was it in an auction? She had already spent a day telephoning each of the well-known auction houses in Dublin, Belfast and London. Mrs Fennell's ears must have been burning. The local switch operator was known locally as 'Rose the Nose'. And right enough, Sylvie did notice a few strange looks during the week in the shop in Slade village. But after a few days, the auctioneers had all come back to tell her that, to their knowledge, a work of that description had never been sold at auction in Ireland or Britain. Her next port of call had to be Paris. Émile had not yet replied to her letter. Maybe he could spread some light on the matter, or at least give her advice on where to start looking for answers. Trying to find more information about the painting was exciting, but the thought of going home filled her with joy. She fantasised about visiting the Rue de Sévigné. And although she knew the apartments that she had lived in had been demolished during the war, she wondered about the other buildings on the street and who lived there now. When she had mentioned to Sam earlier in the week that, if they liked it, they might even move there, start a new life, he had been upset. But maybe she had rushed broaching this subject with him – she knew he was close to his father. He probably rang him and told him, she thought. The last thing she wanted was Peter getting into a state about that, on top of everything else. Hopefully not. Sam's communication skills lately left a lot to be desired. Teenage boys were famous for it. But, even as a child, he hadn't been the most talkative. In fairness, a chatterbox would have done her head in. She would find out soon enough. She had finally reached a decision. She would leave Peter. She had rung him earlier, a stilted phone call, and asked him to meet her at the house in Sandymount the following evening when she knew Sam would be out at rugby practice. She told him she planned to drive up to Dublin the next morning – they needed to formalise arrangements about Sam and money.

It was seven o'clock, the sun was descending, and the light levels were falling. As predicted, the wind had picked up, its whines trembling on the telephone wires. She decided to call it a day. After carefully cleaning her brushes, she left her studio and walked back across the garden into the house. At least it had stopped raining.

Sitting down on the couch, she lit a cigarette, a habit she had taken up only recently. She enjoyed the physical act of smoking, the savouring of the smoke. It helped her think.

A knock came on door and Peter's face peered in the window.

"Sylvie, it's me."

"Shit," she said under her breath.

She went to open the door. "I wasn't expecting you," she said, annoyed. "Why didn't you phone? I told you I would see you tomorrow."

"I was afraid that the old biddy on the switch would be listening in."

"So what? It would give her something to talk about."

"I wanted to see you."

As soon as she let him in, he wrapped his arms around her.

"You can't leave me. I won't let you. I need you." His voice sounded strangled and high-pitched. He started to kiss her wildly on the mouth and she could feel his tears on her cheeks.

"*Stop it, Peter. Stop, please! We have to talk.*" She tried to push him off.

"No more talking, Sylvie – we can make this work. It's simple, I love you and Sam. I need you both. Let's just forget that this ever happened and start again."

"But it did happen, Peter," she said, finally pushing him away from her and looking into his red-rimmed eyes. "And it happened because I was unhappy. The truth is, I don't love you, Peter. You are a good man – I'm very fond of you. But there has to be more."

"Love – is that what you mean or is it sex? Passion, that's what you crave, isn't it?" He pulled her roughly to him and bit her lip so that he drew blood. He pulled her down onto the couch.

"This is what you want." He started pulling at his belt.

"*Whoa there, mate!*" A hand pulled him off her. "The lady seems to be protesting."

Neither of them had noticed Nicholas enter the cottage.

"*You bastard!*" screamed Peter, turning to swipe at Nicholas, who fell to the ground.

Peter hunkered down over him and pounded him wildly with his fists. Blood was pouring from Nicholas's face. Sylvie tried to pull Peter off him but in a blind rage he turned, hitting her with full force. She fell with a crash against the wall, hitting her head, and a stain of bright-red blood tracked her skull on the white plaster as she fell onto the floor.

Peter, his eyes manic, turned to Nicholas. "I'm not walking away this time until I have killed you, you evil bastard!"

"*Peter, don't kill him!*" Sylvie cried weakly. "*He's Sam's father!*"

Peter stopped and turned to Sylvie, but the look of hatred and surprise turned to shock as he realised that she was badly hurt.

He jumped up and ran over to her.

"Sylvie, Sylvie, are you OK?"

She lay, eyes closed, slumped on the floor.

"Sylvie! I didn't mean to hurt you."

Nicholas, his face lacerated and his upper lip swollen and split, joined him at her side.

"We must stop the blood," he said, his own breathing laboured. "Make a compress. Get a sheet from upstairs – rip it up to make bandages. *Now*, Peter!"

Peter got up in a daze of disbelief and headed out of the room.

Chapter 20

"Well, did you find anything, Stephanie? You've been there for three days at this stage. I will have to call it a day at the end of the week."

Stephanie was wearing colourful knitted stockings that came up over her knees even though it was twenty-two degrees outside. Leo would have to talk to the girl – anything loud grated on his nerves and he knew eventually he would get a migraine just from looking at her.

"Thank God! It's so tedious, apart from the fact that I'm sitting all day in that magnificent architectural space. The catalogues are all on microfilm and can only be viewed on those big fiche viewers which are slow and awkward to operate. Anyway, I found this, which might be of interest. It's the catalogue of the last exhibition held here in Vasseur's gallery in 1940 – and an auction catalogue from Bonnard's two years later, in 1942, that features three of the same art works. It's not really a catalogue, more a couple of sheets of typed paper. In fact, I very nearly overlooked it."

Leo's pulse raced. "That's wonderful, Stephanie, well done, and thanks for doing this for me."

"It's not in my job description, but you know what architects say – we are paid for drawing and for scratching out. I'm considering this as non-productive work in the 'scratching out' category." She placed photocopies of the documents on his desk.

"Well, then, you will be pleased to hear we got design approval on that commercial fit-out, and I need you to start the tender drawings tomorrow."

"Thank you, Leo. Thank God! Another day in that place and I'd be afraid I would be classified myself!"

Cheered by this news, she left, closing the door behind her.

Leo looked at the photocopies of the documents Stephanie had referred to.

In the 1942 Bonnard listing, items number 2, 8 and 11 – a Théodore Rousseau, Paul Huet and Charles-François Daubigny, all from the Barbizon School – did indeed match the catalogue titles and artwork descriptions in the 1940 Vasseur catalogue.

He didn't realise that his grandfather had been operating an auction house here in Rue du Faubourg Saint-Honoré during the war. He had assumed he only started operations after the war. But why was his grandfather selling Paul's works which he had told Sylvie in his letter had been destroyed by the Luftwaffe in Lyon?

Leo sat back in his Charles Eames chair and lit a cigarette. He couldn't put his feet up on his glass desk, so he placed them on a low cupboard unit filled with architectural journals.

He thought for a while. He would have to go back to the apartment and go through his father's account books and see could he make sense of this. He should contact Claire, but maybe not yet. He would see if he could get more information. No point jumping to conclusions that could be damaging to his family. There was probably a plausible explanation for all of this. He didn't feel like contacting Sam, he hadn't warmed to the Irishman. Was it because he seemed to have such a high opinion of himself?

He was relieved to find, on arriving at the apartment on the Rue Barbes, that his sister Nathalie was out which meant he did not have to get involved in lengthy explanations. He went directly to the small store off the hall. In the first cabinet he took out the earliest ledger dated 1945. He then searched through the other cabinets and, on a second examination, in the second cabinet at the back, was a hard-backed exercise book. It was pale blue and was a different size to the others. Leo opened it. There were five columns. *Date, Name of Artwork, Name of Vendor, Name of Buyer* and *Sale Price*. The entries were handwritten in black ink in his grandfather's distinctive script. Looking down the list starting from October 1940, Leo saw with dismay that a number of the paintings from the exhibition catalogue of the Barbizon School of paintings had been sold by his grandfather, and beside each artwork the name of the vendor was marked ERR, the Gestapo's art-looting unit.

Leo felt the air empty from his lungs and a cold sweat spread over his body. He was stunned, trying to take in the ramifications of what he had just read. So, the story about them being blown up on the train was a lie. His grandfather had worked with the Nazis to sell Paul's looted art. His grandfather with his medals from the Great War. His grandfather the war hero.

Chapter 21

Rose Cottage, Wexford
August 1982

On the drive down to Wexford Sam had been unusually quiet. Claire had asked him what was wrong, but he dismissed her concern, blaming the heavy weather and a headache.

However, once they turned onto the coast road, they caught a glimpse of the sea and as the car lurched over the humped-back bridge in Saltmills village he seemed to cheer up.

The drive down to the Hook Lighthouse was spectacular. The sun was high in a clear, ultramarine-blue sky and there were panoramic views out to sea on either side of the peninsula. Rough stone walls lined the long straight road which Sam had told her were made by starving farmers during the Potato Famine as part of local subsistence schemes. "The Hunger Walls, my father always called them," he said.

They passed Loftus Hall, a formidable edifice, incongruous in the desolate landscape. It was famous for being the oldest haunted house in Ireland. Once past the turn for Slade, modern bungalows were interspersed with crumbling stone cottages on either side of the road. The occupants of the cottages, Sam told her, had left their homes and emigrated to England and America, and never returned, many dying on so-called 'coffin ships' before they even arrived at their destinations. Claire noticed a rose outside one of the derelict cottages and wondered what had become of the person who had planted and tended the flower so lovingly all those years ago?

Eventually they stopped at a renovated cottage with whitewashed walls and a timber-slatted front door painted red. She noted, sadly, a trellis of roses like the one she had just seen, a bit overgrown, trailing to one side of the door. A shiver ran down her spine. She wondered if Sylvie had planted it.

"This is it." Sam jumped out of the car and opened the door for her.

The key was hidden under a clay model of a gargoyle's head at the front door.

At least the cottage was warm, Claire noticed with relief. Although it was a sunny day, the wind was bitingly cold. Sam told her that Mrs Cody, a neighbour who kept an eye on the place, had turned the heating on the night before.

After leaving their things in the bedroom and a brief tour of the cottage, Sam suggested a walk.

"We'll unlock the studio tomorrow and get down to work, but let's just relax and enjoy this evening. Anyway, I'm dying to show you around. Do you know, it's the one place I feel that I really connect with my mother," he said wistfully.

They headed back up the road towards Slade. a small fishing village, then out along the cliffs. They walked for miles, watching gannets rise in the sky and then swoop swiftly like falling daggers to catch the fish below. As they walked, they searched amongst the waves for seals, stopping every now and again to examine limestone fossils lying loose on the fissured foreshore before reaching the Hook Lighthouse and then circling back once again to Churchtown.

By the time they finally sat down to dinner, steak and chips cooked by Sam, Claire was exhausted. The fresh air and the white wine had made her lightheaded.

Sitting on the couch in front of the fire, Sam curled Claire's blonde hair around his fingers.

"I really like you, you know," he said simply.

"I know. I'm rather fond of you too." She smiled and kissed him lingeringly on the lips.

"But because I have come to really like you – love you, even – there is something I need to tell you, before somebody else does."

"Oh," said Claire, simultaneously pleased and alarmed. "What?"

"It's something that I'm really ashamed of. But I hope you won't despise me."

"Just tell me, Sam." Claire was worried now. She had become emotionally attached to Sam without even realising the intensity of her feelings. They got on effortlessly. Apart from his occasional sulking, she enjoyed his easy good humour. He was always so attentive, such good company. She was filled with apprehension in anticipation of what he was about to say.

"Well, you know when I was working for the bank?"

"Yes."

"Well, one of their clients was a property developer."

"And?"

"Well," Sam bent his head and she could see the bones in his knuckles as he clenched his hands, "Nicholas asked me to get him details of his financial situation. They were both bidding for a site in the city centre. He used this information to discredit the developer and win the tender. The unfortunate thing was that I was found out. I was fired on the spot, asked to clear my desk, and escorted off the premises."

"Why on earth did you agree to do such a thing?" said Claire incredulously.

"Nicholas threatened to withdraw the allowance he was giving me if I didn't. You see, when I was twenty-one he agreed to go guarantor for a mortgage on my apartment in Ballsbridge. He gave me the deposit and an allowance to cover the repayments. As a junior bank official, I wasn't earning very much. I'm not excusing what I did. I didn't want to do it at first – I knew it was wrong. But he persuaded me that it wasn't that big a deal, that this sort of thing went on all the time, and that I needed to toughen up. He made it seem like such an inconsequential thing to do. But it turned into my worst nightmare. After being sacked from my job, I couldn't get a reference and couldn't get another job. So, Nicholas ended up giving me more money to keep me going. Dublin is a small place and word got around. After six months of failed job applications and endless job interviews where I was always rejected at the last minute, Nicholas suggested that I go back to college and retrain. Art history seemed a million miles away from the world of finance. The intention was that Nicholas would eventually buy an art gallery and we would run it together. It's always been a dream of his."

"Oh, Sam, it was a really foolish thing to have done. But I'm so sorry that you've had to endure those horrendous consequences."

"You don't despise me?"

"No, we can all make mistakes," she said kindly, although she felt herself draw back from him, shocked at his lack of judgement. "I do despise your uncle though," she continued valiantly.

"The less you have to do with him the better," he said.

Suddenly she was filled with suspicion. "What about the work on your mother's paintings?" she said. "Is there something else about that you're not telling me?"

Sam looked miserable. "Not really …"

"What? Tell me," she said apprehensively.

"Only that, as well as to build her artistic reputation, the intention is to find out if there is any incriminating documentation in her effects."

"Incriminating documentation?"

"Nicholas told me she was having affairs with several people, including him. I try not to think about it."

"Oh God!"

"There were also the circumstances surrounding how she died. That was never really resolved. He thought there might have been a suicide note, or letters that would shed some light on why she would end her life."

Claire got up and looked down at him, momentarily confused, trying to make sense of what he had just said.

"Why me, why not do it yourself, or get a private investigator?"

"Well, the cataloguing of her work was a genuine

attempt to create accurate records and sell the paintings for the best price. You know how provenance is everything. And Nicholas really needs the money. Earlier this year, one of his main investments ran into difficulties – the builder went bankrupt. The case, and Nicholas's funds, will be tied up in the courts for years. So he needs money badly to keep all of his other balls in the air."

"You didn't answer my question. *Why me?*"

Sam inhaled sharply. "Nicholas asked Professor Dillon for a student who was ..." he paused, then continued, "unlikely to ask any difficult questions."

"You mean someone not too bright."

"Sort of," said Sam miserably.

"Jesus Christ, what a bastard! I don't believe it – he chose me because he thought I was *thick*?"

"I didn't mean it like that, Claire."

"And me meeting you that day, at the dry cleaner's, was that set up? Did you go there deliberately knowing that I worked there?"

"Yes, I did. Professor Dillon told me – he had seen you through the window – he goes to the barber's next door." Then he added with a wry smile, "But I didn't think you would ruin my favourite shirt."

Claire threw the contents of her wineglass at him.

"You *bastard*! How could you? You are a weak, snivelling excuse for a man! All of this, all the time we have spent together – what was that? *More deception and lies!*" Tears were suddenly running down her cheeks.

"No, Claire, you don't understand – this is why I wanted to tell you. I think I'm in love with you."

"You *think!* You *think* you are in love with me! Can you not even make up your own mind up about that.

Take me home. *Now!*"

"Claire, be reasonable, we're three hours from Dublin, I have drunk a bottle of wine at least. I'm in no state to drive you anywhere."

"*Well, in that case you can sleep on the bloody couch!*"

With that she left the room, slamming the door, and stormed up the stairs.

After a restless night Claire got up the following morning with a pounding headache, showered and dressed. As she passed the living room, she saw Sam asleep on the couch. He was still fully clothed. Two empty wine bottles were on the low table beside him. She left the cottage and headed out along the road towards the lighthouse. It was a cold damp morning and the sea was relatively calm, lapping gently across the rocks to the side of the road. But it did not soothe her. Tears welled up in her eyes unchecked and rolled down her cheeks – there wasn't a soul around to notice – as she thought about what Sam had told her the previous evening. She passed the lighthouse with its distinctive thick black-and-white banding, and at the end of the road she sat on a concrete plinth that looked out across Waterford Bay towards Dunmore East.

She had been thinking about what had happened for most of the night as she had tossed and turned in a state between waking and sleeping. His confession had unnerved her. She knew instinctively that his actions demonstrated not only a lack of judgement, but they also breeched an ethical code of behaviour that undermined her previous respect for him. But it was the revelation that Professor Dillon thought so little of her, and the humiliation of knowing that Sam was complicit in this subterfuge, that had hurt her most – it had wounded her ego. God knew this was fragile at the best of times. But was this to be the end of the relationship? Her head told her it had to be, to get out of it now while she still could. But her heart pulled her in the opposite direction – she had not felt so loved and desirable for a long time. None of her relationships since she had left college had amounted to much. She hated the pub scene, had no interest in rugby, a social outlet for many of her friends. At least Sam was someone she could talk to, whose company she really enjoyed. The sex was good too. No, better than good. She loved the time they had spent together – he had melded seamlessly into her life. She suddenly realised how much she would miss him.

It's funny, she thought, as she considered Sam's story, how you look at life through eyes moulded by your own narrow experience. She had enjoyed an easy life, unremarkable, with a loving father and affectionate mother, but Sam's experience had been so different from hers. To lose your mother in such a dramatic way must have been so traumatic for a young boy. His father did not seem to have been much of a support either. Considering he had to depend on that psychopath Nicholas for emotional guidance, it was no wonder his judgement was clouded. He had at least told her the truth. That was something anyway.

When she finally returned, an hour or so later, Sam was up and showered. He proceeded to cook her a breakfast of bacon, eggs and sausages.

When she sat down at the table he said, "I'm so sorry, Claire."

She noticed he had purple shadows under his eyes and looked as if he hadn't slept that well either.

"If I could turn back the clock and start again, I would."

"Look, I don't want to talk about it anymore right now," she said with forbearance. "After breakfast let's look at the studio and see can we sort things out as quickly as possible. I think we should take some space in our relationship. Keep things purely professional between us for the time being."

"OK, if that's what you want. But, Claire, I need you to know that apart from all this stuff about my mother and the paintings, I really care about you."

She nodded sadly but didn't reply.

The studio at the back of the garden was the size of a double garage with a central roof light and a shuttered picture window front and back. The padlock on the door had rusted and Sam spent several minutes trying to open it. Inside, after he had opened the timber shutters, diffuse sunlight struggled to permeate through the filthy glass. In the middle of the floor stood an easel. On it was a painting of a view through an open door of an abandoned cottage criss-crossed with beams of light and fallen timber rafters. It was the brightest thing in the room.

Unlike the studio in Dublin, this space had not been cleaned in twenty years and there were cobwebs everywhere. Claire brushed them off her hair as she walked over to the window. She rubbed a circle on the glassy window with her rubber-gloved hand and caught a glimpse of a view that looked towards the cliff walk and out across the sea.

Canvases were stacked up against the wall and papers were strewn over the floor. A jam jar contained brushes that were stiff with paint. Whatever liquid it had once contained had long evaporated and crumpled tubes of oil paint were scattered on the work bench.

Claire looked through the stack of canvases and was excited by what she saw. Although their edges were black with dust, their faces had remained protected. One after another, she saw images of abandoned cottages where branches grew through tiny rooms, where veined tendrils of ivy grew embedded in patinated walls. One showed a broken stairwell leading to the open sky, the structures laid bare by the elements. The ruins were depicted as traces of the lives of those who had once lived there. The final canvas showed a rose growing outside a half rotten door, with windows open, glass long gone. Claire felt a shiver go down her spine. She could sense Sylvie in this studio, sense her spirit. Over the last few months of examining her work, understanding what moved her, what was important to her, she felt she knew Sylvie. But Claire had not felt this almost visceral connection with her in Dublin. If she reached out, in some sixth sense, she felt she could almost touch her. But what had happened to her here? How had Sylvie died? Surely an artist knew when their work was good, and this was exceptional – the best examples of her work that Claire had seen. Sylvie could not have killed herself, she had everything to live for. Claire would not give up on this project just yet. She owed it to Sam. No, she owed it to Sylvie.

They worked steadily through the day, going through the same process that they had in Sandymount, cleaning and dusting the room first, sorting out the various elements, painting materials, rubbish, artworks, papers. Until, exhausted and hungry, at four o'clock Sam suggested a late lunch in the Templars' Inn.

Claire's eyes adjusted as she walked into the darkened bar.

"What will you have?" asked Sam.

"I'll get it, it's my turn. Toasted cheese?"

"Fine."

She went up to the bar and ordered toasted cheese sandwiches and coffee for them both.

Three men sitting at the bar were staring at a television showing football, the sound blaring in the background.

"Visitor?" said the barman.

"Yes, sort of. I'm staying at Rose Cottage at Churchtown."

Ears pricking up, one of the men sitting at the bar turned to Claire.

"Seán," the barman said with mock formality, "this lady is staying in Rose Cottage."

"Ah, the place where the artist was murdered."

Claire paused, then said casually, "Murdered? I thought she drowned, committed suicide."

"I'll have another pint there, Liam," the man called Seán said to the barman, then turned to Claire. "Oh, that's what they said at the time. But there's them around here that know different."

"Really?" said Claire encouragingly.

"Well, Mikey Mac, a local fisherman, said he saw mysterious goings-on that night."

"Why didn't he go to the guards at the time?"

"Sure why would a man do that? Yeh'd end up in court. It'd cost yeh. Yeh wouldn't be able work fer months. I've seen it all on television. They'd cross-examine yeh about personal things, about yer money, and yer sex life. Sure, who in their sane mind would want to go through all of that? 'Don't get involved', is my motto. Mikey did the right thing. Isn't that right, Liam?" Seán then smiled and turned his back on Claire, indicating that their conversation was over.

"Liam, do you know where I could find Mikey Mac?" she asked.

"Why would you be interested, might I ask?"

"Well, that is her son over there." She nodded her head towards Sam.

"Oh," said Liam, taken aback. "That's different." He leant over to her. "You'll find Mikey Mac here religiously, every Saturday evening after six o'clock Mass."

Claire hadn't been able to maintain her frosty demeanour with Sam after that. She was intrigued. He, however, expressed concern. He had reservations about raking up the past. He told Claire that it had taken him years to come to terms with what had happened to him – issues that he had only recently begun to discuss with a counsellor.

"Look, Sam," she said, "you have told me in the past how much you would like to know what really happened to her. If you don't take this opportunity to find out how she died now, and go with it, you will regret it for the rest of your life."

Sam had, in the end, reluctantly agreed. He seemed more relieved that they had called a truce. But there was still a reserve between them, an unfailing politeness to one another. Also, Sam was still sleeping on the couch.

By the time Saturday came around they had tidied the studio, cleared all the rubbish and sorted through the paperwork. They had found nothing of note to throw any light on Sylvie's death, or Sam's grandfather's paintings. No diaries, or letters worth mentioning. They felt that they had done all they could in Rose Cottage. The canvases had been cleaned and wrapped in paper and were stacked ready to go back to Dublin.

At seven o'clock that evening the Templar's Inn was heaving. Claire eventually got through the throng at the bar.

"Liam, a pint of Guinness and a glass of white wine, if you please. Any sight of Mikey Mac?"

"No, and he's usually here by now. Unusual that he didn't turn up." He grinned. "Maybe someone tipped him off you were looking for him."

"But I only wanted to ask him a few questions."

"Very private, is Mikey Mac, wouldn't protrude on anyone."

"Intrude," said Claire, correcting him automatically.

"Exactly," said Liam then turned away to serve another customer.

It wasn't till nearly closing time that she got another chance to talk to the barman.

"Could you tell me where I could find Mikey Mac? Where he lives?"

"Somewhere in Slade village, I believe, in a caravan."

Mikey Mac's place was not hard to find. The caravan was tucked into the walls of a ruined outhouse in the courtyard behind the old castle, a crumbling Norman edifice that guarded the harbour in the picturesque fishing village.

When Sam and Claire arrived, the old man was sitting outside on an old metal office chair, mending a fishing net. His face was lined and leathery from a lifetime's exposure to the elements. At first glance he could have been anywhere between seventy and eighty. But, by the way he held himself, Claire thought he was probably nearer seventy.

"Sorry to bother you but are you Mikey Mac?" she asked politely.

"I am, missus, and who might I ask are you?"

"My name is Claire Howard, and this is Sam Courtney. He is the son of the artist Sylvie Vasseur who was drowned in 1965. Her body was found washed up on Bannow Beach."

"That was a long time ago."

"Yes, seventeen years ago, to be precise. We believe you know something about what happened that night?"

"Bether off to let things lie. No point dragging up the past. Let her soul rest in peace."

"Well, that's it. Her son can't rest in peace. He never really knew what happened to his mother, why she would kill herself. It's tormented him for years. It would mean a great deal to him to understand the events of that evening." Claire looked at Sam who was looking miserable and not making eye contact, looking at the ground, saying nothing. She felt irritated with him – she was doing all the hard work here.

The old man took out a packet of John Player Blue cigarettes and lit up, taking a drag and inhaling deeply, followed by a deep phlegmy fit of coughing. He wiped the spittle off his mouth with the sleeve of his well-oiled woollen jumper.

"How do I know ye are not reporters, or plainclothes gardaí?"

"Do we look like reporters, or gardaí?" said Claire.

"I suppose not."

"But *are* ye?" he persisted. "Have ye got any identification? I mean, how do I know he's her son? He could be anyone."

"Sam, you have a driving licence, don't you? Show Mikey."

Sam showed the man his licence which Mikey examined carefully then folded and handed it back to him.

"Fair enough so, can't be too careful. I don't want to get involved, mind. I'll deny everything if ye go to the guards. I'll tell you so, missus, but *he* has to go away."

"Why do I have to go away?" said Sam, suddenly animated.

"So that there won't be a witness. It will be her word against mine."

"Why won't you tell me?"

"They won't believe her. She's a woman. A man's word carries more weight."

Claire's eyes widened in disbelief, but she did not rise to the bait and encouraged Sam to return to the cottage.

"Well?" she said when Sam was out of earshot.

Mikey dragged on the cigarette. "Well, that evening – if I remember rightly – and I do – I was walking along the road from the Hook past her cottage. She had arrived a week before. But she had been there before that. Tom Keogh was doin' the building alterations, putting in one of those modren showers in the bath. She was a fine woman, fair hair – yeh'd stop to look at her, and be the bether for it. Even as a child she was a pretty thing. We knew all about her. You see, she was from over in Knockaboy. She lived with the Bank Manager's family in Kilrothery, a miserable ould sod, if I might add. Anyways, she was forinn, French I think, but had come here as a child before the war and went to school in Knockaboy. Jewish, so I was told, but the parish priest soon knocked that out of her. So she was kind of a local. Before that night, I'd met her several times on the road and passed the time of day with her. I don't sleep that well. Probably years of staying awake fishing at night. Anyways, at about four thirty in the evening I heard shouting as I was passing the cottage. It was windy, about Force 4 or 5, but I could hear voices above the wind. Outside the cottage were three cars. A red Triumph sports car, a navy Ford Granada Estate and a light-blue Hillman Minx. The Minx was her car. Naturally, I was concerned that she was alright. A woman on her own. Around that time there had been a spate of robberies on holiday houses – knackers looking for televisions and record players. So, I hung around for a while, but the shouting stopped. Later that night, about two in the morning when I was on my rounds, I saw two men bundling a large roll of carpet into the back of the Granada. The way they were holding it was like it contained something heavy. I was intrigued and suspicious. I went back to my van, made a flask of tea and returned shortly afterwards to the cottage where I sat down on a stone wall out of sight and waited. They didn't return until a few hours later. One of them – and here is the queer thing – he was that man's double." Mikey pointed in the direction Sam had gone.

"Oh my God!" said Claire.

"Exactly," said Mikey. "That's why I'd rather talk to you. I didn't mean that about a womin's word. I was thinkin' on my feet."

"I see. Well, that has been really helpful, Mikey. She took a pound note out of her pocket. "Can I give you this to buy yourself a drink?"

"I don't drink, ma'am. Took the Pledge years ago. Not like some round here that I could mention. Although I go to the pub, for the company and the craic."

When she got back to the cottage Sam was waiting for her.

"I think you had better sit down," she said.

Sam's face was white. He sat down at the table.

"He said there was a navy Ford Granada Estate, a red Triumph sports car, and a light-blue Hillman Minx at the cottage that night. The Minx was hers. And he saw two men bundling something wrapped in a carpet into the back of the Ford Granada Estate and driving it away."

Sam looked at her in horror.

"One of the men looked very like you."

"My father drove a Ford Granada Estate, and Nicholas ... he drove a red Triumph sports car."

"So it was them."

Sam looked at her, his eyes dazed. "I know, Claire," he said, his voice sounding strangled. "I've always known. I was there."

Chapter 22

"Leo, my handsome boy. Two visits in six months. Am I dying and they haven't told me?"

"Grand-mère, don't be foolish, you will live to be a hundred. How are you?"

"You don't really want to know, do you? I'm alive, that is all that matters."

"You are looking remarkably well, Grand-mère."

She had on another elaborate costume in a dark-blue shiny material with her pearls, three strands of exquisite, perfectly matched stones she had worn since he was a boy. He looked around, noting that the sunroom was quiet this morning.

"The inmates are being entertained, they are doing activities," she told Leo scathingly.

Leo was afraid to enquire what these were.

"So, what is it that has brought you back to me so soon?" she asked.

"I wanted to ask you about something. I was looking through Grandfather's filing cabinets and I found Bonnard's sales records. They included the titles of the artworks, the sale price, and the names of the buyer and seller of works he sold during the 1940's."

"Oh, I thought he had burned all of that rubbish years ago," she said testily. "He was such a hoarder, Émile. I used to have to throw out his old clothes and get rid of them without telling him."

"The records were interesting, Grand-mère. I didn't realise that he had worked with the Nazis during the war, dealt with Rosenberg's agency, the ERR, to sell looted art."

The old woman froze. "I don't know what you are talking about. It was such a long time ago. Best forgotten. Now, I find I'm very tired all of a sudden. I must rest. You should go." She closed her eyes to sleep but her face was set with grim determination.

"Grand-mère," Leo persisted, his hand on her shoulder, "I don't want to upset you, I just wanted to talk to you about it, ask you a few questions."

"Go, Leo," she whispered.

He returned there the next morning. A friendly-faced young nurse called him aside as he passed reception.

"Your grandmother had a bad night last night. She was having nightmares – she was sobbing and in a very distressed state. We had to call the doctor to get her sedated. She is still upset this morning." The nurse paused, trying to find the right words. "She can be quite difficult at times, but last night was different."

When he entered the sunroom, he saw that she had not expected him to have stayed overnight. She was less elaborately dressed although still stylish in a twin-set and woollen skirt. Looking closely at her face, he could see that she displayed no physical signs of the previous night's distress. He grudgingly admired the feisty old woman.

"Leo, why on earth are you still here?"

"Grand-mère, I'm not leaving until you talk to me and answer my questions."

"I will call the nurse and tell them you are bullying me," she said petulantly.

He looked around anxiously, but the nurse had left the room. "They won't believe you. They complain to me that you bully them."

"Rubbish!"

"Please, Grand-mère, I need to know," he said, taking both of her heavily veined hands in his. "I'm afraid that if I'm not properly informed about what happened, then I will not be able to deal properly with enquiries that Sylvie's son is making in Ireland."

The old woman looked alarmed. "That girl was always trouble. Didn't I tell you? A brazen hussy even at eight years of age. They spoilt her dreadfully, you know, Paul and Hanna."

"Grand-mère. Tell me about Grand-père's involvement with the ERR."

The older woman closed her eyes briefly then reopened them with a defiant stare.

"Leo, it was all so long ago. They were different times. Young people don't realise. You are all soft, we have cosseted you, protected you. But back then, we couldn't afford to take the high moral ground. Life was all about surviving. Each day was about making it to the next. Paul was a fool. He had only himself to blame." She paused, her eyes locked onto some distant, invisible horizon. Then she said angrily, "I blame him for everything! He put us all at risk for his precious paintings. For what? Things – they were only things at the end of the day. People are more important than things. How is it women always know this, but men seldom do, until it's too late? Paul involved your grandfather and that odious little Irishman, Daniel, in his foolhardy plans. He made some sort of pact with them. Paul made copies of the Barbizon paintings. He left those in the gallery, and those were the paintings that the Nazis looted. However, experts from the ERR quickly realised what he had done. By that stage, the French police were working with the Gestapo, even in so-called Free France. They sent agents to Antibes to question Émile. Question?" She laughed bitterly. "My poor Émile, they took him to the Fort Carré for five days. They held him there, tortured him. When I eventually got him home, he had three broken ribs and his poor body was covered in cuts and cigarette burns. He told them everything. Of course he told them!" She looked angrily at Leo, daring him to protest.

He said nothing, his eyes encouraging her to continue.

"But your grandfather had to protect us: me, your father – who was only a little boy – and your aunts. They asked him to act as an adviser and to help them auction art they did not want, in order to 'buy' what Hitler considered acceptable German art. He was going to have the largest art collection in the world, you know, for a new art museum he was designing in Linz. He held no truck with modernist painters. Émile had no choice. He was one of several French auction houses that were forced to work with the Nazis. After the war these things weren't talked about, until eventually they were forgotten. Anyone with any sense burned their records. I cannot believe Émile, the old fool, kept his." She turned and looked beseechingly at Leo. "We all have painful memories of that time. All we wanted to do was forget. Everyone did what they had to do."

"So, what happened to Paul's paintings?" asked Leo gently.

"Émile told them about the older paintings, the ones they called the Barbizon paintings – they were in the store he had rented near the old market in Antibes. They were sent back to Paris, most of them. Your grandfather told me they were taken to the Jeu de Paume where the ESR stored the looted art."

"What about the paintings sent to Ireland. How did they arrive back in Paris?"

"Well, that was a whole other story. Let me tell you …"

By the time Leo got back to his apartment in St-Germain-des-Prés it was after midnight. He had been on the road for nine hours apart from a brief stop pitstop in Lyon. During the drive he mulled over what his grandmother had told him. He had gone through various emotional stages. Anger at his grandfather for living a lie – particularly when he remembered the cold and distant old man, wearing his medals with pride on Remembrance Day. Eventually he rationalised that he probably had no choice – his collaboration was the only way to save his family. But living the lie was harder to forgive. He wondered had his father, Felix, known any of this but decided this was unlikely. Leo thought affectionately how he was cut from a different cloth and cried at the least emotional provocation: babies, weepy films, would all set him off.

So now it was up to him, he would have to tell his sister of course, but at least his aunts Thérèse and Marguerite had passed away and their children did not carry the family name. But not tonight – he needed to sleep.

The following morning, Saturday, he was woken up by the persistent sound of his bell ringing. He unwound the bedsheets which were twisted around him after a night spent tossing and turning and got out of his bed. It was only 9.00am, he thought angrily. Dressed in boxer shorts, he gingerly stepped out of the balcony window and looked down at the street below to see Nathalie bearing what was probably a bag of croissants from the local bakery.

He released the door to let her in and seconds later she came bounding into the apartment. She was wearing a tracksuit and runners – with a turban thing on her head.

"Nathalie, delightful though it is to see you, it's very early. As you can see, I am not even up yet," he said as she headed for the kitchen and started rooting in his cupboards for plates. "Make yourself at home, why don't you?"

"I was dying to know how you got on with Grand-mère. Your receptionist told me when I rang looking for you yesterday. Did you tell her?"

"Tell her what?" he asked, alarmed.

"About Georges, your new boyfriend."

"No," he said, breathing a sigh of relief. "It wasn't the right time."

"I bet she knows – she's not stupid."

"But she's always asking me when am I going to get married, start a family."

"Oh, she's just winding you up." Nathalie frowned. "If you didn't go about that, then why did you go?"

"Sit down, Nathalie."

"Oh God, is she dying?"

"Yes, but not any time soon unfortunately. I think she'll be around for a few more years, at least." He smiled sardonically. "I found something in Grand-père's files in your apartment, and I wanted to ask her about it."

"What?"

"I wanted to ask her about Grand-père's involvement with the Vasseur's art collection."

"And?"

"What she told me came as a bit of a shock."

"Oh."

"It seems Grand-père was tortured by the Nazis during the occupation. He was forced to help them sell looted-art, mainly owned by Jews, in order to fund Hitler's art acquisition programme."

"My God!"

"That's not all. Knowing this also lands me in a moral dilemma. Do I own up to my grandfather's involvement to Paul Vasseur's grandson?"

"The Irish guy that was over with the art historian?"

"Yes, Sam Courtney. Grand-mère will be devastated if I sully the family name. She strongly advised me to let sleeping dogs lie. But it seems that Sam's mother, an artist who drowned tragically about twenty years ago, approached Grand-père before she died about her father's art and he fobbed her off, saying that the paintings had been destroyed."

Nathalie was as white as a sheet. "And they weren't?"

"No, Grand-père sold some of them for the Nazis."

Nathalie pulled her knees up and wrapped her arms around them – she looked like a frightened child. After a brief pause, she said, "For God's sake, Leo, if you tell anyone it will be in all the papers, on television even! The humiliation of it! People will despise us. Think of how it will affect us both. Look, Leo, everyone has skeletons in their cupboards from the war. Most people, even our respected politicians, rewrote history to suit themselves. Revisionist history, they called it in college. Grand-mère is right, you cannot undo what has happened. Nor should you feel responsible for Grand-père's actions."

"Well, the dilemma is more complicated than that. I learnt other things from Grand-mère about that family. She seems to think that the artist was murdered. In fact, from what Grand-père told her, she's sure of it. It seems that Sylvie had discovered facts that would implicate her uncle in the sale of her father's modern paintings."

"And Daniel killed her?" said Nathalie incredulously.

"No, he was dead at that stage, but his son Nicholas visited Grand-père in Paris just before she died. And Grand-père, who as I remember was a tough customer himself, thought Nicholas was a heartless bastard, capable of anything. To be honest, I didn't like Sam that much either – there was something about him that didn't add up. And because of this I'm afraid that young art historian, Claire, may be in very grave danger."

Chapter 23

Rose Cottage, Wexford
August 1982

"You were there," she said in disbelief. Sam got up from the couch where he had been sitting and stood up at the fireplace. He picked up a fossil from the mantelshelf and examined it closely. Claire's eyes did not leave his face.

"I had gone out fishing that day with Joseph Mullen – it was a Saturday." Sam spoke slowly and softly, still not looking at her. "He was at school with me in Blackrock. His father was the local vet. He had an older brother Malachy and the three of us often used to spend the afternoon fishing, for pollock mostly. We would go out early in the morning and stay out all day. That night we were to camp on the Saltee Island with Malachy's dad. But at the last minute we had to call it off as the wind had picked up, and the sea was getting really rough. The waves were crashing against the boat – Malachy's dad just about got it back into Slade harbour. So, I got home early, unexpectedly, at about seven o'clock. As usual, I walked along the cliff path from Slade harbour and through the fields at the back of the house. As I approached the cottage, I saw my mum through the studio window – she had the light on. She always had the lights on when it was dull. I thought she was probably packing up for the day. She was smoking, looking at her painting. Then I saw her put the cigarette out and head to the house. I walked through the garden and towards the back door and I was surprised to hear my father's voice. He was shouting. So I stopped. I was afraid, I suppose. Those few months previously, they had been arguing constantly. I hid behind a bush and peeked through the living-room window. He had his arms around her, but she was trying to push him off. She was crying and he seemed to be rough with her. He started taking off his belt, and at this stage she was screaming and hitting him. Then suddenly, I heard a car pull up at the front. But they were both oblivious and didn't seem to hear. Maybe she had the radio on, or they were so intent on each other. Then I saw Nicholas in the room pulling my dad off my mum. Then himself and my dad started fighting. My dad seemed to have lost it – Nicholas's face was bleeding, and my dad was hammering away at him, even though he had stopped fighting back. My mum tried to pull my dad off Nicholas, but my dad lashed out and she fell against the wall and slid to the floor, leaving a trail of blood on the wall as she fell. She said something to my dad, and he went to her. Then Nicholas joined him. Then, my dad ran upstairs. Then ..." Sam sobbed and tears ran down his cheeks. His hands started to shake. He clasped them together and breathed in and out, slowly, attempting to calm himself.

After a few minutes he continued, as Claire sat transfixed with horror, staring at him.

"Then … Nicholas took a cushion from the couch and went over to my mum, and, and – he placed it over her face. Her legs and arms were kicking wildly. But after a few minutes she stopped kicking."

Claire, in shock, stood up and took him into her arms, holding him to her tightly.

"Oh my God! You poor boy!"

Sam took a deep breath, wiped his face with his hand and continued, "Then my dad came down the stairs, and I heard Nicholas shout, 'You killed her, Peter, you killed her!'"

"What did you do then?"

"I ran away. I ran through the garden, the field and back along the cliff walk to Slade harbour and I stayed there for hours. There are these ancient hollows carved into the old harbour walls where they used to keep salt. I hid there until about midnight, then I went back to the cottage. I needed to make sure that my mum was dead, that she wasn't just injured. I hoped that my dad and Nicholas would be gone, but they were still there. I went up to the window and looked in. Our carpet was rolled up in the middle of the floor. I didn't know then, but I figured out later that her body was in it. Anyway, it wasn't long before Nicholas noticed I was there. He dragged me into the house, asked me where the hell I had been and told me that there had been a terrible accident, that my father had killed my mother. But he was going to sort it all out. He was going to make it look like it was an accident and that she drowned. He told me to pack all my things and then to go to bed and to stay there until they returned. Then they left the house, carrying the roll of carpet, and put it in the boot of the car and drove off. When they returned an hour or so later with the limp roll of carpet, we drove straight back to Dublin. They didn't find the body till a fortnight later when it was washed up on Bannow Bay."

"But did no one notice that you were both missing, what about your friends? Did they not wonder where you'd gone?"

"Well, I phoned them the next day and said I'd gone home with my father. When the police eventually got involved, I was kept out of the papers, me being a minor. Nicholas insisted on it. The story they told was that Peter came down to take me back to Dublin – their relationship was going through a rocky patch and they were arguing a lot, but he had missed me. He wanted to spend some time with me. He said he had argued with Sylvie when he arrived. She didn't want me to go, but in the end reluctantly agreed. It's ironic really – the truth was she would have been delighted to be rid of me so that she could bloody-well paint in peace. Anyway, then they said Peter had left Wexford at eight o'clock taking me with him. He also told them that she had been drinking alone and was planning to go for a midnight swim. I was made say to the guards that she often did this – and to say that she had been drinking a lot that evening."

"And was any of that true?"

"Well, she would sometimes go for a swim in Dollar Bay in the evening. And she did take a glass or two of wine. But she never drank so much that she was falling about, or that I noticed."

"Didn't the guards see the blood marks on the wall?"

"No, Nicholas had done a good job cleaning up. He

used bleach everywhere and took any blood-stained objects back to Dublin, where he burned them presumably. I was also told to tell them that she was crying all the time. The guards assumed she was depressed. Eventually, they lost interest and assumed it was either a tragic accident, or a suicide."

"Why did you lie to the police? Surely you knew this was wrong?"

"I was only fourteen, Claire! Nicholas had told me that my father had murdered my mother. I was terrified I was going to lose him as well."

"But you saw Nicholas smothering her!"

"Yes, and I told him so, but he claimed I was mistaken, that she was already dead at that stage. I couldn't take it all in – that he would do such a thing. And then I was afraid of him, afraid of what he might do to me – to my father. It was easier to say nothing. Looking back now, I think that at the time I was traumatised."

"Why would he have wanted to kill her?"

"God only knows. Maybe it did have something to do with her father's missing art collection, and that she had found out he was implicated in some way. It's really the only plausible explanation."

"What about the fact that he had an affair with her? Maybe he didn't want his wife to find out."

"No, Evelyn had found out at that stage, she had already thrown him out."

"Did you ever have it out with your father ?"

"He never mentioned it. It was as if it never happened. I tried to talk to him afterwards, but I was only a teenager. He refused to engage with me, and I didn't have the heart, or the skills, to challenge him. He was a broken man at that stage, drinking, gambling. He never got over it – her death and how it happened killed him in the end. But what I feel bad about is that I didn't get the opportunity to tell him before he died that he wasn't the one who killed her."

Sam blew his nose then got up and poured himself a glass of whiskey, bringing one over to Claire.

"And Nicholas, did he ever mention it again afterwards?"

"Well, a few years later when I started working in the bank, he took me away for a weekend to play golf in Puerto Banus. It was then he told me he was my biological father."

"My God! How did you react to that?"

I was shocked – disgusted to be honest – although I knew that they had an affair, I had caught them in the act when I was younger and had hated him after that. But he had looked after me after my father died, when I had no one except my grandmother and she needed looking after herself at that stage. He promised me I would be his heir. I knew he was a very wealthy man. Later, when I had too much to drink, I asked him about that night. He told me how Peter and himself had taken the body to Dollar Bay wrapped in the carpet, taken one of the fishermen's punts lying there, rowed out to the middle of the bay and dumped the body. You know the rest – it was found a fortnight later washed up on the beach."

"How was he when he told you this?"

"He was incredibly matter-of-fact. He said that he had to deal with my father's mess because he was in no fit state to do so himself."

285

"Were the guards not suspicious when they saw that Nicholas's face was pummelled by your father?"

"Well, the drama only kicked off when they found the body several weeks later. By the time they identified her, and got to Nicholas, his skin had healed sufficiently to pass off whatever scars he had as the results of a fall while he was out hill walking. The beach was remote and very few people went there. A couple of dog walkers found her eventually. You see, Peter never actually reported the fact that she was missing. He said he thought she had gone off somewhere, possibly France. She had been talking about visiting her relatives there. This was corroborated by a friend of hers she had met the week before, Deirdre Mathews, if I remember rightly – another artist. She told the police that my mother had been talking about going to Paris."

"But the locals, surely they would have noticed she was missing?"

"Well, she was fairly new to the neighbourhood, and they were used to her coming and going, so it wouldn't have seemed strange to them. Obviously, as we have discovered, Mikey Mac did, but as you heard he wasn't getting involved. The locals had a strange relationship with the guards. I remember, at that time the Sergeant dealt out his own particular brand of punishment."

"But later, when you were older, did you never challenge Nicholas again?"

"I know it's hard for you to understand. But after my father died, I was dependent on him for everything. And as you can appreciate, he is a formidable character. I didn't have the guts to challenge him then, And now I am dependent on him more than ever."

"Sam, he is a murderer, a monster who has manipulated you all your life, as far as I can see, to suit his own ends. I don't know how you can bear to have anything to do with him after what he has done. You must end it." She sat back in the chair, looked around the living space and shivered. "To think that all of this happened here in this room. How can you even come back here?"

"As I said, it's the only place I feel close to her."

"Jesus, Sam. I don't know what to say."

They left early the next morning. Claire dozed for most of the journey, it was easier than talking. After what she had heard the night before, she needed some time to make sense of it all in her own mind and consider what to do next. Should she tell Leo what she had learned? To go to the police at this stage would be futile. They would be unlikely to take her seriously – it had all happened so long ago. But surely Nicholas should not be allowed to get away with murder? Sam was the innocent party in all of this. Despite the shock of what she had learned, she still felt loyalty towards him. But the main question was, why did Nicholas murder Sylvie? As Sam had suggested it must have been something to do with her father's art collection. It was the only motive she could think of. Sam had ruled out fear of his wife's reaction to his infidelity, and she suspected that public knowledge of his philandering was not a big deal for him anyway. Claire felt her pulse racing and those old, all too familiar, feelings of anxiety consume her. Her overriding instinct was that she should walk away – now. But it wasn't as simple as that.

When they finally reached Dublin, Sam dropped her off to her bedsit in Rathmines. The small, untidy space had never seemed so inviting. On the hall table was a letter from Leo. He was coming to Dublin the following week. He had news to tell them.

The next day, after a restless night's sleep, Claire was physically and mentally exhausted. She had dreamt that she was rolled up in a carpet, bundled into the boot of a car and, still conscious, dumped into the sea. She could feel the cold water filling her throat and nostrils. She woke up in terror, choking and gasping for breath, filled with angst that weighed heavily on her chest. Eventually, after consuming half a box of Bach Flower remedy pastilles, at two o'clock in the afternoon she steeled herself to phone Sam. She told him she had a kidney infection – she had just seen the doctor. She had known she was coming down with something in Wexford but with all that was going on she had hoped it would get better in a few days. It hadn't. The doctor told her to take a few days off work.

"Oh, that's too bad, Claire. Poor you! Will I come around and cheer you up?" Sam said sheepishly.

"No, it's OK. Thanks for the offer but I'm feeling really tired and I'm going to take to the bed with a Maeve Binchy novel and wallow in my misery." She tried to keep the tone light, though her hand was trembling as she held the receiver of the hall payphone. She felt guilty deceiving him in this way, but she needed time away from him to get her head around the incredible story he had told her and decide what she should do.

"OK, Claire, I'll ring you later and see how you are.

I found a box of Grandfather's correspondence in an outhouse at Knockaboy yesterday that I'm planning to go through – it should keep me busy for the next few days. We can agree next steps then. Any news from Leo?"

"Yes, sorry, there was a note from him when I got back last night, very mysterious. He will be over next week. He has news to tell us."

"Did he say any more? What kind of news – bad news, good news?"

"Sorry, Sam, that's all he said. We'll just have to wait. Anyway, now I should go, I'm about to collapse on my feet."

"Oh, sorry for rattling on. Look, you take care of yourself – I'll ring you later."

She replaced the receiver, then lifting it again she inserted more coins into the box and dialled her sister Molly's work number. When she finally came to the phone, Claire tried to sound cheerful.

"Can you come around this evening? I need some advice."

"Oh, what's up? I thought you were in a state of romantic euphoria with Golden Boy. Are things still OK there?"

"They were, but something has happened."

"Claire, you don't sound good. I can take a half day – we're not busy now, sales are slow – everyone is waiting to get paid at the end of the month."

"Could you, Molly?" she answered weakly.

"I'll be there in an hour. Put the kettle on."

Claire put the phone down and climbed up the stairs to her bedsit. Once inside the door she bent over double as racking sobs consumed her. She bawled her eyes out for several minutes until, drained, she fell back on the sofa. The strain she been under for the last few days had finally taken its toll.

By the time Molly arrived an hour later, Claire had washed her face, and her eyes didn't look quite so swollen. She didn't want her sister to see the state she was in. However, her attempts were in vain.

"God, you look awful, Claire," Molly said as she greeted her with a hug.

Her sister in contrast was immaculately dressed as usual in a short black fitted dress with patent-leather court shoes, her face an alabaster mask of carefully applied cosmetics.

Despite the fact it was mid-afternoon, Claire was still in pyjamas and a velour dressing gown that had seen better days. She made tea, produced biscuits and proceeded to tell Molly the story that Sam had told her.

"Jesus, Claire, this is serious shit! Nicholas sounds like a psychopath. And a dangerous one at that. Imagine killing his ex-lover and then blaming it on his brother! Sounds like something you would read by Agatha Christie. And Sam, God, he was only a kid – how would you ever get over that?"

"Well, that's just it. I don't think he has. Got over it, I mean."

"Why didn't he just go to the police as soon as he was mature enough to realise the enormity of what his uncle had done?"

"It's more complicated than that. You see, he is totally dependent on him for his income – always has been. Nicholas pays his mortgage and gives him an allowance while he is at college. And then there is also the fact that he is his biological father."

"So! He could always sell the apartment and get a job."

"I don't think it's that easy for him."

"No, Claire, I'm afraid it really is that easy," Molly said emphatically. "Otherwise he is complicit in what Nicholas has done. And you, Claire, what are you going to do? Surely you can't continue with the commission?"

Claire looked miserable. She lifted pleading eyes to her sister.

"That's what I'm agonising over."

"Claire, you can't be serious. This is a no-brainer. You're dealing with a psycho – a *murder* has been committed."

"Well, yes, but it was a long time ago."

"It doesn't –"

"Listen, Molly, this commission is important to me. The money, together with what I inherited from Gran, would enable me to put down a deposit on an apartment. This is not going to happen otherwise. And, maybe more importantly, this project will give me street-cred in art history, help me establish a career as an independent researcher. I'm unlikely ever to be handed an opportunity like this again. To throw it all away, so close to finishing, would be foolish."

Molly, still dubious, asked, "What about Golden Boy – will you still see him?"

"Well, only in a work capacity. I'm sorry for him – he's had a tragic life. But I don't want to share his burdens. I don't have the bandwidth. Anyway, I don't love him anymore. He is just not the person I thought he was. But I'm still fond of him. Hopefully, we can still be friends."

"Jesus, you're an awful gobshite, Claire – even though you were always the clever one you have no sense at all. He's been playing you from the beginning from what I can see."

"I don't think so. He's just emotionally damaged, and it's hardly surprising. It's a pity – he's such a sweet man. Look, Molly, it's been a big help to talk this through. You're right, I'm a gobshite, but I'm going to trust my instincts. I'll finish the inventory and the catalogue of Sylvie Vasseur's works, get paid, and once the job is finished, cool my friendship with Sam – gradually."

"What about the other guy, the French fellah?"

"Oh, Leo. He's coming over next week. He has news about the missing art collection I told you about."

"*Mm*, does it matter anymore, after what you have learnt?"

"Well, yes, it does. If any of the paintings were found it would be news, international news. Again, it would be great for my career. But that's not all – I feel that I owe it to Sylvie Vasseur to finish the story, her story. It's like the final piece of the jigsaw."

"Claire, you are taking a huge risk being involved with any of them. I hope it's worth it. Are you sure you don't want a job in Arnotts? The pay is good, and make-up is uncomplicated. Everyone needs it, and it makes you feel good making other people feel better about themselves."

"You are right, as always, Molly. Sometimes I think that the world of academia has the opposite effect – everyone is conditioned to feel insecure. But the bottom line is, without this commission, despite all the years studying, I will be back with the likes of Stefan, in my Jackson Pollocked shoes, pressing shirts for lazy rich bitches, for the rest of my working days."

Chapter 24

Dublin
August 1982

The following week, he was waiting for her in Jonathan's café on Grafton Street. Nathalie had told him he was mad to get involved. He must be, he thought, as he sipped his coffee. But the girl had struck some chord in him. She had an innocence, a sincerity about her, unlike his stylish Parisian female friends with their red lipstick and Hermes scarves. But, more importantly, he couldn't risk anything happening to her because of his inaction. He could never live with himself. If he did nothing – he would be as bad as his grandfather. He saw her approaching his table.

"Claire, how good to see you again."

She was wearing a white cotton gypsy top and a blue floral maxi skirt.

He jumped up and kissed her on both cheeks. "*Ça va?*"

"*Bien, merci.* What brings you to Dublin? Did you find anything in the library?"

"Do you think you could ask me one question at a time, Claire?"

"Sorry. But your letter sounded so mysterious."

"Well, I wanted to talk to you before I talk to Sam. I just wanted to run a few things past you – as the expert."

"Yes, of course, no problem."

"I don't know where to begin," he said, twiddling a gold ring on his left hand.

"Your ring, should I be congratulating you?" she said enthusiastically, although he thought she seemed a little bit disappointed.

"Yes, my partner and I exchanged vows. It was a big step for me. He's a guy I have known for a long time. But it's complicated."

"Oh," said Claire, shocked, but recovered her composure quickly.

He thought she had probably met gay men before, but he also knew it was uncommon for men to openly admit their homosexuality in holy Catholic Ireland.

"Well, I'm really pleased for you," she said sincerely.

"Thank you." He paused, carefully deciding what to say next. "Claire, I think you need to be extremely careful. I know this sounds a little crazy. But I think that Nicholas may have been involved in the death of Sam's mother because she discovered that he and Daniel had sold her father's paintings."

"That is quite a serious accusation," she said, also choosing her words carefully. Although he knew she liked him, trusted him even, he was still virtually a stranger to her. "But ..." She hesitated. "When we were down in Wexford last week, Sam and I met a local man who witnessed strange comings and goings at the cottage on the night Sylvie died. At the time he didn't want to get involved and avoided the Garda investigation. It seems he saw what looked like Peter and Nicholas bundling a roll of carpet that could have contained a body, into the boot of Peter's car and driving off."

"*C'est incroyable!* Who would believe they could be so cold-blooded? So, she probably was murdered after all." Once he had assimilated the shock, he looked at Claire. "Are you all right?" He took her hand in his. She nodded briefly, but he saw she was looking pale.

Self-consciously, she pulled her hand away and took out a packet of cigarettes and offered him one. He shook his head. Lighting the cigarette, she inhaled deeply. He noticed her fingers were stained yellow.

"I thought you had given up?"

"I had until last week. It's a lot to take in. Still it helps having someone to share all this with."

"Look, Claire, I'm really worried about you. This whole situation is becoming increasingly disturbing."

"I know."

He looked at his watch. "Sorry, Claire. I have to meet an old friend of mine shortly, another architect as it happens. I promised to have dinner with himself and his wife later. Will you promise me to stay away from that bastard Nicholas Courtney until we meet again? At least until I have worked out what's best to do."

Claire nodded. "Don't worry, I've been giving him a wide berth since last week."

"We can catch up tomorrow sometime. I'm in Dublin for the next few days and we need to talk more about all of this. I have documents to show you that indicate Daniel did indeed sell Sylvie's father's paintings. I'm afraid my own father was also involved. But before I talk to you and Sam, there are a few things that I need to clarify. Can I ask you not to say anything to Sam until I have made these enquiries?"

Claire hesitated. "If you think it's important that I don't."

"Yes, I do, Claire. So, see you tomorrow?"

"That would be great, Leo. Unfortunately, I promised I would drive down to Knockaboy at the crack of dawn with Sam tomorrow – but I'll be back by mid-afternoon and we could meet up for a drink somewhere. I'd invite you to dinner, but I'm afraid my bedsit would offend your sensibilities. It's the opposite of minimalist."

"I cannot believe that, Claire," he said, rolling his eyes in irony. "But I understand."

"Look, here is my telephone number," said Claire. "It's a pay phone in the hall. Someone will usually take a message."

"*A bientot.*" He kissed her on both cheeks. "See you tomorrow, my friend."

Leo's next appointment was in a first-floor café just around the corner on Nassau Street, overlooking the playing fields of Trinity College. He had met David Laffan in the Architecture Association in London where both had studied for one term as part of an international exchange programme. David, like Leo, was dressed all in black. But, unlike Leo's pristine style, David – dressed in oversized woolly jumper and corduroy trousers – looked like he had just got out of bed and, in fairness, thought Leo, he probably had.

"Good to see you, *mon ami*, but what have you done to this beautiful city? All I see around me is brutal commercialism and pastiche Georgian facades. Have your planners no understanding of modern architecture?"

"They are all Philistines with geography degrees, I'm afraid, Leo. So, what brings you to Sleepy Hollow?"

"Intrigue, my friend – family business to sort out. I was hoping you could help me. I remember you telling me that you went to Blackrock College. I was trying to find out about a student who was there around the same time as you – Sam Courtney."

"Courtney? Yes, I knew him – well, of him. He was a year above me and a bit of a legend. He was known by everyone as 'Jane'. Short for Janus the two-faced God, mainly because of his vicious temper, and also because he was so good-looking and at that time we thought he was queer. Turns out he is not," said David, smiling at his friend.

"Really," said Leo, not amused.

"Sorry, Leo, we are not as – cosmopolitan as you lot."

"Tell me more," said Leo. There was no point taking offence, he knew none was meant.

"He was a proper weirdo. He used to boast that as a child he killed animals for his mother. She was an artist. Seem to remember she drowned tragically. Maybe that was what had him the way he was. Anyway, he would tell her the dead animals were roadkill and the two of them used to sketch them. Weird, huh? Afterwards, he left them to decompose and then collected their skeletons. He had quite a collection that he kept in a battered leather suitcase under his bed. He also got involved in a couple of particularly nasty fights. Most young fellahs will beat the bejaysus out of one another if sufficiently riled, but as soon as they floored the other guy they would back off. Or someone more sensible than them would pull them off. But not Jane, he just couldn't seem to stop – didn't seem to have an off-switch. One young fellah ended up having to have stitches. The teachers finally copped on to him when he killed Matron's cat – he put it in her underwear drawer. Ironically, the cat was called Lavender. He was caught in the act and expelled. His uncle pleaded with them to let him stay, even offered to pay for a new AstroTurf pitch. But the powers that be had decided at that stage his behaviour was unacceptable and were adamant that he had to go. He was a nasty piece of work alright, but on the other hand he could switch on the charm like a light bulb. Hence the name Janus. On the face of it, he seemed a gentle sort of chap, a good athlete and particularly good at rugby, as I remember. And of course, with those blue eyes and blonde hair he looked like butter wouldn't melt in his mouth."

Leo climbed the steps of the Victorian terraced house on Haddington Road an hour or so later. He winced at the choice of colour – the door was painted a luminous orange. As he rang the bell, he noticed a thin-faced woman cautiously looking out between the curtains of an adjacent casement window. When she finally decided to answer the door, Leo was faced with a small woman in her sixties with dyed red hair. She was skinny, wearing jeans and a white T-shirt studded with fake gemstones. After he had assured her that he was not selling life insurance or coloured televisions, but that he wished to consult the professor on an academic matter, she reluctantly let him in. Then she left him sitting in the hall on a rather uncomfortable baronial-style chair while she went to find her husband. As he waited, Leo examined the framed prints of various species of insects that filled the walls. A rather strange choice of artwork, he thought, for an art historian.

After several minutes had passed, the professor finally appeared, nervously straightening a thin leather tie that he appeared to have put on hastily.

"Monsieur Bonnard." The professor held out a large flabby hand in greeting. "You wish to speak to me."

After a brief appraisal, which Leo seemed to pass to the professor's satisfaction, he invited Leo up to his study.

Leo followed the older man up the staircase and into a first-floor room that looked out over a well-tended garden, a stand of apple trees visible in the distance. The somewhat untidy and musty room was lined with modern bookcases. Leo sat down as the professor fumbled in a half-hearted attempt to tidy away some of the papers strewn over the desktop.

"How did you find me?" the professor said abruptly, looking over half-glasses.

"It wasn't that difficult – I'm no Hercule Poirot," Leo said, amiably. "I used the telephone book."

"Ah, I see. Well, Monsieur Bonnard, your academic enquiry – how can I help you?"

"Not to beat about the bush, professor. I believe that you were an associate of my grandfather's, Émile Bonnard, and helped him with Paul Vasseur's collection of modern paintings."

The professor, his eyes like a startled rabbit's, pursed his lips and tried to appear puzzled.

"Sorry, I don't know what you are talking about."

"I have reason to believe that you wrote the provenance for their sale in 1952 at Bonnard's, my father's auction house."

"You cannot be serious?"

Leo opened his slim black leather briefcase.

"I have never been more serious in my life, professor. I have copies of the relevant documentation here endorsed by yourself. Obviously, these are totally fictitious – they vest ownership of the paintings with Daniel Courtney. Whereas I have documentary evidence that they were owned by Paul Vasseur. Here, this is a transfer of ownership signed between Paul and Daniel Courtney, on the 20th October 1941. Unfortunately, professor, if you had done your homework, and being a respected researcher even at that time – I think your first book had been published on early twentieth-century French art that year – a rather expensive-looking tome as I recall – you would have established that Paul's death occurred in Auschwitz on the 14th September 1941. Dead men cannot sign forms, I think you will agree. The Gestapo were always such meticulous record-keepers. Although I accept that these records may not have been readily available, even to distinguished scholars like yourself, until many years later."

The professor rose from his chair as if to grab the documents. But Leo was too quick for him and moved them out of reach.

"Needless to say, copies of these documents are with my lawyers in Paris."

"Jesus Christ, what do you want? Money? You have wasted your time – I have no money!" The professor put his hands over his eyes, sweat glistening on his forehead. "This will ruin me, destroy my career, a lifetime's work. I regret the day I ever got involved with that bloody family."

"Look, Professor, from what I can see, my father's involvement in this affair was not something I'm particularly proud of either. I'm not here to exact revenge. Nor have I any wish to drag my own family's name unnecessarily through the courts. However, Sam, as the main beneficiary to his grandfather's estate, may well feel differently. More importantly, I believe that Claire Howard is in danger."

"Claire? What has she to do with this?" said the professor, distracted momentarily from his misery.

"My grandmother believes that Sylvie Vasseur was murdered because she had discovered information that led her to believe that Daniel had sold her father's paintings."

"Her sudden death was a dreadful shock," said the professor in an agitated manner, "but Nicholas assured me that she had taken her own life. It did strike me as a little ... convenient. I'm ashamed to say that I didn't question what had happened at the time or interfere in any way. I had just got tenure in Trinity and I was afraid for my own family."

"You don't have children," Leo said coldly.

"Yes, but for my wife and myself."

"*Mm.*"

"You have no idea how intimidating Nicholas and your father could be, they were ruthless men. But murder, no. I didn't believe that he had murdered her. She was a difficult woman, a narcissist personality, I think they

301

would call it now. She lacked empathy, she was cold and heartless. Beautiful, of course. Her son is very like her."

"Sam."

"Yes."

"He is studying here with you in Trinity, I believe. He told me he got fed up with the world of finance."

"Well, it was more a case of the world of finance got fed up with him. His uncle made me take him. He couldn't get a job anywhere. Dublin is like a small town, you know, and people were genuinely shocked at what he had done."

"And what had he done?" asked Leo.

"Well," the professor shuffled awkwardly in his chair, "he was living in the Bank Manager's house in Mullingar, and he seduced his teenage daughter. He was fired immediately, of course. His uncle, Nicholas, had to make a substantial payment to the girl's father to keep it out of the courts."

Leo had arranged to meet Nicholas the next afternoon at five o'clock, in Hartigan's pub at the end of Leeson Street, near Nicholas's office. It was a real Irish pub with wood shavings on the floor, dark wooden bar furniture, and a ceiling yellowed with the patina of years of tobacco. Leo winced at the smell of stale beer and cigarettes as he entered. It was quiet enough, an hour or so before the lunchtime rush began in earnest. In one corner of the bar, two elderly gents were avidly watching a television showing yesterday's horse racing at the Curragh.

The barman nodded at Leo – he had asked him to let him know when Nicholas arrived. The prompt wasn't necessary. From his grandmother's description, he recognised him immediately. He sauntered through the door, dressed stylishly in a dark navy suit, blue-and-white pinstripe shirt and a yellow tie. Leo thought that the tie was a mistake.

Nicholas headed towards the bar, ordered a whiskey and then walked over to where Leo was sitting.

"Leo, I presume – you have quite the look of your grandfather."

"Thank you. I'll take that as a compliment."

"It's good to meet you. I was intrigued by the message you left at my office."

"I didn't want to alarm you, but I needed to talk to you about a family matter."

"Yours, or mine?"

"Both as it happens, but I won't waste any of your time unnecessarily. Claire Howard and your nephew Sam contacted me recently to enquire about Paul Vasseur's gallery and his art collection."

"Contacted you?" said Nicholas, surprised. "They wrote to you?"

"No, they visited me at the gallery in Paris. I use Vasseur's old gallery as an atelier. I'm an architect."

"I see."

"Well, I became interested myself," Leo chose his words carefully, "and in going through my grandfather's files I came across documents which suggested that some of the Vasseur paintings, known by my family as the 'Barbizon paintings', were sold by my father after they were requisitioned by the Nazis."

"Looted, you mean."

"Yes, looted," agreed Leo with resignation.

Nicholas's face was expressionless although Leo noted the pupils in his dark grey eyes had contracted.

"I also found documents from 1952 relating to Vasseur's modern paintings. These are provenance documents endorsed by Professor Dillon that I understand to be forged. They include the transfer of ownership of the artworks from Paul to your father Daniel Courtney."

"How extraordinary! But, do you know, I find all of this subterfuge hard to believe."

"Yes, I'm sure that you do. However, I believe that you were also involved in these, let's say, transactions."

Nicholas started to get up from the table. "I'm not sure where this is going, but I do not like what you are insinuating. In fact, it sounds downright libellous."

"Please sit down, Nicholas. You must believe me when I say I do not wish to drag up the past unnecessarily. Although it might not be possible, ultimately, to prevent that from happening. That depends very much on the next ten minutes and whether you are willing to cooperate with me. I'm concerned about the safety of Claire Howard."

"Claire? Why? Forgive me if I say you sound a little melodramatic."

"No, I don't think I am. Not from what I have heard today about your nephew. He has quite a reputation for a violent temper. I have just been talking to a colleague of mine who was at Blackrock College at the same time as Sam. He was telling me about him. How he came to leave the school."

Leo noted that he had had Nicholas's full attention, his eyes locked unwaveringly on Leo's.

"He's actually my son," Nicholas said, his mouth grim. Leo was momentarily taken aback.

"It's a long story," said Nicholas wearily.

"Another time, maybe. All I really want to know right now is, where is Claire? I have been trying to contact her for the last hour. She told me to ring her around four o'clock, she was to meet me later this evening, but she is still not home. She told me that she was going down to Knockaboy early this morning but expected to be back mid-afternoon."

"Yes, that's right, she has gone down with Sam to visit my mother. They are probably stuck in traffic. Or else they decided to stay overnight."

Leo leant over to Nicholas, lowering his voice. "My grandmother believes that Sylvie Vasseur was murdered."

"Now that is simply ridiculous."

"I thought so at first, that she was being histrionic. But then I met Claire yesterday and she told me she had met a witness from that night. A local man who saw unusual activity going on in the cottage, and now I'm inclined to think my grandmother was right."

"Well, why didn't he report it at the time?" said Nicholas dismissively.

"He had his reasons. But now he wants to set the record straight, do the right thing and go to the police." From what Claire had told him, Leo knew he was stretching the truth here. He watched Nicholas carefully. Confronting him like this was a gamble but, with Claire possibly in danger, time was not on his side.

"Does Sam know this?"

"Yes, I believe so."

The blood seemed to drain from Nicholas's face.

"It was so long ago," he said after a brief pause. "No one will want to know."

"I think you are wrong there, my friend," replied Leo. "Sylvie Vasseur's story has always been one that has excited public attention. 'Beautiful young artist drowns in tragic circumstances' was one of the headlines at the time. And I believe with her works about to come on the market that there would be huge public interest."

Nicholas rose again to go, his poker-face once more in place.

"I think it's time you told me the truth about what happened that night," said Leo gently, looking up at him.

"Or else?"

"Or else I'm going to the police to formally declare that Sylvie's murder was connected to the sale of her father's stolen art collection and Nazi looted art. I have already got a confession of sorts from Professor Dillon that should make them take me seriously. However, as you could imagine, he too is anxious to preserve his own reputation." Leo looked up at Nicholas. "My advice to you is to play ball with me. If I find Claire in one piece, then I will disappear into the sunset and no one will be any the wiser."

Nicholas sat back in the chair. There were beads of sweat on his forehead. "Why do you think that Claire is in trouble?"

"You tell me. But why don't you start by telling me what really happened that night?"

Nicholas picked up his glass and gulped down a mouthful of whiskey. He paused and then, cupping the glass in both hands and as if in a trance, slowly, carefully started to speak.

Nicholas explained about his affair with Sam's mother, and how at the end of that summer, after they had split up, he had heard from a mutual friend that she was planning to move back to France. He had been down visiting his mother in Knockaboy and she mentioned Sylvie was at the cottage.

"So I decided on the spur of the moment to drive over to the Hook to try to dissuade her from leaving."

"Why?" Leo asked.

"Because she was the only woman who ever kept me interested. She was beautiful, wilful, and intelligent – physically she was amazing." Nicholas looked defiantly at Leo. "I knew she was complicated, narcissistic even. But I could handle her. Also, she was taking my son away from me. When Peter told my ex-wife Evelyn about us, she left me to live in America with my young daughter, Sarah. She had a brother living in Chicago who she was close to. Initially I had agreed to it. It suited me at the time. There is no divorce here in Ireland, you know. But once she left, she refused to let me see my daughter – she broke off all contact. Sam became even more important to me then. I didn't want him living in France and also becoming a stranger to me. But that evening when I arrived, I was surprised to find Peter there. Peter, the idiot, was forcing himself on Sylvie – she was screaming at him to stop. I tried to pull him off, but Peter turned on me and started beating the shite out of me. Sylvie tried to push him away, but he lashed out at her as well, punching her directly in the face. She fell, hitting her head off the wall. Blood was coming out of her mouth and the back of her head. Peter froze, stunned. I remember screaming at him to tear up a sheet for bandages, to stop the bleeding. Eventually he pulled himself together and ran upstairs. It was then that I noticed the boy staring wild-eyed at the scene from the kitchen. As he saw me, he turned and ran out to the garden. I ran out after him and dragged him back to the house. I tried to reason with him. I told him not to be alarmed, that his mother was very sick, that there had been a terrible accident. That I needed to take her to the hospital in Wexford and that his father was ripping up sheets to make a compress to try to stop the bleeding. 'Will my dad go to prison?' the boy asked. 'Yes, if they find out,' I told him and said that he would have be very brave and help me. I asked him to stay there while I opened the car and started the engine. 'Will she tell them?' he had asked calmly. 'Will she tell the police – will he go to prison?' 'Possibly,' I said, without thinking, 'but let's just help your mother first before she bleeds to death.' I told him to get a cushion and put it under her head and I ran out the front door, but as I returned I saw him with the cream satin cushion pressed over her face. Sylvie's legs were kicking and he was saying something like, 'Sorry, Mummy, I really don't want to go to France. I want to stay here with Daddy.' I could hear muffled screams, and I could see she was digging her nails into his face drawing blood and her legs were flailing about. He was wincing with pain, but he held firm. He was only fourteen or so, but he was strong and fit from playing rugby, big for his age. He was a big ... beautiful child. I screamed at him to stop but by the time I got to her and pulled him off, her limbs had gone limp and the kicking stopped. Just then Peter come back down the stairs with the ripped sheets. Sam had already removed the bloody cushion, placing it carefully under her head. 'Daddy, don't worry, she's dead now.' 'Oh my God, I have killed her!' Peter cried. 'She cheated on you, Daddy," Sam said, glaring at me. 'She was planning to take me to France – I wanted to stay here ... with you.' Peter looked at Sam in horror, he froze at the enormity of the situation then threw himself at Sylvie and, stroking her bloodied hair out of her eyes, sobbed inconsolably. 'Oh, my darling, my darling, what have I done?' I decided on the spur of the moment to let Peter believe he had killed her. Animal instinct, I suppose. I was protecting my son. I was in shock – I could feel my pulse racing. But I needed to think. I could see my life before me, the life that I had worked so hard for draining down the tubes. I left the sobbing Peter and went into the kitchen, took a tea towel and mopped the blood from my face and hands. I opened the fridge and took out a bottle of wine and poured myself a glass to steady my nerves. Then I went out into the garden and sat down on the wooden bench at the back of the house, facing Sylvie's studio. You might think this was callous, but I needed to think carefully how to save my family, to save myself. It was a clear night, although wild and windy, and the moon was nearly full. I lit a cigarette and tried to work out what to do. I remember it as if it was yesterday. It was surreal. Beyond the cliffs, I could hear the roar of the sea, the sound of humming electricity wires overhead vibrating in the wind. And every few minutes, the rotating beam of the lighthouse illuminated the garden. I tried to process what had just happened. My son had murdered Sylvie and both he, Peter, and I would be implicated. I knew that those next few minutes were critical. To call the guards and say it was an accident was too risky, they would be able to tell in an autopsy that she had been smothered. No, we would have to get rid of the body. On either side of us were derelict cottages, crumbling stone walls inhabited only by ghosts. The nearest house, the Kennedys', was a good distance away, far enough not to be aware of the comings and goings of their neighbours. I smoked the cigarette and drank the wine slowly and eventually came up with a plan. After what seemed like an age, but was probably only a very short time, I went back into the cottage. At this stage Peter had stopped sobbing, and he was sitting on the floor, his back against the wall beside Sylvie's body, staring into the distance. Sam was sitting calmly beside him, his hand placed proprietorially on Peter's arm. 'Come on, brother,' I said to Peter, 'we don't have a lot of time. Listen to me, you've got to pull yourself together. We have to get rid of the body.' He threw me a look of withering contempt. 'Nicholas, how the fuck can you think of such a thing? We will have to call the guards – tell them it was an accident.' I told him that they would never believe him, his hands were covered in blood, and that Sylvie had the marks of his fist on her face. To scare him into action I told him that if he was convicted, and I had no doubt that he would be, I had seen cases like this before in the courts, he would get twenty years. Maybe, for good behaviour, they would let him out after fifteen which was still a long time, and what would Sam do while he was in prison? Who would look after him? I told him I wouldn't, that was for sure. He asked me was it true, what Sylvie had said, that I was Sam's father. I had to admit it. I told him I'd wanted to tell him for years, but Sylvie wouldn't hear of it. But I pointed out that I had nothing to do with Sam, that he had been his father from the start. The last thing I wanted was a dependent. I remember saying, 'Please don't confuse me with someone who gives a fuck about children'. I begged him to believe me – we didn't have much time. Sam, of course, was listening to all of this and had begun to cry hysterically. *'You're not my father! Peter is my father! I don't even like you!'* I think he even called me a pervert. In the panic of the moment, I had forgotten he was there. I begged Peter once more to trust me. But he persisted in being difficult. He said, 'Why should I trust you – you have never given me any reason to trust you before? Sometimes, I despair that we are related, that we came from the same gene pool.' I told him that right then he didn't have any other option. Then I searched the cupboards – I knew Sylvie would have Jameson somewhere. I found a bottle, opened the top, and prising Sylvie's mouth open, I poured the whiskey down her throat till it spilled out of her bloodied mouth. Then I made Peter drink some which seemed to calm him down. We waited till two in the morning when there was less chance of meeting anyone coming home from a night's drinking in the local pubs – although, licensing hours were largely ignored in that part of the country – the nearest Garda station was in Duncannon at least five miles away. My brother

311

eventually come to the realisation that he had no other option than to do as I suggested. I had told Sam to pack his things, then go to bed and stay there. With difficulty, we rolled the Indian rug that covered the stone floor around Sylvie's body which we then manhandled into the boot of Peter's car. There was no way it would fit into my sports car. We drove steadily up the long straight Hook road, passing Loftus Hall. At the next junction, we took the turn towards Fethard village and drove along the coast road until we reached an unmarked track. It led to a sandy beach where we had fished for mackerel as children from Uncle Daniel's small wooden boat. There were always a few punts tied up where the beach met the sea grass. Together we pulled the body from the boot of the car. We brought it down to the water's edge. It was hard going – I remember the wind whipped our jackets and trousers so that the fabric flapped around our arms and legs. The tide was just about to turn, and although waves lapped up on the beach, I could see white horses in the sea beyond the protection of the cove. We dragged a small wooden punt down towards the water's edge to Sylvie's body, and I started to unroll the carpet. At that point, Peter seemed to fall apart again. 'I can't bear to look at her like that.' Tears were running down his face. I told him to pull himself together and started to remove the cotton dress Sylvie was wearing. But he totally freaked out, he was hysterical. '*What the hell are you doing, leave her alone, you bastard!*' he shouted above the sound of the sea. He lunged at me and I had to fight him off, at the same time trying to explain that I was trying to make it look as if she had been going for a swim. Anyway, I managed to strip off her dress so that she was left in her bra and pants. Then we lifted the body into the punt, and I rowed out into the bay to the edge of the protected cove where the punt rose and fell in three-foot-high waves. Once we were caught by the current, I shouted to Peter, and we lifted the body and pushed it over the side. I remember Peter saying the Lord's Prayer repeatedly as we rowed back towards the beach."

Nicholas was expressionless, although Leo could see beads of sweat on his clammy forehead.

Nicholas took a gulp of his whiskey. "You must think I'm a monster, and I must admit that I can be a selfish bastard. But that night, I was protecting my brother and my son. You see, when Sam was born, at first he meant nothing to me. Children are all the same really, snivelling, snotty leeches. But he was such a beautiful boy. Sylvie was quite strict with him and he had good manners. And as he grew up, he was clever, amusing company when he chose to be, good at sport. To be honest, he wasn't interested in me at all. Or Sylvie, really. The only person he had any time for was Peter for some strange reason. Ironic really. He caught Sylvie and me having sex once, and he bitterly resented us both after that. But, despite this, I felt some bond with him. In fact, after Sylvie passed away, and then Peter, I had to take responsibility for him. I told him I was going to make him my heir and he began to see some advantages in me being his father. But, always, there was something not quite right about the boy. He was a bit odd. At first, I thought, well, he's probably just a chip off the old block, self-centred like me. But it was more than that, there was a cruelty there that even I found quite shocking. There was the time, he was about eight, when he deliberately ruined one of his mother's paintings in a jealous rage. She'd done a portrait of the daughter of a friend of hers who she was quite fond of, a pretty little thing. In a fit, he had slashed the almost finished canvas with a knife. From his mother's reaction, I knew he had done similar things before. She told me that he killed animals for sport and then collected them like trophies. When he was ten, I persuaded Sylvie to take him to see a psychologist in London who specialised in childhood behavioural problems. Dublin is such a small town, you know. He told her that he would probably grow out of these behaviours and that that they could relate to approaching puberty. But Sylvie knew at that stage that there was something seriously wrong with him. I think as he got older, stronger, she was actually a little bit afraid of him."

Nicholas sat back in the seat and lit a cigarette, inhaling deeply.

"Sorry, Leo, do you smoke?"

"Yes, thank you."

The two men sat smoking in uneasy silence. Leo was stunned by what he had just heard. Eventually he asked. "What about Claire, his relationship with her? Is he genuinely attached to her?"

"Well, he has not managed to maintain relationships for any length of time in the past. We needed an art historian, and their relationship meant that he had some control over her, I suppose. There is a resemblance to his mother, although Claire is a good deal heavier. I thought that was why he was attracted

314

to her."

"How come you chose her?"

"Well, I had asked the Professor to recommend someone who wouldn't pry too much into our family's private affairs. Someone who wasn't – how can I say – overly diligent, or curious. He recommended her, said she hadn't been able to get a job after she graduated and had ended up working in a dry cleaner's. I hadn't followed it up, but shortly afterwards Sam and I were at some public lecture in the Art History department and the Professor pointed her out to us. Sam sort of stalked her after that, and we decided to hire her to do the inventory of the studio."

"And now ... do you think he's serious about her?"

"Yes, I think he is serious about her, but not in the way you mean. He likes to own things."

"So, I was right to be worried about her safety."

"Well, I wouldn't have let her come to any harm. I would have called him off when the work was finished."

"How can you be so callous?"

"It is what it is, Leo – he's my son. I have to deal with him as best as I can."

Leo, feeling he was about to explode with anger, took another drag of his cigarette.

"So, what are they doing in Knockaboy?"

"Well, he found papers recently belonging to my father that suggest that the painting, *Girl on a Swing* is actually there, somewhere. Sam was beside himself with excitement. Unfortunately, my mother is suffering from mild dementia, so she's not much help in trying to locate it. I have been pretty much tied up with bankruptcy proceedings involving a property development I have an interest in. The case is in the courts now. I asked him to wait a few days and then I would go down and help him. But he wouldn't wait and insisted on going with Claire to see could he find it."

Leo stubbed out the cigarette in the ashtray. "We must go there now. From what you have told me she could be in real danger."

"We?"

"Yes, we, Nicholas. You are coming with me. I only hope I don't regret not going to the police immediately."

Chapter 25

Any vestige of hope that Claire had of rekindling their relationship had evaporated after Sam's disclosures in Wexford. She was shocked. She hoped, at least, they could continue to be friends.

However, since he had picked her up earlier at her flat in Rathmines she had felt uneasy. Sam seemed wired – with a pent-up energy she had not experienced before. Although, she thought to herself, even that was an improvement as since their time at Rose Cottage he had been withdrawn, morose even. But as they drove along the coast road towards Wexford, Claire felt her initial unwillingness to come on the trip dissolve. The early morning sun shed an effervescent light over the sparkling sea and, when she closed her eyes, she luxuriated in its warmth on her face.

She had suggested to Sam that they should postpone the trip and see Leo instead, go over recent events and give him a proper welcome to Dublin. Though she couldn't say so, she was of course anxious to learn what he had discovered in his father's ledgers. But Sam had insisted on going. He wanted to get to Knockaboy before Nicholas, to find *Girl on a Swing* first, or even clues to its whereabouts. He reminded her that it was the final part of the puzzle before they could finally close off the inventory.

"It would solve all of my problems," he told her. "I could pay off my debts and finally cut Nicholas out of my life. And then, maybe, maybe, we could start again."

Claire gave him a wan smile. "What makes you so sure that the painting is in Knockaboy?"

"Yesterday I found a letter to a French conservator in an old file that was in the box in the outhouse. Remember, the box I was telling you about. In it, Grandfather claimed that a painting he owned by Mateus had been damaged in transit from France and needed some minor repairs. Mateus often painted over old canvases. In this case it seems that the paint on the original painting was not of a good quality. Grandfather described a crack along the lower left-hand side. The conservator came to Knockaboy. There were receipts for his flights, the train journey to and from Wexford and his stay in the Royal Hotel in New Ross."

"That is strange. I wonder why Daniel didn't take the painting to Paris?"

"Well, people would have asked questions, wouldn't they? He would have had to produce a provenance."

"Probably."

The car was at a standstill, traffic was slow – a funeral cortege was blocking the main street in Gorey.

"Can I look at the photograph of the painting again?"

"Sure," said Sam. "It's in the file on the back seat."

Claire leafed amongst the old carbon copies of letters and found the black-and-white photograph of the painting – a young girl sitting on a swing dressed in a white lace dress set against a background of flowers and trees. It was typical of Mateus's work, she thought. The painting managed to capture the spirit of the girl, transfusing it with a primeval quality that almost brought her to life.

"The flattened imagery is so powerful." she said to Sam. "It reminds me of early Egyptian and Chinese art. It was as if they knew that to copy life in a realistic way failed to capture its essential spirit. But it was the Japanese who animated abstraction. Mateus seemed to really understand this, I think." She studied the face of the young girl and the unwavering way she looked directly at her, the viewer. Once more Claire felt a connection with Sylvie, that she couldn't quite explain. Maybe it was because she knew so many intimate details of her life and death. "Your mother looks so feisty!"

"She was no wallflower certainly. She was beautiful. Sometimes I wonder was that an advantage, or a disadvantage."

"Why do you say that?"

"Well, really beautiful women don't have to try so hard to empathise with others, to be liked. And sometimes don't ever develop those skills."

"I'm not sure that's fair. I know a lot of beautiful women who are also really nice people."

"Like you, Claire," he said with a smile.

"I wouldn't ever call myself beautiful, Sam."

He placed his hand on her thigh and rubbed the silky fabric of her skirt up her leg slightly.

Her senses tingled at the unexpected physical contact but she gently pushed his hand away.

319

"Sam, we agreed."

"Sorry," he said, staring at the road ahead of him. "You look quite like her, you know."

"Apart from the fact that we both have fair hair and blue eyes, I cannot see that much of a resemblance. She was at least a foot taller than me, and, I'd guess, several stone lighter."

"In my eyes, the resemblance is remarkable." He turned to smile gently at her.

Claire felt unsettled by the comment.

By the time they reached Knockaboy, Claire was tired. She had pretended to sleep for the last hour just to avoid talking to Sam. His intensity was annoying her.

"We are here," he said as they turned off the road onto a dirt track leading up to the house.

Claire had heard Sam talking about Knockaboy so often and had expected something a little grander. It was, however, a typical, rather unremarkable, Irish farmhouse.

As they parked on the granite chippings outside the house, a large black Labrador puppy bounded towards them. Sam had warned her about the dog that Nicholas got to keep his grandmother company.

As Claire got out, tentatively, the animal in his exuberance pinned her to the side of the car.

"Jasper, get down! You stupid mutt!" said Sam, pushing the dog away.

An older woman appeared at the front door, all smiles and arms open in welcome.

"Come in, dear, come in. Welcome to Knockaboy, you must be exhausted after your trip."

As they entered the kitchen, the Angelus bell was

sounding on the radio, marking midday. Sam's grandmother paused and crossed herself as she faced the picture of the Sacred Heart on the wall with its red perpetual light shining beneath it. Out of respect for the older woman, Claire and Sam performed the same ritual. When the bells finally finished, they sat down around the large wooden table which was covered in a plastic cloth of brightly coloured flowers.

"Daniel always said, a family that prays together, stays together. We shared a devotion to the Sacred Heart, you know," she said to Claire.

Sam's grandmother was not what Claire had imagined. She had pictured a more formal woman, neat and tidy, organised. Instead she was homely, well padded, and slightly unkempt. Her hair, once permed, was limp and although she had removed her housecoat as soon as they had arrived, the green crimplene dress underneath was spattered with food stains. She had made tea for them, a salad of ham and boiled eggs, with beetroot that bled into the pale green crinkly lamb's lettuce and had turned the edges of the eggs pink. This was followed by some homemade tea brack of a tough rubbery texture that Claire suspected was none too fresh.

When they had finished eating, the older woman turned to Claire.

"Sam tells me you are looking for a painting, Claire. How exciting! What does it look like?"

"Like this." Sam pulled out the photograph from the file to show his grandmother.

"Lovely, isn't it, my dear," she said, addressing Claire. "I love the flowers."

"Have you ever seen it, Gran?" Sam asked. "It's of

my mother as a young girl. It's by Mateus, the famous Portuguese artist."

His grandmother looked at it again carefully. "No, I can't say that I have. Your grandfather's paintings were mostly of geometric shapes and unrecognisable women," she said dismissively. "More tea, anyone?"

She then proceeded to tell Claire how Daniel had first become interested in art, and how he had regularly attended auctions in Dublin. Several times she asked Sam what Claire's name was, and Sam politely told her each time, as if for the first time.

When tea was finished and they had washed and dried the dishes, the old woman said, "My goodness, you poor things, you must be starving after your trip from Dublin. Sit down and let me make you some tea. Would you like a ham salad, and I have some lovely brack that I only made today?"

Claire looked beseechingly at Sam. She suspected that they were in for a long afternoon.

When Sam's grandmother left the kitchen to use the bathroom, Sam whispered, "Sorry about that – Gran's got even battier since I saw her last time."

He suggested that they start looking immediately for the painting. Claire agreed enthusiastically, anxious to get going.

"Have you any idea at all where he could have hidden it?" she asked.

"No, but it's about eighteen by twenty-four inches. There cannot be that many places in the house that you could hide something of that size. If it were anywhere obvious in the house Gran would have seen it. But because of all the alterations over the years there are a lot of nooks and crannies in the attic spaces. I think we should start up there."

They both changed into jeans before heading up to start the search. Sam, using a pole concealed in a nearby airing cupboard, pulled a hatch door down and a collapsible metal staircase gave them access to the roof space.

"Before this was fitted, about ten years, ago, only my grandfather and Nicholas ever came up here and they had to use a ladder. I was only up here once when I was about ten, I followed Nicholas, but he told me to go back downstairs immediately, insisting that it was dangerous."

When Claire got to the top of the steps, she stepped tentatively onto the floor which was covered with plywood panels loosely laid across the timber joists. The main attic space was head-height and felt hot, already warmed from the day's sun. Tiny shards of light shone through cracks in the slates and dirty, yellowed insulation hung down from the rafters. Outside she could hear the trees rustling in the wind and a horde of crows squawking, heading towards the woods at the back of the garden. But in the attic, it was quiet, with only the muffled sounds of the radio coming from below. Claire sneezed – a musty smell filled her nostrils. She could see a fine layer of dust on the old suitcases and boxes piled everywhere. Although, there was an order, all receptacles had been carefully marked: delft, old curtains and household bric-a-brac. Claire got the impression that no one had been up there for years. As she got her bearings, she could see that off the main space were smaller rooves, one over a side extension and one to the rear.

"We should be systematic about this," said Sam. "I'll start in the side extension, and you start here."

Claire was relieved, the side roof was lower and looked less negotiable.

Once they got started, she found it hot and dirty work. She rummaged through bags of bedsheets and old woollen blankets marked with brown stains from the damp and smelling of moth balls which made her queasy. She was also conscious of spiders and other creepy crawlies, never knowing what her fingers would find. She should have brought plastic gloves. Every so often Sam would shout in delight at some object he had discovered that reminded him of his past: his grandfather's ancient timber tennis racket in its original leather case – old stuffed toys belonging to his father as a child – a Waterford glass chandelier that used to hang in the hall. When he came across a box of old photographs, he placed them near the hatch and promised Claire they would look through them afterwards.

"*Jesus Christ!*" Claire screamed suddenly in fright, as she uncovered a glass display case containing a stuffed otter. Sam rushed to her side.

"This is the first animal I ever shot," he told her proudly.

Claire shivered. The flea-bitten animal's glass eyes seemed to stare back at her, malevolent and unforgiving.

They spent at least the next hour or so going through all the boxes and bags but found no sign of the painting. As time passed, Sam's earlier enthusiasm dimmed, and once more he became quiet and morose. Claire tried to concentrate on the task in hand, although her eyes were constantly drawn to the glass eyes of the otter. She was getting tired and her back was beginning to hurt. She was just about to suggest to Sam that they take a break when she heard the phone ringing downstairs.

A few minutes later they heard Sam's grandmother at the foot of the ladder.

"*Sam! It's Nicholas! He wants to talk to you!*"

"*Oh, tell him I'll ring him back!*" called Sam belligerently.

They heard her shuffling back down the stairs.

But the old woman returned a few minutes later. "*He says it's urgent!*"

"*For God's sake, tell him I'll ring him later!*"

"*We'll be down shortly, Mrs Courtney!*" Claire called down, surprised at the way Sam had shouted at his grandmother.

Five minutes later the phone rang again.

"*Claire, there is a man called Leo on the phone – he sounds foreign. He wants to speak to you – he says it's urgent!*" came from below the hatch.

"*Tell him Claire's busy!*" Sam shouted.

"No, I'll talk to him," said Claire. "It must be important if he has tracked me down here."

Sam grasped Claire's arm. "*Tell him you'll call him back later!*"

"Sam, you're hurting me!" she said, pulling her arm away, shocked to see his face contorted with anger and his eyes filled with rage. "I'll talk to him now!"

She crouched down to descend the ladder. But, unexpectedly, Sam pulled her back roughly with his full force, knocking her over. She toppled, losing her balance, and landed spread-eagled on her back across the floor.

He lunged on top of her, his knees on either side of her body, pinning her down.

"What is he to you, Claire, that French bastard?" he snarled. "Do you want him to fuck you? Is that it? You do know he's a queer!"

Claire's heart was pumping as she tried to push him off, but he was too strong for her. His eyes were bulging, and his lips were pulled tight across his teeth. He looked like he was having some kind of fit.

"*Sam, what the hell is wrong with you?*" she shouted. "*Let me go, for God's sake! Sam, you're scaring me!*"

"*Sam, what's going on up there?*" came his grandmother's voice. "*Is Claire all right?*"

"*She fell over, Gran, but she's alright! Go back to the phone and tell him she's not here!*" Sam shouted.

"*But I've already told him that she is, dear!*"

With that Sam, releasing her, banged the trap door shut. A feeling of cold terror engulfed her.

With difficulty she turned over and crawled towards the trapdoor on her hands and knees. She grasped at the handle and tried to pull it up.

"*Leave it, you bitch, leave it!*"

She sat back, cowering in terror, looking up at him.

"You have let me down, like all of the others." He ran his hands through his hair, his face filled with a look of desperation. "How is it that everyone lets me down in the end?"

His grandmother was calling below. "*Sam! Sam, what's going on up there?*"

"*How can you be so cruel?*" Sam hissed at Claire.

"What is it – am I not good enough for you?"

His face hovered menacingly over hers. She could almost taste the smell of the musky aftershave he used. She felt her throat constrict with fear.

His grandmother had fallen silent, no doubt gone back downstairs.

"No, Sam, no, I'm really fond of you but –"

"Fond? Who the fuck wants 'fond'. Don't you want me?" he asked pathetically.

"No, not like that. Look, Sam, let's go downstairs and talk about this."

"It's too late, Claire. It's too late for everything. This was my last chance, but the painting isn't here. That bastard Nicholas sold everything years ago. He sold my birthright, all my mother's paintings, the ones I should have inherited."

"You knew this all the time?" Claire said, astounded.

"Yes, of course I knew. He said I was going to get the money anyway – I was his heir. But he drip-fed money to me, *my money*. I want to make him pay for what he has done. But most of all, *Girl on a Swing*. I need to find her, my mother. She's valuable. I need to sell her."

"You're going to sell it?"

"Yes, of course I'm going to sell it! You think I care about her, another fair-haired bitch? Just like you, only interested in fucking around?"

"Sam, please, I want to go downstairs."

"Not possible. We have a job to finish."

Tears were running down her face. "Please, Sam, you just said yourself, it's not here, I want to go downstairs."

"That's tough, Claire. I'm fed up with your fucking teasing. I thought what we had was special, that we had a future together."

He dragged her over to an old chair and pushed her down on it. He pulled at a roll of coiled-up curtain rope and tied her hands behind her back to the chair. Then he bound her feet together, pulling the cords tight.

Looking around frantically, her eyes caught those of the otter and a cold chill ran down her spine.

"Sam, please, please, let me go. We can talk about this."

He slapped her across her face with the back of his hand. The force knocked her sideways, the room started to spin, and she tasted tears and blood on her lips. Her head was throbbing, and she felt a sharp pain in her battered face.

Sam grabbed a black bin bag full of old clothes and emptied them onto the floor. She watched in horror as he found a scarf and roughly tied it around her mouth between her teeth. The taste of the dusty material pushing back her tongue made her gag. He then left her and proceeded in a frenzy to check the contents of the lower attic to the rear, ripping open boxes and emptying bags.

Claire sat there, petrified. She tried to hear sounds of the old woman below, but all was quiet. But then she could smell burning, as smoke wafted up into the attic from below, faint at first, then the smell intensified and became stronger. She tried to scream but the binding contorted the sounds.

Sam looked around, distracted from what he was doing. He smelled it too.

"*Jesus Christ!* The crazy old bitch is burning the house down."

"*Sam, Sam!*" came a scream from below.

Sam rushed over to open the trapdoor and smoke billowed through the opening.

"*Jesus Christ!*" he said as he disappeared down the staircase, leaving Claire coughing and spluttering. The smoke caught the back of her throat as she watched it start to fill the space until she could no longer see anything. The last thing she remembered was the piercing glass eyes of the otter.

The journey had seemed endless to Leo, as Nicholas drove at speed to Wexford, on a road that seemed to pass through every village and town on the east coast of Ireland. By that stage, Leo had been really worried about Claire. After an amount of badgering, Nicholas had given him the phone number at Knockaboy and they had stopped several times at telephone boxes to try to ring the house. But each time there had been no reply and the phone rang out. In Enniscorthy, Nicholas had eventually got through to his mother, but the old woman was rambling. She had gone to call Sam and left him hanging on for ages. When she had returned to the phone, she told him some long-winded story about how she had shouted at Sam, but he was busy up in the attic – and how she was baking scones for their tea. A second call by Leo was equally unsuccessful. Eventually they gave up trying to get through.

It was after eight o'clock and starting to get dark when they finally got to Knockaboy. But as they approached from the main road, they noticed a plume of black smoke coming from the house.

"Jesus Christ, the house is on fire!" said Nicholas as he drove along the driveway, which was little more than a dirt track, at breakneck speed.

The car screeched to a halt as they reached the house, granite chips flying everywhere. Thick smoke was pouring out of the windows and an older woman was watching events unfold as Sam, wielding a garden hose, directed water into the kitchen while a black Labrador puppy ran howling around the garden.

"Where is Claire?" Leo shouted, jumping out of the car.

"It's the range, I don't know what the old bat was burning, old shoes probably." Sam had broken the glass in the kitchen window, and they could see smoke pouring out of the oven, but the flames seemed to be contained within it.

Nicholas grasped Sam by the neck from behind so that water sprayed everywhere.

"Where is she, you lunatic? Where is Claire?"

"She's in the attic, won't come down for her tea," said the old woman helpfully.

Nicholas let Sam go, and he and Leo raced into the house, pulling their jackets over their heads and followed by the dog.

Smoke was everywhere. The two men, coughing and spluttering, crawled on their hands and knees to the top of the stairs where they found the attic door open. Leo climbed up the metal staircase. He found Claire unconscious but still breathing. She was tied to a chair that had fallen to the floor. Hastily, he ungagged her, untied her hands and legs and lifted her to the hatch where Nicholas was waiting. The two men manoeuvred her through the opening and carried her down the steps and then down the main staircase. Although the house was still filled with smoke, at this stage the fire was extinguished and there was black sooty water everywhere. They helped Claire out into the garden and sat her on a kitchen chair in the middle of the lawn. Her face was covered with a mixture of dried blood and black smears, and she had an angry red welt down one cheek. Still unconscious, her breathing was laboured, interspersed with a racking cough, as she attempted to clear the smoke from her lungs.

"*Jesus, Mary and Joseph! Is she still alive?*" Nora was standing by, wringing her hands. "Do something, Nicholas! Sam, look what you've done!"

"I'll get her some water from the car," said Nicholas.

Sam looked on, an anxious and concerned expression on his face.

"Is she alright?" he asked.

"Let's hope so, for your bloody sake!" Leo said, looking up from smoothing the hair from Claire's forehead to glare at him.

As Leo gently wiped the blood and grime from her face with his handkerchief she started to revive.

"Leo, what on earth are you doing here?" she said faintly.

"I came to find you, my friend." He turned to Sam, furious. "You won't get away with this."

Nicholas returned with a bottle of water and held it to Claire's lips to sip.

"We should call the police, now!" Leo said. "If you don't, Nicholas, I will."

"No need to call the gardaí," said Nora. "What would the neighbours think? Why don't we all sit down and have a nice cup of tea. I've just baked a few scones."

"I'm so sorry, Claire, please don't let him call the police. I don't know what came over me. You mean everything to me." Sam was now down on his knees beside Claire, pushing his head into her lap. He lifted his head and tears spilled out of his pale-blue eyes. "It was as if demons possessed me. I'm so sorry."

Claire, saying nothing, looked desperately at Leo who moved towards the house.

"Wait, Leo, I'll go. I'll call the police," said Nicholas, glaring at Sam. "Maybe I should have done it years ago and avoided a lifetime's grief."

Nicholas walked into the house, leaving Sam looking around wildly like a hunted animal.

"Sorry, Claire," he said then turned and ran across the lawn towards the woods at the back of the house.

"Surprise, surprise, the phone isn't working, the line must be damaged," said Nicholas, returning, his face like thunder. He turned just in time to see Sam disappear into the trees. "*Leave him!*" he shouted as Leo started to go after him. "*He can't escape for ever!*"

Leo came back and Nicholas offered him a cigarette.

"After all of this, did you find the painting?" Nicholas asked Claire.

"No," she said weakly.

"Jasper," said Nora plaintively. "Where is Jasper? The old woman was looking around frantically for her dog.

Nicholas, hastily discarding his cigarette, turned and ran back into the house. He returned several minutes later carrying the lifeless animal.

"He's dead," he said woodenly then turned his back to them and walked to a cluster of bushes at the far side of the lawn. Nora followed him sobbing. Nicholas laid the animal down gently on the grass and put an arm around the distraught old woman.

In the distance they could hear the sirens coming along the road from New Ross. A neighbour must have phoned the fire brigade. A few minutes later a fire engine and Garda car screeched to a halt in front of the house.

"*Is everyone out?*" shouted a fireman.

"Yes, and the fire is out," replied Nicholas, rejoining the others.

The firemen jumped down from the vehicle and entered the house to inspect the damage.

The New Ross Sergeant and a young guard got out of the squad car and approached them.

Nicholas, leaving the group, strode over to meet them.

"Sergeant, I am so sorry to have put you and your men to such a lot of trouble. But, as you can see, the fire is extinguished. Sergeant Conroy, if I am not mistaken? I think we were at school together in Kilrothery."

"Courtney, yes, I remember," he said belligerently, obviously not impressed, taking his notebook from his pocket. "How did the fire start?"

"My mother, she's a bit distracted these days." Nicholas winked at the sergeant whose face, slab-like, continued to show no emotion. "Well, she left scones baking in the range, forgot about them. But we managed to get the fire under control, as you can see. Windows are broken – smoke damage – house is a mess

– but no one hurt, thank God. So there's really no need to –"

"And this young lady?" the sergeant interrupted, walking past Nicholas to Claire. He knelt down on one knee beside her. "Are you all right, miss? Do you need me to call a doctor?"

"No, Miss Howard is absolutely fine, Sergeant – she, Claire, got a bit of a fright, that's all," said Nicholas.

"Yes, sergeant, she should see a doctor," said Leo assertively.

"And you are?" asked the guard.

"Leo Bonnard, a friend of Claire's."

"Were you in the house?" the sergeant asked Claire.

"Yes, I was with Sam, we were in the attic …"

"Sam Courtney tied her up, restrained her. We got here just in time. She could have died," Leo said angrily.

"Sergeant, my friend here is also suffering from shock." Nicholas held his hands up, palms facing out, to the guard. Then he turned to Leo, hands still outstretched as if to calm him also. "My nephew Sam has, unfortunately, had some kind of breakdown, sergeant. You have just missed him – he ran off a few minutes ago. As you can see, Miss Howard is a little shaken, has a few cuts and bruises but otherwise she's fine."

"Miss Howard, do you wish to press charges?"

"No … no, I don't think so," said Claire uncertainly.

"Well, no, need to decide that now, miss. Restraining someone against their will is an extremely serious matter. Looks like he gave you a fair clatter as well."

Claire put her hand to her swollen cheek but said nothing.

"We will search the area and see can we find your

nephew, Mr Courtney – and I will also hold you personally responsible for making sure that everyone here comes to the station in the morning to make full statements. Then, and only then, will I decide if it's necessary to bring this any further. Meanwhile, you should take this young lady to Doctor Timmons in New Ross to check her out, and I will have a look around here." He turned to the young guard. "McEvoy, take their details."

Then he headed into the house where the fire officers were still examining the damage.

Afterwards, as Leo thought about the events of the afternoon, he realised no one had mentioned the painting. Nicholas had not specifically asked them not to. But they all understood that nothing would be gained in the short term by explaining the complicated history of events to the Wexford police.

After the gardaí left, Nicholas took Claire to the local doctor and gave him a sanitised version of the day's events. Fortunately, the doctor advised Claire her lungs would probably recover after a few days, and all she needed was bed rest after her ordeal. He also gave her sleeping tablets.

Nicholas had booked them all into the Royal Hotel in New Ross for the night and, as soon as they arrived, Nora and Claire immediately retired to their rooms. Nicholas arranged to have tea and sandwiches brought up to them later.

After dinner in his room and having rung his office to let them know he wouldn't be back for a few more days, Leo headed downstairs to the bar to meet Nicholas for a drink. Although the last thing he wanted to do was spend time with Nicholas, he had accepted his invitation, knowing that they had unfinished business

At that stage, it was quiet in the hotel. As he passed through the foyer, the receptionists giggled and whispered. Word must have spread on the local grapevine about the fire and Sam's escape, thought Leo. In the resident's lounge a couple of businessmen were drinking pints at the bar while a ginger-haired barman diligently emptied ashtrays. Nicholas was already there, sitting at a table near the window. He was looking out pensively over the quays of the River Barrow where fishermen were tying up their nets and stacking boxes after a long day out at sea. A scene that seemed incongruous to Leo in its tranquillity after the day's dramatic events.

"Leo, what can I get you?"

"A whiskey, I think, is in order," he replied.

Nicholas clicked his fingers at the young barman, who came over to them.

"Claire OK?" asked Nicholas after he had ordered Leo's drink.

"Yes, I just rang her room. She's exhausted – she's going to try and get some sleep. She'll see us at breakfast. Any word about Sam?"

"Yes, I have just come back from the guards. They picked him up outside New Ross, not long afterwards. They took him to the station. Sergeant Conroy rang me and said he was extremely agitated. Doctor Timmins had already examined him. He established Sam hadn't taken his medication for weeks."

"Medication?"

"Yes, he's on medication. Conroy let me see him after the doctor had finished. He was still in a state, despite the fact the doc had given him something to calm him down."

"Will they charge him?"

"Conroy says he'll keep him there overnight until he's interviewed us all. Even if Claire drops the charges, if he believes he has grounds Conroy will charge him. He always was a self-righteous little shit, even when he was a kid."

"I hope he does. Did you see what Sam did to Claire? I know he is your son, but the man is a bloody animal. He was completely out of control!"

"That is just it, Leo, he was not in control. The medication he takes – is supposed to take – helps manage his condition, avoids these kinds of aggressive incidents."

"And what exactly is his condition?" asked Leo coldly.

"He has a sociopathic personality disorder."

"Is that like a psychopath?"

"No, although the conditions are related. Both are characterised by a lack of empathy, but the actions of a psychopath are controlled, well thought through – those of sociopaths less so. They are prone to emotional outbursts, are deceitful and lie. They usually can't maintain relationships. They can form shallow attachments. But if they do, they tend to be fixated on only one, or two, people."

"And in Sam's case that was Claire."

"I am afraid so."

"You said in Dublin she reminded him of his mother, Sylvie."

"Apparently. As I said, I can't see it myself. But there you go. I called her 'the dumpling', just to piss Sam off."

Leo's mouth was set in a grim line, but he refused to rise to the bait. The man was impossible, he thought to himself.

"I have a friend, Karl, who I go hill walking with – he's a psychiatrist. Actually, he's Sam's psychiatrist. He explained to me that we all see people in unique ways, have different relationships with them."

"So what was Sam's relationship with his mother like?"

"Not good. She was damaged herself by the loss of her parents. She wasn't exactly the maternal type either. All those years ago, when she discovered she was pregnant, she didn't want the baby. I wanted her to get an abortion – we were both so young. However, she wouldn't agree to that – for her it was a step too far. Instead she married my brother Peter. The whole situation was extremely difficult for me. Obviously, my parents didn't know. They thought Peter was the father. But she soon realised that it had been a mistake and she struggled in those early years. And as she became obsessed with painting, there is no doubt Sam was neglected. She tried to make it up to him as he grew older, but it was too late. For Sam anyway. Cigarette?"

"Not just now. So why Claire?"

Nicholas lit up and, crossing his legs, he leant back in the chair. He looked once more out at the scene on the quays.

"Well, Karl suggested that Sam was looking for Claire to fulfil those emotions that were lacking from his mother. Although he would have left her eventually, he always did."

The apple doesn't fall far from the tree, Leo thought to himself.

"Is it inherited, this condition?"

"No – you're mixing that up with psychopathy. You are born a psychopath, but sociopathy is usually developed as a result of a trauma, in Sam's case feelings of abandonment."

"Condition, or no condition, Sam is a murderer," Leo said slowly. He could no longer contain himself as he clenched his fists on the table.

Nicholas looked coldly at Leo, his face a mask. "It happened a long time ago, Leo. Seventeen years to be exact. It was a passionate outburst, fear of losing his father probably pushing him over the edge. It was a once-off, and the act of a minor. Until today's incident, other than a few insignificant brawls, Sam's tendency towards aggression has been stabilised with medication. There is nothing to be gained by dragging up the past. Nothing. I would have thought that you of all people could see that."

"It is not your, or my, decision to make, Nicholas. But I intend to be honest with the guards when I speak to them tomorrow."

"What good would it serve? Even if there was a trial and that half-witted fisherman testified, a good defence barrister would make mincemeat of him. As I have already said, it was a long time ago, and other than this episode today Sam has led a harmless existence. I doubt very much that they could make anything stick, even considering today's events. All that would happen, Leo, is that we would both be forced to air our family's dirty linen – which wouldn't go down too well with the clients of your fashionable architectural practice, I would imagine. Another whiskey?"

At the Garda station in New Ross the following morning, Dr Timmins consulted with Sam's psychiatrist in Dublin who confirmed that Sam's violent actions and impaired judgement might have been because he had not been taking his medication. As a result, after a rather heated exchange with Nicholas, Sam had agreed to visit his psychiatrist for an emergency assessment. Nicholas promised the sergeant he would collect Sam from the station later that day and take him directly to his doctor's clinic.

While Leo and Claire waited to be interviewed, Leo relayed Nicholas's account of the previous evening, of Sam's current distressed state and his history of mental health issues. Claire pulled a compact out of her bag and looked in the mirror at her swollen eye and felt the crusted blood on her scarred cheek. And, although she was still badly shaken by the previous day's ordeal and didn't want to see Sam again – ever – she also remembered all the good times they had spent together. She had been subject to her own demons at various stages of her life. And almost despite herself, she could not help but feel some sympathy towards him. Who was she to judge? By the time Sergeant Conroy called her in, she had persuaded herself, and to a lesser extent Leo, that she would not change her mind – she would not press charges. So after detailed interviews with them all, the Sergeant concluded that the fire was an accident. He would review the case in a few weeks' time when Sam's psychiatrist and the local doctor provided formal reports.

It was nearly noon by the time they had finished in New Ross. Leaving Sam in the Garda station, Nicholas drove Claire, Leo and his mother back to Knockaboy to inspect the damage. As they approached the house, Mrs Courtney started to sob. Leo felt sorry for the elderly woman and wondered what would become of her – somehow, he couldn't see her sharing Nicholas's penthouse apartment in Ballsbridge. The once white render of the house was stained black and the glass in the windows was cracked. The kitchen window was completely open to the elements. As they wandered through the rooms the smell was overpowering, the carpets and timber floors ruined, the furniture soiled, and everywhere was stained black.

"It's not as bad as it could have been," said Nicholas. "I don't think that there is any structural damage. Thank God for insurance."

Mrs Courtney looked around her as if she could not believe what had happened. Her home, her life, was destroyed. But as they moved into the devastated kitchen with the blackened range, the red light under the image of the Sacred Heart continued to glow as brightly as ever. As Claire approached it, she saw that the glass had cracked, and part of the paper print of Jesus had burnt away, partially exposing beneath it the face of a young girl. A face that looked out at them with grim determination.

"It was here all the time!" said Nicholas incredulously.

"I kept telling you," said Nora. "Your father always told you to put your trust in the Sacred Heart."

Chapter 26

Dublin
November 1982

The restaurant in the Shelbourne hotel was moderately busy – a few businessmen and well-heeled ladies lunching with their friends. It would do. Claire had thought carefully about where she would meet them. It was a little stuffy here for her liking but at least they would be able to talk. She didn't want any distractions.

She had not seen Leo since he had returned to Paris a few days after the fire. Claire felt that he had left secure in the knowledge she was safe, and he had done his duty.

She breathed slowly and deeply, trying to still her gnawing anxiety. Her sister's words were ringing in her ears. "Focus, Claire, you will only get one shot at this."

She smoothed the white linen tablecloth and fiddled with the knife. She had dressed carefully: a midi-length green skirt, and a short black velvet jacket over a new white satin blouse. "As if you mean business," Molly had said. The waiter had certainly treated her with more respect than she usually received from service staff. He obviously hadn't seen her handbag, a black army-surplus special that she had pushed under the table out of sight.

She looked up as Leo entered, dressed in a black leather jacket and jeans. Several women raised their heads to gaze at him.

"Looking as lovely as ever, Claire." He kissed her on both cheeks and sat down opposite her. "The dark green suits you. I think that unlike most blondes you are a winter person."

"Leo, you always say the nicest things."

"They are simply true. You have lost the haunted look you had the last time we met."

"It's hard to believe it was two months ago," she said with a smile.

"Have you recovered? The whole experience must have been traumatic." He placed his hand over hers, his fingers long and nails well-manicured. She winced at the contrast with her own, which were nicotine-stained with nails bitten to the quick – she drew her hand away, placing both of them out of sight under the table.

"I still have the odd nightmare, but I'm OK. I'm getting there. Wine helps." She smiled as she raised her glass and took a mouthful of white wine.

The waiter, hovering, asked Leo what he would like to drink. He ordered a bottle of Bordeaux.

"I'm intrigued by your summons. Is everything OK?" Leo asked.

"Yes, I remembered you were attending a conference in Trinity this week, but thanks for meeting us."

"The pleasure is mine. I am delighted to see you again. But I did wonder what was so important that it could not be discussed over the phone."

"There are a few things I need to agree with you both. But Nicholas just phoned to say he has been delayed. He is on his way. I'll wait till he comes, if you don't mind. No point saying it all twice. At least we can relax for a few minutes."

"How mysterious. Any more developments with *Girl on a Swing?*"

"Well, as you know, the original painting was destroyed. But the copy was a good one. It must have been, it fooled us all. Looking at the pigment used, the conservator thought it was made in Paris in the 1940s. Probably by one of several accomplished Russian counterfeiters around at the time. Paul must have had it made with the others. The conservator still thinks it's worth preserving. If only for record purposes. But still, it was a huge disappointment."

"Does Nicholas know?"

"Yes, he was raging when he found out. Until then he had been like the cat who got the cream. He was banking on the insurance payout to solve all his financial difficulties. Any money he will get now will have to be spent on the house so Aunt Nora can live in it."

"So he hasn't put her in a home?"

"No, he's too mean. In Ireland it would cost a fortune. She has been staying with her neighbours, the Cusacks. But with Sam still out of action it's going to be difficult for him to sell the house in Sandymount. So now he's banking on the sale of Sylvie's paintings."

"Are those not also Sam's by right?"

"Well, it seems that Sam signed a document authorising Nicholas to sell these on his behalf before all this happened."

"Another Grimm's fairy tale?"

"No, for once, it appears to be genuine."

"And how is Sam?"

"Good – considering. I still think of him. Fond memories for the most part, poor fellow. The guards rang me up a week or so later, to tell me Sam had subsequently admitted himself to a private psychiatric clinic. His medication was altered, and he is undergoing therapy. They told me that if I am still not prepared to press charges, they are not going to pursue the case any further. According to Nicholas, he is doing well, and I now have a better understanding of how the trauma of his mother's death exacerbated his condition."

"Have you seen him? Sam?"

"No. I'm still not ready to do that. Not yet anyway. But he wrote to me. He told me he didn't know what came over him. He claimed that Nicholas drove him to the edge of madness in his attempts to control him and steal his inheritance. He hoped we could still be friends." She smiled sadly. "He talks of his 'issues' rather than accepting he has serious problems, and doesn't seem to accept any personal responsibility for what happened."

"That's more or less what Nicholas predicted would be his response," said Leo.

"I must admit, I was upset after receiving the letter. Although Nicholas has since given me a personal undertaking that Sam won't try to contact me again. I do wonder, though, if it is really safe to release him. Presumably, they will do, at some stage. I cannot get it out of my mind that he actually murdered his mother."

"Neither can I," said Leo. "But I had a long chat about it with Nicholas after the fire. He told me Sam's doctors are confident that aspects of his condition such as anxiety and aggression can be managed with drugs. Nicholas described Sylvie's murder as an atypical incident fuelled by fear and rage. Sam had been terrified his mother was about to decamp to France with Nicholas, who he despised, and that he would be forced to go with them and leave Peter who he idolised. Sam was a minor when he killed Sylvie which would be considered if he were ever tried. The fact is, it was so long ago. It would be almost impossible to prove in a court of law. Anyway, Claire, distressing though the knowledge of what happened in the past is, there is absolutely nothing you can do to change it, and nothing for you to worry about now. Contrary to what we read in novels, very few sociopaths are murderers. Most of them are chief executives of successful businesses and pillars of the community."

Claire didn't look convinced.

"From what I have been told, a lot of Sam's problems stem from his relationship with Sylvie. During the time you spent together, did he talk much to you about her?"

"Apart from his own version of her murder – which, according to Nicholas, he still maintains happened – no, he didn't talk about her in any meaningful way – just what you would expect really, that she was distant and often cold towards him. He idolised Peter – he still thinks of him as his father. But he did make a comment about his mother that I thought strange at the time. He said that beautiful people didn't have to try so hard to be liked, were less likely to empathise, or try to please others. But I think he was wrong about that aspect of her personality. It was more complicated than that.

Looking at photographs of her, I think she knew she was beautiful. But she didn't seem to flaunt it. Flaunt may not be the right word. She didn't seem to use it. It was as if she understood that it was a barrier in her relationships with others. Other than her parents, she had never really known love that wasn't contingent on her beauty. Her foreignness growing up in rural Ireland didn't help – it certainly marked her out. Not to mention being made feel beholden to the dysfunctional Courtneys. As a child, it's hardly surprising Sam absorbed some of Sylvie's feelings of abandonment and isolation."

"She had a tragic life, don't you think?"

"Not entirely. I think art brought Sylvie happiness. It was something she was good at – it was a link with her father – it helped her make sense of things."

"Well, it certainly wasn't a happy life," said Leo.

"Whose is?"

"Oh, most of us muddle along." He twisted his ring absentmindedly. "But what about you, Claire? Presumably, you got paid for the commission."

"Yes. Actually, with a generous bonus as well."

"Good. You certainly deserved it. Have you seen much of Nicholas?"

"Yes, a few times. Since the fire, he has taken an avuncular interest in me. It's a bit disturbing if I am honest. He even sent a plumber to fix the shower in my flat when I told him it was banjaxed. I suspect he is trying to buy my silence. How about you? Have you sorted things out with him?"

"Well, I think so," he said. "On the night of the fire, after you went to bed, we sat up talking, and drinking of course, at the hotel bar. After much discussion, we agreed to let sleeping dogs lie. The paintings that Daniel stole were Sam's by right, and as Nicholas's heir he will ultimately benefit from the fact they were sold. Nicholas has, in fairness, been subsidising Sam one way or another for most of his adult life. He has promised not to disclose details of my father's collaboration with the Nazis. The fact that Émile auctioned them will be seen as unfortunate, rather than duplicitous. It will go some way to preserve our family name. In return, I keep his confidences concerning what happened that night and Sam's involvement in Sylvie's murder."

"Well, that's sort of what I want to talk to you both about. Where we all go from here. Oh, speak of the devil, here's Nicholas," she said, smiling nervously.

"Claire, good to see you, my dear – and Leo, welcome back to Dublin." Nicholas, tanned despite it being November, was dressed for business in an expensive navy suit with a white shirt and a blue-and-yellow striped silk tie. He sat down beside Claire and took his cigarettes out. "You don't mind, do you?"

Not waiting for an answer, he lit up and inhaled elegantly, his elbow on the table, and raising the other arm he clicked his fingers at the waiter.

"Jameson Red," he demanded abruptly, then looked with one raised eyebrow and a sardonic smile from Leo to Claire. "What's this all about? Charmed as I am with the prospect of your company, I am rather busy at the moment."

"I too am in the dark, Nicholas," said Leo.

"Well, what is it, Claire?" Nicholas said patronisingly, as if dealing with a child.

"As you know, I have finished the inventory of

Sylvie's works. Sam had intended writing a biography of her life for inclusion in the auction catalogue. And as Sam is not in any fit position to do so now, I started to write one myself."

"Is this about extra money?"

"No, not exactly."

Nicholas glared at her.

"I have decided –" She stopped. "I have decided," she started again as if reassuring herself, "that I will write her biography myself, in book format."

"*Absolutely not! I won't have it*," said Nicholas.

"Please lower your voice, Nicholas," said Leo, looking around the restaurant, "and cut out the aggression. Go on, Claire."

"You can't stop me, Nicholas," Claire said firmly.

"There is the small matter of the contract you signed. I'll take you to the cleaner's."

"It is my determination that I won't be returning to *any* cleaners that has led me to make this decision. To write Sylvie's biography would establish my career as an academic."

"And why, may I ask, do you presume that I have any interest in your career?" he said, eyes narrowed.

"It would increase, considerably, the value of Sylvie's artworks at auction. And ... I would not include Sam's role in her murder. In fact, I won't talk about it at all, other than the inquest's findings."

"This is blackmail," Nicholas said quietly.

"Not exactly ... just ... seizing an opportunity." She placed her hands flat on the table, stretching her fingers so that they wouldn't see them shaking. "Sylvie's story needs to be told."

"Really," Leo said warily.

"Yes, Leo. I had hoped that once you thought about it you would support me, help me even."

"Why?"

"It shouldn't be swept under the carpet, what happened – the idea of Degenerate Art, Daniel's role, your father's role, Nazi collaboration."

Leo sat back in his chair, suddenly deflated. His brown eyes looked plaintively at Claire.

"You cannot be serious, Claire. Have you gone mad? What about my family? It would *kill* my grandmother!"

"Leo, she is over ninety," Claire said, determined.

He tilted his head – he was no longer smiling.

"Not to mention the damage to *my* family's reputation," said Nicholas, "and the embarrassment this will cause *me* in the business community." His face was like thunder.

"Is this not appropriating Sylvie, commodifying her – in just the same way as you accused the Courtneys of doing?" Leo asked.

"I suppose I am." She paused. "Look, Leo, I can never repay you, or Nicholas for that matter. You both saved my life."

"Funny way to show it!" spat Nicholas.

"But this is a story that must be told," Claire continued. "Of course it's an opportunity for me. I could establish a reputation and at least get a decent job where I can afford to pay my rent. It certainly beats my current occupation working at the make-up counter in Arnotts department store. It was that or go back to Stefan's dry cleaner's. If he'd have me."

"Ah, the famous incident with the pink shirt you

told me about," Leo said coldly. "I need to think about this, Claire." His hooded eyes evaded hers.

Nicholas watched Leo, waiting to see what else the Frenchman would say.

After a long pause, Claire begin to fidget nervously.

"You were prepared to deal with disclosure when you initially found out about all of this, Leo – when you thought I was in danger," she said gently.

Leo took his cigarettes from his jacket pocket and lit a Gitanes with a flick of his Zippo lighter.

"But you are not now, and I don't like being cornered, Claire."

Claire bit her lip.

The waiter returned to the table, "Can I take your order for food?"

"We're not ready." Nicholas dismissed him with a wave of his hand.

Leo dragged deeply on the cigarette and blew a perfectly formed smoke ring in the air. Then, leaning back in the chair, he tilted his head to one side while still focusing on Claire. He appeared to be considering what to say.

"If I'm honest with myself," he said eventually, "this knowledge of my father's actions has already become a burden to me. I also need the story to be told. At least I have no children to saddle with the legacy. My sister will be shocked, but she is resilient, she will get over it. Being a victim of the occupation was always the accepted tradition in our family, being complicit will certainly be harder to acknowledge. But I have always believed that, all these years later, my country is still only coming to terms with what happened during that time. For most people, the story of the resistance was the compelling narrative. But, you know, there were many different experiences that cannot be divided neatly into categories of collaborator, or resistor. It was more complicated than that. As my grandmother says, we did what we had to do." He placed an elbow on the table, his head bent, and rubbed his temples with his long fingers. "Although this is not in any way an excuse in the face of such terrible evil." He looked back at Claire, then stubbed his cigarette in the ashtray with one precise movement. "Yes, Claire, I will help you."

"Well, you might have gone soft in the head, my friend," said Nicholas. "But I, for one, will see you both in court."

"Will that be the civil court, or the criminal court?" Leo said with resignation. "Think about it, Nicholas. Really, your father and my grandfather's crimes are historic. We can paint them in that light anyway. There are other advantages for you, financial ones. A biography of Sylvie's life would increase, considerably, the value of her works."

"Will it make that much of a difference?" Nicholas asked grudgingly.

"Yes, I think so. Let's face it, you couldn't make it up. It will cause a resurgence of interest in her work, spawn a few exhibitions."

"Was she that important? Will she be remembered in ten, or twenty years' time?"

"Yes, I think she will – her story will be anyway. She will be remembered as the girl on the swing in Mateus's portrait, the art collector's daughter, an artist who drowned tragically."

"And her portrait if it had not been a copy?"

"Would have been worth a fortune."

"Pity," said Nicholas. "And you would promise that the circumstances of her death would remain unaltered."

"Yes, I can sign a contract agreeing to this. I will deal only with the historic crimes and overlook the more recent ones," said Claire.

"Ironic, isn't it?" said Leo. We can face the sins of our father's but not our own. If Mateus had only known the trail of destruction his painting would create."

"It seems, Claire, that Professor Dillon seriously underestimated you," said Nicholas, swallowing down the rest of his whiskey.

Epilogue

The cleaner had left the apartment. Nicholas had heard the front door close twenty minutes or so ago. Still, you could never be too careful. He poured himself a large whiskey in a Waterford glass tumbler. Then he locked the door of the lounge area and approached an elegant side unit. that he used as a bar. With a flick of a switch that was concealed in a drawer, the bookcase on the far wall slid aside to reveal the painting.

He walked over, sat down on an armchair and gazed at the portrait – devouring it.

As ever, she seemed to be staring back at him, brazen, wanton, even at so young an age. The artist, Mateus, had certainly felt this too.

Nicholas smiled to himself and took a slug of his drink, feeling the warmth from the whiskey radiate through his chest.

She would have laughed at how things had turned out. It was disappointing they had discovered that the painting behind the Sacred Heart was a copy. It would have been the icing on the cake if they had assumed it was the original. He remembered Daniel telling him how Émile had asked the Germans for the painting, long after the ERR discovered it was a fake – for a price of course. Émile had some misguided notion of giving it back to Paul. But then he had become involved with the ERR to sell the genuine Barbizon paintings. There was also the fact that Émile couldn't bear looking at it when he finally learned what had happened to Paul and Hanna. But when Daniel, who had even less scruples, heard about its existence he asked Émile for it, and Émile was glad to get rid of it.

The original painting had always been in the bank in New Ross. His father had considered the copy as an insurance policy, his pension. When he retired, Daniel had intended to move to Kilkenny, buy a house there, and maybe even open an art gallery as a pastime for his old age. He had planned to burn the house at Knockaboy down and claim on the insurance – including the insurance on the painting. At the time, Nicholas had procured forged documentation: a letter from Paul leaving the painting to him.

The public sale of the original *Girl on a Swing* would have raised all kinds of questions regarding provenance. And who knew what records were still in existence, yet to be discovered? Even if Daniel had made a private black-market sale, there was always the risk that at some time in the future Sylvie would get to hear about it. But an insurance claim was a different kettle of fish, provided that Daniel could negotiate with the insurers and keep it under the radar. Of course, his father never got to carry out the arson. The old man passed away sooner than he expected. But the possibility of following through on the plan had always intrigued Nicholas. However, the personal risks in its execution were huge. Forensic science was so much more sophisticated now than it had been in his father's day. Fortunately, his demented mother had saved him from this dilemma by burning the house down herself. In light of the conservator discovering it was a copy, the plan was doomed to failure anyway. Good old Nora. The poetic justice of it all.

And there was one fortuitous outcome he had not anticipated: that 'the dumpling' would immortalise Sylvie with a biography, potentially a bestseller. The value of her paintings would rocket. At least he could pay off his debts.

He lit a cigarette, inhaled, and fantasised how he would be invited to go on radio chat shows, maybe even television. He would tell the interviewer how shocked he had been to hear of his father's criminal activities, that his father had been a remote figure when he was growing up – but, then, he would commiserate with the interviewer, most fathers of that generation were. And although he was deeply hurt and ashamed of his father's actions, at least he could thank him for inspiring his interest in art. He would enjoy that.

Yes, more by accident than design, things had worked out beautifully for him. He had regrets, of course he did. He still regretted he had killed Sylvie all those years ago, but he didn't really have a choice. Did he? He had planned to do it quickly, painlessly. When his mother had told him Sylvie was there, he had driven over hoping to surprise her, catch her unaware, but that fool Peter had got in the way. However, he hadn't had to alter his plans that much. He had intended all along to fill her up with drink, smother her, and set up a fake drowning. He just hadn't considered having to deal with Peter in this scenario. It was unfortunate he had to frame first Peter, and then Sam, for her murder, but needs must. As it turned out, he was glad she died then, it was better that way. He could never imagine Sylvie growing old gracefully, or quietly for that matter. However, there was still Sam to deal with. His son remained furious with him. But he would crawl back, eventually, once he was ready to leave the clinic and he realised he had no money.

"*Sylvie, Sylvie,*" he whispered longingly.

She had even cast her spell over poor old Mateus. Although, somehow, he had known. He turned the canvas over. Written in the artist's scrawly handwriting in faded black ink were the words of a poem, of sorts.

'*Stippled sunlight through beech trees and the smell of roses wafting on a summer breeze. A young girl on a swing. The swing rising higher and higher, and the child squealing in delight. Until one strong push and then, as if propelled, the child goes flying through the air, her white lace skirts trailing like the wings of a wounded dove before finally lying broken, shattered on the ground. A shimmering halo of red blood spreads around her fair hair.*'

The End